Serpent's Smile

E D Skinner

Visit the author at https://www.edskinner.net/

ISBN-13:   978-1-963180-07-7 Hard cover
              978-1-963180-06-0 Paperback
              978-1-963180-05-3 Ebook

To Anita, for always being there, no matter what.

Acknowledgements

My special thanks to Makella Brems, Lynne Bender, John Gluth, Tony Brong, Robert Bureker, Ricky Lee, MSgt Robert Parker, R. Dan Pauley, David Rogers, Scott and Jackie Brems, Wendy Templeton, Terri Chadwick, Allison Templeton, Jon Milan, and Roger and Barbara Bond for their comments, suggestions, and expertise. And to all those who've provided encouragement and understanding, I am most grateful.

This work would never have come to fruition without the skill, experience, and encouragement of physicians Ross Bremner, Talal Hilal, Daniel Ahn, Jonathan Ashman, and Kirk Anderson, and the dedicated nurses and skilled technical staff at the Mayo Clinics in Scottsdale and Phoenix, and at St. Joseph's Hospital, also in Phoenix Arizona.

PART ONE

HOPE SPRINGS ETERNAL

"May you live in interesting times."
Chinese curse

Chapter 1

Morning
Wuchang, China

"Lili," Sartaq blustered into the cell phone that scrambled their Cantonese, "I no have *spare* suicide bombers!"

He swept an empty hand back across the black hair on the side of his head. The white bristly whiskers from the long scar made a crackly sound.

"I making five ready for Singapore," he continued. "They almost done. But more? No. Not ready for year." He remembered his confrontation with Wang yesterday. The boy's increasing resistance made him doubt the choice. "Maybe longer," he added.

A long, narrow boat rowed by eight students with alternating oars, left then right, hissed past on Donghu Lake.

Sartaq scowled at the sight. Foreign things, especially American, were a favorite at Wuhan University. And with seventy thousand students, they'd taken over most of the suburb of Wuchang containing the main campus. Across the bridge, downtown Wuhan was even more changed. There was little he or Lili remembered from forty years ago.

Her voice started in his ear with his nickname, "Taq," but then morphed into a nasal sound like the chants of the Tibetan street beggars near the hotel. After a moment, it changed to an animal groan with bird chirps. Feng Min had explained that his app could make odd sounds if a lost packet interrupted the encrypted data between the phones. He said it was inherent in something called UDP. The boy was a computer genius, but incredibly naïve in his creation's uses.

"... is what you ask for," Lili's voice resumed from the app. "Islamic State will facilitate your project, both the transportation and the explosives, but they want proof you can deliver."

"I don't care—" he began, but his sister's voice continued from America.

"Use the Party-parent's meeting for the demonstration. It's perfect. We'll bring the cash. That gives you two months to prepare your warriors."

Sartaq scowled. His little sister knew nothing of turning parent-hating college students into maniacal jihadists.

But then he sighed, knowing that once she'd decided, that was it.

And it'd be up to him, as usual, to make her plan work.

Their mother had taught them how to manipulate people. Twice widowed, she'd started during the Cultural Revolution, and without Party rank or official sanction, she now directed thousands in Shenjiawan. Lili, her second born, managed American software engineers in Silicon Valley, but also guided the actions and finances of the Chinese Democratic Movement in the United States. And Sartaq, Lili's older half-brother, bent naïve college students into violent fanatics for Xinjiang and Uyghur independence.

"Oh, all right," Sartaq said.

"Singapore is your project," Lili said, her voice gleeful at his resignation. "We'll bring the cash when I visit in October."

There was that *we* again.

"Lili," he said, leaning forward as he walked next to the lake as if he could tower over her, "adding someone, especially outsider, is bad idea. Much risk."

The app made a drumming sound before Lili's voice resumed. "... stopped at border and turned back. I can't risk that. But when a pretty Chinese woman is with American businessman, they are waved in."

Again, she'd made up her mind.

Sartaq sighed and looked out at the lake. The day was going to be oppressively hot again. Wuhan was called "The Oven" for good reason. There'd be no relief until November. He'd rather be in the grassy shade of the tree on campus where he preached from the Qur'an to indoctrinate his recruits, but the app needed a more reliable WiFi connection than he could get there. Here by the lake with student dorms nearby, the coverage was the best he'd found.

But after the usual fruitless haggling with Lili on the phone, Sartaq was tired of listening. He wanted quiet, shade, and something for breakfast.

"All right," he said, nodding at her earlier suggestion. "New construction downtown across Chang Jiang. I get explosives there."

The app made a swooping sound and went dead. Feng Min had explained that was the chain of VPNs dropping out, another English-letter abbreviation Sartaq didn't care to understand.

Pausing with his back to the lake, he pried off the back of the phone, removed its battery, and put everything in a pocket of his green coveralls. Their next scheduled contact was in three days. She'd want to know if he had the explosives, and what he had accomplished toward the additional recruits.

He hated her interference, her *micro-managing* as she called it. But he'd waited twenty years for this opportunity.

A Bao bun with spicy pork would be good, he thought, scanning the signs of the open-fronted shops and ignoring the ones in Arabic. They wouldn't have pork.

Chapter 2

Morning, Twelve Hours Later
Surprise, Arizona

Blake Spencer straddled his red Cannondale bicycle in the pre-formed concrete tunnel beneath Bell Road. Here on the west side of the Agua Fria, he was in the town of Surprise, his home, that split the dry riverbed with Phoenix.

He moved a hand to block the glare beaming in and read the text message on his cell phone.

$7000 2 wks China?

A car slapped on the expansion joints overhead as it passed, the sound reverberating from the tunnel's rectangular concrete walls.

"When and where?" he said in annoyance. "China's big."

Standing in one place, even in the shade under the roadway, the Sonoran Desert's heat was fierce. At least when he was moving, the air whisked away his sweat and with it the calories, the joules of energy from his body. But down here, there was no convection. Sweat dripped from his nose, from the underside of his arms, and on the inside of his thighs.

Surprise, where Julie'd insisted they buy a house, would hit a hundred and fifteen today.

His mind supplied, forty-six.

The conversion, Fahrenheit to Celsius, came automatically. His mind was always doing that, supplying answers. Most of the time, he ignored them.

But Julie, he couldn't. Dead, cremated, and in a jar inside a crypt he'd never, ever visit, none of that changed the fact that her death was his fault, and there was nothing he could do to forget it.

Work gave relief for a few hours, but alcohol was more effective even though it had other consequences. He'd learned—calculated actually—when and how much to drink to compensate for what his liver metabolized. The graph from the spreadsheet showed hours versus ounces, and he could keep his dark thoughts sedated for days at a time. But a week or two of drunken peace cost weeks to recover, and during that time, his brain was no good for work.

Blake rubbed the dried crust from his blue eyes and scratched his cheeks through the brown and increasingly white hair. Three weeks with no bookings was a pleasant break, but he was bored and wanted to do something. He loved the chase, immersing himself in some morass of details, and plucking out the gem of explanation behind a computer screw-up.

He knew, and they did too, it was much more about ego than dollars.

But right now, he needed the income, the cash flow, for bills. Income for his kind of consulting was spotty. When it came, he paid the outstanding bills, got ahead of the utilities for a couple of months, and then invested the rest. In retirement, he could be fat and happy, but he knew to let the investments do their job. You had to leave the money there.

But right now, he was hot. Damn hot.

Blake took off his baseball cap, wiped his forehead with the back of that hand, then looked to see which hat he'd grabbed that morning. On the front was the picture of a tank with a lightning *Zot* shooting out its cannon, the souvenir cap from Raytheon in Tucson.

Standing in the tunnel's shade, he put the hat back on his head and then angled the cell phone in his other hand to read the sender's name.

Megyn Zhang.

His grin popped in surprise.

"China Doll!"

He'd met her six years back at her employer's Sunnyvale office. They'd hired him to teach her engineers the intricacies of VxWorks, a real-time operating system they would be using for a flight management computer. Comac, a mainland Chinese corporation, manufactured avionics. She, in turn, managed the engineering group in Sunnyvale that did final customizations for western companies.

Arriving for the first day of class, she'd briefed him on the five individuals he'd soon meet, all Americans with fifteen to twenty years' experience. They would be a fairly typical audience. Blake's job was to take them to the next level.

At the end of the first day, Blake commented as he packed his computer that he would eat at a Mountain View sushi bar he'd heard about with a specialty in *ankimo*.

"The one on Castro," she confirmed. "And yes, the Monk Fish liver paté is excellent."

He invited her to go along.

"*Omakase*, please," she told the sushi chef as they settled at the bar. "Both of us."

Blake admired her initiative. They talked, drank, and sampled the chef's imaginative creations until closing.

They did Afghani in Sunnyvale on Tuesday, steak and lobster with live jazz in San Jose on Wednesday, and then *dim sum* on Alameda Island Thursday, his last day in the area. It took his polite insistence and her assurances in Chinese to get the "special meat dumplings."

Out the end of the underpass, heat waves rose from the desert. It made the distant saguaros ripple in the glare.

He tapped a reply into his phone.

Hi Megyn. Great to hear from you. Which 2 weeks? What topic? Where?

* * *

He pressed Send and glanced up at a parched, yellow-green Palo Verde just back from the riverbank. He raised a hand as he spoke to it. "Seven grand for two weeks isn't bad. And if they pick up the travel, this could be good."

Swinging a leg over as he mounted the bicycle, he pushed off in low gear. Guiding the front wheel between the water-rounded rocks in the dry wash to the concrete ramp from the street, he powered up the slope. Shifting to maintain optimal leg power, he reached his home in eight minutes.

Chapter 3

Showered and sitting on the living room couch in navy-blue boxers with his first cup of coffee, he wondered if he should check his phone or notebook computer first; she'd move from one to the other, depending on which was closest at hand.

You like her.

He blinked in agreement with his mind's comment.

Nothing on his phone, he opened his notebook computer; the email client dinged.

The return address on the top message, *zhang.m@whu.edu.cn,* made him grin but then cock his head.

"Zhang.m is probably her," he told the room, "but why from *whu.edu.cn* not Comac?"

He knew *cn* resolved to mainland China, and *edu* meant it was an educational institution there, but what was *whu?*

He typed the whole address into a browser and hit enter.

After several unusually long seconds, a website came up. Huge, red and black Chinese characters dominated a photograph of a grassy, tree-dotted campus. In the extreme upper-right corner of the webpage, a GIF of a tiny US flag waved mechanically. He clicked it, and moments later, the screen re-painted with the same picture, but now with "Wuhan University" in place of the Chinese characters.

Blake scrolled down, and a different image came into view. A European-looking man with wire-rim glasses wearing a white collared, blue shirt and striped bow tie appeared to be mid-sentence. His hand, similarly frozen in the moment, gestured toward a white board filled with mathematical formulae. "Nells Madsen," the caption read, "Nobel Laureate, Guest Lecturer, International Experts Program."

In the past, Blake's emails with Megyn had been through her employer. She'd been in California for twenty years, and she seemed as American—as California—as could be.

But this email from her through a mainland China university raised questions. Had she quit her job and moved back to China? Was that at Comac's request, or had she taken up a professorship at the school?

He read the email carefully. It started with three paragraphs that sounded like a copy/paste from some legal department, but then, after a blank line, he could almost hear her voice.

Hi Blake!

I've discovered a new East European place in Mountain View. You'll love it. Just a few doors from our sushi bar. Get the borscht. Both the red and the white. They're wonderful! My treat.

FYI: The China class is my alma mater, Wuhan University. Pls reply this email, not Comac. No secrets, just not their business. (I'm logged into the school via the net.)

Thanks, M.

Satisfied with her explanation, Blake launched Google-Earth and typed in "Wuhan, China." The view swept across the Pacific and into China before starting its plunge down. It slowed and then hovered high above a large, sprawling city with a river zigzagging up and through. A legend identified the water as "Yangtze" with "Chang Jiang" in italics.

Blake brought the email up again and scanned for the key factors: Teach ... College students ... Two, five-day seminars ...

Consecutive weeks ... Same material twice ...

He pursed his lips. "Expenses?"

The legalese was roundabout but said the school would make the air, hotel, and local transportation arrangements. It didn't specifically state they would pay, but in the next paragraph, it added that any *exceptional* expenses would be his responsibility.

He bobbed his head. "They're paying for meals."

Mainland China, the epicure in his head grinned. *This could be interesting!*

Blake leaned back on his couch to plan.

For Megyn's booking, he'd need five days of lecture material. That would be about nine hundred slides, give or take. He'd be teaching college students so he would focus on fundamentals rather than odd-ball quirks. Thinking of the training materials he'd written before, much of this course could be copy/pasted. And the rank beginner material he knew without needing to look anything up.

Easy-peasy.

But then a different thought stopped him.

I don't know Chinese.

On the mouse pad, he stroked and tapped to begin a reply to Megyn's email.

Hi, M. Great to hear from you. Did you move back to China?
YES, I'm interested, but I don't speak Chinese.
How can this work?

Her reply dinged when he was in the kitchen leveling the grounds for another pour-through.

Hi, Blake.

I'm pleased you are interested! In addition to my employment at Comac, I also organize this program for my university each year in Wuhan. We bring in a foreign expert to teach a class. We prefer Americans. Experiencing you firsthand is best. :-)*

Don't worry. You can do everything in English. The school will supply a Mandarin translator.

When can you go?
M.

He didn't recognize the :-)* emoji at the end of her first paragraph. Google search returned, "Kissy face."

He straightened. She's flirting?

Their relationship even after several meetups had been friendly. No more than that. He was married, she knew that, and they'd both acted accordingly.

But now Julie was gone. He was free, free to act, free to follow through...

Should he tell Megyn about Julie, that he was single again?

That would suggest he was interested. And he was. But that needed to be communicated in person.

He put that thought aside and checked his calendar. He had bookings in Cedar Rapids, Tucson, and a probable repeat in Huntsville. Plus, he'd need about ten days to create the materials. And the university's existing calendar was an unknown. They might have some considerations to factor in.

He picked dates that would work for him as a first offer. *What about the weeks of 23 and 30 October?*

Megyn answered immediately. *Perfect! I'll email the contract tomorrow. Drag-and-drop a signature onto the PDF and send it back. The department will make the arrangements.*

Another ding. *Been anywhere good lately?*

He typed. *Fab meal at a little discovery in Cleveland: Luigi's Ristorante, east side of town if you're ever there. Best meal yet. Home-made Limoncello and tira misu.*

Ding. *Lady fingers?*

He grinned. *Spongy and gooshy like you like 'em.*

Ding. *Yum! Back to my engineers. Ciao! :-)**

Another kissy face; he smiled.

In the kitchen, his pot of water screamed.

Chapter 4

Two and a half months later
Friday and Saturday, October 20-21

Blake bounced up from his aisle seat when the plane's gong sounded.

He stacked his black computer case atop his black roller suitcase from the overhead and then waited. Seated over the wings, he knew from long experience it'd take three to five minutes for the passengers in front of him to exit the plane.

His next flight was three hours off. With a thirteen hour sit to Shanghai, he wanted a long walk before boarding that one. He'd used the sidewalk outside at the SFO curb before and knew it was nine minutes around. He made a dozen circuits before going through security at the international terminal.

The sign at gate G4 confirmed his United #857 was on schedule for its 1:15 pm departure. He scanned the lounge for a place to sit.

Her eyes and demur smile riveted him.

China Doll!

In his mind, Roy Orbison's high tenor wailed in joy at the end of "Pretty Woman."

Megyn looked as perfect as a wedding cake. She wore her auburn hair pulled back into the same bun, but with lips and nails painted a milky pink, she seemed less dramatic. One hand draped over the other and rested on a tan linen skirt below a jacket of the same coarse fabric. A frilly-collared blouse with bright flowers bloomed up from the collar.

Her eyes never left his as he crossed the lounge.

He righted his stack of two bags, computer and zippered suitcase next to her nearly identical set.

"Megyn. What a surprise!"

When she stood, she tilted her head up slowly to meet his eyes.

"Nice to see you, Blake."

He felt like hugging her but her hand was already out. The gentle press of her fingers matched his, lingered, and then pressed a second time to keep his hand.

Blake's face felt warm. He took a quick breath and tasted something in the air. Pinot Grigio? Light, simple, sweet...

He gestured at the airport lounge with his left hand. "What are you doing here?"

"Traveling to Wuhan," she said, turning her head to follow his gesture.

"No ring?" She asked quizzically.

Blake felt acutely uncomfortable. He needed to tell her— wanted to tell her he was single again, but how? What words? Here in the airport lounge?

As he debated the situation, he heard himself answer.

"She died."

"I'm sorry," she said with a sudden frown. She released his right hand but kept her eyes on his face. "I have the seat next to you. Is that all right?"

He wanted to shout, "Oh Hell, yes," but suppressed the words even though he felt his face brighten.

She smiled back, and it was done. All the times they'd met for a meal in various cities as their travels occasionally coincided, all the feelings he'd had to keep bottled up, all of it rose up in his chest.

He gasped and sighed without thinking but let the smile all the way out.

"Shall we sit?" she asked, and smoothed the back of her skirt and did so. She patted the black and chrome seat next to her.

"I don't understand," he said, turning his luggage stack and sitting. "Do you always escort your guest instructors?"

She seemed amused and rocked her head side to side. "I'm going to visit my mother. She lives near Wuhan."

She answered his next question before he could ask.

"Yes, the same flights, hotel, everything." She blinked and paused as if deciding something.

"Do you know Shanghai?" she asked, her face serious again.

The school had made the booking, and he'd guessed they gave him the layover to help with the jet lag. Another two-hour flight to Wuhan and a rest day there would've been less expensive. But he'd never visited Shanghai, so he didn't argue the opportunity.

But now, an evening with Megyn in China's most glamorous city...

Shanghai's twenty-five million residents ranked it among the top five in the world. And for elegance, no other came close. Megyn's beauty and practiced composure were the perfect mate for the spectacular city.

Blake thought of his windbreaker, short-sleeve shirts, office-caliber pants, and comfortable shoes in his suitcase. He'd look like a dork.

He was a dork.

"Umm," he choked, his heart throbbing with a cold-sweat threatening, "that'll be...convenient. Same shuttle bus? For the downtown hotel, I mean? And flight to Wuhan?"

She reached across and put her hand on top of his where it rested on his thigh.

"And after breakfast, too."

She squeezed.

Four hours out from San Francisco, the Aleutians crept toward their tiny airplane on the seat back monitors. They'd finished the bland dinner an hour ago and mutually rejected everything on the airplane's two dozen channels.

"I've got some music and movies on my notebook," Blake gambled. "Maybe we could do some of those?"

He pulled the notebook from his computer bag along with his

wireless earbuds. He handed her one and stuck the other in his ear. "I'll set the audio to mono so we hear everything."

He browsed to his Music directory.

"What do you like? I'm not picky about genre as long as it's good music."

"You choose," she said.

"Linda Ronstadt?"

Her eyebrows arched a "Maybe."

He clicked the play button on the screen. But halfway through the first chorus in "You're No Good," she frowned and took out her earbud. "Too bossy. I think I need more than just sound. Maybe a movie?"

He guessed she'd seen the Videos directory on his screen. He double-clicked it and pointed to an inner folder. "I've got all four TV seasons of 'Rumpole of the Bailey.' Do you know it?"

She shook her head.

"It's about a courtroom barrister in London. He's gruff but funny. Defends low-caliber crooks. He refers to his wife as,"—he lowered his voice to sound like Leo McKern—"'She who must be obeyed.' Understated and droll. Very British. I love it."

Megyn crinkled her pink lips. "Some other time, maybe."

"Some Sci-Fi?" He asked, double-clicking the next folder. Icons for "Soylent Green," "Forbidden Planet," and "The Expanse" appeared. He frowned at the offering. "Probably not the first. 'Soylent' is dystopian. Planetary over-crowding, food riots, desperate mobs, wealthy in guarded enclaves... Charlton Heston and Edward G. Robinson. Good," he shrugged, "but kind'a dated now."

She shook her head. "I'm not a fan of science fiction, Strangelove excepted."

He laughed and hit the Back button. He double-clicked a folder named "Film Noir" and several dozen icons filled the window.

"One of these, maybe?"

Several seconds passed as she studied the titles. "I don't know these. They're old, aren't they?"

Blake nodded. "40s and 50s, black and white. They're very dark —the characters and stories, I mean. Everyone will be flawed, even the good guys. And lots of them finish badly. For the characters, I mean."

She looked interested. "You pick. Give me a good example."

"Ah," he stroked up with two fingers on the mouse pad and double-tapped an icon. "That's easy!"

"Double Indemnity" filled the LCD as Walter Neff—"that's Fred MacMurray," Blake whispered in her open ear—began his confession into the long-handled microphone of his dictation machine. Blake's lips tracked several of the lines he knew by heart.

When one of the flight attendants nudged his shoulder and offered a tray with cups of coffee and tea, Megyn stayed riveted to the movie. He took four creamers for his coffee and one for hers.

On his notebook's screen, Phyllis was hinting she wanted Neff to not only murder her husband, but to also make it look like an accident. She intended to collect on the double indemnity clause of the policy she'd just bought from Neff.

In her seat, Megyn fidgeted. They'd had two small bottles of wine, ice water, and several cups of coffee.

"Take a break?" He whispered close to her ear.

"No," she snapped, pulled out the earbud, and dropped it in his lap. He clapped his knees together to catch it.

She stood up. "Let me out."

He barely had time to grab the earbud, close the notebook, and then yank it to his chest before she flapped up his tray, shoved past, and disappeared toward the back of the plane.

What the hell?

Had he missed something? Said something wrong that she'd then stewed about for an hour? Maybe she didn't know Fred MacMurray had started as a heavy, long before Flubber?

But this was *film noir*! Everybody is flawed. That's the whole point.

Feelings were not his strong suit. In his ten years with Julie, she'd hammered at his insensitivity. He eventually learned to recognize her glances and vocal stresses, but she'd find other reasons to complain.

"I'm an engineer," he'd confessed in frustration, "not a

therapist."

In hindsight, that was their point of no return. Not long after that and late one night after yet another shouting match, she'd screamed, "I'm fucking anybody but you." It pushed her train well onto a different pair of rails. Her suicide a few months later, in bed with another man and co-suicide, released him from the marriage, but locked in his guilt.

Megyn was leaning on the stainless-steel prep table partitioned off at the back of the airplane.

Blake leaned forward and copied her position, ducking his head so their eyes would be at the same level.

She glanced in his direction.

He opened his hands and started, "If I said or did something…"

She sighed, "No. I'm all right." Her voice sounding annoyed.

"Was it something I did?" He asked.

"No," she hissed, opening then closing her hands. "I don't know what came over me."

He waited.

After a moment she gave a quick nod. "Yes, I do. It's that woman in the movie."

"Phyllis?" He asked. "Barbara Stanwyck's character?"

She rocked her head. "It's so… shallow."

He offered a shrug. "Well, she is the *femme fatale*."

In the dark, a shadow visibly raced up her shoulders and neck. She snapped, "*Nobody* is *that* shallow."

He'd never thought about it. *Film noir* was always bad people in bad situations, doing bad things, and getting their comeuppance, or not, in ninety minutes. They had to cut a lot of corners to make it fit.

"It's just a movie, Megyn."

She stewed in silence.

He tried to think of movies with strong female characters that didn't use sexual manipulation.

"Bette Davis in her later roles?" He asked. "She's done some powerful characters. Her Queen Elizabeth is outstanding."

She bobbled her head again.

He pursed his lips. "What about 'Hidden Figures?' African

American women, three in particular, who do math calculations for NASA in the Mercury program. Strong-willed, very intelligent women in a heavily prejudiced environment. I grew up in the South. The movie definitely nails it."

Again, she said nothing.

"No sex," he added hopefully.

She shook her head. "Sex is fine. It's part of us, and not just for reproduction." She turned her face to search his eyes. "It completes us, who we are; it's much more than just a creature function. Love, companionship, sharing difficulties, worries, struggles..."

It was like she'd looked at the deepest part of his psyche and then put it into words.

All he could do was nod, but the phrase soul mate ran through his mind.

She straightened and wiped a hand down a forearm. "I just don't like it when a woman—or a man, for that matter—is stereotyped. Real people are complex, complicated..."

Bent by life, he thought but didn't say, and started back to their seats.

The airplane's ventilation system hissed as he clicked and swept through the movie titles on his computer.

"'My Cousin Vinny?'" he asked. "Marissa Tomei is a riot. Sassy, sexy, and smart as a whip."

Her character was a lot like Megyn, he realized.

But she shook her head. "I guess I'm tired. I think I'll get some sleep before Shanghai."

He checked his watch. "Eight and a half hours to go," he said, closing the lid of his computer. "Me, too."

Shifting to get comfortable, she paused with the little pillow in one hand and searched his eyes. "Did you know yours are the color of blue Jasper Wedgwood?"

Without waiting for an answer, she set the pillow against his upper arm and snuggled in.

Whatever had set her off earlier, it'd been forgotten.

Volcanic wasn't the word to describe her character, but it was that, nonetheless. Deep, he thought. Smoothly meshed gears silently turning all the time.

An impressive individual.

Wearing both ear buds, he continued the movie.

Blake never slept in airplanes. He knew too much: the engineers, the programming, the interaction of mechanical actuators and high-tech sensors. He'd read the design accommodations, the guesses that had to be tested in combinations and sequences with no way to imagine the unimaginable. And knew they would sometimes befuddle the pilots, rip the aluminum, and scatter parts—and parts of passengers—in the ocean's depths.

Megyn slept on his arm, her throat puttering softly, as Walter Neff descended into madness, murder, and self-destruction.

"Here," Megyn said as they prepared to deplane for Customs in Shanghai. "Put this away."

Blake stared at the fat, manilla envelope she'd put in his hand. It was more than an inch thick.

She pushed his hand with the envelope toward his chest. "It's for my mother."

He hesitated.

"It's under the limit," she assured him, her voice rising. "I have one, too. If I carry both, I have to pay the duty, but split like this…"

He nodded.

Apparently satisfied, she leaned forward to get her purse.

He thumbed the flap. Inside were three rubber-banded stacks of bills, each one about a quarter-inch thick. Chairman Mao looked back at him from the first stack. The upper corner of the bill said, "100." He knew the conversion. A hundred RMB was about seventeen bucks.

"How much is all this?"

Megyn shrugged. "They won't ask."

She turned to peer into the tiny mirror she'd set up on the seat-back tray table. She unscrewed the top from a tiny glass bottle, and turning her face in the mirror, painted her lips with fresh pink.

Blake used his thumb to peek at the second bundle. A thin,

Asian man with a long, stringy beard looked back from 200,000 of something.

The third pile was from Singapore. The 100 on top was worth about seventy US dollars.

Megyn cupped her hand over his. "Don't flash that around."

He hedged his misgivings. "Megyn, why does your mother need cash in three different currencies?"

She stuck out her tongue and touched it with a fingertip, then peered into the mirror and began smoothing an eyebrow.

"Some of it's for her needs: groceries and things. And some is salary for her workers. They come from all over." She inspected both eyebrows in the mirror. "Korea, Vietnam, India... They send the money home. This just makes it more convenient for everyone."

Blake remembered his mother paying for everything in cash in the 1960s. His father complained he couldn't track the household budget without check stubs, but she said, "You don't expect everyone to go to the bank, do you?"

"We'll use the Nothing to Declare exit," Megyn declared.

She was staring at him, waiting.

Should he risk breaking the law—Chinese law—for her? If caught and it was just a little over, he could try claiming ignorance and hope they'd let him pay the fine. But if it was a lot, and it looked like it might be, would they put him on a plane back to the US? Or more likely, would they lock him up and wait for a judge to decide?

Then again, they could probably walk through the Nothing to Declare exit without being challenged. He'd done that in every country he'd ever visited including China.

Beautiful Megyn? Sitting beside him and smelling wonderful even after an all-night flight? And now with an evening of possibilities in Shanghai...

He blew out the air he'd been holding and stuffed the envelope into the pocket of his windbreaker. And zipped it shut.

She smiled, and as Blake watched, tucked three bottles, two compacts, a black and a brown eyebrow pencil, and a little round mirror into her small purse. Inside, he glimpsed a dark red passport with five gold stars inside a circle, and behind it another, a US passport with its dark blue cover.

Dual citizenship, he realized.

"So," she asked, "how should we dine? Elegant gourmet, back alley hidden gem, secret lover's rendezvous?"

She reached over the armrest and put her hand on the top of his leg. She glanced up at the passengers standing in the aisle then slid her fingers down the inside of his thigh. Her pink nails clawed at his leg, and she purred in his ear, "What do you want?"

Downtown Shanghai was like Piccadilly Circus grafted onto Times Square in the middle of the Loop in the heart of Chicago after someone had injected it with steroids thrice over. The economic capital of the country, every major Chinese corporation owned an architecturally unique tower animated with multi-story videos and escalating, roving neon. The aggregate bill for electricity would've made Las Vegas leave the table.

Blake stepped back from his hotel room window and unzipped his roller suitcase. They'd only be in Shanghai the night, and at nearly eight o'clock, there was no time to buy a new suit before dinner. Shanghai would have to take him as he was, an American dork with an elegant Chinese woman.

He reminded himself that Julie'd been dead—by her own hand—for ten months, and the abandonment—we abandoned each other—had started long before that.

He needed to move on.

"Forward," he announced to himself, "Not back."

He hummed as he took out his best white shirt. It was for Mondays when customers would see him for the first time. Looking at it now, it seemed shabby, washed and worn too many times, and it needed a touch-up with the hotel iron. On such short notice, the best he could do would be that shirt with the new brown pants and the leather shoes he'd polished and bagged. He wished he'd brought a tie.

What's done is done, his inner voice counseled.

Meta-thinking, he called it. Thinking about his thinking. If his inner judge was making positive statements, he figured his conscious and unconscious minds were aligned. Same with his body. If something felt good and his mind was thinking happy thoughts—or no thoughts—then everything was good.

He closed his eyes and stood completely still. It took only a few seconds for an unconscious smile to pull up his cheeks.

He nodded, said "So be it," and turned to the closet for the hotel's iron and board. Minutes later with the white shirt and tan Dockers cooling on wood hangers, he showered and shaved. He dressed and went out the door in twenty minutes.

Outside Megyn's room, light fluttered in the peephole before her door opened a few inches. She peeked around the edge. "You look nice. Come in."

A piano played from the radio as he stepped in. He recognized "Songbird" from Fleetwood Mac's Rumors album. He had the vinyl from way back, the CD at home, and the MP3 on his computer.

"That's my favorite album," he said as the door *kerchunked*.

She flowed past him like a spirit.

Her purple, blue, and pink translucent gown billowed as she turned in front of the floor-to-ceiling window. Silhouetted in Shanghai's blinking and flashing neon, Blake followed every move as she bent forward—gentle shoulder, small waist—raised a leg—compound curve of hip, thigh, knee, calve, tiny ankle and slim foot raised in the air...

Penché.

The word came unbidden. It was a ballet term, but he'd never been and knew nothing, he'd thought, of it. And her turn, he somehow knew, was a *pirouette*.

Blake's breath shuddered. She was ten times more beautiful than he'd dared to dream.

One arm draping the air, she pirouetted in bare feet to Christine McVie's caressing words with the music. Megyn's toenails, he noticed, were now scarlet. They matched her fingertips and glistening lips.

There was a rap at the door behind him. "Room Service."

"Would you admit them?" she fluted, putting on a robe.

Blake groped for the handle. When he pulled the door open, a starched-white, cloth-covered table glided through propelled by a man in a tan and brown uniform.

"Here by the window," Megyn waved, her fingertips sparkling with the downtown lights.

They started with the Napa Chardonnay and the bamboo baskets of steamed pork dumplings. Next came the Merlot from Chile—surprisingly robust, more like a Cab—and a crackling Red Snapper with sweet-red pepper on crackly skin. The radio began Samual Barber's "Adagio for Strings," and when Blake fumbled a bite with his chopsticks, she swept around the table and leaned over his shoulder. Her sleek, auburn hair, released from captivity, glided across his neck like a satin sheet, cool and smooth. Reaching in past his shoulder, she probed and separated the delicate filet on his plate with the same ivory chopsticks as if they were extensions of her fingers. Her warm breast pressing his ear, she lay the chopsticks aside and used two bare fingers to pluck a morsel from the succulent, inner flesh. She guided it into his open mouth. His teeth automatically trapped her fingers. She paused before drawing them out and letting his tongue explore every island, ridge, and delta in her fingerprints.

Blake—his mind utterly silent—complied with every nuance of movement, gesture, shift of arm or leg, and she with his. She was a little girl, coy and shy. She was a tigress who took what she wanted, the eager innocent quivering at his touch, but guiding, knowing how to lead while seeming to follow.

Only the Pinot Noir remained un-sampled that night.

Chapter 5

Next Day, Sunday, October 22nd
Shanghai to Wuhan, China Eastern #2506

The morning started in bed.

Fluffy white robes, graceful feet with scarlet toenails versus his boney ones, spoons ticking as they stirred heavy cream into delicate ceramic cups of strong coffee, the crunch of Jian Bing crepes, thick bacon, poached eggs in cups, sausage links that snapped when bit, her mellifluous chuckle before "Here, did you see this?" followed by raucous noise from his notebook computer and a YouTube video quickly turned down...

Mid-morning, he returned to his own barely used room, showered and changed back into travel clothes. He repacked, and on a sudden urge mussed the covers on his unused bed, felt silly about doing it, and finally huffed and smiled at himself.

Checking out—Megyn was in Navy blue today, pleated skirt, vested jacket, clear finger and toenail polish. The airport preliminaries for the domestic flight to Wuhan passed with a minimum of conversation. Hands meeting and clasping momentarily while walking the concourse, an arm out, "You first," a thank-you nod, gesture toward the bathroom, waiting, a hand toward the gate, boosting bags into the overhead...

When China Eastern's flight 2506 climbed out of Shanghai and turned west, he couldn't hold back the words.

"I'm falling in love with you," he whispered in her ear. It was all he could do to keep from tasting it with his tongue.

She hummed a sigh and lay her head on his shoulder.

It was the best morning-after he'd ever known.

Don't rush this, his mind cautioned. Don't make the same mistake.

His relationship with Julie had been chemistry, too, but very different. They couldn't keep their hands off each other, but it always felt rushed, like it'd disappear if they took too long. Getting married had seemed like the right thing to do, but it became a horrid lesson for him, and fatal for her.

Megyn shifted on his shoulder.

"Where are we?" She asked.

He looked at his watch. "More than halfway. About an hour to Wuhan."

Julie was burgers and fries, Jerry Lee Lewis, and beer, or the house rosé if they dressed up, but that, other than sex, was about it with her.

Megyn listened—really listened—to straight-ahead jazz, complex orchestrations, light but nuanced chamber music, and 70s rock and roll. And then she could discuss it, put into words what she felt, what she thought. And the way she looked at him, was like her mind was working, exploring, probing for ideas. She always had something unexpected to say or ask. And now there was sex. Indescribable sex. Animal, mindless, soul obliterating sex.

But would that be enough, or would this just become like before? Where was the fault? Was it him? Or something in Julie? And what about Megyn?

Different, yes, but in the right way?

"That'll be Anhui Province," she piped toward the window, her hair up in the bun again with the jadestone, gold pin holding it in place. "Hefei is the capital," she mused. "We memorized them in school. Thirteen of the fifty biggest cities in the world are in China. Shanghai and Beijing are in the top ten, and Wuhan is bigger than New York City."

Far below, the landscape was varying shades of green even though it was late October. No roads or railways were visible from this altitude, but the cities were obvious. A large river almost directly below meandered in a mostly east-west direction. Blake guessed it would be the Yangtze. Emptying into the Pacific at Shanghai, it ran four thousand miles across the center of the country. Ocean-going vessels could navigate nearly a thousand of them.

Blake leaned back away from the window. "You were lucky. We had fifty pairs, states and capitals, to memorize in Mrs. Rodner's eighth grade Geography. Everyone hated her."

"How come?"

"You had to do what she wanted, no discussion. She sipped at a bottle of Coke from the deep drawer of her desk. It got lighter and lighter throughout the day but never ran out. Someone saw her topping it up with a bottle of Wild Turkey between classes. In the afternoon, if the bell didn't wake her, we'd tip-toe out."

"She passed out?" Megyn shook her head. "Our bad ones were Party zealots, Chairman Mao devotees."

Suddenly, she got a worried look on her face and glanced across the aisle and then between the seats, forward and back. She pushed herself up on the armrests and glanced around the cabin.

"Something wrong?" He asked.

She shook her head. "We're in China now. Can't talk about some things."

Would they arrest him if he said something bad about Mao, took a picture of the wrong thing, was misunderstood?

But he was a US citizen. They could throw him out, but as long as it wasn't a capital crime like drugs or murder, that was probably all they could do.

But Megyn carried a Chinese passport. She was still a citizen. Consequences would be different for her. Or could the US intervene because of her dual citizenship? Who would take precedence?

He purposely took the discussion back into safe territory.

"Mrs. Rodner at my school was an awful example," he said.

"Teachers are just people, of course. They have problems like everyone else. Most of mine did a good job. They cared about their students. I respect that. When I'm at a job with eager students, I go all in for them. And not because it's good for business–which it is—but, well, I guess I just like people. The ones I get in class are usually married, have young kids, and want to make the world a better place."

He wove his head. "Of course, a few classes don't work out. Expectations are different, or something happens in the news," he laughed, "or it snows two feet and flights are cancelled."

He chewed his lip a moment. "There was this one guy... He was in charge of the group and asked me to give everyone a grade so he could find out who to fire. I told him there is no test, no grade for the class, and that besides all that, that was his job, not mine. Mid-morning, the security guy showed up and walked me out the door. Class over. Go away and don't come back. I billed them for my actual expenses and the one day I started, but they never paid. Won't go there again."

He opened his mouth for a deep breath, caught the scent and taste of Megyn's hair, and closed his lips to savor it. His mind supplied a word, *fecund*. And images of seeds pushing out shoots, one going down, another stretching up to break the surface, then twisting up for the sun...

Megyn's scent was like that. Rich, earthy...

Fertile?

Blake loved babies—tiny fingernails, pudgy toes, giggles and poops—but in their six years, Julie had been adamant. "No. Not ... now." He was afraid to guess what her hesitation was really saying.

Having a baby with Megyn...? Would she want to? Could she? Would it be risky?

She shifted on his shoulder.

"What was your school like?" He asked, forcing his mind back into the airplane and the hiss of air. "Growing up, I mean."

Megyn shrugged. "Confusing and regimented. Schools re-opened the year I started. Most teachers had no experience."

"I'm sorry, re-opened?"

"Mao suspended—closed—schools in 1966. Intellectuals were purged." She hesitated. "Some were beaten, stoned, driven away. Some were..." She paused for a deep breath. "They reneged in 1970, but nobody wanted to teach."

Blake huffed. "That shouldn't have been a surprise."

"So," she continued, "the Party chose the teachers. Almost none were qualified. And that's when I started First Grade. It was little more than babysitting."

Five years younger than me, Blake realized. *She's forty-eight.*

Another thought came.

Menopause?

He wanted to Google an answer, but not here, not where she might look over his shoulder.

Last night had been... spontaneous... and unprotected.

An uneasy thought crowded in:*Was she trying to get pregnant? That happened, he was sure, not just in* movies.

Megyn interrupted his mental wandering.

"Mother still has my Red Book. We carried them all the time. Teachers orated from it, and we repeated it back, line by line. All the books—math, history, everything—had to have Party approval. 'Mao said this' and 'Mao said that' was common in every book. 'Build the new China,' they said. It was all very heroic, but also naïve, and in hindsight, transparent."

Blake grimaced. He'd seen the news reports of the programming being done on the children in China, the Party indoctrination. But despite it, Megyn had obviously become an effective, independent woman.

"Party dogma filled everything," she said. "In math, a word problem might ask, 'If comrade Xin produces three hundred and fifty kilograms of cotton on eight *mou* of land and then the Party rewards him an additional four *mou* next year, how much is his new duty?'"

"Five twenty-five," Blake answered without thinking. "And what's a *mou*?"

Megyn grinned. "About an eighth of an acre." She turned to him. "You're so much like my engineers in Sunnyvale. Do you all do that?"

"What?"

"Word problems. Do you all do them in your head?"

Blake shrugged. "The answer just comes."

Megyn closed her eyes and leaned back in the seat. "I remember this dance my sister-comrades and I learned. We were eight or nine. We stomped the rhythm with our bare feet, *Ta-da, Ta-da, Ta-da-da*, then again, *Ta-da, Ta-da, Ta-da-da*. And the words fit the rhythm—funny I don't remember the words now except that you had to look mean and angry. We started with the left foot —stomping out some evil—and then switched to the other foot each time around."

Her knees bounced under the edge of her Navy-blue skirt with the rhythm of her bare feet, her shoes neatly positioned to the side on the floor.

"I'd tilt my head one way or the other to track where we were. Our uniforms were dark green cotton blouses with matching caps —I sewed on the red star—and matching skirts with pleats. I was awarded a Chairman Mao button for memorizing and got to display it on my collar. The only one in my troop of eight. I added some hand movements and extra steps. At assemblies, they put us up front. Those girls were like my sisters, all connected, chanting together, moving the same, our feet slapping the concrete as one..."

She looked at Blake.

"The Communists knew how to indoctrinate kids, and they're getting better and better."

She paused. "That's why you're going to the university is so important. They need to see what real people are like. They need to see you, hear your ideas, understand what human really is." She leaned back. "It's too late for the adults. They've been entrained to one interpretation of events by repetition and hearing nothing else. The Communists know to keep drumming it in and block any other messages." She began shaking her head. "We were good little Communists, me and my comrades. Later, when I realized how they were programming us, I was so ashamed."

"You were, what?" he asked, "Six years old? Kids don't know

any better. That's what school and parents are for, to teach them right and wrong, how things work, how to think for themselves. But if all they get is one side, how would they know otherwise?"

She shook her head. "No, we knew. Eventually, if not before. New books came out almost every year. In them, things changed. People that had been heroes became traitors. Teachers collected the old ones so you couldn't compare, but one year I left mine at home when they gave out the new. That night, I compared them. The section on the Nationalists and Chiang Kai-shek was shorter in the new book and very different. The old book said they were helping Mao and the Communists fight the Japanese invaders, but in the new, they were traitors to the people.

"The next day, I stupidly asked the teacher. I thought I could trust her. But she grabbed both my books, accused me of lying, and sent me home. Mother read the note she sent, then had me tell her what really happened. When I finished, she said this was a key lesson in life. 'Things change,' she said. 'Accept them as they are. And then again at how they become. But never question it. That was your mistake, allowing the teacher to know that you noticed. You must keep such things secret. You and I don't make the world, daughter, but for those who are clever, we can sway those around us. Be clever. And be subtle.'"

Megyn took a long breath and sighed.

"The next day, I did as Mother directed. I went to the teacher and started crying. I said I was wrong, and that I was sorry. I added that, the old book was wrong and that it was right for the Party to destroy it. After that, I was her pet student. Mother was right about her, about a lot of things in the real world."

"She sounds like a clever woman."

"I'm lucky that way, to have someone close I can trust."

She studied Blake for a moment, then put a hand on his arm.

"At University, some of my friends were openly critical of the government. The Party doesn't like that. So, those students were watched, and if you didn't want to become suspect too, you kept your distance, publicly for sure, and in private, if you weren't absolutely sure of everyone."

Blake waited.

She leaned close and spoke almost in a whisper. "I got my Master's in the spring of 1989 and moved to Shanghai to work for Comac. Do you remember that summer?"

Blake thought for a moment. "I was a software engineer at Motorola then, but no, nothing special."

Her fingers squeezed his arm. "1989? Student protests? Tiananmen Square?"

"Oh, yes," he said, excited, "I remember that!"

"Sh!" she cautioned.

Blake lowered his voice. "That student in front of the tank? The way he defied it, daring the driver. And when tank turned to scoot around him, he stepped in front to block it again. Incredible defiance and courage. I'll never forget that."

Megyn was nodding.

"Some friends were in graduate school at Shanghai University. We shared an apartment there, me working at Comac, them in school."

She glanced over the seat backs in both directions, then leaned in close. "You can't talk about this," she said, a deadly serious look on her face.

"Okay."

"I'd be arrested if they found out."

Blake nodded and felt his heart rise up. She was going to tell him something, some deep secret. He didn't know—didn't care— what she was going to say. What mattered was that she trusted him. Totally!

She began. "For the protests on that day, my friends and I were assigned to a train station in downtown Shanghai."

"It wasn't just in Beijing?"

"No. But in Shanghai and the other cities, the Army moved in to break us up. Guns, armored cars, tanks... They didn't hold back like you saw in Tiananmen Square, probably because everyone could see what was happening there."

"We ran," Megyn went on. "Hundreds of us. Two of the men I knew were shot in the back. Many others arrested. But the Party didn't know about me, so I could go on as if nothing had happened. A year and a half later, Comac moved me to Sunnyvale to start the office there, and I lost track of everyone.

"Then, one morning in the coffee shop where I stopped on the way to work, an Asian man I'd never seen handed me a note. It told me to create a gmail account and the name to use, and to send a message to a certain other account. I got an answer from someone who turned out to be one of the young men that had disappeared after the protests. He'd escaped to North Vietnam, worked a ship to Kuala Lumpur, and then into the United States as a political refugee."

She smirked, "Since then, we've cultivated our own little network of dissidents."

Blake was astonished. "That's incredible! I mean, you were there, it really happened to you—and you've kept it up since then, too?"

A chime sounded and the seat belt sign came on.

She took a deep breath. "Remember, you can't mention this here."

Blake looked at her perfect makeup, every hair in place, the ironed blouse, the arrow-straight pleats in her skirt... She didn't look like a rebel, but she was!

She squeezed his arm. "Sometimes, I'm not sure which I want more, love and security, or for everyone to just live their own lives like they want."

After a moment, she added, "When this is all over, maybe we could spend some more time together."

Blake's heart leapt up.

"I've got some time before the flight home. Maybe do some sightseeing? You could show me your China, not the one tourists see."

"Or," she said, "we could go somewhere else. Australia or New Zealand, maybe."

Blake didn't know the mileage but was sure those were quite a way, and likely to be expensive once they were there. Not knowing if she would pay her own way or not, he hedged.

"South Korea is very cosmopolitan. Not as over-the-top as Shanghai, but I know some places in Seoul you might like."

She nodded. "Or maybe somewhere more adventuresome?

Hanoi or Bangkok?"

Blake offered, "I have a cousin in Chingmai. He could show us around."

Another slow nod then, "I hear Singapore is nice."

Blake's eyes lit up. "Yes, Singapore. I know a guy there, too. The Hawker stalls are the way to eat. Eight, ten, a dozen vendors in one place with picnic tables. Pick the longest line and order what everyone else is getting."

She nodded on his arm. "Sounds fun."

"That's him," Megyn announced, her head nodding toward a man just past the roped-off Arrivals area.

Blake's work with defense customers was no secret. He listed his customers on his website. Boeing and Raytheon, both big in the defense arena, were prominent. And he knew that some Chinese companies built military products remarkably similar, suspiciously similar, to ones he'd worked on. The Chengdu J-10 versus the General Dynamics F-16 was but one example. But anyone who knew security measures in US defense corporations would also know that Blake's work exposed him to no secrets. To a foreign power—if they'd done their homework—Blake wouldn't be very interesting.

But he couldn't be sure.

Blake sized up his driver-to-be.

The man looked young and bored. A college graduate, Blake guessed from his apparent age and because the University was paying him. New-looking, dark gray suit, white shirt, and plain blue tie.

A nondescript chauffeur.

But then again, if he was actually a party minion assigned to watch and report on Blake, his apparent indifference would be a good dodge.

"Blake," Megyn said to them both, "this is William. And William, this is Mr. Spencer."

Blake put out his hand and smiled. "Nice to meet you, William."

The returned handshake was a polite squeeze accompanied by a small bow, but the young man's eyes never rose to Blake's face.

He motioned to the glass exit and mumbled half a dozen syllables. Blake guessed it was Chinese.

Megyn explained. "William says your van is outside. He will drive you to the hotel. Tomorrow at eight, he will take you to the classroom. He'll drive you back for lunch, and at one-thirty, take you in for the afternoon session. Class is over at five—back to the hotel for dinner and sleep."

Blake kept his face still. Either Chinese was a lot more efficient than English, or Megyn had added a lot on her own.

She pointed across the reception hall. "I'm getting a rental for the drive out to Mother's. You can contact me in an emergency. Use my usual number; it forwards to me here, but I'll be an hour or two away, depending on traffic."

Blake couldn't hide his disappointment. "When will I see you?" He pointed to William. "We could drive out to your place?"

Megyn's eyes narrowed. "Not appropriate. Mother is... traditional."

Blake felt his ears redden. He'd probably sounded like a hormone-driven teenager.

She went on. "We have an outing next Sunday to the provincial museum with two senior students. I think it is informative."

Blake nodded.

She hadn't mentioned Saturday. Apparently, it would be open, a down-day as he called it. What could he do? And what should he not do? This was Communist China. The mainland. How much free rein would he have when off William's leash? Would there be a suggested list of places he could go? What if he turned left instead of right? Would someone intercept him with the pretext of helping? He could try some sight-seeing—not his favorite activity —but, well, just about everything here would be different. And his cell phone had a reasonably good camera. But if he aimed his camera in a direction they didn't like, would they stop him before clicking the shutter? Confiscate his phone? Sneak in and borrow it while he slept, and...

Stop that, he told himself. If they did that, he had nothing to hide. He could be completely open and honest. He had nothing to hide, and therefore nothing to fear.

Blake's preferred spare time activity was to explore. Sometimes, it would be the immediate neighborhood. Sometimes, he'd take a bus or subway and go somewhere on the map that looked interesting. Near Kyoto Japan, he rode a cog train partway up Mount Hiei because it was on the map near a subway station. And at the high end, there was a cable car to the top, so he then took that. There, he bought a sandwich and drink, and seeing a sign marked "Kyoto" and pointing to a path, he started down. Stopping to sit on a rock in a bamboo forest, a man dressed all in white and wearing an extraordinarily long hat made of straw trotted past. They nodded at each other and then the man was gone. Later, he learned the man was a Tendai novice, and that they ran instead of sitting for their meditation. Eighteen miles a day for one hundred consecutive days was the requirement. If the man had stopped for half of Blake's offered sandwich, he would've had to commit suicide.

From Blake's preview of the area on Google-Earth, a forest-covered mountain, Mount Luojia, was part of the school campus across the street from the hotel. One of the three Geocaches Blake had noted from another website was on the mountain. He'd brought three US Sacagawea dollar coins, one for each of three nearby caches. He'd use the geocache app in his Android phone to get close. Then, scrambling under bushes or shifting a few rocks, he'd find the container, usually a coffee tin or old ammo box. Inside it would be a logbook and a pile of cheap trinkets. The protocol was to sign the book, take something, leave something, and much later log his "discovery" online at the sport's main website.

Blake smiled as he again imagined the next person's surprise at finding a dollar coin from the United States in the middle of Communist China.

He raised his arms and took a step to hug Megyn.

"Sunday then?"

Her eyes flared as she drew back.

"Oh," he exclaimed, looking left and right. "Sorry."

Megyn gave him a faint smile, nodded, and then turned. Her rolling suitcase with the computer bag stacked on top thumped across the joints on the marble tile floor. Her goal was a yellow and brown booth next to a side door.

Blake smiled and shook his head. He hadn't expected a Hertz rental counter in the middle of China.

He grabbed the handle of his own luggage stack and motioned for William to lead the way.

Chapter 6

Out through the dark-tinted side windows, everything was gray concrete, gray grass, gray trees, and gray sky. The van reminded Blake of those used by state department agencies. Passengers could see out a little, but not vice versa. If someone wanted to do them harm, they'd have to aim at the whole van, not any individual inside.

But Blake didn't feel comforted. The van marked him as different, a person of some interest.

The ride took more than an hour, and except toward the end, there was nothing to see except the roadway with its raised edges and highway signs.

Two hours later, William said, "Feng-Yi," and pointed ahead and across to the left. A tall, slim white building with an orange roofed, square penthouse sat back from the road at the next traffic light.

He zipped the van through a gap in traffic and bumped up a sharp ramp to the hotel's glassed-in entrance.

Inside, plain white-marble tile swept across the floor, up the walls, and wrapped the columns. Even the acoustic ceiling tiles on the ceiling matched. Surgically clean, the monotonous white was a far cry from the kaleidoscopic exuberance of Shanghai.

To the right, a two-foot, wood picket fence—the same white—sectioned off a dining area that occupied half the lobby. White-marble tables and white-cushioned metal chairs continued the sterile impression. A few customers sat solo and paired. The *tick* of chopsticks and *clack* of white ceramic echoed across the lobby.

Straight across the lobby, the white iceberg of the check-in desk jutted up from the floor. A uniformed clerk, mercifully dressed in tans, stood. Hunched forward, eyes down, elbows on the podium, he appeared to be reading.

A gift shop to the left was dark with its door shut. Inside, Blake spotted a glass-fronted refrigerator with green and clear bottles of water, small bottles of wine on the next shelf, and cans of beer on the third. Overseas, Blake needed bottled water to drink and brush his teeth, but with the lobby shop closed, he might have to wait for morning before getting his supply.

William called and waved from the check-in desk, the clerk smiling.

Blake handed over his passport and waited. In some countries, the hotel would hold his passport while checking with the Police. Without it, he couldn't board a plane to leave.

The clerk flipped past the photo page to find the double-page, stamped and signed Chinese work Visa Blake had gotten in LA ahead of time. They'd reviewed the official letter from the school and the affidavit from the Phoenix Police department that said he wasn't a known criminal. Blake spent the night in LA before getting his passport back with the two-page stamp. It stated he would have a one-month window in which to arrive, teach, and then leave. Not the most welcoming of documents.

The hotel clerk hand-wrote in his logbook, then returned the passport.

Blake exhaled in relief and put it in his shirt pocket, safer there from pickpockets than the ones in his pants.

The clerk nodded as he offered a brass key fastened to an elongated, green plastic diamond.

Blake couldn't help smiling. It was the same as the Holiday Inn keys he remembered as a child in the 1950s. The room number, 1124, had been heat embossed into the plastic and then hand-painted white.

The monotony of white changed to blond in his room. Wallpaper with two broad vertical stripes in marginally different shades established the color pallet. One repeated in the carpet, the second in the flowers on the polyester bedcover, and then back to the first for the desk and television.

Blake hesitated, key in one hand, the handle of his roller bags in the other, to study the TV. It looked to be an old glass-tube model with controls for what he guessed would be volume, channel, vertical, and horizontal hold. There was no remote waiting on top. This part of China was still using analog television transmission.

The setting sun beamed straight into his face from a large window looking out to the west. The air was thick with fog or smoke, and Blake could look directly at the sun with only a tiny squint.

"West," he said aloud to set his internal compass.

Five miles that way would be the bridge over the Yangtze—Chang Jiang—with Wuhan's downtown on the other side. "Eleven million people," he said aloud. In the United States, only New York and Los Angeles had more, but they were dwarfed by Shanghai.

China's population was staggering.

He sat on the end of the bed and waited for the TV to warm up. Next to him, a heat-sealed bag with slippers—white fabric with matching plastic soles—waited. He took off the shoes he'd been wearing since Shanghai and put them on. Walking to the door and back to the bed, they were a good fit.

The picture on the TV bloomed then slowly shrank to size.

He remembered the channels he'd watched growing up. NBC and CBS—5 and 3—were first. Then ABC started transmitting on 13. Years went by before PBS showed up on 10 from a studio at Memphis State, later renamed University of Memphis. All of them played the national anthem before going off the air each night. He preferred the Air Force fighter planes in the CBS version. If his jet lag was true to form, he'd get to see what China showed at the end of their broadcast day.

Most of the hotel's channels showed incomprehensible soap operas, either in contemporary or historic settings with fancy costumes. Two of the others, 7 and 9, displayed ping-pong and soccer matches, and 13 was the weather channel. Blake scooted back on the polyester bedspread to the top of the bed and stacked the pillows to watch for the Wuhan forecast. There was a plain yellow circle with "33" on the map where the city would be.

"Ninety-one degrees Fahrenheit," he told the room. "Hot and sunny. No jacket."

He switched to the soccer game and shifted back up to the pillows. He folded on leg atop the other and noticed the edge of that slipper's sole had turned dark gray. Pulling that foot up and touching the bottom, his fingertip came away like he'd wiped it through a used ashtray.

"What the Hell?"

He scooted forward again and bent over. He pawed the carpet, and his fingertips came up gray. He patted his toe and a small puff billowed up.

Sniffing, it smelled like a barbecue grill.

He'd smelled it walking from van to hotel but thought nothing of it. People often barbecued on the weekends in Phoenix regardless of the temperature.

But, putting together the scent, the puff from the carpet, and the dense smog that'd clogged his nose and irritated his throat, it all fit another thing he'd noticed. A few blocks before the hotel, they'd driven past a man with a flat-bed cart stacked with five-inch sections of dull black cylinders. Two people, both women, were standing and talking to him. One was holding out money.

"They cook with charcoal," he mused. "Thousands of years, wood and charcoal."

Outside filling the air and embedded in his room's carpet, ash from open fires used for household cooking had polluted China for thousands of years. And it still did.

Blake's hand unconsciously went to his shirt pocket. Next to the passport was a slip of paper with the SSID and passphrase for the hotel's WiFi connection.

The contrasts—charcoal pollution, analog TV, and computer WiFi—seemed incongruous, but here they were.

"Wow," he said in a whisper.

Chapter 7

First Day of Class, Monday, October 23
Wuhan University, Wuchang, China

The next morning, William stopped the van in front of a four-story building. He pointed. "Classroom."

Blake followed him up the four steps and inside.

A four-story open space filled the atrium, and the hard slam of the door behind them echoed for a full second. Hazy shafts of sunlight angled through windows, bounced off the polished concrete floor, and partially illuminated dual stairways in the middle of the back, one headed up to the left, the other to the right. In the corners, each turned ninety degrees and then continued up to walkways around three sides of the atrium on each floor. Like the building's plain exterior, the concrete of floor, stairs, and walls were interrupted only by glossy blue doors, one in each wing, east and west, on each floor.

William gestured to the stairs. Hoisting his heavy computer bag, Blake followed him up to the left.

At the third landing, William waited. Blake set his computer bag on the floor that circled the atrium and rubbed his arm. William pointed toward an open door in the back left corner of the building. He said something in Chinese. Through the door, Blake saw a tall white urinal, its porcelain gleaming in a shaft of sunlight.

He recognized what William had said now. It had sounded like "You shit" but without the final "t" and that rude interpretation fit. It meant "bathroom" and was one of the few Mandarin words Blake had practiced before the trip.

"Shay, shay," Blake said, nodding.

William started up the stairs again. "Three," he said in English, gesturing up.

In the US, the top floor would've been number four, but in most of the world, it was three. C programming and some other languages did the same. The first element in an array was "0". Here, it would be the "ground" floor. Above that would be 1, then 2, 3, and so on.

Inside the railing on the top landing, William was holding a blue door open. "Classroom," he said again.

Blake entered and stopped to look around.

The room was huge. Blake guessed seventy-five feet wide, and two-thirds of that, fifty, deep. An aisle down the middle split twelve rows of long gray tables with nine gray-steel, backless stools on each side.

"Nine stools times twelve rows times two sides," he mumbled to himself. *Two hundred and sixteen,* came the answer in his head.

He nodded. "Big class!"

Blake never taught more than twenty at one time, twelve being optimal for participation. He liked a free-flowing class with lots of interaction. Too many people let them hide in anonymity. He'd have to work to engage this group, and then control the flow to stay on topic while watching the clock.

Three large Sony glass CRTs weighed down each table and marked the location of white-box workstations tucked underneath.

"Three times twelve times two."

Seventy-two computers.

Again, he nodded.

At two grand per workstation with the expensive Sony CRTs, the room held $150,000 worth of computer equipment. If all the classrooms in the building were the same, there was half a million dollars of equipment in this one building. Even at Chinese prices, it was a significant investment.

Blake stepped over to jiggle the mouse at the closest CRT. A login box appeared on the screen. It had the distinctive look of Ubuntu Linux. Curious, he typed "root" for the username and clicked the Login button without entering a password. The screen erased and a green-on-black terminal window appeared on the display.

He grinned.

Most embedded software engineers either logged in or elevated themselves to "root" status for most of their work. It was dangerous, but many preferred it as an expedient to keep up with racing thoughts. Having a "root" login with no password expedited the process.

He typed *uname -a* at the prompt and pressed Enter. The computer answered.

Linux moe17 4.19.66-v7+...

Moe17? Blake chuckled aloud. Would he also find larry17 and curly17 elsewhere in the room? And what about shemp17? He wondered what other Americanisms these kids would favor.

Tall, green shades covered the windows on both left and right walls, the only color inside the room other than pale white on walls and ceiling, and gray linoleum on the floor. Three air conditioners hummed and blew cool air on each sidewall. The overhead fluorescent lights added to the chalky look. Turning around, a single red box with a white cross attached to the back wall drew his eye.

"First-aid kit," he said.

At the front of the room, Blake's lectern would be a short, glossy wood box with angled top. It sat on a wide table. A large white projection screen hung on the classroom's front wall. Next to the lectern were cables and connectors for the projector, Ethernet, and a power strip with two prong slots, no ground holes.

Everything connected, he clicked the display on his notebook to full screen on the first slide of his lecture. "Embedded Computer

Considerations," filled the big screen behind him.

He was ready.

Students arrived in twos and threes, chattering in Chinese and glancing in his direction.

They all wore what appeared to be brand new clothes. The males wore Docker-like slacks and printed short-sleeve shirts, and the females had pleated, dark skirts with white or pastel blouses. Everyone's shoes were well-polished.

At three minutes before the hour with all two hundred and sixteen stools occupied, the students chatted softly among themselves with the occasional glance at Blake as he stood quietly waiting next to the lectern. A young woman in a two-piece black and dark brown herringbone-tweed suit stepped into the room and pulled the door shut making the latch click. Conversation ceased.

She walked down the center aisle, the click of her shiny black pumps on the floor the only sound other than the hum and blow from the air conditioners.

She stopped in front of Blake, her back to the room.

"I will translate for you," she declared.

He offered his hand. "Nice to meet you. Please call me, Blake."

She responded with four stiff fingers and a thumb press to the back of his hand.

"I am Miss Chou. For everyone's benefit, I will speak to the class in Mandarin. I will introduce you, announce breaks, the lunch hour, and the end of each day. We will start at Nine, take two hours at Noon, and stop at Five."

She turned to glance at the clock at the back of the room.

One minute 'till.

Blake thought of a dog on a leash.

"You will," she resumed, "speak one sentence, then stop. I will translate. I will nod for you to continue."

At the back of the room, the second hand twitched straight up and was joined by the snap of the minute hand moving into alignment.

She turned on her heel, back stiff and straight, and began

speaking to the class in Mandarin.

It sounded like someone berating a small child. And more than her voice, there was something in the set of her shoulders, her formal attire, her stiffness that grated on his nerves. Although he couldn't understand the words, he wondered if the students had the same impression.

Six hours of that per day for five days, then another five days next week, would strain his patience. Blake had taught through translators before. It doubled the time to deliver the material. His estimate at the slide count, nine hundred pages, had not factored this in. He acknowledged the miscalculation to himself. He had twice as much material as needed. He began mentally revising the delivery. He'd skip the repetitive introductory pages and recaps around each section, that would help, but he'd still need to gloss over a lot of meat.

Blake always brought more content than needed. You could never tell where questions might lead. And this was just a difference in degree. He'd dealt with before. Watching the clock, he could extemporaneously follow up some question and add fifteen minutes. Or coming across a rudimentary slide, tell the class to let him know if they had any questions but then flip to the next slide. More often than not, no one would object.

For insurance, when a customer paid for four days of content, he made sure they always got that plus a little bonus. But here, that'd be more like a 100% bonus. He'd have to cut, literally, half the material. For that, he needed to know what they already knew. That meant feedback. Their questions would tell him what they did and didn't know.

Miss Chou finished her initial harangue, turned to him, and after a moment, flared her eyes at him.

Blake smiled, politely, at her impatience. He said, "Thank you," and clicked the Page Down button on his computer's keyboard. From the corner of his eye, he caught the flicker on the projection screen as his first slide appeared.

Blake never read the bullets aloud. They could all read or wait for the Mandarin translation. Instead, he began to outline what it said, then caught himself up short when he realized he'd spoken a complete sentence.

The translation to Mandarin took much longer than he'd expected, but maybe he'd said something that required more explanation. Idioms, he knew, would be a problem. Perhaps he'd let one slip in without realizing it.

When she nodded to him, he spoke one sentence and then stopped. As her voice scraped out each Mandarin syllable, his mind started suggesting titles.

Ms. Clicky-clack. Prissy Missy. Tweed-y Bird. Barking Jay.

Blake swept his eyes around the classroom. No one smiled, frowned, or reacted in any way as she yapped. Two hundred and sixteen faces watched as if they already knew what she was going to say.

Cultures could be so very different.

In Japan, no one showed expression during his lecture, and they only asked questions on breaks or after class. In Germany, the written material was gospel. Students would argue if he brought up an exception not on the slide. He learned to pencil in corrections on the slide as he spoke, and then told them to add them to their notes as well. That precluded their arguments. And in Brazil, no one entered the classroom before the appointed start time, and then they ignored his attempts to begin for another five. In Italy, that delay was another fifteen minutes in the morning, and half an hour later after lunch.

Halfway through slide number eight, a hand went up from the right side of the classroom.

The translator held up a finger and continued until her Mandarin ran out. She rotated slightly on her heel to precisely face the raised hand, stuck out her hand palm up, and nodded. A boy in a blue and white striped shirt rose, and keeping his arms rigid at his sides, fired off his question in the sharp syllables Blake now recognized as Mandarin.

Blake waited for her translation so he could answer. But instead, she apparently answered the student, at considerable length, because the boy nodded and sat down.

This was a problem. Blake needed to hear, and to answer, their questions. He was the teacher, not her. Her job was translation, not explanation.

She turned to Blake. "You may continue now."

He pursed his lips. He'd have to pull her aside on the first break and set things right. For the moment, however, he was stuck.

But after a few more slides and tedious translations, another hand rose. As before, the translator finished her delivery, then granted the questioner permission to speak. And again, she answered without consulting Blake.

"You may continue now."

Blake ground his teeth. Their questions would tell him what they did and didn't know. With that, he could start tuning the content to these kids, to what they already knew, and what they didn't. He needed to hear those questions!

On the first bullet of the next slide, three hands shot up like rockets.

But this time, when she gestured to the nearest, he stayed in his seat and tilted his head, his eyes slightly narrowed as he spoke. And the instant he finished, another student popped up and practically barked at her. And when he finished, two in the back row stood, gestured, and added to what sounded to Blake like an open revolt.

The translator's shoulders slowly rose at each new barrage. And the heel of her right foot would rise an inch, pause for a break in the bombardment, but then stomp down when it didn't come only to rise again.

She's pissed!

A smile tried to pull up the ends of Blake's lips. He put up a hand to wipe it away.

And when she finally found a gap to jump into, her voice was like a heavy cleaver chopping through a cow's leg bone. Shards flew left and right in her verbal butchery.

But the classroom was in revolt, and four more students stood and began shouting her down.

Blake needed to stop it, to regain control, but how? He had neither the language nor any understanding of the culture.

The translator turned to him, her face and eyes red, and snapped something—in Mandarin, Blake guessed. She then stomped one of her black patent leather shoes on the floor, turned, and stalked up the aisle as students continued their verbal assault. She flung the door hard against its stops, and when it rebounded and slammed shut, she was gone.

Silence descended on the classroom.

Stunned and blinking his eyes, whatever had just happened, Blake knew it had also killed his class. His slides were in English. He spoke only English. And this was mainland China where everyone spoke Mandarin.

His seven grand fee? *Pfffft!*

All those hours of preparation, travel, the two-week hole in his schedule... Wasted.

"It's okay," a thin voice said.

Blake looked for the speaker.

In the middle of the sixth row, a hand waved. "We understand you fine." A young man was nodding.

"You understand me?" Blake asked.

Lots of heads bobbed.

A young woman with pretty eyes in the first row smiled. "We understand English mostly good. And if some don't, we help." She raised her hand, palm up toward him. "You teach. We listen."

A triangular-faced young man next to her with black-rimmed glasses and an open notebook computer on his lap said, "You teach now, please? English Okay." He pushed his glasses back up on his nose then positioned his hands over the keyboard, ready to type.

Blake grinned in amazement. They'd understood him all along.

And when *Clacky Shoes Herringbone* got something wrong, they knew it.

They weren't asking questions; they were correcting her translation.

And when she argued with them about it, they drove her out!

Blake's grin went from ear to ear.

He knew these kids. They were rude, direct, and said it like it was.

They were engineers!

Engineers were direct and precise with their questions,

impatient when they didn't get an answer, angry when they knew it was wrong, and could be vicious with pretenders and charlatans.

Blake knew engineers because that's what he was. It had cost him full-time jobs more than once, and that was why he'd become a consultant instead of a full-time employee. Companies needed what he could do, put up with the laser focus and abrupt, bordering into rude commands he would issue while working a problem, and then shove him out the door when done.

He billed in half-day increments and for actual expenses. And other than that once, they paid—in full—within thirty days.

He turned his head slightly to the side and raised an eyebrow. "Testing, one, two, three?"

A voice answered, "Four, five, six."

"Seven, eight, nine, ten," several more chorused through the accompanying sweep of laughter.

Blake grinned, then made a funny face at them. They growled and grimaced back like kids playing.

The boy in the front row with the glasses pushed them up again, his face both annoyed and amused.

When the ruckus died down, Blake pointed to and repeated his explanation for the first bullet on the projector. When he stopped, several heads nodded.

"Any questions?"

No hands rose, and several heads shook *No.*

The next bullet took less time.

Blake caught on. The nods showed him where to speed up, and their absence when to slow down. He talked around the points on the slides, watched the class, and then added examples and comparisons where needed, or moved on to the next point.

Faces watched him, turned to the screen, and then came back. Some looked down to hand-write notes or click the keys on notebook computers.

And the questions began.

A hand would rise, or a voice would interrupt. "Sir?" He would stop and let them ask their question—sometimes wrestled out in tangled English—and he'd try to answer. Sometimes it took a couple of attempts to understand the confusion or to communicate his answer. Occasionally, his words would be translated by one student for another, and the class would talk back and forth, before it would die down and someone would say, "Thank you; please go on."

He started moving around the room as he liked to do and used the computer's wireless remote as he did. He spoke from the back, stood next to someone who looked sleepy, moved to the far corner, worked his way back to the lectern. He used a red laser to point out a word on the projection screen or something in the room—the air conditioners, the red box with emergency bandages on the back wall—to make a point. Or sometimes he'd just use his hands to mimic someone's fuzzy hair and then work that into his presentation. Smiles and laughter told him they understood, or that at a minimum, they were paying attention.

Uptake would depend on what they already knew. If they had the basic ideas to which new information could be attached, they'd learn. If not, and with two hundred plus of them, there wasn't much more he could do.

Still, he was pleased. The class was going well, and he could adjust his delivery as he felt appropriate rather than doing a hatchet job.

The clock on the back wall was twenty minutes past mid-morning break when he noticed the time.

"Let's take a break now." He pointed to the clock. "Fifteen minutes."

Blake bustled up the aisle but many of the other males beat him down one flight for the line at the single urinal bathroom.

The room nearly empty and two minutes of break-time left, he tapped the mouse pad twice to wake his sleeping display. Unfortunately, the mouse pointer was sitting directly over the Close icon, and on the second click, the slide viewer program quit.

He smiled, shook his head, and launched the file browser. When he clicked into the Documents folder on the way to today's lecture, a tiny photograph of Julie appeared in the bottom corner. The image must've been in that folder for months, but he hadn't noticed it.

He grabbed the picture with the mouse intending to drag it to the Pictures folder, but a voice stopped him.

"Who's that?"

Blake looked up. "I'm sorry?"

The young woman in the front row with pretty eyes was pointing at the projection screen. "Who is she?"

"That's my... wife." He left out "ex" on purpose.

"We were just married. Six, not quite seven, years ago."

"Is that your home?" The young woman went on. She was cute with a fair complexion, swooping nose, balanced features, and brown eyes. She reminded him of Megyn.

He double-clicked the picture to full screen it.

"That's our house in Surprise, Arizona," he said, turning to point to the projection screen. "Surprise is a suburb of Phoenix."

With two hundred-plus students, Blake wouldn't be able to learn many names, but if he connected with a few, that'd help build everyone's trust.

"If you don't mind," he asked, "what's your name?"

She flicked her head tossing her bangs aside, and then smiled. "I'm Zoey!"

Flirting? Blake kept his expression friendly but neutral. She was probably thirty years his junior.

"Hi, Zoey," he said and tilted his head. "Is that a common name in China?"

"Oh, no. That's my American name. We all take American names in English class. My real name is Tong Yan. Tong is my family name."

She pointed up to the screen. "Isn't Arizona above California?"

"Arizona is next to California, not above it." He bent down to the keyboard. "Let me show you."

In a moment, Google-Earth's blue-green sphere spun into view on the projection screen as it steadied over the center of North America. He clicked, swiped, and scrolled until only the southwestern states filled the display.

"This is California." He wiggled the mouse pointer over the state to attract attention.

Zoey nodded. Her eyes were on the screen.

"It covers more than half of our Pacific coastline," he said. "San Francisco is about here," he jiggled the pointer. "Los Angeles—is down here. Over to the right, this is Nevada with Las Vegas down in the corner with all its casinos. South and east of that, or just plain east from southern California is my state, Arizona."

He looked up to see if she was still following. Next to her, the boy with the slippery glasses had returned. And looking up, he saw the classroom was nearly full. Everyone was watching the screen.

"I was just showing Zoey and—" he gestured to the boy with glasses next to her and raised his eyebrows.

"Alex," Zoey said, opening a hand toward the boy who nodded.

He looked to be nineteen or twenty, younger than Zoey but males that age always looked younger than the girls. He had fidgeted a lot during the lecture, his eyes always moving from the slide to Blake, down to the laptop he'd brought then back to the screen. Blake guessed he was ADHD and had learned to turn it to his advantage.

Blake was the same, albeit self-diagnosed. Reading about the condition, he came across the term *hyper-focus*. It meant he, and probably Alex, could channel the nervous energy into a single, laser-like beam of concentration. The distractions their minds threw forced them to compensate by focusing on detail after detail. Alex could be a top-notch engineer, but also like Blake, he would be challenged by social skills.

Blake continued to the class. "I was just showing Zoey and Alex where I live in the United States. This is Arizona," he said, gesturing toward the big projection screen. "Think cowboys and Indians. We still have a lot of both in Arizona," he repeated as several faces silently mouthed his state's name. "But they're not on horses like you see in the movies, and we don't shoot each other anymore."

There were some chuckles, but some coursed eyebrows and pained expressions.

He wondered if he'd said something wrong but continued anyway. "If you saw the earlier picture, that was my wife, Julie.

Taken when we were first married."

"Do you still live there, in the same house?" Zoey prompted.

"Yes, I do."

Blake realized he'd said *I* not *we*. He hoped they wouldn't pick up on it. The failure of his marriage, not to mention Julie's suicide, was not something he wanted to discuss. Especially not with college kids in China.

He zoomed the view.

"This is Phoenix. Up to the left are the suburbs of Glendale, Peoria, and Surprise where I live. They are all parts of greater Phoenix, like Wuchang is to Wuhan. There's even a river, the Agua Fria, separating them. But unlike your Yangtze, there's no water in it. And it's quite small. Less than a hundred feet across."

Alex said, "Thirty meters."

Someone asked a question in Chinese while looking at Blake, but then someone else started to answer. As with the earlier discussions between students after the translator left, their speech sounded more liquid, smooth and rolling, instead of choppy and angry.

"Excuse me," Blake asked when they seem to have finished. "Your speech—the way you are talking—it's different. Is that still Mandarin?"

Alex shook his head and pushed up his glasses. "No. Among ourselves, we use what you would call Cantonese. It's our own language."

Blake cocked his head. "Your own language?"

"Most of us grew up in Guangzhou," Alex explained. "That's south of here, about half-way to Hong Kong. Westerners call our city Canton, and so the language we use is named Cantonese. It's what we learn at home and use with our families. Most students here already know it, or the ones from somewhere else learn it because it's so common. And it's more—I think you would say— eloquent. We only use the Beijing street language—Mandarin— when we have to. It doesn't have the finer aspects, so it takes longer to express yourself."

Zoey waved impatiently toward the screen.

"You were going to show us your house?" She was smiling and

looking at him. She flicked her head again and her black hair flashed in the light. She blinked her eyes.

Amused, Blake smiled and said, "Yes, I'll show you the house." He looked at Zoey. "My *wife* picked it."

He clicked and zoomed Google-Earth until six houses, three on each side of a black street, filled the screen. He wiggled the mouse on the roof of one. "This is it. I'll switch to street view so you can see what it looks like from the front."

The view tilted and rolled upward on the big screen like the room was on a roller-coaster. In a moment, the front of his house steadied on the screen. The picture showed it soon after sunrise, and Blake realized it was a recent picture. The Google picture car must've gone through the neighborhood in the last few months because the flower beds were empty, and the paint looked dingy as it did now. His garage door stood open, and the back of his blue Honda Accord showed in full sunlight. Google had fuzzed out the license plate, but a lot of stuff inside his garage was visible.

"That's my car," Blake narrated as he moved the mouse, "my water heater, my bicycle—it's a Canondale made somewhere here in China—and back there, that blue thing is a reloading press, and to its left—"

Zoey raised her hand. "What's a reloading press?"

Blake hesitated.

Could he talk about guns and ammunition in China? To students? No one had given him a list of forbidden topics, and America's love of guns common knowledge, but it was also contrary to China's "no guns for citizens" policy.

How much could he say?

But he was here, and they'd asked. Megyn said they wanted the students to get to know an American, and he did shoot, and he did make his own ammunition. That would, he felt, qualify him as a red-blooded American.

He decided to take the plunge.

"The reloading press makes ammunition for guns. I buy lead bullets, empty brass shells, primers, and propellant. The press puts them together into cartridges. I have to be precise, and obviously very careful. Measurements to a ten-thousandth of an inch—"

"2.54 micrometers," Alex provided before Blake's mind did the conversion.

Blake nodded his approval.

But Alex wasn't done. "You own many guns? Machine guns, too?"

"Just handguns," Blake answered.

Alex prompted by raising his eyebrows.

"Give me a second."

Blake clicked and dragged on his notebook's mouse pad to expose his Documents folder again. Double-clicking into Pictures and then the Firearms folder, several tiny snapshots lined up. He typed control-A on the keyboard, did a right-click, and chose Open from the menu.

Picture after picture of guns opened, each one covering the one before. When done, the last filled the huge projection screen.

He walked to it.

"This a 1911," he said, patting the screen. "It shoots a 45-caliber bullet." He held up his hand in the projector's light and made a half-inch gap between thumb and forefinger. "About this big around and not much longer."

Zoey frowned in the front row. "I don't like guns."

Blake answered in measured tones. "I believe all life is sacred. Life's purpose, I believe, is to increase life, to improve it. But by that same token, I believe that if someone is going to take a life, then stopping them preserves life."

Zoey was still frowning.

"I know that seems somewhat contradictory. And I agree. This is a huge, complicated, and to some, a terrifying topic."

Zoey's nod looked polite but nothing more.

After a moment, he walked over in front of her.

"What would you do," he asked, "if you were walking alone at night, say down by that lake or on the mountain next to the campus, and someone came at you with a big knife?"

Zoey shook her head and folded her arms across her chest. "I don't go those places at night."

"Good for you. And like you, I don't put myself in danger, at least not on purpose. But sometimes don't we stumble into situations or circumstances, or danger finds us in what we thought was a safe place? You've heard the expression, 'Bad things happen to good people'?"

Zoey's face contorted like she was in pain.

He'd made this too personal for her.

"Alex," Blake said, turning to him, "what about you?"

The boy looked up and away for a moment, mouth open, his tongue exploring his upper lip. "I'd look for another way to go."

In the back of the room, a boy in a Che Guevara sweatshirt stood. He asked in an accusing tone, "You kill someone?"

"No," Blake answered. "And I pray—" he left out God not wanting to enlarge the discussion, "—I never have to."

The boy in the sweatshirt rebutted angrily, "But you could?"

Over on the right, a girl in a white blouse with a pink scarf tied around her neck turned and said something equally angry to the one in back but in Cantonese.

The boy cocked his head and started to answer, his voice getting louder.

Blake held up his hand.

"All right, everyone," he said louder than usual. "It's a fair question, and it deserves a fair answer."

He took a breath and the boy in the back sat down. "I suppose if I was sure someone was about to kill me or someone I loved and there was no way to get away or prevent it, then, yes, I would try to stop them. If I had a gun, I would probably shoot."

"But just wound them," Zoey suggested.

Blake shook his head. "I would shoot to stop them. Center of mass."

She shook her head. "America is very dangerous. Murders all the time. Aren't you afraid?"

He shrugged. "To be honest, most of the time, I don't think about it. The average American's experience of in-person gun violence is low. Most people live their entire lives and nothing like that ever happens except in the news. I shoot guns, yes, but only at the gun range. Paper targets. Nothing else. It's more for the camaraderie, for the friendship of others, more social than self-defense."

Zoey shifted in her seat. "Our news says America is dangerous for tourists."

Blake had to shrug again. "If you don't know what you're doing or where you are, I suppose that might be true. There are dangerous neighborhoods, places where I wouldn't go. But I might not know which ones to avoid. I might not realize it until too late."

Alex took off his glasses and started rubbing a lens with his shirttail.

"Across the river," he mused without looking up, "Wuhan has dangerous places. Near the deep-water shipping yards, for example." He put his glasses back on and looked at Blake. "You American. You *look* American. US passports are valuable, and some think you have a lot of money. You should be careful here."

Zoey snapped at him. "The Police are cleaning up those areas. And it's Hankou more than Wuhan. Wuchang is safe; the campus is safe."

Alex ignored her. "Do you take a gun when you go shopping? In America, I mean?"

"Sometimes. They tell me that's bad—being inconsistent about carrying. But if I'm running to the grocery for a Stouffer's Mac and Cheese or picking up a Classic Crust pizza, I don't bother. The gun is heavy, and if it's in my pocket, anyone who knows what to look for can tell. Or if I put it in a holster, then I've got to wear a shirt with the tail out or put on a jacket to hide it. In the summer in Phoenix, that's as much a tell as the imprint, the outline of the gun, on your clothing."

Alex's eyes stretched into circles. "You keep it secret?"

"Always," Blake said firmly. "You don't advertise. If there's a bad guy and he knows I've got a gun, he'll attack me first."

Alex looked up, lips parted, and nodded. "I see. A gun makes you a target. I hadn't thought of that. Same thing when you travel? Do you take guns with you?"

"Sometimes yes, sometimes no. It depends on several things. First, there are some cities in the US that forbid guns. Chicago and

New York, for example. If I showed up there with a gun, they'd lock me up and I'd lose my guns." He gestured to the screen. "I paid eight hundred dollars for this 1911, and then put in another five to have it Accurized."

"Accurized?" Alex asked. "What's that?"

Blake held up both hands, and touching fingertips, made one big circle. "A 1911 fresh from the manufacturer will shoot its bullets into a five or six-inch circle at twenty-five yards. That's good, but not good enough. Our Bullseye guns are then tuned by experts. They shoot much tighter groups. This one," he tapped the screen behind him, "will do a two-inch group."

A murmur of surprise rolled through the room.

"You good," Alex said with a chuckle.

Blake shook his head. "The gun can shoot a two-inch group, but I can't. I'm still learning."

He glanced at the school clock on the back wall and realized they'd been talking about his home and guns for an hour.

He crossed to the podium. "Let's get back into embedded computers before we stop for lunch. I'm glad to answer all your questions—anything you want to know—but I'm also supposed to tell you what I know about computers and real-time systems."

As he talked through the next slide, his shoulders felt relaxed and comfortable. His words came easier, like he was talking to friends instead of strangers. They'd bonded a little, the students and him. They might not agree, but they'd heard his perspective and expressed their feelings. He was not an outsider anymore. Just a person, like any of them, who happened to be standing up front, nothing more.

That evening, the tremor in Blake's hands mirrored the feeling in his stomach. He knew the symptoms of jet lag and what to do about it. Right now, he needed a filling, easy to digest dinner, and then a good night's rest.

The hot pot last night with the open smorgasbord of ingredients in the lobby restaurant had been ideal. He'd chosen recognizable ingredients from the long white, cloth-covered table and then boiled them to death in the Chinese Sterno powered pot of soup on his table. It reminded him of a New England boiled dinner except there was no corned beef, no carrots, cabbage, or potatoes. Just mystery vegetables and mystery meats.

But tonight, the long table had disappeared. Instead, the one server that spoke a little English steered him to a table, and then handed him a bright red, fold-open menu.

Inside, entrees numbered 1 through 8 described in English filled the left-hand page. A second set, also numbered 1 through 8 but described in Chinese characters, covered the right-hand page.

The left-hand dishes sounded like ones he could order at a Denny's.

The hamburger steak with gravy and onions reminded him of a dinner in Austin. Tired of the Texas barbeque two nights in a row, he opted to stay with their excellent beef, albeit ground, and asked for extra vegetables.

Blake pointed. "I'll have the number four with gravy and onions, mashed potatoes, and carrots." He handed back the menu and added, "Well-done."

The girl jotted on her notepad, gave a quick bow, and disappeared through the kitchen's swinging door.

Blake leaned back in his chair to gaze out through the hotel's glass front.

It'd been a tumultuous day. The translator's rigidity threw him off at the beginning, but then the student revolt drove her off. He wondered if there would be repercussions, but the rest of the day had passed without her return, no official reprisal, and not even a politely worded reprimand. And the students, most of them it seemed, understood his English.

He heard his server's heels clacking on the hard floor toward him.

"Chef say you no can have that," she said and handed him the same menu.

Blake sat for a moment. Are they out of hamburgers? Or gravy? Or maybe the mainland Chinese chef doesn't know how to make American gravy?

He pursed his lips and scanned the left side of the menu again.

"Number eight, then. Dover sole."

The fish, perfectly done with a light coating of butter, had been perfect at the restaurant in Boston's North End. A side of angel hair, *aglio e olio*, completed his dinner.

His Chinese waitress plucked the menu from his fingers and clomped back to the kitchen.

The long talk with the students about guns and violence in America had been risky thing, but if they didn't kick him out of the country, maybe he fit in better than he'd feared. And the gaps in their understanding were obvious, and suggested the intentions of country's censorship, but that they also realized these highly educated kids needed to be more worldly than their general citizenry. The official news, promulgated by the Communist Party was, they seemed to know, one sided. These future leaders needed to be wiser. Hence, Blake's invitation and today's developments.

"Chef say you no can have that," his server said from behind.

The menu appeared in front of him already open.

Maybe the chef had flunked American Cuisine 101 in cooking school?

He pointed. "Number one. Roast pork with vegetables."

Trenton, New Jersey and the Hilton's dining room. There was no walking the streets or exploring the neighborhoods there. Teach, eat, and sleep all in one place then get the heck out of there.

She was smiling down at him.

"No," she said.

Well, he thought, at least we're communicating now.

He swept his hand down the entire English side of the menu.

"Anything?"

Wearing the same smile, she said, "Chef say you no can have that."

The English side was just for show, apparently.

Blake's eyes shifted across to the Chinese list. Was there any order to them? Simple dishes at the top, challenging specialties toward the bottom? Meats, then fishes? Strict vegan? There were no any divisions, no sections.

Random or sequential, he wondered. With dinner from the

same menu for the next twelve nights, he'd call tonight number one to make it easier to remember if it was edible or not.

He pointed to the first entry.

"This," he said.

Her smile revealed pretty, white teeth. "Good," she said before turning and clacking her shoes to the kitchen.

Worst case scenario, how much weight would he lose by living on wrapped nut bars and bottled water for two weeks? Could he get a real PayDay in the gift shop, or would it be a Chinese clone?

Next to the kitchen's swinging door was a small, glass-fronted refrigerator. Brown and green bottles with various labels glittered inside with drops of condensed humidity.

Beer was one of the few things safe to drink just about anywhere. The brewing process would fail if everything wasn't tightly controlled and scrupulously clean.

At a hundred and fifty calories per bottle, he'd need at least ten a day to accumulate a respectable caloric intake.

One for breakfast, three for lunch, and ... six for dinner? Or three in the dining room plus three more before bed? For twelve days?

Hopefully not.

But right now, a beer—one, maybe two—would help him sleep.

He walked over to the refrigerator and crouched down to look.

Several labels had English as well as Chinese printing. There were also a couple with the simpler Japanese strokes for sound syllables mixed with Asian characters, and two others were in the distinctly Korean script with upper and lower divisions.

His waitress came out of the kitchen and stopped beside him.

"You like beer?"

He nodded.

She opened the glass door and took out a tall boy bottle, its label all Chinese, and motioned for him to follow.

Back at his table, she grabbed the top, gave it a quick twist, and handed him the open bottle.

"King Long," she said. "You like."

She was right. It was cold, had a clean, not overly hoppy bite, and he felt the slight buzz by the time his dinner arrived. The plate of colorful vegetables and thin, gently done slices of white meat in a creamy sauce looked wonderful.

He poked a slice of meat with his chopsticks. It didn't react.

Scooping carefully, he brought it close to his face and sniffed.

"Chicken?" he mumbled aloud.

He put out his tongue to try the sauce.

A little sweet.

"Okay," he shrugged and popped a slice of meat into his mouth.

He smiled his relief. It was chicken, and perfectly done. Juicy, tender, and not the least bit stringy.

He waved to his server. "Spoon, please?"

She obliged.

At the end, he tilted his plate to scoop up the last of the sauce.

He leaned back in his chair and sighed. "Maybe this is going to work out after all."

Chapter 8

Five Days Later, Saturday, October 28
Luojia Mountain, Wuchang

At the end of the week, the first five-day seminar ended on track and on time. The students had asked a wide range of questions, many of them about life in America and his beliefs, just as Megyn had said. He'd given honest answers, they'd discussed his points of view not always agreeing, and everyone, Blake included, received an education. He couldn't ask for a better outcome.

With nothing on the agenda for Saturday, he was on his own. A hike up Mount Luojia across from his hotel would feel good after the limited movement all week in the classroom.

He dressed for comfort in running shoes, old jeans, a soft cotton shirt, and the dark green baseball cap with the Lockheed "Skunk Works" patch, a black skunk with a white stripe on its back, sewn on the front. It was one of Blake's favorites; a memento from a job he'd done for them in Palmdale, California.

Forty-five minutes later, Blake huffed for air and his legs burned but he was at the top. A long-running ridge line led to the left and right, both directions channeling through mature trees and underbrush. Where they led was anyone's guess, but here the sound of wind through leaves and bird calls had replaced the hiss and noise of traffic. And looking straight up, he could see blue sky again.

According to the geocache app on his cell phone, "Serpent's Smile" waited 517 yards to his right. He'd brought Sacagawea dollars from the bank to leave in the cache. It would be an extravagant gift considering that the traditional trinkets in a geocache were worth only a few pennies. But the next person to open the cache would be astonished. Blake smiled as he imagined their exclamations.

Cell phone in hand with the arrow of the geocache pointing the way and the distance ticking down with each step, Blake headed for the cache.

Suddenly, a deep voice somewhere ahead bellowed. Like the classroom conversations between students, the speaker's emotions came through without needing to understand the words. The one ahead sounded like a military commander reprimanding an underling.

Blake froze.

No overt restrictions had been raised all week, but he'd been sheltered and corralled. William shuttled him between hotel and classroom. And there, he had two hundred potential censors. Or informants.

But now, he was alone. And in spite of the trees, there'd been no possibility of anyone following. There was no way they could've remained hidden the whole way up. If this was a restricted area, there'd been no one to warn him.

There were signs on the campus paths, in Chinese, that might've announced some boundary. He'd assumed they were directions to classrooms and dorms, but if one had been something else, he could be in a restricted area.

The shout, he was sure, had not been in Mandarin. After a week of hearing Cantonese, his ear picked up the finer nuances.

As Blake stood waiting to see if some uniformed official was going to appear to walk him off the mountain into prison, a different voice hollered back. Both voices had come from beyond a clump of boulders a few yards ahead.

Blake dropped his cell phone into his shirt pocket. Crouching low, he slunk forward. At the boulders, he laid his hands on the cool granite and inched his way up.

In a space ringed by trees where the ridge-top broadened out into a long elliptical area, two small groups faced each other. The first, about fifty yards from Blake, had their backs to him. Two men with a woman in the middle. Probably students by the look of their clothing. The man on the left had long, mussy hair white as a sheet. Smoke from a cigarette drifted up from his left hand. The woman—*girl*, his mind corrected—had long, straight black hair. She shifted her weight from foot to foot. The male on the right pinched at something on his face, guided his hand into the pocket of his pants, and then withdrew it for an inspection of the fingertips.

The second group, maybe ten yards beyond the first, included another student. He was being held around the neck by the muscular arm of a much older man standing behind him. A dark strip of what looked to be fabric was stretched across the student's open mouth and tied behind his head. His eyes, wide in terror, looked as big as the lenses of his black-plastic glasses.

The boy looked a lot like Alex that'd sat in the front row of class. This boy's head was a little thinner but could've been a cousin.

Blake examined the big man holding him. Dressed in green overalls with yellow work boots, he appeared to be about as tall as Blake and maybe a similar age, but his forearms were half again as large.

But his head and face set him apart from anyone Blake had seen in China. First, the man's eyes were much too far apart in his round face. And he had a muddy, reddish complexion instead of the combinations of yellow and tan of the students. His most distinctive feature, a chalk-white scar, started in his hair and then ran down to the bottom of his jaw.

Blake grimaced.

Whatever'd made that scar must've almost killed him.

The man bellowed something and jerked his arm. His prisoner, the frightened boy, danced on his toes as he gagged and coughed. Both his hands clasped and pulled at the arm around his neck, but without any effect. The big man's upper-body strength was apparent, and far beyond the boy's ability.

The woman in the middle of the trio pushed out her arms, palms up, and shouted, "Sartaq!"

Blake mouthed the two syllables.

Sar-taq.

It sounded like a plea. Was she begging? Or had it been a name?

The big man barked at the trio and then glared as if expecting something. But seeing only the backs of their heads, all Blake saw were their nods.

That seemed to satisfy the big man because he gave a curt nod, took a breath, and then hoisted his prisoner completely off his feet.

The boy's arms began to flail as the scar-faced man patted for something on his belt. Sunlight coming through the trees glinted on a long, shiny blade as it came out of his black scabbard. It swept up and then paused beneath the boy's upraised chin.

"Jesus!" Blake hissed as he inhaled.

A dark blotch appeared at the boy's crotch, then spread down the inside of his right leg. A slower stain crept down the inseam of his left.

The boy's legs paddled the air like he couldn't keep up with a runaway bicycle, and around the muzzle across his mouth, his shriek was pure panic.

At this, the trio reacted with begging voices and gestures, but they didn't move.

Blake heard "Sartaq" again mixed in with the yells.

The blade at the boy's throat gave Blake no room for action. With no weapon, no gun, not even a walking stick, Blake could shout and wave his hands, but a simple tug would slit the boy's throat.

The three on-lookers were much closer, and they spoke the same language, and seemed to know the man. He was big, for sure, but there were three of them. They could spread out, keep talking, delay whatever was about to happen, and then charge, grab the arm with the knife, wrench it away, and rescue that poor kid.

Why didn't they do something?

But no, they just stood there. Watching.

I've gotta do something!

Blake slid down behind the boulder and fumbled his shirt pocket for the cell phone. He hit the Home key, tapped in his security code, and mashed the phone's green icon. Eventually, the keypad appeared.

He stopped. What's Emergency in China? Is it 911? Or 112? Or 999?

Blake had been too many places to remember which to use where.

He poised his finger to try all nines when a gargled shriek cut through the forest. Birds leaped from branches and flapped to get away.

Blake scooted up the boulder to look.

Across the treeless opening, the machete was halfway across the boy's neck and still gliding left. Above the shiny, silver blade, a black gap had already yawned open. Suddenly, a spurt of glistening red arced out. It lingered in the air a moment, then fell with an audible slap onto a large sheet of black plastic.

Where'd that come from? Why is it there?

Blake's mind forked into two streams. The OCD part counted passes of the knife.

One.

The other latched onto that incongruous detail, the large square of plastic sheeting on which the man and boy stood back toward one edge.

The girl with the shiny black hair, her back to Blake with her arms out toward the man and boy, crumpled to her knees.

The killer's eyes flared.

Sexual ecstasy?

He hoisted the boy's chin higher. The movement opened the black incision wider as blood coursed out and down the front of the boy's green and blue checkered shirt. At the same time, a small rivulet coursed off sideways along the sloping bottom of the man's arm and then raced in narrow lines down his coveralls.

The muscles in the man's arm bulged as the machete reversed and pressed deeper into the boy's neck.

Two.

Blake shouted at himself. *Stop counting!*

But knew his OCD wouldn't quit.

In the trio of spectators, the boy with white hair had bent forward with his back arched like a cat. Yellowish liquid splashed in the dirt in front of him. The girl turned away, her body overwhelmed by a shiver. The other boy stood frozen: one hand glued to the shiny black hair on top of his head.

The machete reversed again.

Three!

The victim's arms and legs whipped in a huge spasm, then flopped loose like a marionette with its strings cut.

The blade stopped two-thirds of the way across. The big man grunted and the muscles in his arm bulged until the machete suddenly leaped forward.

It cut through.

The body, released from the head, dropped to its knees, one hand landing inside the cupped other like it was sitting Zazen. Ever so slowly, the torso slumped forward. It made a soft *frump* in the utter silence when it landed in the blood.

The boy's head—dripping from the neck and perched in the crook of the big man's arm—held grimaced lips, blue and angular, where they'd wrenched out above and below the gag. The eyes behind the glasses were pinched closed.

The big man's body wrenched with an orgasmic shiver.

In the silence, the expression on the severed head slowly eased, and then the eyes opened. They blinked—twice—and appeared to focus on the trio. The ends of the blue lips began to wriggle.

It's talking!

Blake remembered reading how such things happened after a guillotine execution. And elsewhere, someone said four minutes without oxygen would start to permanently damage the brain. Was the boy still in there? Did he know what had happened? Could he see his own headless body lying in the blood before him?

Blake closed his eyes.

Oh, God, let him—the head—the brain inside—let it stop. Please, God!

The breeze hissed through the leaves, but no birds called or sang.

When Blake forced himself to look again, the boy's eyes had angled up as if to heaven. They didn't move. They didn't blink. His face was still.

Dead still.

In his hand, Blake's cell phone chirped.

The electronic twitter of a cell phone was unmistakable. Sartaq glared at his trio of followers in front of him. Deng Lan, Hu Jian, and Tan Ling all shook their heads.

Sartaq's gaze flicked up and beyond them at some movement.

A dozen paces back atop the large boulders, the crown of something round shifted sideways, then moved up and became a dark green baseball cap with some kind of squirrel, black with a white stripe on its back, on the front. Tufts of gray hair stuck out from beneath the hat. The head wearing it moved up a little more and milky blue eyes became visible. They were Western eyes, not Asian, and the color reminded Sartaq of some English china that was on permanent display in a university showcase.

The eyes flared, and then the eyes, head, and hat all disappeared behind the boulder.

Sartaq screamed, raised his bloody machete, and charged across the clearing.

Wang's head, dropped from the crook of his arm, splashed onto the bloody plastic and rolled onto an ear before stopping.

Hu Jian, Deng Lan, and Tan Ling scattered as Sartaq swept through. He slowed to curve around the boulder and then bounded up two pillow-size rocks to the ridgeline's trail. A cloud of dust was drifting off with the light breeze.

The man—*Witness!*—was somewhere ahead.

Sartaq had prepared for everything—the time when students would be sleeping in on a Saturday morning, his best knife, the sheet of plastic to catch the blood—but not some visitor, some stranger, some foreigner.

His heavy boots clomped as he ran. He cursed them. Barefoot, he'd be much faster but there was no time to stop and unlace now. Besides, he knew all of Luojia's paths. He'd walked and run them all his life. The slope fell away on both sides in this section, campus to the left, shops to the right, and was far too steep to use. And this section had no branches, and the dust in the air confirmed the witness's flight.

Leaping to shortcut all the bends and turns, Sartaq closed the distance. He could see his target now. Short-sleeve shirt, blue jeans, black belt, blue running shoes with dark gray soles.

He grinned. Nobody but an American would wear a baseball cap.

And Europeans, like the University students, would wear all new clothing. Only an American would wear old, worn-out clothes.

The slang terms for Americans that Sartaq had heard in the Islamic State videos came to mind: *Whitey, Cracker, Great Satan.*

Remembering them, his mind raged.

Why do you get so much when we have so little? All men are not created equal. Your father is not murdered. Your teachers don't hate you. Grandfather didn't beat you, scar you, hurt you...

But this man was fast. Sartaq's lungs heaved for air and his legs burned. The boots felt like bricks on his feet. He wasn't used to running. Swinging a hammer at a forge, his arms were powerful, but not his legs.

Suddenly, the American leaped off the ridge and disappeared to the left.

No, Sartaq railed. *Campus that way! Must not get there.*

Sartaq was a campus fixture under the big tree with his Qur'an where he preached. They would recognize him, and his clothing was drenched with Wang's red blood.

He paused where the American had jumped. The slope was nearly vertical, but he could see a cleared path in the dead leaves farther down where the man must've come down and slid.

Sartaq tried edging down the steep slope, but a root caught one boot and he pitched over. His hand tore branches from bushes as he tumbled until his hand, its grip like the steel vise in his shop, fastened on a young sapling. Arm wrenched as it stopped his fall, he rolled to look downhill, but the American was nowhere to be seen.

Between the tree trunks and through the scrubs lay a black asphalt walkway.

It was one of the campus walkways.

"Shit!"

English profanities, learned from American movies watched in the dorm with his followers, had superseded all those Sartaq knew.

Through the leaves, he saw the American—hatless now, with shaggy, gray hair—pitched forward on hands and knees on the black pavement.

Sartaq watched as two university students bolted up from a concrete bench and ran to the American. One on each side, they dragged him to his feet.

Sartaq's mind raged.

Lili will be a witch. She doesn't know Wang, about the boy's treason, about the execution that I had to do. It was not in her plan. Damn her plan!

There was nothing he could do. If they saw him and all the blood, they'd surely call the authorities. There'd be a search, long before Sartaq would have a chance to complete the cleanup and disposal he planned.

My plan, he wanted to scream, not Lili's plan!

Blake's palms burned like they were on fire.

On elbows and knees, he'd skidded to a stop on the path's rough asphalt. He let himself tilt and roll onto his side, the brush of air across his palms torching up the pain.

The forest behind him... looked like a forest. No crazed killer with a machete.

Where is he? Blake wondered. *Big man, round head, white scar, clomping boots, blood-drenched machete.*

Blake had jumped off a cliff, plummeted to the soft slope where it came out to meet him, then he'd run, jumped, and careened the rest of the way down. He ran the last of the slope until suddenly out of the forest and into the campus and then tripped in the ditch next to the path.

Blake scanned the trees for movement.

Did I get away? He wondered. *Is it possible?*

Two students leaned down beside him, each one putting a hand on one of his shoulders and an arm. He writhed against the burning in his hands and knees.

"You Okay?" One of them asked.

Blake waved a raw palm toward the forest. He tried to say, "Murder," but it came out like a donkey's bray.

The students looked at each other. One of them shrugged.

Blake was pretty sure the killer had locked eyes with him over the boulders. Those eyes had been too far apart, freakish. And the white scar.

Thank God for good running shoes.

The killer had been in clomping work boots. Yellow. Clumsy.

Maybe I did get away?

"You fall, yes?" One student asked. He pointed to Blake's bloody palms. "Go doctor."

They pulled to get him up.

"We help," the other said. "You stay Feng Yi?" He gestured toward the noisy traffic that would be on the other side of the campus wall. "Big hotel, yes?"

Blake nodded.

They pressed him forward. He took a step but then stopped to scan the trees again.

Where's the killer? He's had time to get here. Is he watching from somewhere?

Blake's knee buckled, but they caught and boosted him back up. They encouraged him forward again. The hotel seemed so far. Could he make it? Or would the killer find them first?

Chop, chop.

He managed another step; his knees screamed at the insult. Unable to close his fists for the pain, he kept his fingers curved, rigid, but the breeze burned his palms anyway.

I made it!

It took forever to reach the high concrete wall. Then, they worked him sideways through the narrow pedestrian gap that left the campus. Down the sidewalk to the traffic light, he moved a little better by then, and his hands no longer dripped. But wide-eyed drivers, stopped at the light, pointed and stared as the two students helped him hobble across the street. By the time they reached the marble steps at the hotel entrance, Blake was shambling by himself.

"Thank you." He waved them away. "I'm okay now."

Unable to close either fist, he threaded the clawed fingers of both hands through the handle and pulled open the glass door. He lurched through before it closed.

The voices echoing in the marble-lined lobby stopped. Every face turned to look. Blake pulled himself taller and began shuffling faster, still in baby steps, and grimacing or blinking at the pain. He shuffled across the expanse of sparkling white floor. He didn't dare make a fist against the pain; that would've opened the wounds and left a trail.

When the elevator door opened, he staggered and leaned against the wall. He jabbed the "11" button with a knuckle. An eternity later, he was inside his room. He fumbled the chain onto the latch and worked the desk chair under the handle.

All the time, one thought had hounded him.

Police! Call the Police!

He half fell to the desk with its tan, plastic phone. Reaching for the handset, his eyes glanced in the mirror. His blood-streaked face, wild hair, and crazed-animal eyes gaped back at him. He looked like a werewolf that'd just devoured a small child.

What will they think? He wondered. *Gun-crazy American?*

Looking like this, would they believe him? Would they think he was the murderer trying to blame someone else?

Not like this, he thought, still looking in the mirror. He needed to look rational and tell a factual, believable, coherent account of what he'd seen. And they'd probably cross-examine him for hours, so his facts needed to be consistent, to match in each repetition, but not word for word.

Think this through. Get the facts straight.

And this is China. Simple words that a translator won't screw up. A translator like...

Little Miss Prissy Tweed came to mind.

God, not her.

She translated him wrong, the students said. He wouldn't know if his story was being told right or not.

Reduce it. Keep it simple.

What would be easy to translate?

Homicide?

Murder?

Decapitation?

Sawed off the kid's head?

He remembered the plastic sheet. Someone had to put it there. It was there on purpose.

Premeditation?

Would that be translated right?

Panic was rising in his chest.

Blake clamped his eyes shut.

I'm overthinking this. Simplify. Calm down.

He opened his eyes.

In the mirror, he still looked like a madman. A homeless madman that'd been living in the wild. Hiding on that mountain. Killing and eating birds and rats. Watching students from secret hiding places...

Oh God, he thought, *I'm so screwed.*

No! Wash your face. Comb your hair.

But his heart still thudded in his ears.

He raised his hands in the mirror. They shook like he'd tossed down four shots of espresso. His whole body shivered—*shock?*—and in the mirror, his face glistened with sweat next to scabbed-over scapes from twigs and branches.

Flop-sweat, he diagnosed. *Hypoglycemia.*

Need sugar. Fast sugar. Candy. Chocolate bar. Candy-coated peanuts.

The red plastic telltale on the mini fridge by his knee flipped halfway across the room when he wrenched the door open.

He chomped a handful of M&M clones, but they stuck halfway down. No bottles of water, in the fridge, he washed down the swallow with a shot-bottle of Jack Daniel's Red. The sizzle on his tongue was nice and a warm glow bloomed in his stomach. The

Snickers look-alike slid down with two swallows of Seagram Seven. His ears felt warm.

He held up a hand. It wavered, but no longer shook.

Music, he thought. *Something calm.*

He could move his fingers a little now. He pushed up the lid of his computer and thumped the mouse pad with the side of his thumb. He double-thumped his MP3 collection and started "Fast Car." Tracy Chapman's warm croon oozed from the tiny speakers.

He'd eaten enough sugar. He just needed to wait for it reach his small intestine where it'd be absorbed into his bloodstream.

But now the craving for more, for a sugar-fix, clawed at him.

In the fridge, only salty snacks remained. They wouldn't help.

But there were two more shot bottles, a clear one with a red and white label, and something in transparent green. Not sugar, but alcohol always worked when Julie's ghost started raging and screaming.

Through the lips and over the gums...

He couldn't remember the rest.

He tossed an empty toward the desk in a high arc. It bounced off something, and when he turned his head to follow, the entire room rolled like a ship at sea. He put both arms back and caught himself.

He nodded to the wild lunatic in the mirror. "You're fucked."

"No shit, Sherlock," he answered.

The reflection was holding a small green bottle in its hand.

He tried to scoot forward for a better look, but the bedcover seemed glued to his butt. He rocked forward, but then the room spun again. He flopped back on the bed.

"Okay," he said to the ceiling, "Jes' for a sec—"

And closed his eyes.

Part Two

On a Mission

"He who will not risk will not win."
John Paul Jones

Chapter 9

Demise of the Cultural Revolution, Forty Years Ago Shenjiawan (near Wuhan) and Kashgar (Xinjiang Province)

Standing at the lip of the tiny stage for the school recital, twelve-year-old Sartaq pushed back the fear, but more so the anger. In the audience before him, Mother Shen's eyes flared at him in her otherwise unchanging, public face. She sat next to People's Education Committee Party Leader Chen in the front row.

"War is..." Sartaq started, but then his mind went blank.

He looked to the side. Standing with her uniformed dance troop, Lili was mouthing the words at him. But without pitches, even his own mother's maiden name, *Shēn*, would be wrong if he pronounced it *Shěn*, or *Shèn*.

Just three years ago, schools had reopened when Mao's Cultural Revolution fell out of favor. Sartaq was nine and his little sister six, but because schools had been closed for so long, they started first grade together.

Sartaq was the worst in his class. They wanted him to do everything in Mandarin, but it was an ugly language. He was like his mother, defiant, but didn't understand about playing along. She was the master of that with her sometimes overnight guests, as she called them.

Today, if he failed to recite the assignment of two short sentences, the entire community would witness his embarrassment. His little sister Lili, the school's star pupil, had already finished all the Party-sanctioned fourth grade materials. They'd let her start on the older, fifth-grade books even though they were left over from before and hadn't been corrected by the Party.

Suddenly, as if by magic, words came out of Sartaq's mouth.

"War is continuation of politics."

Over to the side, Lili grinned but stopped herself before clapping her hands. She looked especially neat today in the squarely pressed Chinese Army uniform with her green cap and red star.

Mother Shen's eyes smiled at him from the front row. Party Leader Chen next to her gave a tiny nod as if to say, "Go ahead."

There was more?

He hated Mandarin. It sounded like you'd been caught doing something bad. It had none of the grace of Chinese, the language they spoke at home. Foreigners called his native language Cantonese, but they lived in China, so it was Chinese.

But the school forced them to learn things in Mandarin.

In the weeks before, he'd read aloud three times—with Lili's help to say the words right—his assignment from Mao's Red Book. He knew the Hanzi characters well enough and could say most of them—in Chinese—without help. But Beijing said them different. How were you supposed to know when to say the Beijing words or the Chinese words?

A chair scraped on the floor as everyone waited.

Lili's success moments ago didn't help. Her group had finished with their fists high after a final foot stomp and boyish shout. Party Leader Chen had been the first on his feet to applaud. Mother Shen rose beside him. Chen leaned over to say something, his mouth unmistakably shaping her given, personal name, Daiyu. Only husbands and parents were permitted to use personal names. Why did she let him do that?

"If Mao is out now," Sartaq had asked Lili one evening, "why do we still use his Red Book?"

"He's important leader," she'd explained, flush with the fervor the school poured into every young student. "He's father of revolution." She tapped Sartaq's copy. "He pushed out Nationalists to free us."

Lili's fanaticism for Mao, for the *New China*, sickened him. Three years older than her, he saw through their attempts to drum in the ignorant faith. But when he'd complained to his Mother Shen, she had pursed her lips and told him, "Lili is young and impressionable. But she's also very smart. Give her time. As she sees and experiences things for herself, that will change. Someday, she will understand their lies and treachery. And she will do something about it."

Someone in the back of the room coughed.

Sartaq remembered that the next line of his quotation started the same way, but then said war was something else. But what? And how could it be one thing in one sentence, and then something else in the next?

He tried, "A political... *character*?"

No, that was at the end, not the beginning.

Party Leader Chen shifted in his seat, his fat pigface now an angry frown.

"War," Sartaq started over, "is... is..." his guess came out in a rush: "is combination of politics?"

"Stop!" Party Leader Chen commanded and bounced to his feet.

He turned to face the audience.

"Comrades," he said, "We've been patient with this boy. Given him great patience. But as you can see, this school's resources—of which we have no excess—are being wasted. This cannot continue. Tomorrow, this effort—well-meaning and kind, but obviously of no value—will cease.

He turned to Sartaq and barked, "Sit!"

Did he mean here, right here on the stage? Sartaq looked around for help.

Chen swept his hand in dismissal. "Go," he boomed.

In a flash, rage overwhelmed Sartaq. He remembered sounds: a whine in his throat, the rasps of someone choking, the scraping of chairs, voices clamoring his name, but nothing else.

Three men were holding Sartaq.

Before him, Chen's arms and legs lay splayed out with his eyes closed. Blood flowed from his nose and ran back the side of the nearest cheek and across his ear.

Another man knelt and pressed his fingers into Chen's bulbous neck. "Heart's beating," he said. "Just knocked out." The man glanced at Sartaq, the glimmer of a smile on his face.

"Who has cart?" A woman asked. "We should take home."

Neither Mother Shen nor Lili said anything that night. Only Jee, the family's Korean cook and housekeeper, provided any consolation. She buttered and massaged the bruises on his knuckles. At one point, she looked him in the eye and breathed, "Good for you."

The Party edict arrived in the morning.

It said that, under authority of the *Up to Mountains and Down to Countryside* movement, Sartaq was designated as *privileged youth*, and is promoted to the Yao cooperative in Anhui Province. Transportation to be arranged and provided according to policy. There, he would continue his education from farmers and workers. Such service was to continue until he had fully developed his talents as judged by the cooperative leadership committee.

Mother Shen was sad but resolute.

"Life gives many lessons," she said to him in front of the staff. "Some are hard, but those are often most valuable. Look on this, my first born, as practical education in ways of world."

Privately, she added, "And do not forget who has done this to you."

Did she mean Party Leader Chen? Or the leadership committee? The Party, or Beijing?

The travel orders said he would leave by train in two days.

But Sartaq didn't wait. Early the next morning, without word or note, and carrying only a small roll of clothes and a bundle of food, he left.

East Turkestan—Xinjiang as Beijing called it—was where his dead father had lived. His aunts and uncles would still be there, he hoped.

It was thousands of kilometers, but rail lines and trains, highways with trucks, and if nothing else offered, the sun would direct his feet. Descended from Mongolian warriors and bearing his real father's name, Khan, they would understand that actions —his actions—were stronger than words.

"I'll stay there," he promised himself. "And become a warrior like Khan Genghis."

"I am Khan Sartaq!"

A year later, a blast of cold air from the Tajikistan pass swept down Sartaq's spine. He reached down to pull the pants legs to cover his ankles, but they were almost a hand's-width short. His thirteenth birthday had passed a few days ago, unknown to his blood-cousins, aunts, uncles, and grandparents on the Khan farm.

Xinjiang's cold swept down from the Arctic above Russia. It forced unlikely comrades. He curled tighter and spooned the warm back that arched and shifted against him. His arm over the huge, curved flank, he stroked her belly and the bristly hairs, sparse and pliant, bent at his touch. When his caress reversed, they felt more like stiff twigs. The sow turned to gaze at his face, then snorted and lay her head on the frozen mud.

Beyond the rough, broken boards that walled in her sty, dry gusts stirred flakes of snow in the wagon furrows between frozen ridges.

Arzu sat in a dark, sheltered corner next to the farmhouse, her hazel eyes watching him. He didn't know how long she'd been there. Her lips parted to reveal white teeth and the slender tip of her pink tongue.

Daughter of his father's younger sister—"First cousin," she'd told him—she wore a box-like, gold-trimmed hat with dangling beads on her head. She was wrapped in an embroidered vest and black bodice that lay open at the top in spite of the brutal cold, the pale skin of her chest beautiful in the morning light. She sat cross-legged, the banded-wool skirt taut between her knees. A few centimeters of pale thighs drew his eyes inward toward the dark cavern beneath her skirt. After several mindless moments that warmed his blood, his eyes rose from her dark mystery, travelled back up to her chest, and then her eyes.

She grinned at him.

Sartaq rose and stepped over the sty's low fence. He put his hands in the worn pockets of his pants to warm them and walked over. He stopped in front of her knees. She rose without retreating, their faces aligned and close. Her breath nuzzled his upper lip. It reminded him of the sweet, moist loam in the Shen fields far to the south where his mother and half-sister lived.

Safe by the back wall of the farmhouse where no window could see, Arzu pressed tight against him. She slid her fingers inside the waistband of his pants on both sides and pushed them down. They dropped to his ankles. He stepped out of them as her icy fingers grazed across his belly and then turned to descend and wrap around his warmth.

His eyes fluttered and shut.

And a man's voice bellowed to his left.

Startled, Sartaq opened his eyes and snapped his head to look.

Sweeping toward him, back and forth, was the big, knobby end of a long cane. At its far end, Khan Iochi, his grandfather, sputtered and cursed in what must've been Uyghur.

The burled handle of his cane looked like a bunched fist that'd been dipped in black. It swung closer and closer. Sartaq raised an arm and skittered on the frozen dirt to the side away from the cane. Arzu's touch, warm and eager, was gone.

The old man followed driving Sartaq back and around the corner, down the side, and around to the front of their unpainted gray-wood house.

An old woman's cackle sounded from the porch.

Sartaq tried to cover himself with his hands.

She was leaning forward in her plush chair, its cotton stuffing streaked with black where it stuck out. The color matched the few remaining strands of her hair that hadn't turned the color of the clouds. She'd tucked the faded sky-blue dress inside purple trousers that were secured with a thin twist of hemp. Bundled inside a heavy, brown wool jacket with gold buttons, she sat outside puffing on a pipe when it wasn't raining or snowing.

Four girls, Sartaq's Khan cousins, stood on the porch, two on each side of the old woman's tattered throne. They leaned on the rail, each with a hand to shade their dark, Uyghur eyes. They hissed and giggled.

Without warning, the old man lunged and swung at Sartaq's hips.

Sartaq twisted and thrust forward to evade the cane, his hands darting to protect his back, but too late. The smack of hard wood against his sun-darkened skin made his stiff manhood waggle in the icy wind.

The girls on the porch squealed in unison, Arzu with them now.

The old woman pointed at his member. She began twitching her swollen-jointed finger in the air, imitating his organ's shimmy and shake.

Sartaq bent to cover himself, but Khan Iochi's cane found his back again. His hips thrust forward from the strike.

The girls howled anew but then faded as they picked up a chant from the old woman.

"Piroytki, Piroytki, Piroytki."

Half-breed.

Sartaq was the son of a Uyghur man and a Han woman, and both races reviled him.

He straightened and quit trying to hide his manhood. Half-breed or not, he was still a man.

Look, he thought, glancing at his cousins. *This is strong, young man!*

The old hag's voice rose an octave. She began fluttering her tongue in a yowl that mocked his manly shimmy.

"Uh-lu-lu-lu-lu-lu."

The girls joined her ancient wail.

"Uh-lu-lu-lu-lu-lu."

The old man circled the club high over his head, faster and faster. At the back of a turn, he twisted his hands and pulled his elbows down. The club swooped and grazed the dirt spitting tiny pebbles into Sartaq's face.

He closed his eyes, and a moment later, the cane's rock-hard, roughly carved head took him at the bottom of the jaw. It split his flesh up the side of his face and well into his scalp.

He remembered hearing the shocked gasps of little girls, but then nothing after that.

Sartaq cried out the moment he awoke.

Eyes closed, he raised his hand and touched what felt like thick, rough fabric looped over his head and under his jaw.

He took slow, shallow breaths without moving. The fiery edge of pain on the left side of his face slowly dulled into a throb with the beating of his heart.

Lying on his back, he forced one eye open.

Long, milky-blue spokes started in the ceiling behind him and converged around a center ring an arm's length across. A cap of some sort sat atop the ring but askew and revealing a crescent of blue sky. Wisps of smoke drifted up between two posts that held up the ring. Every segment of spokes, ring, and posts had a wooden, squarish look. He guessed they'd been shaped, painted, and embellished with the thin, white squiggly lines that ran along each piece. A *shushing* sound came from the spoked ceiling and walls, and everything shifted this way and that with the creak of wood joints.

Down beyond his feet, half a rusty steel drum radiated heat. A steaming wok sat atop the fire. He wriggled his toes in the warmth and wondered what had become of his shoes. He remembered kicking them off along with his pants, and then the thrilling touch of Arzu's fingers.

A door opened to his right. A man in his thirties entered. He had a square, leathery face with a round cap on his head, the same kind as worn by the Uyghur men. Black eyebrows arched up emphasizing his long, thin nose.

He said something. The words had the sound of Uyghur.

Sartaq tried not to move his jaw as he gritted out, "I speak Chinese."

The man seemed to ignore him as he picked up two plastic jugs by the door and carried them next to a wok.

After straightening, he said, "Southern Provincial Capital. Westerners call your language Cantonese."

Sartaq huffed his understanding.

"Welcome to my home, young Khan Sartaq."

Sartaq studied the man but didn't remember meeting him before.

"My name Qassim," he said, "*Major* Qassim. We have history, you and me."

Sartaq didn't remember falling asleep, but when he opened his eyes, the slim window above his head was dark. Down beyond his feet, Qassim's voice chanted softly, the words foreign. After a pause, the man rose with his eyes closed. Dressed all in white with his head facing right, he mumbled something, turned his lead left, and then mumbled some more.

Muslim, Sartaq realized. Qassim practiced religion. He gave a silent harrumph.

Back in Shenjiawan's one-room school, the teacher had pointed out Xinjiang and four other colored areas on the map of China. "Special Administrative Regions," she said. In America—another place they were studying—they also had special areas. They called them *reservations*. And like the Chinese Special Administrative Regions, the American reservations also had their own laws. And even though it was officially discouraged, some practiced religion.

In Kashgar, Sartaq had seen the funny caps, and the bowing, kneeling, and putting their faces down on rugs. On Fridays, he'd watched as people in their best clothes filed into the big, yellow Id Kah Mosque, but only after each one stopped first to wash their feet.

It seemed strange, and not a little silly.

All the gyrations and ministrations fed no stomachs, made no plants grow taller, and influenced no officials. On the contrary, Party members seemed to regard worshipers as ignorant and superstitious.

Religion, Sartaq concluded, *was a waste of time.* Anyone with half a mind could see that.

Qassim was looking at him with a pleasant smile.

"Good evening," he said. "Feeling better?"

"What you want?" Sartaq growled in disgust.

Major Qassim cocked his head as his smile turned to amusement. "Me? From you?" He laughed. "You really are Khan!"

"How..." Sartaq started, then grimaced from a stab of pain.

"... did I know you're Khan?" Major Qassim finished for him. "Word go around. I'm surprised you lasted this long."

When Sartaq had arrived last spring, his Khan grandfather warily agreed to let him work the farm but wasn't permitted in the house. He learned to muscle the plow behind the ox, castrate sheep, gather eggs without breaking them, shovel out the hog pen, and any and everything else they demanded.

His girl cousins would sometimes stop to watch him work. They would pause with the bucket of food destined for the hog pen and let him pick out what he wanted. Sometimes it was better than what he could forage for himself.

Months passed and he shifted to fixing fences, repairing roofs, cleaning out trenches for water to the field, and his body became larger and stronger. The girls started bringing extras from the dinner table and sitting to talk or just watch him eat.

It was strange. Back home, everyone looked away from his face, and other than his family, they avoided him. But here, while their eyes avoided his face, the girls would scan his physique. Sartaq's hands, arms, thighs, and calves had all grown with the labor. And when he took off his shirt in the sun, their gaze flicked shoulder to breast, stomach, and sometimes paused, for just a moment, just below his waist.

Sartaq knew his head was too big and his eyes too far apart, but the girls found his body... interesting?

Later, after being banished when the harvest finished, he made a production of leaving the barn and walking down the road toward Kashgar. But he returned late that night for the hog pen against the back of the house where Arzu, the oldest, became his benefactor. She'd sit close as he ate the food she brought. He'd quivered at the first touch of her fingers on his arm, her kiss, the taste of her breath, and then the warmth when she straddled and slid him inside...

"Soup?" Qassim offered.

Returning from his daydream, Sartaq forced a nod.

Qassim boosted him up into a sitting position using two stiff cushions with geometric designs in their stitching.

"I knew your father," he said. "He was one of old man's sons. His favorite, I think. And I saw you, baby in mother's arms, but you wouldn't remember that." He filled a yellow-glazed bowl with broth. "You have Khan look, no one feature, of course, but their odd mix, how they differ but are alike."

He knelt with the bowl and dipped in a metal spoon, raised it to his lips, and blew across it. He leaned forward. "Open."

It was spicey like Szechuan but different. The meat was goat—a tough, old gamey buck—and root smells with aromatic leaves. Much better than what they cooked at the farm.

Sartaq's eyes must've wandered around the walls and ceiling.

"*Yurt*," Qassim instructed. "One hour pack and move. Very handy sometimes."

Qassim set the bowl on the rug next to him.

"I avoid Party officials. And Khans. Your grandfather blames me for what happened. I've been watching you—for week now, off and on—and saw what he did. They abandoned you, unconscious, in front of house. There was lot of blood and I think they expected you to die. But, like I said, I knew who you were, and if Iochi didn't like you, then I thought you might be worth knowing. So, I picked you up, bound your face with shirt, and carried you here."

Sartaq thought of Arzu, how she'd drawn him on. "I was tricked."

"Betrayed," Qassim corrected. "That was cruel." He picked up the bowl and offered another spoonful. "If it'd been me, I'd've taken club and beaten old man's head into mush."

Sartaq swallowed and then struggled to say the syllables. "My father?"

Qassim nodded. "Yes, I knew him. It was—What are you now? Ten, eleven?"

"Thirteen," Sartaq answered.

"You were year old then, so eleven years ago."

"Are you Chinese Army?" Sartaq asked, eyeing him carefully.

Qassim laughed easy. "Not that one."

"Muslim?"

"Yes," he said with confidence. "Allah guides my day." He paused for a moment and then smiled. "Perhaps *he* sent me to farm..." but let the words trail off.

He leaned close to look at the bandage around Sartaq's head. "We should change this soon." He reached into his shirt pocket and produced two round tablets and two oblongs. "Swallow these."

Sartaq hesitated.

"Aspirin and Streptomycin—big ones. We go easy on Aspirin. It thins blood, but now will help you rest." He shrugged. "Everything risky. Must try things. Take chances."

Sartaq chewed the pills and grimaced at the taste. He accepted two spoons of soup to wash everything down.

He put a hand up to the left side of his face and the cloth bandage. "This?"

"Battlefield surgery," Qassim said, pleased with himself. "Twenty stitches. They usually come out in few days but for size of that, we wait longer. Gonna have big scar." He winked. "Girls love them. But gauging from your recent public display of apparatus, that'll be no problem for you, anyway."

Sartaq blinked away an offered spoonful.

Qassim raised the bowl to his own lips and finished it. He poured a little water in the bowl and then stepped out the door with a rag. He came back in and set the bowl on a low table by the fire drum.

"Your father," Major Qassim began, "was Khan Batu, and I was there when the Communists shot him."

Sartaq's face must've made his curiosity obvious.

Major Qassim leaned close and muttered. "If you repeat any of this, they will kill us. Do you understand?"

Sartaq nodded for him to go on.

Qassim frowned. "I'm not kidding. What your grandfather did to you is nothing compared to Communists."

Sartaq nodded again, but bigger and slower.

"I was officer in charge," Major Qassim explained. "We go out to ambush four regular Army soldiers that took same position every night. Hit and run was plan. Guerilla tactics. Make soldiers afraid."

Sartaq nodded for him to continue.

"But somebody betrayed us. They knew we were coming and had planted troops in secret to ambush us. Your father went down in first volley, others seconds later. By grace of Allah's hand, I was in rear. They didn't see me.

"Afterwards, I had to tell families. Most of them knew risk, so while they were very sad, they also understood. 'Soldiers die,' one father said. But Khans blamed me even though many Chinese soldiers were waiting." He studied Sartaq's face a moment. "My money—if I were betting man which Allah forbids—would be that one of Khans, brother perhaps, told Communists knowing they would kill everyone including your father."

Qassim poured steaming milk-tea into a decorated mug. The painted design was like those woven into the rugs on the yurt's walls and floor. No faces or figures. Just straight lines with meaningless squiggles, nothing like the Arabic script on the spine of the book by the man's bed.

"I hate them," Sartaq said, taking the mug and carefully sipping at the hot, salty brew. "They ruined my life. My dad was first, but when I was five, Communists killed my little sister's father." He glanced at Qassim who nodded. "He was teacher. At college. Since then, Mother... She's been... Party officials... Leader Chen..."

The thought of what his mother had done, had to do, over and over... It disgusted him, but he knew she'd had no choice. She'd done it for them. But even so...

The pain in his cheek flared.

"Ow."

Qassim nodded slowly. "I'm sure what your mother did was necessary. Life can be very hard. She had you and—you said—your little sister to raise. With no father, she would have to rely on her own family. If she could rise above that, well, she must've," he paused, *"influenced* people."

"I hit him." Sartaq grimaced as he twisted his face to get all the syllables out, "Party Leader Chen."

Major Qassim tilted his head forward to stare at Sartaq.

"You struck a Party leader?"

Sartaq grinned despite the pain. "Knocked him out. One punch. Felt great. Everyone frowned, but their eyes smiled. I had to leave then."

"No kidding."

"They tried to send me to some farm in Anhui, but I came here instead. On my own."

"You might do well commanding others," Qassim concluded. "I am Major. Pretentious title for our little group of *activists*, but it helps get things done. Like we were doing when your father got killed."

That's what Sartaq wanted, to *do* things, to hit the Communists, to hurt Party officials like Chen.

He grunted as he tried to sit up higher, but Qassim put out a hand. "Not today. You need to mend first."

"Teach me about your God," Sartaq said, trying to sound like he meant it. "How does he make you do things?"

Qassim had just risen from his morning prayer. "He doesn't make me do anything," he answered. "I do choosing. The hard part is figuring out what is His will."

Sartaq kept his face earnest and innocent. "How do you know that?"

Qassim raised a hand to his forehead. "It starts here," he said, then moved it down to his chest, "but you know it here. Qur'an and Hadith point way, but you must feel it. When you experience *taqwa*, that is it."

"I don't understand." Sartaq shook his head.

Major Qassim grinned. "Good. Now we can begin."

In the coming weeks, as his wound slowly healed, Sartaq complied in every respect. And he was an excellent student now that the subject of his study had a purpose he relished. He memorized the movements, and the spoken Arabic for each of the five daily prayers. And he could quote and explain the parts of the Qur'an dealing with *infidels* and *idolaters*.

But more than the words and movements, he watched, measured, and memorized his teacher. He learned the broad flow of concepts, from simple to complex, particularly those that beckoned—that demanded—action. Violent action.

Jihad—the struggle, the striving—became Sartaq's secret focus. But it wasn't the practice as much as the reason. It taught him what to find and groom in individuals to shape them into warriors willing to sacrifice themselves.

The keys, he learned, were in everyone, in their hurts, the wrongs they'd suffered, the pains and resentments of a life, no matter how short or long.

To everyone except Qassim, Sartaq appeared to become a devout follower of Islam.

But in their private conversations late at night in the yurt, the Major groomed Sartaq, openly and willingly, for a different role.

Sartaq would become a recruiter and trainer for the Uyghur resistance. They had a country—East Turkestan—to be re-established. Stolen from them in 1949, they'd hurt the Communists and drive them out.

And when that had been done, when the Uyghur country had been freed from the Communists, Sartaq would return to the Khan farm. They'd welcome him as a hero, but he wouldn't forget the Khan's abuse. He'd smash the old man's head and throw it to the pigs, and then take Arzu for his own, to possess any time he wanted.

His face scarred but healed, Sartaq left a few months later. When he reached Shenjiawan, the spring planting had finished. Mother and little sister both said the look in his eyes was much wiser than his thirteen years would otherwise suggest. They looked but didn't ask about the angry red scar that would slowly turn white and leave a matching streak in his hair.

Best of all, Party Leader Chen was gone, and the farm in Anhui no longer needed workers.

"I will work in Wuchang," Sartaq told Chen's replacement. "I strong. I will fix pots and pans, spoons, make knives sharp so people cook and eat."

"It is humble ambition," the man said, sitting next to Mother Shen in her finery. A shop near the University and a few tools would be made available to help him start.

Sartaq scouted the mountain behind the shop for cast off bricks and assembled a wood-fired forge. But it had many shortcomings. He redesigned it and switched to the charcoal used for cooking, and then the soft coal used by businesses for heat, much of it gathered a lump at a time from spillage.

The kitchens of the University provided a steady flow of work. And neighbors brought him additional business. Sharpening knives became an important sideline. Seeing the profit there, he began crafting them from scrap metal.

And, in the evenings, his occasional forays onto the campus to talk with students, to teach them about Allah, to have them read from a Chinese translation of the Qur'an he'd carried from Xinjiang, went unnoticed, or ignored, by school officials. Later, they dismissed him as harmless, a mental cripple which served his purposes.

And as Major Qassim had predicted, the students with the most anger proved to be the most eager for his teachings. When one of them was ready to graduate from both the University's academic program and also Sartaq's teachings, it was easy to convince them of their futures. Months, sometimes years later, Sartaq would hear about one of them, possibly with one of his long knives, in some anti-Party incident.

That was well and good.

But Sartaq longed to strike as he'd done Party Leader Chen, to do the smashing, crushing, the chopping of flesh and bone. He'd never forgotten the thrill, the satisfaction of hurting someone he hated.

Years would pass before the opportunity would arise, but then it would be for thousands!

Chapter 10

Present Day
Wuchang, China

At dusk, Sartaq closed the roll-up front door of his Wuchang metal shop but left it unlocked.

He climbed back up to where he'd covered Wang's double-bagged body with dead leaves and carried it to a concealed spot closer to the line of shops. He needed darkness to carry it through the front door, because he could no dare going through the back where it might rip open. When he thought the streetlights only a minute or two from coming on, he hoisted the load and strode up the sidewalk to his shop.

Inside, with the roll-up pushed down and bolted, he set Wang in the far corner. "A few days," he said to the rounded part he guessed was the boy's head. He set the deadfall on the back door and squeezed out.

Sartaq headed down the sidewalk, turned at the lake, and then uphill on the lane to his third-floor, one-room apartment.

Inside, he needed no light. He felt for his largest piece of furniture, a four-drawer, wood dresser liberated from the back of a professor's moving van. Inside was the thick envelope from Lili with two passports, matching credit cards, two one-hundred RMB bills, and two twenties in Singapore money.

"If the taxi to Wuhan airport is hundred RMB," he'd asked her, "what good will only two twenties be in Singapore?" She'd dismissed his question with something about the *conversion rate* being different. He didn't understand, but with Lili, that was common. She thought it was okay, so he left it at that. And if she was wrong, then he'd have to make something up.

As usual.

Feeling for the clothing Lili'd purchased for him, he struggled into them. Nothing fit, the collar rasped his neck, and the leather shoes cramped his toes.

He sighed.

Reversing his path, just before the shop he cut between the cars and trucks on the avenue and walked up the ramp to the hotel and its line of taxis.

"Let's go," he barked at the first one. "Airport." He added with an angry look, "And I know way."

He didn't, of course. The closest he'd ever been to an airplane was watching them high overhead. Lili'd said flying was easy, they'd tell him everything to do, and he could sleep most of the way there.

But as usual, she'd left things out. When the pretty flight attendant told him, "Fasten your seat belt," Sartaq did not know what to do.

She repeated, "Your seat belt?"

He shrugged his ignorance.

She bent forward. "You're sitting on it," she said, pawed next to his leg, and brought up the strap. She buckled and tightened it for him then left.

"First time?" The man in a business suit across the aisle asked.

Sartaq started to nod but switched to a head shake and turned away.

Lili'd said it was a nine-hour flight to Singapore. He settled back and closed his eyes as the plane trundled across the airport's concrete. The bumps were annoying, but much less severe than those on the bus out to their mother's. But when the plane's engines roared and the back of the plane dropped then leapt up, he yelped.

The man across the aisle looked at him, shook his head, and went back to his paper.

Some sound—jet engines from a plane climbing far overhead, or maybe the groan of a truck's diesel—woke Blake.

He forced his eyes open and saw a blue rectangle skewed to a parallelogram.

He shifted his back and realized he was laying on the bed. The blue shapes were on the ceiling, lights from eleven stories below projected through his hotel room window.

Turning his head slowly to the side, his alarm clock showed 10:50.

He remembered being chased by a machete-wielding madman, running, jumping, and tumbling down the mountain, and then skidding, hands and knees, across an asphalt-covered campus path. Two students helped him back to the hotel at—what? An hour or more before noon?

On the table near the mini fridge were four empty shot bottles: a Smirnoff's, two Johnny Walker Blacks, and a Gilbeys.

He'd researched the numbers for his debaucheries. The half-life of alcohol was four hours. Twelve hours had passed, so half of half of half left him with almost a whole shot still in his bloodstream.

He patted his abdomen on the left side. "Hang in there, liver. You're not done yet."

A white light blinked from the night table. He retrieved his cell phone and tapped in the unlock code.

One new text message. Megyn. 9:42 a.m.

"Where," he asked the room, "was I when that message came in?"
On the mountain. At the murder.

He understood. His phone had beeped when her message arrived, and it was that sound that gave away his presence.

Blake tapped the icon to see what she wrote.

Find Serpent's Smile cache? Blue/wht ceramic snake? Played there many yrs ago. Owners were family friends. Dead now. CU tmw.

He pecked a reply.

Need help. Pls call. Emergency!

Sitting alone in the darkened lobby restaurant, Blake checked his watch again. It was after one. Megyn had said half-past Midnight.

Across the lobby, a clerk sat at the main desk, feet up, eyes shut.

Blake turned the empty bottle of King Long beer in his fingers. He'd given the clerk 100 RMB to open the cooler next to the kitchen door, and they each took one.

Emptied in two long draws with a loud belch after each, the alcohol started through the walls of his stomach in less than a minute. In three, the hangover, the pain in his hands and knees, and the killer with the great big knife didn't seem as severe.

Bottle empty, he chiseled his thumbnail under the edge of the label.

If you'd had your gun...

He blinked and shook his head. Carrying a gun in China, especially for a foreign visitor, was utterly impossible. And shooting a big man like that with only a nine-millimeter would've enraged him; a double-tap doubly so. Bleeding out would take minutes, but in the meantime...

Besides, Blake had been fifty yards back. An exacting Bullseye aim would've been needed, but with that knife moving across the boy's neck, there would've been no time.

Too late, he told himself. *Nothing I could do.*

A movement of pink through the hotel's humidity-misted glass drew his eye. It came up the steps. In the darkened lobby, she was halfway across before he was sure.

There were lines across her forehead and a clump of chestnut brown hair stuck out. It bounced with each step. Her usual Mona Lisa smile was upside down, and when she arrived at the table, her scent—sour—did, too.

She dropped her purse on the table and dragged out a chair.

"I got here as fast as I could."

Her expression looked concerned and sympathetic, but her tone reminded him of when she'd stormed off to the back of the plane.

Where should he start? The hike? The murder? Passing out?

"Blake," she said, her voice rising, "it's the middle of the night. I've been dealing with issues all week. What's the emergency?"

Jump in, his mind directed.

"I saw a murder."

Half the bottle's label ripped loose in his fingers. "Damn."

She blinked. "What? You saw someone killed? On purpose?"

He wanted to yell, *"Of course, it was on purpose. That's why they call it murder."*

But he didn't.

He closed his eyes, took a breath, exhaled, and continued as he went back to work on the label.

"In the forest," he said, tipping his head toward the fogged glass across the front of the hotel. "Up on the mountain, on the ridge line..." He stopped picking at the label and looked into her eyes. "This guy cut off a kid's head!"

One end of Megyn's mouth flinched and her eyebrows arched.

He went on.

"A student... a boy... freshman, maybe. He had a pale, innocent face... New-looking clothes like they all wear..."

Megyn wavered in her chair, her voice turned sincere. "You saw it? A student... decapitated? By another student?"

Blake shook his head. "No, no. The victim, he was the college boy. At least, I think he was. The killer, though, he was older. My age, maybe? Big man. Huge arms. Weight-lifter type. Green coveralls, yellow construction boots." He raised his hand. "He had this sc—"

"On the mountain?" She interrupted and hooked a thumb over her shoulder. "Here? On Luojia?"

He nodded. "Up on the ridgeline. The boy... his head might still be there. And the body... I don't know."

He stopped. He didn't want to tell her he'd panicked, that he'd run. But he had. He'd run away in wholly fucking terror.

"It was too late," he said, his voice taking an edge. "The boy was... or was about to be..." He shook his head. "I think that's when I got your text. My phone beeped, and then the killer looked up. I ducked down but... Next thing, the killer screamed and came charging toward me. So, I, uh, took off? Then, I was out of the forest on my hands and knees—" he held up his scab-covered palms, "—on one of the paved paths."

Megyn gasped. "You need to take care of that. Does the hotel have alcohol?"

"Two students," he shook his head, "I don't know their names. They helped me back to the hotel. Didn't see the killer again."

He gave her a sheepish grin. "Apparently, I run pretty good. I intended to call the cops, but my blood sugar was wonky. Adrenalin burns it up, you know? So, I ate some candy bars and... a few drinks from the refrigerator." His face felt hot. "Two, I think."

He looked at her eyes. "Four, actually," he confessed. "Real fast. I guess I passed out. Then, when I woke up, I saw your text from this morning, the one that alerted the killer."

If she hadn't sent that text message, the killer wouldn't have known he was there. This was all her fault.

He shook his head.

"So, I texted you back—tonight, I mean—and, well, here we are."

When she didn't answer, he added, "Thanks for coming."

Megyn leaned forward.

"Blake, call the Police. You should've done that immediately. You can explain you were in shock, took a drink to calm down, several—do you have the empties if they ask?—and passed out. Say that you're calling them now because you just woke up."

He nodded. "I thought about the US Embassy. Maybe I should call them, too."

She nodded vigorously. "Excellent!" Another pause. "In fact, call them first. See what they say to do."

Blake felt hopeful for the first time. Dragging her out in the middle of the night had been the right thing to do.

He felt the tension in his shoulders drain. "That's what they're for, isn't it?"

Megyn stood. "I'll ask the front desk for a phone book."

"Wait." Blake took out his cell. "I'll Google it. The wireless here is real good."

The call answered on the first ring.

A recorded voice announced, "This is the United States Consulate in Wuhan, Hubei Province, Peoples Republic of China." It switched to Mandarin for a dozen syllables and then back to English. "If you are a US citizen and need emergency assistance after hours, call the State Department hotline. The number is..."

Blake made a scribbling motion with his finger. Megyn grabbed her purse to hand him a small notepad and a brown eyeliner pencil. Blake jotted down the long string of digits.

Punching in the new number, he smiled but grumbled, "Seems like they could switch the call if it's an emergency. What if you couldn't write it down or something?"

It rang once before picking up, but clicked twice more before a man's voice asked, "United States Citizen Services. Are you a citizen of the United States?"

The voice echoed like it was at the end of a long tunnel.

"Uh, yeah," Blake started, then the words came tumbling out. "I saw someone killed— I mean murdered. I'm in Wuhan— I mean Wuchang, that's a suburb of Wuhan."

Silence.

"In China?

A keyboard clacked from the other end.

"So, should I call the Police or what?"

"Just a moment."

More keyboard.

"Everything is going to be all right," The words were reassuring but his voice sounded mechanical. "It is good that you have contacted the State Department. We will notify the appropriate jurisdictions on your behalf. Someone will be provided to advise you during interviews with the authorities. Say nothing without them."

Blake covered the microphone. "They said they're going to call the Police. And they're going to send someone here."

Megyn leaned back and nodded.

Blake had never needed his government while traveling. "They're good!" He grinned even bigger. "Not like that *Sartaq* fellow."

Megyn's cheek flinched. "What?"

The man on the phone said something at that same moment.

Blake held up a hand and said, "What?" into the phone.

The man asked, "Sir, what's your name and where are you?"

"Do I need my passport number?" Blake stood. "It's up in my room."

"No," the man said patiently. "We can look it up. Now, please tell me your full name."

Megyn touched his arm. "Where did you hear that?"

He covered the microphone with his hand. "What? The name? It's Sartaq. The girl said it once real clear, and then I heard them all say it along with other things."

"Sir," the voice on the phone repeated, "please tell me your full name, your exact location, and what number you're calling from."

"Don't you have the number from the system?" He asked.

"China blocks it. Now, please, let's start with your name."

"Oh, Okay." He sat down imagining a guy in a white shirt with a headset sitting in front of a computer. "It's B-l-a—"

Megyn jerked his arm and exploded. "Hang up!"

The voice on the phone said something again.

He brought it back up to his face. "Just a second." He put it face down on his leg. "Megyn, what's wrong?"

"Don't say more. Just hang up!"

"I don't..."

Her hand like a claw, she reached for his cell.

He automatically jerked it up out of her reach. "What're you doing?"

She commanded, "Give me the phone!"

Across the lobby, the dozing clerk's chair thudded on the floor.

Phone high and out of her reach, Blake said, "But you told me to call the Embassy!"

Around the edges of her lipstick, the skin had turned white. Her eyes flicked in tiny little moves, back and forth between his.

And then a moment later, her face calmed, color returned

around her lips, and the Mona Lisa smile reappeared.

"Yes, Blake," she crooned, "you're right. I said that, so you are correct. But I need you to hang up now."

She leaned forward and put her hands on his legs just above his knees. She squeezed. "I've thought about it and changed my mind. Trust me, Blake. Please hang up now."

Blake opened and closed his mouth like a goldfish in an algae-clogged tank. His blood was surging again, and he felt that warm glow in his crotch.

"Trust me, Blake, please." She slid her hands up his thighs and squeezed again. "Hang up. I'll tell you why as soon as you do. It's... complicated."

His mind dull and foggy and his groin feeling that wonderful ache, he brought the cell phone back up to his face.

"I'll call you back."

He pushed the red disconnect icon and put the phone in his pocket.

Megyn scooted back.

Blake waited. Should he invite her up to his room? Her squeezes left no doubt.

But then she said, "There are a lot of things to consider."

Her eyes locked on his, she started, "In the first place, how does the Embassy know you're not the murderer?"

The muscles in Blake's crotch pulsed. "What?"

"I know you didn't do it, but people might call just to cover up a crime, to divert attention. They don't know who you are, so..."

The only feeling left in his crotch was the need to pee.

"I'm just trying to imagine," she went on, "what kinds of contingencies they—the US Government—must have in their book. Maybe they'll keep you under wraps, get your story, and cross-check other sources."

She waved a hand dismissively.

"Time is good, actually—your delay, I mean. It gives us some leeway to figure out what to do."

He smiled to be polite. Her mind seemed to be going a mile a minute.

"But there's a problem," she said, her face scrunched. "Your class."

Blake tucked his chin back a fraction of an inch.

"My class?"

Was she worried about him, or had this become something about her job and the school?

She babbled on. "The Embassy will probably hide you. What do they call it, a safe house? Or they might want you to stay here, in Wuhan I mean, until everything's straightened out. They would certainly need you to testify in court. That might be quick, or it could be slow, I don't know."

Megyn's face seemed twisted, older, almost a caricature.

"No," she shook her head, the loose clump of hair flagging back and forth. "So, I guess it boils down to this: If you tell anyone what you saw, even though you are innocent, you will probably be stuck here for months. And, if they think you did it, then it'll be even worse. You'll need a lawyer, a Chinese lawyer, and be stuck in court. And if convicted..."

She took his hand from the beer bottle. "Blake, you can't tell anyone. Not the Embassy, not the Police, not now, not ever."

Blake realized his jaw was hanging open.

"Megyn," he pleaded, "that kid was murdered! The killer cut off his head, for God's sake. And not just a chop. He had to saw it off!" He gestured at the glass doors across the lobby. "That lunatic is out there. That was no crime of passion, Megyn. Premeditated murder, pure and simple. He even had this big piece of plastic all spread out on the ground for the blood. The killer must've planned it all out, every step of the way."

The check-in clerk had rocked back in his chair and closed his eyes again.

Megyn looked down and curled her fingers as if examining the nails.

Blake shook his head.

"I'm calling the Embassy."

He took out his cell phone and keyed in his unlock code.

"They can tell the Police. I can show them where it happened, and from your text, I know exactly when. And they definitely said, 'Sartaq.' That's the murderer's name. I'm sure of it."

Megyn's swipe was swift and vicious.

The phone flew out of his hand and hit the marble floor twenty feet away. The back, battery, and body of the phone skittered separately across the polished tile.

"Not now, Blake!" She yelled, and then added in a calmer voice, "I mean, not yet. It's…"

The clerk was watching them again.

Megyn stared into Blake's eyes for a moment, then rocked forward and swept her hands under her thighs to straighten her skirt. She pushed her face toward him. "It's too risky. Please?"

This was nuts. The day, the murder, the booze, the beer, the late night, and now Megyn… It all piled up on him. He wished he'd never come to China. Or if he'd kept her out of this, handled it himself like he should have, then she wouldn't be telling him one thing while his gut said something else.

He closed his eyes, focused on breathing deep and smooth three times, then opened them.

Her eyes were focused through him to somewhere far away.

He resigned. "All right, Megyn."

Her eyes focused on his.

He held up a hand.

"I'll do what you want. I won't say anything to anyone. But right now, it's late, and I need to pee. And get some sleep. God knows it's been a day."

She smiled and patted his hand. "I understand. That poor boy is dead. You can't change that. It was an awful experience, I'm sure. Just let it go."

He felt like he should say, "Yes, Ma'am," but didn't. He waved a hand toward the glass doors. "I still don't know if this killer—this Sartaq—got a good look at me."

Megyn put a fingertip on her cheek and tilted her head like a schoolmarm. "Are you sure that's a name? Perhaps you misunderstood. You know you don't speak Mandarin or Cantonese, so…"

Blake ignored her. He knew what he'd heard.

He stood up and collected the parts of his phone. He put it back together and watched until the little green, cold-boot Android robot appeared. "Looks like it's okay. I'm going to bed now. Tomorrow's Sunday and I know you had plans for us to visit the museum, but I'm going to skip that. I'll eat here and stay in my room. Maybe download a book or stream a movie. God knows I need the distraction."

Megyn rocked her head. "No. The museum trip is set. It's not for you. It's to give the students more time to interact with you, part of what you were hired to do."

Blake opened his mouth, but Megyn put up a hand. "I'm sorry, it's in the contract. Your performance has to be up to the established practice. We do it every year. It's required and the students expect it."

Blake wanted to see that clause but was sure if he fought it, he'd end up in a Chinese court with a Chinese judge. He had no choice.

"All right, I'll go."

Megyn beamed and stood up.

"William will be here at half-past nine. Alex and Zoey will come over from the student dorms to meet us, and we'll all ride in the van together. Lunch will be there, and then there's a dinner planned for the evening. You'll like it, really."

Blake stepped back and pointed toward the elevator. "I'm going to get some sleep."

Her single, sharp nod was like someone giving him permission.

Chapter 11

Sunday, October 29
Singapore (2000 miles south), and Museum and
Dinner in Wuchang, China

The Singapore border official compared Sartaq's face to the one in the passport. He stamped an empty page and slid it back through the slot.

"Welcome to Singapore, Mr. Ma."

Lili had briefed him. "After passport booth, use green exit but wait for several others and walk through together. You have nothing to declare."

He glanced at the digital clock near that exit.

1:43AM.

He had to get to the shipping company before three when the guard changed.

"Not much time," Sartaq mumbled to himself. He paced behind the luggage carousel where everyone waited. His new leather shoes creaked. And hurt.

At twenty minutes past the hour, the suitcases started coming up. Sartaq trailed a family with three kids, each with a brightly colored roller bag, through the green exit.

As Lili'd predicted, no one challenged him.

Outside, the air felt thick with humidity like the worst of the summer nights in Wuchang. He would only be in Singapore one day even though Mr. Ma's reservation said two, but he hadn't slept on the airplane as Lili had suggested.

He patted his pocket with the second passport in a different name. Lili'd said to use that when leaving. It already had an entry stamp. Their new Islamic State partners had seen to everything.

He waved to the first taxi, and its back door swung open. Climbing in, he took out Lili's note and carefully said each syllable, "Cow-den Ship-ing, Pe-sek Road, Ju-rong."

Without thinking, he added in Cantonese, "Take fastest way."

The taxi driver blinked at him in the rear-view mirror. "You're going there now?" He'd answered in the same Cantonese. "Everything's closed."

"Yes, yes, I know," Sartaq snapped. "How long?"

"Twenty minutes," the driver shrugged, "depending."

The flag dropped on the meter and 4.88 appeared on the display next to 2:33.

"Is that for whole trip?" Sartaq asked, thinking of the two 100 Singapore bills in his pocket. He'd have a ton of money left over if that was true.

"First quarter mile. It'll probably be about fifty out to island."

The driver pulled out from the curb and navigated to a meandering road from the airport building.

He glanced back at Sartaq in the mirror again. "Plus fifty percent surcharge after midnight."

Sartaq wasn't sure how much that'd be, but he got an uneasy feeling Lili'd hadn't given him enough.

Typical, he thought. He'd have to figure it out.

"You take credit cards?"

The man nodded. "Visa, MasterCard, American Express, Diners Club, and Discover."

He hoped Ma Feng's credit card was one of those.

Singapore was lush and well-manicured even in the dark. They passed a sign with three English letters where the roadway widened into a divided highway. He could read the American letters, ECP, but did not know what they meant.

He glanced over the seatback at the taxi's speedometer. It sat a little below seventy, the same as city streets in Wuhan.

"Too slow," he complained. "Is there faster way?"

The driver turned his head to glance at him. "There's only one way to island, sir." He pointed out the window straight ahead.

When the taxi rocked to a stop in front of a low building in an industrial area, the dashboard clock said 2:58.

They'd just made it.

Sartaq said, "Wait," and grabbed the door handle, but it wouldn't move.

"Pay what's on meter, sir."

Sartaq's throat growled as he retrieved Mr. Ma's credit card and set it in the little metal trough between the seats.

"Please hurry!"

The driver took it and slid it through a slot in a handheld box with a glowing screen. He pushed a bunch of buttons and then waited.

The clock changed to 2:59.

A scroll of paper chattered softly out of the little box. The driver passed it back with the credit card and a pen. Sartaq slashed a wavy line and shoved it back through.

His door swung open.

"Five minutes," the driver shouted as Sartaq hustled up a concrete walk bathed in light from a tall post. "That's all I can wait."

A small sign hung from a wrought-iron post next to the red brick building. Hand-lettered in several languages, the Hanzi portion said, "Yang-Xi Shipping."

An arrow pointed right to a brick path.

Sartaq raced around the corner, his leather soles sliding on the mossy bricks.

He stopped at the brightly lit guard shack next to a high, closed gate. A fat man in a gray shirt with a gold-thread badge sewn over the pocket sat inside. He didn't look up from his paperback.

"Box," Sartaq wheezed. "You have box for me."

"ID?" the guard said as he turned a page.

Sartaq opened Ma Feng's passport and pressed it to the glass.

The guard leaned forward to read the page and compare the

picture to Sartaq's face.

The clock behind him said two minutes after.

"You're late," he said, closing his book. He leaned back, crossed his arms over his chest, and stared.

Sartaq yipped, "My box?"

"You first," the man said. "And my replacement should be here already. You better hurry."

Sartaq fumed but took the envelope out of his pocket that Lili'd prepared. He shoved it through an opening at the bottom of the glass window.

The guard slid it into his lap, looked both ways, and then counted the contents. Satisfied, he slid it inside his jacket, then bent over and came up with a cardboard box about the size for work boots. A red label with white printing in four languages said, "Fragile: Do Not Drop."

He set it on the counter, slid the glass window all the way open, and shoved the box out.

Sartaq jumped to catch it. He glared at the man but he'd already returned to his book.

Lili'd given him four things to do on this trip. The first, getting the dynamite, was done.

Sartaq held the box to his chest and took baby steps around the slippery path to the front.

"Where to?" The taxi driver asked as he slid into the back seat again.

Box on his lap, Sartaq read the syllables from Lili's sheet. "Ma-ri-na Bay Sands Ho-tel."

The man's eyebrows went halfway up his forehead.

"Yes, Sir!"

When Sartaq entered the long, curving lobby, it was dark and quiet, not surprising at four in the morning.

The uniformed clerk behind the check-in desk greeted him in muted Beijing Mandarin. Sartaq handed over the forged passport and credit card as Lili had instructed, and said in Cantonese, "I have room. Ma Feng."

The agent typed on his keyboard and answered in kind. "I see you'll be staying with us for two nights, Mr. Ma?"

Sartaq nodded quickly. That was a lie.

The clerk handed him Mr. Ma's passport and a small paper envelope with a white plastic card sticking out. "Room 5416." Then he held out a red plastic card. "This is your gaming card. It has 475 RMB credit, compliments of Marina Bay Sands Hotel."

Sartaq turned it in his hand. One side had a silver sketch of a lion's head. On the back was the dark stripe like on his credit card, and below that a lot of tiny print in several languages.

The clerk droned, "You may use it at any of the machines or tables in casino, but not in restaurant or bar. At end of stay, we will refund any balance over that in cash." He finished with an open hand gesture. "Take elevator to fifty-four."

Sartaq raised his eyebrow. "Fifty-*four*?" *Four* was bad luck in China. The word sounded the same as *death* if said wrong.

"Is that problem, sir? We can give you something lower, if you wish."

"No," Sartaq smirked. He was bringing death to Singapore. Bad luck was his mission.

Looking at the lock on the door marked 5416, there was a slot for a regular key, but they'd only given him the white and red plastic cards. After a moment, he realized the black slot was about the same width as them. He tried the white card, and the slot turned green as the mechanism inside the latch clicked.

He turned the handle and pushed in.

The lights came on automatically.

The room looked like a picture in a magazine. All the fabrics were brown or gray, and the woods black or brown. Two huge beds sat on the right, the covers folded back on the farthest to reveal taut, snowy sheets. Topped with two white and one charcoal pillows, they bested the downtown store windows in Wuhan. A mahogany chest stood on the left wall next to a long, oak desk with flat-panel TV and a tray with a gold handled bucket and a pair of drinking glasses wrapped in paper.

It was better than any place he'd ever experienced, and for the night, it was all his.

One corner at a time, he gingerly set the tape-sealed box from the shipping company on the desk.

Drawn by the lights through the thin curtain, he pushed it open. The entire wall was glass, floor to ceiling, and wall to wall. Singapore's skyscrapers sparkled to his left across a small bay. Several older one- and two-story buildings sat to the right, bathed in yellowish spotlights behind a perfect green lawn.

The digital clock by the bed said 4:17.

A yawn overtook him. He'd executed Wang, chased the American, hidden the body in his shop, and bounced in an airplane for hours, all today.

He needed to sleep.

Sartaq's new clothing, shoelaces still knotted, landed in a heap on the floor. Sliding in naked, the icy, slick sheets made his breath shudder. They caressed his skin whenever he moved.

A memory drifted up.

He was ten. Mother Shen sat in front of a mirror brushing her long, dark brown hair. She looked at him and smiled. Next to her on a small cushion was his little half-sister, Lili. She combed, stroke for stroke, in her own mirror in time with their mother. She gave him an identical smile.

He remembered lying in bed and hearing the grunts, moans, and bellows of his mother's guests. Party leaders from various committees—agriculture, housing, finance—they disgusted him. It was necessary, he knew, but he still hated them, hated what his mother had to do.

The one thing he had in common was appearance. They were ugly by birth. Sartaq more so by inheritance, and his grandfather's cane.

His father's Uyghur and his mother's Han blood produced what others whispered was an *abomination*. His head was too big, his eyes too far apart, his black hair finer than it should be, but unruly and wavy. And then there was the scar.

But his body chemistry functioned like theirs.

The young women on the campus were almost universally attractive, with many stunningly so. His body responded to their scents, but he dared not make overtures; their revulsion was quick and obvious. Even when he could afford a whore across the

Chang Jiang bridge, they would squat and flush him away before entertaining another customer.

Sartaq rolled to his side on the bed that seemed as big as his entire apartment. The sheet glided across his thigh like the hands of a paid lover, her foreplay to the main event.

The air conditioner purred in his ear as he closed his eyes.

Sunlight beamed in Sartaq's face as a chilly draft blew down his back. He passed a hand across the prickled hairs on his thigh. Naked on the bed with no pillow, no sheets, and no blanket, his penis was hard, the muscles in his groin tight and aching for release.

He rolled to let the sun warm his back, but that channeled the frigid gusts from the room's air conditioner down his chest, stomach, and thighs. His arousal faded.

He needed to pee.

Standing at the white ceramic toilet in the white ceramic bathroom, a wave of relief shimmied up his body. He scanned the labels on the containers next to the sink as he waited for his bladder to empty. Shampoo, conditioner, body wash, hand lotion, and a tiny little box marked "Face Soap" that couldn't possibly last a single use.

He flushed the toilet and began opening every one of them. Each was full. He marveled they must top them off after each guest, and wondered if they would charge extra if he took some home?

But Lili's instructions had been clear: "Take nothing. Leave nothing. Do not attract attention."

He shook out his clothes and put them on, then worked his bare feet into the stiff, leather shoes with the laces still tied. The ballpoint pen from the desk went in his shirt pocket, cell phone and two credit cards in one pocket of his pants, and the two passports and remaining cash on the other side.

Lili's second task for him was to hide the box of explosives somewhere for two weeks.

"Why now?" He'd asked Lili. "Why send explosives now instead of day before needed?"

"Getting explosives into Singapore is difficult," she explained. "And it was up to Islamic State. We must deal with what they decided."

Sartaq sighed. Same as with Lili's plans. They dictated, but he made it work.

He planted the package on his left hip and held it with one hand across the top. Joggling up and down for a test, it stayed in place.

Lili'd said to use a linen closet. When he'd given her a blank stare, she'd explained, "Each floor will have housekeeping room. Look for sign."

Why didn't just she just say that in the first place? But he knew not to ask. Her explanations would go on and on. She liked to show how smart she was. She'd gone to high school, college, and then even more college. So, he followed her plans, usually without asking, and then fixed them when they didn't work.

The door that said "Housekeeping" was nearest the elevator. He tried the handle, but it wouldn't turn.

Of course, he nodded, Lili's plan hadn't said how to get a key.

He looked back down the hall, but it was empty. At the elevator, he pushed the Down button. It took two stops to find what he wanted.

At the far end, a woman in a tan, one-piece dress with a white bib stood next to a cart almost as tall as her. It had a big, open-mouth cloth sack on one side, shelves with toilet paper, folded linens and towels, and spray bottles with different color liquids on top. Morning light streamed into the hallway from a doorway beside her. She picked up some sheets and disappeared into the room.

Sartaq power-walked to the cart, looked in to see her billowing out a clean sheet, and started searching for a key. He guessed it would either be a metal one to fit the lock, or another plastic rectangle like the one in his pocket.

He spotted a white card with a lanyard on the bottom shelf, but before he could grab it, the maid came out of the room with a wad of sheets.

She said something. It wasn't Mandarin or Cantonese, and he

didn't think it was English.

She stuffed the bundle into the bag and waited.

"Soap?" Sartaq asked in Cantonese. "Wash hair?" He mimed scrubbing the top of his head with his free hand.

She reached into the cart and handed him one of the small white boxes.

He gave her a nod and then ambled down the hallway, turning as if looking at room numbers. When she disappeared, he bolted back to grab the lanyard, and then ran back up the hall and let himself into "Housekeeping."

Chrome-steel supply racks filled most of the four walls, including the space above the door. Filled with boxes and neat stacks of toilet paper, facial tissue, and all the things he'd found on his sink, the containers had signs in Hanzi, Arabic, and English. On the back wall, a low tub sat on the floor beneath two mops hanging from hooks. The space on either side of the tub was empty, but the black marks on the floor suggested the storage spot for the laundry carts in the evening.

"We will use human nature," Lili had told him. "People believe written word."

Sartaq set the explosives down, reached up to the rack over the door, and took down two large "Toilet Tissue" boxes, one from in front of the other.

He emptied the first by adding the rolls to the half-empty top shelf on the left. Then, he eased his sealed box of dynamite in and re-closed the flaps, one inside the other, all the way around. With the pen from his pocket, he crossed out "Toilet Tissue," and just above it, copied the four English letters, X-M-A-S, from Lili's note. He repeated the markings on each face including top and bottom, then boosted it onto the rack over the door, added the other box, and used it to push his to the wall.

When he slipped out into the hall again, nothing had changed. He walked past the cleaning cart, dropped the housekeeping key on the floor next to it, and then pushed through the door into the stairwell. He stopped, closed his eyes, and repeated to himself, *Floor fifty-two, fifty-two, fifty-two.*

One flight down, he took the elevator to the ground floor.

Two of Lili's tasks for him remained: find the six columns and figure out how to get away in ten seconds.

Sartaq stuck his hands in his pockets and walked to the glass doors at one end of the foyer. Outside, a man stood idle at a tall desk.

Workers like that annoyed Sartaq. He worked hard but got paid only when someone bought his work. Waiting earned him nothing. Why pay someone to do nothing? He shook his head in disgust.

The instructions from Islamic State had been relayed through Major Qassim. Lili had read them aloud, and he imagined how it would look.

The explosives would cut away the six supports, two per building, all on the same side. Each of the three towers, their inside legs gone, would then fall over like a drunk who'd lost his balance.

And, better than 9/11 in America because the hotel buildings would fall to the side, they would then crush the casino across the street. More dead!

Sartaq knew it would be a lot, but Islamic State's prediction of ten thousand dead, three times the 9/11 success, made him giddy.

He'd be a hero! He would walk through Kashgar where people would wave, cheer, and shower him with gifts.

And then he'd go to the Khan's.

He couldn't decide which would give him more pleasure, the parade or his wrath on those people. Arzu's face and the coolness of her hand came to him. Maybe he'd spare her.

Strolling through the hotel lobby, Sartaq passed a man in a gray uniform sitting at a desk. Behind him, a square column ran from floor to ceiling, each face about as wide as Sartaq's two outstretched arms.

Casually walking around it, Sartaq looked at the pictures on each face. One was a group of people at a beach. In the next, minor figures were skiing on a snow-covered mountain. In the last, they tossed a colorful ball in a swimming pool.

When he got back to the front, Sartaq stopped, nodded to the man, and picked up one of the paper brochures from a stand next to the desk. He smiled as he opened the pamphlet, not from what he saw, but because he realized the column behind the desk had to contain one of the building's support beams. He'd found the first one.

He put the brochure back, nodded again to the man, and made a fist behind his back. He popped out one finger, turned, and continued through the curving lobby.

When all five fingers were out, he saw the sixth ahead. It looked exactly like the others, a floor-to-ceiling box.

Next, he needed to pick the one that would give him and Lili a way out.

He started through the lobby in the opposite direction, checking the walls on the outside of the curve for additional exits. Opposite the column with the potted palm, a green sign of a running figure glowed above a gray steel door. It had a shiny metal push-bar across the middle. It was an Emergency Exit. Never locked.

If they were to use it, there needed to be somewhere on the other side that would shield them when the bombs went off.

But without opening it now, he needed to explore what was out there.

Sartaq looked down the long tunnel of the lobby for the closest end. He planned to count his steps so he could do the same on the outside to find the same door, but soon lost track. Looking back, when he reached the end, he could see the potted palm. His column was there. He tried to memorize how far it looked.

Stepping outside, he walked along the narrow service road on the outside of the hotel. At what he guessed was about the same distance, he found the gray steel door. Across the roadway was a low concrete wall, about waist high. If he and Lili laid down, it would shield them.

That was the last of his tasks in Singapore for Lili.

Back inside the lobby, the clock over the check-in desk showed a few minutes before Nine. He had all day and most of the evening to pass.

The red card—the free money—was in his pocket. The hotel man said he could use it in the casino, and that he could then take home all his winnings.

A sign with flickering lights said "Casino" and pointed to the top of an escalator.

Sartaq grinned as he rode down.

If he played carefully, he might take home more money than Lili'd provided. She'd be proud of him.

Blake and Megyn, along with the two students, Alex and Zoey, climbed into the van at nine o'clock on Sunday morning. William drove them to the Hubei Provincial Museum where he parked and then joined them at the entrance.

They started in one corner with the earliest artifacts. Zoey commandeered leadership for their visit, and translated every placard and footnote, added her own asides, and made certain they missed nothing of China's twenty-two thousand years of history. Only Zoey seemed annoyed when the museum closed at the end of the day.

"But we're not done."

William drove them a few blocks to Tsing-Tsing.

The restaurant was across from the main gate of the University, and just a block from Blake's hotel. The interior looked like any large Chinese eatery in the States. Shiny metal gongs and hand fans painted with outdoor scenes hung on the white walls surrounding the sea of red carpet. Black lacquered tables with identical chairs and red-cushioned seats filled the space. In the center of each round table, a blond wood rotating tray awaited the dishes from the kitchen.

They sat at one of the smaller tables as a piano solo started on the restaurant's sound system. In a few moments, Blake recognized it. He touched his ear. "That's Mozart's Piano Sonata in C Major. I love this."

They listened for a few moments. Zoey said, "It's like a ballet."

Blake nodded. "That's what I think of, too. A very young dancer, thin and lithe. But not a professional dancer. Someone younger with innate talent. All in white: tutu, body stocking, toe shoes. Her feet grace the floor as she pirouettes, tilts, and points."

They listened until the end.

Megyn turned to Zoey. "What did you like best at the museum?"

"Oh, that's easy," she gushed. "The Mongolian room. Genghis wasn't Han, but what he accomplished, unifying the country like that back in the thirteenth century, that was wonderful."

Megyn looked at Blake and gave him an amused smile.

Zoey's endless lecture at the museum threatened to resume. "The Khans were from Mongolia, first Genghis, then Kublai. They have a savage history!"

Blake nodded, unsure how to fend off another thousand years.

"Up in the north," she gestured behind her, "Genghis was a brutal man. His armies raided as far west as today's Poland, up into Russia, across most of southeast Asia, and all of what is now China." She looked around the table to be sure everyone was listening. "Isn't that incredible?"

Blake tried to divert the discussion to more immediate needs. "What should we order for dinner?"

Zoey didn't seem to have heard him.

"We talk about our money in yuans," she said. "That's from the *Yuan* dynasty. The official name of our money is *renminbi*, RMB, but nobody says that. Genghis' grandson, Kublai, started it in 1271 until the Red Turban Rebellion," she blushed, "but I'm getting ahead of myself."

Blake glanced at Megyn and flared his eyes.

She interrupted before Zoey could reset her chronology. "That's amazing, Zoey. Your knowledge of China's history is encyclopedic. Is that your major?"

Zoey blinked and looked embarrassed. "Uh, no. I'm going to be a Software Specialist. Web design and databases. I just love my country. Don't you? It's so... historic!"

Megyn nodded. "My father was a professor in the Chinese history department here at the University. You would've liked him."

"Is he retired now?"

"He's dead."

"Oh!"

Blake looked away to keep from smiling at Zoey's embarrassment. She'd walked into that, and Megyn had set the hook perfectly.

A waiter in white shirt and black pants arrived with pencil and notepad.

Megyn turned to Blake. "What do you think? Should we task our students with selecting the meal?" She turned to Zoey. "What do you think?"

Zoey, her pride apparently restored, beamed at the offer. She waved-in her companions and they huddled with whispered comments before announcing their selections.

Alex went first. "Szechuan Boiled Fish!"

Their server began writing.

"Chairman Mao's Red Braised Pork," Zoey chirruped.

William put his arms across his chest. "Baozi!"

"Little Bao buns?" Blake guessed.

Megyn grinned. "Very good!"

William hadn't finished. "King Long beer," he added.

Blake didn't know the students could have beer. He'd assumed they would have to be twenty-one. But if they were going to order it here, then it must be okay.

Blake leaned in to catch William's eye. "Orion? Orion beer?" He pointed toward the bar. To the others, "It's from Okinawa. The silver label on the brown bottle."

Zoey translated for William. He nodded vigorously. "Good, good!" He pointed around the table, eyebrows up. Everyone nodded. William held up five fingers to the server and gestured with both hands. "Big'a beer."

With five tall-boy bottles on the table, Zoey, Alex, and William ignored the menus and fired off a dozen more dishes. The man scribbled on his notepad to keep up. And by the interruptions and discussions that caused him to erase and rewrite many times, their dinner promised to be special.

An hour later, with nine of the serving dishes completely empty, Zoey, Alex, and William chatted among themselves.

Blake leaned closer to Megyn. "It's moments like this, watching those three talk and laugh, that show me how much alike we are."

Megyn nodded but pursed her lips. "Most people can afford to be just that, uncomplicated with transparent lives, good friends..."

She paused, her eyes distant and dreamy.

Blake added, "And family?"

When she didn't answer, he said, "Megyn, is it all right for me to ask about your family, about your mother?"

Megyn flinched like someone had pointed a bright flashlight in her face.

Blake back-pedaled. "I'm sorry. I didn't mean to pry."

"It's Okay. She lives on the other side of Wuhan, out in the country. I don't see her often, and she only writes for critical things. But we're very close. We think alike. She can be demanding. Sometimes we clash."

"I'm sure she appreciates everything you do for her," he said, and then started, "The money we snuck—"

Megyn's slap on the table made the chopsticks leap from their rests. William, Alex, and Zoey stopped and stared. Diners at the next table turned to look.

Megyn blushed.

"I'm sorry," Blake began, "I didn't..."

Almost too soft to hear, Megyn spat half a dozen harsh and guttural syllables between her teeth. Blake recognized Mandarin.

The students instantly looked down at their laps.

After a moment, Blake leaned over. "Megyn?" He half-whispered, "I'm so sorry. That was... I didn't think about what I was saying. Sometimes I let my thoughts out without thinking."

"It's all right," she sighed. "Besides, this is a watershed. Everything will soon change."

Her eyes looked distant, distracted.

Blake guessed she must be referring to something with her mother. Was the old woman sick? Was Megyn here for a last visit? Or something financial? After all, that was a lot of money he'd helped her bring in. Maybe the woman was in debt, unable to pay her bills.

Megyn put a hand on his arm. "Blake, the things we want in life..."

She began again. "The things we've worked for, the things I've done from the States..."

She sighed. "I've made... sacrifices in my life."

Megyn was obviously trying to tell him something—baring her soul by the sound of it—but whatever it was, he didn't have a clue.

What had she meant by *sacrifices*?

She'd never married but didn't say why. He'd guessed several reasons, not the least would be her living in the US but with a mother still in China. He assumed she'd never met the right man, a *Chinese* man. Family expectations and pressures could be persuasive.

Or had she meant more than marriage? A family with children? Lots of them? Or maybe it was her mother who wanted that for Megyn, but time was, well, running out?

He offered, "Megyn, if there's anything I can do, anything at all..."

She shook her head. "Blake, this trip is... It's important. Beyond important. As I said, this is a watershed moment, and not just in my life."

Her expression looked resolute.

"You're not Chinese, Blake. You're American. *Very* American. You grew up with the American government, American social practices, American education. That's such a different world than here. There's just no way you can understand. You have no basis, no experience of what it's really like."

Blake's temples thumped. Everything she said was true, but he still felt denigrated. He'd travelled. He'd experienced many cultures firsthand. And he'd sure as Hell experienced emotional pressure. Julie's defiance, her open promiscuity, had crushed his hopes and feelings. Withdrawal and alcohol became his only escapes.

Megyn paused for a long moment, her eyes down, and then said, "I want you to do something."

"Okay," Blake said.

Her eyes still down, she asked, "Do you do field trips?"

He blinked as slowly as he'd ever done in his life.

"What?"

"A field trip," she repeated mechanically, her eyes coming up and scanning the wall behind him. "Take the class somewhere and teach, you know, on the spot?"

He shook his head. "Not usually."

Her eyes stopped on something high on the wall behind to Blake's right.

She said, "Take the class on a field trip." A muscle in her cheek twitched.

Blake's mouth slowly opened as he tried to imagine it.

A field trip here? With two hundred students?

He shook his head. "I wouldn't know where to go, what to say, or what to do."

"Well then," she shifted in her chair and looked down at her hands, "we'll have to make it something easy."

She scooted forward and with the demeanor of a third-grade teacher started issuing instructions.

"Take them to one of the old buildings on the campus. Perhaps the Old Library. It's just a few hundred yards from your classroom. Yes, the Old Library will be perfect. Take them to the Old Library."

Alex and Zoey were listening, their faces blank.

"The Old Library," Blake echoed.

Megyn blinked as if coaxing along an idea.

"Give them an assignment," she nodded. "Tell them to come up with mechanisms to automate the building, something to improve the place, convert it for a new use. They should have plenty of ideas."

Alex pushed up his glasses and said, "That building is very stuffy. No circulation. Either too hot or too cold. And it smells. We could do a blue-tooth network with sensors and fans in different areas to equalize the temperatures and bring in fresh air."

Megyn looked at him and smiled. "There, see? That's perfect. The building needs fixing up, and your students can figure it out. It's a perfect challenge. Thursday at 4:30. Plan to stay an hour. They won't mind if you go a few minutes over that day."

Megyn tilted her head and looked in his eyes. Her face looked profoundly sad.

Then something must've clicked in her mind.

She said, "Give them half an hour." Her eyebrows pulsed once. "And stay there." Her eyes went back to the wall behind him. "Have them meet you in the main hall at five o'clock to present their solutions. They will love it. They're quite enamored with you, you know?"

In all his years, no one had ever tried to railroad one of his classes. He was hired to teach a subject, one in which he had a lot of experience. And he focused only on what they wanted, kept the class that way, and on schedule. That was his job.

But he acknowledged, this class was different. The students weren't professional engineers, and Megyn apparently had a big role in it. She was acting on the University's behalf, and she'd booked him. It was her responsibility so, he guessed, it was all right for her to call the shots.

"Well," he said, "that would be a break from the classroom. Looking at slides and listening to my voice for five days might get old by then. Perhaps a change would be okay."

Megyn looked at him, smiled, and reached over to press his hand. She added two pats before withdrawing her hand. "You're here to be yourself, to be an American for them to experience."

She looked at the far wall again. "I'll tell Xiaosheng. He's the Dean of the software school. I'll tell him your plan."

My plan? When did this become my plan?

Blake could feel the blood rising in his face, but before he could object, Megyn leaned close and slid her hand down between his thighs. She squeezed. He gasped as the blood drained from his brain, and the crotch of his pants tightened.

"I'm glad that's all set." She smiled, but her eyes were looking down at her folded hands.

He looked down at them just in time to see a drop of water splash on the back.

Chapter 12

Monday, October 30
Wuchang and Shenjiawang

From the taxi's back seat, Sartaq watched the thief stuff two chunks of his expensive hard coal into the pocket of her flower-print, blue dress. Then, she casually leaned against the concrete block pillar between his shop and the grocery next door to scan the approaching pedestrians.

Sartaq's flight back to Wuhan was supposed to land hours before the coal delivery. But it was more than an hour late, and then traffic slowed his taxi. He was hungry, tired, and now the grocer's wife was stealing his coal.

"Thief!" He yelled in the backseat.

The driver paused from counting Sartaq's change.

"Read meter," he groused. "It is what it is."

Sartaq thumped the back of the seat. "Not you. Her!"

Change finally in hand, Sartaq shoved the back door open, but when she saw his face, she bolted. Sartaq knocked into a young woman with a baby and a sack of vegetables, and his money went flying. By the time he'd collected it, the thief had already disappeared into her husband's grocery.

She'd stolen from him before, but the husband would do nothing. Sartaq needed to take direct action with her. But now wasn't the time. He had a more important task to complete: disposing of Wang's head and body.

Looking at what was left of the pile of hard coal outside his roll-up, he hoped there would be enough.

Sartaq used hard coal when working high-quality steel. Typically, that meant it would be from Japan or South Korea. American steel was rare in Wuhan, but it also required very high heat.

One of his students researched cremation. "Three hours with coal," the boy reported, "six with wood."

"I'm going to kill you," he shouted at the grocery, hoping the woman would hide and leave the rest of his coal on the sidewalk alone.

Sartaq bolted down the walk and then cut around to the back. He pushed through the bushes, unlocked the back, caught the deadfall, and entered. He then unlatched the front that could only by undone from the inside and thrust the door up. It banged into the stops.

A flash of blue fabric and tan sandals disappeared to the right.

"Damn it," he bellowed, too late.

Turning on the bare bulb in the center of his shop, he grabbed one of his flat-bladed scoops and shoveled inside what she'd not already stolen.

His white shirt soaked in sweat and streaked with black, he re-bolted the front from the inside, jammed the back door shut, and stripped.

He started a small fire in the forge to get the draft started.

When he untied the end of the nested construction bags, the stench was extreme.

It would become much worse.

Four hours later, his eyes stinging, only Wang's blood-caked head remained. Up on the mountain, it'd rolled across the plastic when Sartaq had chased after the American, and now the blood had solidified in the dead boy's hair, and in his eyebrow and eyelashes on the left side.

Sartaq's forge had an extra wide mouth, built that way to

accommodate sizeable scraps of metal, but Wang's flesh seemed to take forever. After the first piece, Sartaq started slicing it into slabs like the butcher shop. That helped. But bones and their bubbling marrow needed even more time. And then he had to shatter and crush what was left.

Sartaq pondered the head. It was too big to fit through the forge's opening, and after removing the jaw, there was no way to carve it up.

"Just meat and bone," he said.

He put it face-down and hit it with the drive shaft from a Shinjin truck. The scalp split wide, and in the bone, a new crack oozed. Another whack and one side of the skull bounced open. Pulling, cutting, and gouging finished the worst of it.

Burning his blood-caked clothes and the wash rags he used to clean his body were the last to go. The fabrics flared quickly in the coal's heat, but the plastic soles of the yellow boots sputtered and sent thick, wispy smoke up the vent.

Someone banged on the roll-up door.

"Closed," he yelled. "Go away."

"What you cooking?" He recognized the grocer's whiney voice. "Smells bad. Neighbors complaining."

Sartaq shouted back, "Roast pork," and smiled at his own joke. Wang was a traitor; That made him unclean, and to the grocer who was Muslim, the same as a pig.

"You cooking pig?" The grocer yelped. "Forbidden!"

But Sartaq knew his way around the Qur'an. The Islamic rule that permitted collecting and selling fertilizer also applied to pork. While it was forbidden to *eat* pork, if a *fatwa* was issued by the *Imam*, it could be raised and sold to infidels.

Sartaq had proclaimed himself a Prophet of Allah. He was above any Imam and could easily grant himself permission.

"Allah gave me dispensation," he countered, "You want some?"

The grocer shouted back through the metal corrugation. "No, no. Smells bad, terrible bad. Smell like burning liver and old copper wire. Stop. You stop now!"

Under the bottom of the closed roll-up, Sartaq could see the shadow of the man's feet shuffle back and forth.

"You hear? Stop cooking!"

Sartaq kept turning the crank of his forge's blower. Inside, the soles of his old boots spit tiny blue flames. A few more minutes and they'd be nothing but ash.

There was a final "harrumph" from outside, and the shadowed feet tracked uphill and disappeared.

Sartaq looked carefully into the forge and with the slim, spade-nosed shovel picked out the last pieces of charred bone. He dropped them into the flat-bottomed bucket sitting by his anvil, and then broke them down smaller using a piece of rebar. The truck's drive shaft crushed that down into gravel, and then into rough sand.

He dumped it into the plastic bucket with the rest of Wang's sand.

"You easier to carry now."

Dressed in new coveralls and boots he'd bought before the execution, he undid the inside bolt on the front roll-up but went out the back and locked that from the outside. He walked around to the front, opened it long enough to retrieve the bucket, and then locked it on the outside like a normal night.

Carrying what would look to anyone like a bucket of coarse sand, he headed downhill to Donghu Lake stopping to buy a Bao bun, spicey pork, of course, and a fruit water. Munching dinner and carrying Wang, he walked along the shoreline to their tree. Decades ago, he and Lili used to go swimming there. The tree was much bigger now and beneath its wide overhang was a deep, shaded pool.

Bao bun in one hand, he dug his other one deep into the bucket and cast the pebbles in an arc across the water. Moments after it made a soft rush of plops across the water, a big silvery carp wallowed up, mouthed a sinking fragment, then spat it out.

He nodded his agreement.

"Wang no good."

Three hours later, Sartaq strode out of the shadow of the high stone wall that surrounded the Shen-family estate.

The Korean woman standing next to an old woman in a

wheelchair glanced at him, bowed, and then scurried back to the big house.

"Good afternoon, Mother Shen," Sartaq said when he stopped behind the wheelchair.

Shen Daiyu turned her head and swept her piercing blue-green, gold-flecked eyes up to his. Her thin, scarlet-painted lips neither smiled nor frowned. It would've cracked the dry rouge she used on her lips and the powder caked on her face. The practice and the look emphasized instead of hid her seventy-two years.

"Come around front," she commanded, a gnarled finger flicking to show the direction.

Her eyes ticked with precision as she scanned him from head to foot.

"You stink," she snarled.

Sartaq had bathed more times in the past two days than he usually did in a month, and his coveralls were brand new. But the stench from the incineration when he sniffed a sleeve was unmistakable. The new clothes, hanging in the back of the shop, had been smoked in Wang. No wonder people on the bus out to Shenjiawan had avoided him.

"Where's Lili?" He groused, hoping to change the subject. "She called me."

The old woman gestured toward the small table at the edge of the patio. "Take me over there where air moves. Put my back to it so I don't smell you."

He slipped around behind and gave the leather and chrome wheelchair an angry shove. He kept both hands near the handles, but let it roll forward. Her head joggled as the wheelchair bounced across the rough flagstones. It reminded him of the yellow, plastic kitty that'd sat atop the Singapore taxi's dashboard, it's head on a spring. If his mother were to raise one hand, she'd be a perfect match.

"Careful," she shouted, but she seized the arm rests instead of waving one of them up in the air.

He grabbed the handles, stopped the chair, and then started again, this time at a creep. "This okay?"

She slapped a hand at him over her shoulder. "Stop fighting me!

You know better than this. Do as told. No drama."

He recognized the words. Only Lili would say, 'No drama.'

Earlier that morning, Lili had called on the phone to demand a midday meeting.

"No," he'd argued back. "I have plans for then."

He didn't mention he'd be incinerating Wang's body.

It sounded like she was going to insist, and then he'd be stuck. But for once, she simply asked, "Okay, when?"

Sartaq stifled his surprise.

"Four o'clock," he offered. "Maybe later. It's two or three hours on bus, you know?" She wouldn't remember that detail, of course. She always drove one of those expensive rental cars.

"Well," Lili had groused as if she needed to be doing something else, "be there as soon as you can," and hung up.

It had to be Wang's execution. Deng Lan would've told her.

Deng started showing up at his Qur'an readings not long after Lili's last visit. At first, Sartaq was unsure of her presence, but when he mentioned it to Lili on one of their secret calls, she'd huffed about his being prejudiced against women. She insisted he let her stay.

The girl smiled at him a lot and always sat close. Very close. She was too young to take seriously, but his body's reaction to her nearness, her smile, her scent was undeniable. So, he indulged himself. And she cooperated. Eagerly. Not long after, she volunteered for their first real action. That was after just a few months of study.

He was sure then. Deng was Lili's spy.

Sartaq stopped the wheelchair at the patio table and set the brakes.

The old woman scowled and put a hand to her nose and mouth as he tucked the heavy, wool lap cover over her boney thighs. Years ago, the Tibetan horse blanket had been a brilliant yellow with galloping red ponies. They reminded Sartaq of his Uyghur father, of their kinship to the Khans and Mongol warriors. But after fifty years, the colors had faded, and the fibers turned fuzzy with wear.

He circled around to his seat—downwind, as instructed—and

waited for Jee, his mother's Korean helper, to finish serving. The enormous, flat-faced servant never made eye contact with either of them as she poured two steaming cups from an ornate pot. She backed away after a quick half-bow.

He started, "Momma—" then stopped. Jee was waiting a few steps back. Sartaq shifted his gaze toward Jee, back to his mother as she watched, and then twitched his head toward the house.

"That's all, Jee," Mother Shen said. "I'll call you when we need something."

Sartaq turned the hot cup with his fingertips and waited for the slap of the spring-tensioned kitchen door to the house.

"Lili *ordered* me, Momma," he began. "That's two or three hours, plus time here, and then two or three more to go back. When my shop closed, I make no money, and my customers go other places. Not good."

The old woman reached out with her knobby fingers to pick up a little white pill from the ceramic dish. She sat it on her tongue and drank her entire cup of steaming tea.

Sartaq grimaced. The scalding liquid inside her mouth and throat should've burned, but she didn't react. Too many boiling soups, he wondered. Or perhaps the nerves in her brain didn't work anymore.

She set the empty cup in its saucer and gazed past him, out over the low, stone wall.

Without looking, he knew that all the fields were bare this time of year. This was normally when she would make her plan for the spring plantings. She would decide which farm would grow what, and how much it should yield. She specified what it should bring in the market, and what her commission would be.

She would then have each of the agricultural committee members—one at a time—visit. The arrangements, as she called them, were consummated in privacy. Things were much quicker now, but she still completed them in secrecy.

She used to be a beautiful woman. Now, she was rich.

Days later, the committee members would meet, discuss possible arrangements, and then approve exactly as she had specified in private.

"Daughter Li won't be here," his mother announced. "A meeting in town."

He bolted up. "Lili's not coming?"

"Sit!"

His mother's bark was only one notch away from her slap.

He sat.

"You and I will meet," she declared.

Sartaq sighed. Lili must've visited earlier and convinced the old woman. Mother and daughter were much alike, even though they used different family names. Sartaq's father was Khan, shot by the Communists when he was an infant, whereas Lili's father was a Zhang, a college professor who disappeared in Red August. Lili and Sartaq's mother resumed the family name of her parents, Shen, and put her life back together at their estate. Lili kept her father's Zhang name, and Sartaq kept his Khan's.

Sartaq sighed and waited.

His mother would now lecture him at great length with many unnecessary details, then seem to ask what he thought. Lili said it was something called a *rhetorical* question. He'd learned to purse his lips, wag his head, and then say, *it's an excellent plan.* Doing otherwise would only provoke a repeat of all the details.

Mother Shen Daiyu was, more than anything, a schemer and a manipulator. She could sit for hours working up a plan and then maneuver the players like cardboard cutouts in a shadow-puppet show. Of late, her plans tended toward repeats of ones from the past, but they still had to be completed.

Zhang Li, Sartaq's little half-sister that he called Lili, inherited all the conniving, the extraordinary beauty, a defiant streak, and then earned a Master's degree and added twenty years' experience in America. She was her mother's equal or better.

Refusing or disagreeing with either Lili or their mother was impossible. And when the two conspired together, it was unthinkable.

So, Sartaq learned to insert his own ways into the nooks and crannies of their complicated plans.

Mother Shen narrowed her eyes. "Daughter Li uses beauty well." Her eyelids flared and her pupils switched back and forth between his eyes. "Beware women and babies, my son."

Sartaq pursed his lips but said nothing. They would need to do something with her soon. When the agricultural committee members realized the extent of her mental decline, they would expel her.

The family would lose all their prestige and privileges.

"Mother," he corrected, "I am fifty. I know what makes babies."

But she wasn't listening. Her eyes, looking beyond him toward the brown fields, were empty. She'd stay that way for several minutes, he knew, until the pill kicked in.

The spells had started three years ago. They were rare then, one or two a month, and lasted only a few seconds. "What was that?" She would say after missing a few words. It was the first clue. But then she worsened. More recently, she was having several attacks each week. Lili had explained what it was called, but the doctor-words she used were big. The pills were supposed to fix it but maybe she'd waited too long? Or needed a bigger dose?

He turned around to get the sun's warmth on his face and waited.

The Shen's had owned the land below for four-hundred years. Historically, they dictated to the farmers what to plant and where to market what it produced, and everyone prospered under the Shen's guidance.

But when the Chinese Communist Party took over in the 1920s, they took away the land. They leased it back to individual farmers who were expected to produce and make payments in product or coin. The Party gave no direction and assumed the farmers would continue as they had in the past. But to survive the cold winters, the farmers grew first what they needed to eat. And they planted and harvested those same crops year after year, and in the same places. Over time, appropriations grew even though yields declined. It was a closed circle, one ill causing the other in an endless loop. Soon, everyone was starving.

Mao's Cultural Revolution, half a century later, made it worse. He blamed the elites and so all schools were closed, and teachers fired. Many of them were labelled *Enemies of the People*. They executed some. Others vanished without explanation. Lili's father, their mother's second husband and history professor at Wuhan University, suffered the latter fate, and his young, now provider-less, family was expelled from university housing.

Resuming her surname by birth, Mother Shen Daiyu moved her two small children, Sartaq and Li, out to the former estate where the family was still permitted the small house on the mountain overlooking the fields.

In time, she convinced, manipulated, seduced, and blackmailed local party officials. And they let her direct the ancient estate and all of its environs. *Managing the cooperative*, they called it.

And, just as the Shens had done for centuries, she directed what the farmers must grow, where they must sell, and for how much. In her first five-year plan for the Party, food and industrial crops were rotated across the fields according to her dictates. Production quotas were fulfilled for the first time in a decade. The agricultural committee was happy, the Party was satisfied, and none of the families working the land went hungry.

In the next cycle, they assigned additional tracts for her supervision. And at her insistence, they granted her full participation in the agricultural planning committee. Again and again, she succeeded. They assigned her more farms. And after twenty years, she controlled more land than had ever been owned by the Shens.

Mother Shen Daiyu had dominion over thirty thousand *mou* of prime agricultural land in the heart of China's breadbasket. She moved into the big house and had a staff of five to clean, cook, and serve her needs and those of her children.

Everything Sartaq could see from the patio vantage point plus all the land wrapping around Shen-hill prospered under her guidance.

"So," she said, her empty cup clattering onto the saucer, "Li says you murder young college boys now."

Sartaq closed his eyes against the anger that welled up. He was right; Deng had told Lili.

"Don't hide your soul from me, Khan Sartaq!"

He opened his eyes, nodded, and steeled himself for what must be coming. "Yes, Momma."

She began as if reciting a recipe. "Your sister Li makes plans and brings money. You are man so you do steps. You do attacks. You make things change. That's what men do. Your father took rifle. He was supposed to kill Communists. He was soldier, and soldiers die.

"But you, my son, you lead. You command soldiers. You direct fight. And when fight is done, you survive. That is your job. You live. You live so you lead again and again. Soldiers die. Leaders lead."

He toyed with his empty cup. "Yes, Momma. My students, my troops, my soldiers: they fight. And they die. But I live so I can lead more. I know this, Momma. Thank you."

Her eyes narrowed and she studied him for a moment. "This execution you did," she asked as if questioning the weather in town, "that was not in your sister's plan?"

"No, Momma," he explained. "It couldn't wait. Wang was traitor. *Kafir*. He talked with others, tell them things, try to ruin plan. I make him stop. Make example for others."

She was looking at her fingernails. Her head gave the slightest of nods.

"Very well," she said. "Li's plan was in jeopardy. You were decisive. You took action. You saved plan. Good."

Sartaq grinned.

"It worked really good, Momma. Everything happened just as I hoped—just as I made my plan. I got everything ready, my people to watch, secret place, and I did it. And when I got back from Singapore, I finish job. Wang gone. All gone. Fish gravel. Then, I meet Hu Jian, Tan Ling, and Deng Lan one at a time. Make them promise to Allah again. They are ready, Momma."

His mother nodded once. "Daughter Li said there was witness?"

He blanched. "Yes. American."

Mother Shen waved the fingers in her lap like she was dismissing a fly.

"Americans experience such things every day. Violence does not surprise them."

"Yes, Momma. And I scared him good. He ran. Maybe he go

home to America."

His mother leaned forward, crooked an arthritic finger at his face, and smiled.

"You've done well." She reached out and traced her red fingernail down the scar on his cheek. "We worried about you, you know? Not good student, argued with your teachers, left for year... But you became man. Powerful man."

She smiled like she did when he was a little boy. "Improvising is okay when you have to." She tilted her head and gave him a stern look. "Just tell sister Li next time. No more secrets."

"Yes, Momma," he lied.

She patted his hand. "I have already spoken to Daughter Li. She won't bother you about this anymore. We have plan for American." Her eyes narrowed. "Li very persuasive."

So, Lili promised to get rid of him? Sartaq smiled to himself. Poison? Or maybe a Bird Spider in his bed?

After a moment, he shook his head. "Momma, she likes him."

The old woman shook her head. "She is my daughter. She will do what I have instructed."

Mother Daiyu leaned forward in her wheelchair to fix his gaze. "And you, you will also do as you've been told!"

"Yes, Momma," he said, bowing his head.

But she was wrong about Lili. His little sister was a woman of the world, and every bit as shrewd and calculating, perhaps more so, than their mother. She would protect the man because...

He'd have to take care of the American.

Improvise.

"Jee," Mother Shen cheered toward the house. "More tea. Make sure it's hot. And red bean cake for obedient son."

The gold flecks in her eyes sparkled with the setting sun coming over Sartaq's shoulder.

"You are leader," she cooed, stroking his bowed cheek to coax up his face. "Mongol warriors in you. Lead like ancestors. People will follow."

Chapter 13

Sartaq eased his canvas satchel to the dirt leaning it against their Sidrah tree. Named that by one of his early recruits who said that was where Muhammad first encountered the angel Jibrīl, the tree served as Sartaq's meeting space.

Lili knew Islam served Sartaq, not the other way around. Like any of the hammers, tongs, and punches at his forge, it was a tool. With a good quotation and then provoking a student's emotions, he could heat their passions. Fashioning their hatreds, like battering a piece of steel into a machete, just required hammering in the right places.

Inside Sartaq's satchel lay four bombs. Six sticks of dynamite with a blue-sparkle bicycle grip and trigger button is what today's warriors would see, carry, and detonate. But the trigger was fake. Sartaq knew some would, as the American's say, "chicken out." Covered in black tape so they wouldn't notice, each bomb had one of Feng Min's remote trigger boxes. Sartaq would send them in, secretly leave, and then detonate the explosives minutes ahead of time before they could run away.

"Soldiers die," his mother taught him. "Leaders lead."

And to lead again and again, he must not die.

Two boys in dark blue suits with scarlet stars on their lapels strolled past on the asphalt footpath toward the Old Library. Their formal clothes identified them as sons of Party members. They'd be meeting their fathers for the annual meeting.

That was his target, the Old Library and the father-son Party rally.

They glanced in his direction, but when he made momentary eye contact, they looked away. Most students avoided him as well as Islam.

Sartaq smiled at their arrogance. They'd be dead soon.

Today was just practice, Lili had said. A rehearsal. But to Sartaq, this attack would kill more than any of the other ones he'd helped create. But they'd all been indirect. They'd used his knives. They'd employed his students turned killers. But Sartaq would only see the aftermath of those acts on the dormitory televisions.

Today would be different. He'd see it himself.

Three students, two boys and a girl, came up the path from the same direction. Dressed casually, they were today's sacrificial warriors.

Sartaq put on his most confident face.

They stopped at the tree and took their usual places with Deng Lan to Sartaq's right, Hu Jian with his snow-white hair and perpetual cigarette to his left, and acne-faced Tan Ling straight across.

Sartaq stretched up to look across the sports field. Above its grandstand was a large university clock. Throughout the campus, they ticked in lock-second precision.

Four-thirty, Sartaq said to himself. Half an hour to when he'd tell them to press their detonator buttons. But the clock in the Old Library, the building, and everyone in and around it would disappear two minutes earlier.

"Of all your comrades may do in life," he began, "today you will better them. Angels will sing your names, not theirs."

Sartaq opened his satchel and took out the first of the four bundles. It was the size of a loaf of bread and glistened with its coating of black electrical tape.

"Hu Jian," he said and handed one to the boy with white hair.

"In few minutes, we march together to Old Library. Inside, you walk to table under center dome. Watch big clock. When fast hand on clock is straight up for five o'clock, complete your heavenly act."

The boy's head twitched down and up in acknowledgement.

Sartaq continued. "Have no fear. You will feel warm hug of Allah."

Hu placed his bomb into the empty paper grocery bag he'd brought.

The second boy, Tan Ling, picked at an acne sore under his chin when Sartaq held out the second bomb. "Here is your gift," Sartaq said. "Exactly at five. Yes?"

"Allah be praised," the boy said. He put the bomb inside his black leather briefcase and pressed the latches shut.

The third bomb went to Deng Lan. She slipped it into her pink pony backpack and lowered the flap. She twisted around to set it behind her, but kept her eyes locked on Sartaq's. As she turned, her knees rose and made an open tent of her skirt. Sartaq remembered Arzu in Xinjiang, another temptress who'd betrayed him.

He'd learned to enjoy the experience but quash any sentiment. Animal needs, yes, but nothing more.

Sartaq withdrew the last bomb from his satchel. He held it up. "My present is like yours," he said. He turned it in his hands. "Such a simple path to *Firdaus*, Heaven's highest level."

He guided it back inside his satchel and then checked the distant clock on the sports stadium.

"Perform *Salah* now and then—"

Tan Ling interrupted. "Isn't it too early for *Maghrib*?"

"True," Sartaq gave a nod, then looked away. "But it is special day, and since we all here, we skip *Adhan*. Please begin with *Iqama*."

He stood and turned to *qibla*, due west toward the sun, with the satchel next to his ankle. Beneath the branches of their tree he could see the Old Library's main entrance.

He began the chant.

Allah is Greatest.

Allah is Greatest.
I assert that there is no god but Allah.
I assert that there is no god but Allah...

His mind made up, Blake turned off the computer projector.

"Okay class," he announced, glancing at the clock, "it's 4:30. I know some of you were expecting a field trip today, but a better use of our time will be to hear about an example embedded system created right here by one of your peers."

He motioned toward Alex in the front row next to Zoey.

"This young man has designed, built, and programmed exactly that."

To Alex, he said, "The floor is yours."

Blake stepped back and sat in the chair by the window as Alex moved to the podium, a small gray box in each hand. Setting them on the table next to the lectern, he retrieved a handful of loose batteries from his pocket and set them by the two boxes.

"These," Alex said in English as he held the two boxes above his head, "are the transmitter and receiver I designed. The transmitter," he wiggled the box in his left hand, "can trigger many receivers." He waved the one in his right. "They use WiFi radio signals so there are no connecting wires. Through them, you could turn on a bunch of lights, trigger multiple MP3 players at different locations, or anything else you might need to do at a distance with a very high precision of synchronization."

From his chair next to the wide column between two windows, Blake scanned the room. Everyone was paying attention.

"The receiver," Alex continued, turning the box in his right hand and panning it around so the class could see its main face, "has a power switch and three LEDs: Green for power, yellow for armed, and red for the final countdown."

He put the boxes down, loaded three AA batteries into the receiver, and flipped the power switch.

Holding it up, he announced, "There, the power is on now." Using his thumb, he turned the switch off, and the green LED turned off. "And now it's off."

He set it down.

Holding up the other box, he said, "This is the transmitter. It has the same switch and LEDs, but also this control." He tapped the large red pushbutton on the box's face. He took a step forward around the lectern. "Those in the front can see it's labelled 'qu.'"

Alex turned toward Blake. "That means 'Go.' It even looks like a running figure, don't you think?"

Blake squinted, but the Hanzi character was too small from where he sat. He nodded anyway. "Yes, thank you."

Alex faced the class again. "The thing that makes these special is they can make everything happen at the same instant. I emphasize the word, *instant*. To do this, when they're first turned on, they coordinate their clocks within a few microseconds of each other. Then, when the 'Go' command goes out, it includes the time—calculated to be ten seconds from the button press—for activation. After that, there's no need for any communication. Everything is automatic. Since each receiver has the same time, each will fire its relay at the same instant."

A female voice asked, "Why ten seconds? Is that to let them synchronize?"

"No, you weren't paying attention," Alex said with a polite smile. "They synchronize when each receiver connects with the transmitter on WiFi. That delay, ten seconds, was just the requirement."

Another voice offered, "Maybe someone wants to get away?"

Alex shook his head. "It's wireless so you don't have to be right there. I tested at two hundred meters, and it worked just fine."

Blake injected, "Alex, if I may?"

Alex nodded and turned to face him.

Blake spoke loud so everyone could hear him from his seat.

"Sometimes we get requirements but don't understand why they're there. But specifications are like that. We don't have to understand what the designers are thinking; just what they want. That's what specifications are for, to tell us what something is supposed to do, not why."

A young man in the front row on the left side waved to Alex.

"Isn't WiFi too hit-or-miss? We did a paper on that last semester, and in a dense environment with many stations, collisions, delays, and retransmissions are common. How do you get the timing so exact?"

"Excellent question," Alex bubbled and pushed up his glasses. "I cloned an open-source implementation of NTP, the Network Time Protocol, and then enhanced it—"

The same boy in the front row spoke up again. "Wouldn't the Precision Time Protocol be better? And which repository are you using? Did you keep it open-source?"

Alex smiled but shrugged. "I didn't know about PTP when I started. For the repo, I started at SourceForge. At first, I didn't plan to make it public." He smiled sheepishly at Blake. "Chinese copyright law said it's okay to do that."

Blake nodded.

In the US defense industry, it was common knowledge that foreign agents would try to steal or buy copies of specifications. Consequently, documents were kept under lock and key, and the engineers were told only enough to build their individual parts. Unexplained requirements were, therefore, *de rigueur*.

Alex turned to the class.

"But once I saw how well my changes worked," he grinned, "I didn't want to limit my career opportunities. So, I switched my repository to Github and enabled public access. That was great because, right away, I discovered that the engineers in chats were very receptive to my questions. They gave me some excellent suggestions and I made it even better."

Alex leaned on the lectern, making rock forward and teeter on the front edge.

"My improvements extended the packet exchange during the initialization phase, and to watch for a repeating answer within the desired tolerance."

Alex held up one box. "The receivers are WiFi clients. They link to a transmitter—" he held up the other box "—the access point."

The boy in the front row asked, "How did you measure the accuracy across multiple receivers?"

Alex grinned and pointed toward the window close to Blake. "That tree by the sports field? The big one where groups meet up? I turned on a receiver and set it there where no one would notice."

Through a gap at the edge of the green window shade, Blake could see one tree taller than the others at the edge of the track and field area. Students in dark business suits with ties, sometimes with an older man in similar attire, walked up the pathway to the right before passing out of view.

Alex pointed toward the floor.

"I put the second in this building's lobby. And another in the center room of the Old Library, and the fourth was with me at the main cafeteria along with the transmitter. The farthest out was almost three hundred meters from there."

"Why three hundred meters?" A boy in a green and red striped shirt asked.

Alex pushed his glasses up and gave a shrug. "Another of the requirements. Anyway, with all of them placed and ready, I turned on the transmitter, waited a few seconds to let them all synchronize, and—"

A hand rose.

"How do you know when *all* the receivers have synchronized?"

Alex grinned. "Very good! That's a design flaw. The transmitter has a light it turns on when one receiver has synchronized, but that's all you know. With this design, you have to wait long enough for them all to get ready, but since it only takes a fraction of a second, it really doesn't matter. I suggested adding a display and show how many receivers have synchronized but the delivery schedule wouldn't allow it.

"Anyway," he finished, "I collected all the receivers with their power still on. In the lab, I then hooked up a logic analyzer to sample the pulse from the counter-timer chip in each receiver to check the timing. All but one was within ten microseconds."

A male voice in the back row sounded annoyed. "Is this for explosives? To replace the special cord they use to time the explosions?"

"I don't know the application." Alex pushed up his glasses.

The boy in the back said, "They use a star configuration so one blast doesn't break the signal before it gets to the other detonators. My uncle is a civil engineer and helped build the

Three Gorges dam. They used up nearly a hundred miles of it."

Alex held up his two boxes. "With these, you wouldn't have to use any."

The same boy objected. "But your boxes get destroyed."

"The receivers, yes, but only if they are close to the explosives, and they're very inexpensive. The main board is a Raspberry Pi Model B, about thirty Yuan, but the schematic is open-source; you could make your own for a lot less if you bought in bulk and left out the unnecessary parts. I used aluminum utility boxes because the guy funding the project wanted them right away, but you could design and print a plastic one for a lot less. Maybe fifteen Yuan or less for the whole thing."

Blake tuned out.

His two-week gig in China was almost done. Tomorrow would be the last day. He'd be glad to get out.

Relieved.

He nodded.

Megyn came to mind. *Maybe somewhere with her?*

He glanced at the clock at the back of the room.

4:54.

He prompted Alex. "Why don't you show them what's inside and then go through a cycle before we finish for the day?"

Alex picked up the receiver box, pulled the clam-shell halves apart, and held up the one containing the electronics.

"The larger board you see is a standard Raspberry Pi. There are several chips and connectors that aren't used for this application."

He pointed to a smaller board next to the first as he ambled down the center aisle, showing it left and right. "See the big heat sink on this board? These are special, from a French company. Nobody in China makes them." Alex winked. "Not yet anyway. It puts out a full hundred milliwatts." He looked at the boy in the back whose dad was a civil engineer. "And yes, that board is expensive. We need to get a local source or make it ourselves to reduce the cost. It's not open-source, but someone could trace it out and reverse engineer the design…"

Back at the lectern, Alex inserted the batteries into the receiver again. "I'll take you through an entire sequence. First, the receiver —"

A girl halfway back on the right interrupted him. "Can we get the source code?"

"Sure," Alex said. He put down the receiver and walked to the whiteboard. "Email me for a link." He printed in large letters: feng.min@yahoo.com.cn

Walking back to the lectern, he commented, "They use the WiFi SSID E-T-I-M."

"Too many abbreviations," someone wise cracked, a grin in their tone of voice.

"What's it mean?" Another asked.

A third voice, louder than the others, piped in. "E-T-I-M? Isn't that what that terrorist group painted on walls?"

Alex shrugged. "It's just four letters."

"It's a Xinjiang separatist group," a student toward the back explained. "My mother was there when they did that attack in the Kashgar market. And that's the same one that did the car bomb in Tiananmen Square."

Alex pushed up his glasses and opened his mouth to speak, but another student cut him off. "Didn't they also do the train station attack in—where was that?"

"Kunming?" someone asked.

"Outside the train station," the previous student answered. "They used handmade machetes to hack and kill dozens. I saw the pictures."

The afternoon sun in their eyes, Sartaq and Deng Lan were in front as the four of them approached the Old Library. The pink pony backpack slung over one shoulder, Lan meandered a little as they climbed the four steps. Her hand brushed Sartaq's, and she glanced up at him. Sartaq smiled at her but shook his head.

Too public, and no time.

Inside the library's small anteroom, Sartaq looked through the arch to the central hall and the official school clock.

4:54.

Four minutes to go.

He pointed to a bench at the side of the anteroom. "I will be there," he said, and then turned to point through the arch into the large, common space at the center of the library. "All of you go to big room, to table in middle reserved. I put sign there for you. Read books. Watch main school clock. At few seconds before 5:00 but not before, turn around and look for me. I will be where you can see. We then press buttons together." He raised his hands. "Allah will welcome in paradise!"

Sartaq pivoted on his boot and walked across to his bench and sat down. He shifted his backpack around to his lap, made eye contact with his followers, and nodded.

The three of them turned, and looking back occasionally, ambled into the main hall where they passed out of view.

Sartaq quickly set his backpack on the floor and pushed it under the bench with his foot. He walked fast to the building's side door, pushed it open, and left.

He took quick, long strides up the path and went left at the fork. The spot he'd chosen was about two hundred paces from the Old Library. There, the walkway curved around and behind an outcropping of boulders. As Tehran had confirmed, they would shield him from the blast.

He took the transmitter box from his pant's pocket and looked through the trees to the clock over the sports field grandstand.

Three minutes before the hour.

One minute to go.

Sartaq's hands were trembling. Months of planning and an amazing number of large denomination RMB bills passed from Lili through Sartaq to Feng Min for these little gray boxes.

He turned toward the boulders that blocked his view of the Old Library, held the transmitter above his head, and flipped the power switch. The green LED gleamed in the cool shade.

"Wait for yellow," Feng Min had told him.

Alex walked over near the window where Blake was sitting and held the receiver up for everyone to see.

He flipped the power switch. The green LED came on.

"It's now listening," he said, "for a WiFi transmitter

broadcasting E-T-I-M."

Sartaq kept his eyes on the transmitter he was holding above his head.

Hurry up little boxes!

The yellow LED winked on much brighter than the green.

Ready!

Sartaq caressed the top of the red button with his thumb. The bump in its center reminded him of a nipple on a chilly morning. He smiled as his body chemistry surged at the thought.

In the shaded classroom, the yellow LED on Alex's receiver dazzled Blake's eyes. His eyebrows bunched.

"Alex?"

"That's odd."

The boy stared at the receiver in his hand.

Zoey offered, "Doesn't that mean it's synchronized?"

"But that's impossible." Alex picked up the disassembled transmitter from the table. "I haven't put the batteries in. It can't be sending the signal."

Sartaq mashed the red button. It made a *scrunch* before the *click*.

The red LED flashed on and began blinking.

Sartaq turned and squatted down with his back pressing the boulders. Up through the trees, he could see the top corner of the four-story computer building. Its concrete walls glowed yellow in the late afternoon light.

As Tehran had instructed, he squashed his hands on his ears, opened his mouth, and yawned.

"Oh!" Alex said when the red LED on his receiver lit up.

Students bolted up from their seats. Several shouted.

A corner of Blake's mind started counting the winks of the red LED.

One.

Alex shrugged, "Now I'm—"

Two.

"—stumped. This receiver says it has—"

Three.

"—the 'Go' message."

Four.

Rubber-footed stools burped across the linoleum. Half a dozen students bolted for the exit.

Looking up, Alex shouted, "It's Okay—"

Five.

"—see?" Alex held the receiver up. "Nothing's plugged in—"

Six.

"—Nothing can happen."

The room became dead still. Alex turned the box in his hands, his eyebrows furrowed.

Seven.

Zoey started saying the count in Cantonese as Blake's mind tallied the English.

"Bat." *Eight.*

"Gow." *Nine.*

"Sup." *Ten—*

The breathless *thump* came from behind. Blake felt it pass through his chest and arms. Two feet beyond Alex's upraised arm, the white concrete column between the windows looked like a double-exposed photograph. At that same instant, hundreds of tiny, bright points of light began shredding the long, dark green window shades as they streaked across the room. They sparkled like diamonds.

The perforated shades billowed inward. Bigger slits appeared as angular chunks of glass tumbled through. Spinning in the air like three-pointed throwing stars, they raced in before arcing down toward the wide-eyed students. Hands and arms began to rise.

One shard, a long skinny spike, pierced deep into the side of Alex's head. The impact made his body rebound in a wave and flung the black glasses from his face like a helicopter.

The entire building lurched beneath Blake's chair. The back legs snagged on a seam in the linoleum and the chair started over backwards, Blake's arms rising as he went.

A whole-body pulse like the strike of a wrecking ball rocketed through the classroom. The overhead fluorescent light tubes popped in unison.

A thin, disappearing arc of white fog flashed over Sartaq's head at the leading edge of an iridescent wave of air. When it reached the concrete building, it reflected like light in a mirror and flowed away, disappearing through the trees.

Everywhere, leaves began falling.

Despite his cupped hands and yawn-opened ears, Sartaq felt the shockwave as it passed through his body.

The sound reverberated from every brick and concrete building on the campus.

Sartaq jumped up, ran around the boulders, and looked back down the path.

High overhead, hundreds of objects were rising: pieces of blue-green roof tile, long boards, shattered stubs from tables and chairs. But there were hundreds, thousands of smaller things.

Sartaq wondered if some were parts of bodies. Fingers? Eyeballs? Organs from inside like Wang that he'd had to quarter to speed up the incineration?

Everyone close to the bombs, Hu Jian, Tan Ling, and seductive little Deng Lan—Lili's spy—would have been instantly obliterated. Farther out, he guessed, people might've been thrown against the inside of the Old Library's walls before they too were blown out.

The cloud of debris had started back down.

Raining furniture, he thought and smiled. Maybe some blood and flesh? A few bones?

One piece, the shape of a filing cabinet, seemed fixed in place as he watched. It got bigger and bigger. At the last moment, Sartaq bolted to the side before it crashed into the asphalt path, spilled its drawers, and keeled over. A deep dent in the asphalt looked like it'd been made by the point of an Egyptian pyramid.

And more was coming.

Sartaq bolted another hundred steps. He stopped in front of the four-story classroom building with the blue doors. Big pieces were hitting the ground but well away from him now.

The *tap*, *smack*, and *tick* of smaller objects filled the gaps between heavier and more distant *bangs* and *thuds*. All other sounds were mute: no voices, no birds, not even traffic from the street on the far side of the sports stadium.

The entire world was holding its breath, stunned at Sartaq's victory.

He skipped, twirled, and hooted his joy.

Chapter 14

Shortly Thereafter

Doctor Chen pulled Blake's ear lobe down and snaked in the tip of his otoscope.

"Small split," he said, popping the probe's plastic cover into the trash. "Edges touch. Heal by self. No water. No finger. Two, three weeks. You go now."

The emergency room physician was very young, not much older than the seniors in Blake's class.

Blake nodded. "Thanks, Doc." He stood up from the examining table and looked around. The Emergency Room bustled with moaning, crying, and unconscious patients, many still arriving.

The doctor bobbed his head toward the door. "You go. Americans not safe."

Blake walked out, spotted an idle taxi, and took out his cell. He tapped Megyn's icon at the top of his Recent Calls list.

The voice on the other end warbled, "Hello?"

"Megyn?" Blake asked. "Is that you?"

"Blake!" she shrieked.

He heard fumbling sounds, a loud clatter on a hard floor, more fumbling, and then finally more words.

"You're alive?!"

"Megyn, something's happened," he said.

"Blake, I thought..." she began in a rush and then paused. When she resumed, she calmly stated fact. "You weren't in the library."

"No, that's right. We were doing a show-and-tell in the classroom, and—"

"Wait," she interrupted.

There was a *sproing* like a long, metal spring being flexed, the slap of something like a lightweight door against a wood frame, and then the *clack* of shoes on tile.

"Oh, Blake," she finally resumed, "I was so afraid... The library... The TV said..."

"I'm okay," he stopped her. "There was an explosion at the university in another building. I'm okay, but it's bad, really bad, Megyn. The other building was destroyed. Nothing left. Anyone inside—" He paused. "Up in our classroom, all the glass windows blew in. No warning or anything. Lots of injured. And some dead. I was lucky. One of the support columns shielded me."

"You weren't in the library?" Megyn asked.

She sounded relieved, but there was something else in her tone. Impatience?

"I called as soon as I could," he said, but realized he'd been so busy, so overwhelmed, he just hadn't thought of it. "I'm sorry."

Her relief gushed out. "Oh, Blake, I'm so glad you weren't there." He sincerity was unequivocal as she rushed on. "The field trip... Terrible idea, I'm sorry. I'm so glad you didn't go. Please forgive me for suggesting it. I was confused... Everything's so complicated..."

He remembered her imperious command to take the class to the library. That'd been no suggestion, he thought, but let it pass.

"Remember Alex," he continued, "the boy student that went to the museum and then dinner with us?" He forced back a surge of emotion. "He's dead, Megyn."

"That's... unfortunate." The word came out clinical, disconnected, like a doctor discussing a recent cancer diagnosis with another physician.

Blake coursed his eyebrows but went on as he headed toward a line of taxis half a block from the hospital. "We did what we could in the classroom. When the emergency medical people arrived, they pushed us aside. There was nothing else we could do in the classroom. A few students and I went outside and over to where the explosion came from. The students had to tell me there used to be a building there, but there was nothing left. Just piles of debris. No structure at all."

"I'm not surprised," she said, then added, "The TV is saying it was leaky gas line down in a utility tunnel."

"No," Blake said, very sure of what he remembered. "A gas explosion would've cracked or blown the roof off any such tunnels. Or left a mark where the flame vented, but I saw nothing like that. Instead, there was a big black scorch mark—almost a perfect circle—right in the middle of a big, clear expanse. No holes or vents. Just a black circle. Whatever blew up, that was the center of the blast. It was on top of the concrete floor, not underneath."

Silence.

"Megyn? Are you still there?"

"Just thinking." Another pause. "Well, whatever's happened, we'll have to deal with it."

We? Blake wondered. Since when was this a *we* problem? He was the one nearly blown up. She'd been... What? Dozens of miles away?

"Well," Megyn sighed through the phone and relief came back into her voice, "thank God you're alive. And it did not hurt you?"

"Just my ear." He mechanically put a hand up. He could hear the sound it made when he touched the ear, but it was distant, muffled.

"I can hear a little through it. The ER doctor said it'd heal by itself."

"A doctor? You're at a hospital? I'll come get you. Which one?"

He turned around to look at the building, but the name was in Chinese. "No idea, but it doesn't matter. There's a taxi here."

He leaned down and waved at the driver. The man nodded and motioned him in.

"Hold on a sec," he said, climbing into the back. He pulled the hotel's matchbook from his pocket and handed it to the driver. "Feng Yi hotel," he said.

The driver flipped the match book over to look at the back,

handed it back, and punched a button on the taxi's digital meter.

"Megyn," Blake continued into the phone, "right after the explosion, I looked down through the blown-out window of the classroom. I saw him again. The same guy, the one that murdered that kid on the mountain. Sartaq. He was down on the walkway, dancing and spinning like a Whirling Dervish as stuff fell around him."

Megyn made a sound, somewhere between a *hmmm* and a chuff.

It was then that it hit him. That man did it, the man Blake had seen committing murder, and Blake hadn't told anyone except Megyn. He'd allowed the murderer to run loose, and now this.

Blake was now responsible for the explosion.

If he'd called the Police five days ago... If he'd told them about the murder on the mountain, that a man named Sartaq had done it, they might've caught him before he could kill again.

Assuming he did the bombing, his mind objected.

He argued back. *The man was dancing in the street!*

But by not reporting the first murder, Blake was now an accomplice to an even larger crime. And lots of people—*college kids, for God's sake*—had died because of his selfish fear.

"Interesting," Megyn said, as if her mind were elsewhere. "Maybe he lives near the school? That would explain the coincidence—his being in the neighborhood, I mean."

Blake had been some nasty places in the world, but the violence here was a thousand times worse, much too close, and his fault.

If he stayed, prison—a Chinese prison—was inevitable.

"Megyn, I'm leaving," he announced. "I'll pack when I get to the hotel."

"I see."

Her curt answer made him pause for a second before going on.

"I'm calling the State Department to tell them what I know. They can deal with the Police, but I'll be gone. I don't know if that madman is targeting just kids or the entire school or what, but I'm leaving."

He could hear her breathing.

"I'm leaving, Megyn."

More breathing.

He realized he wanted her to go, too. But not just because of the danger. He just wanted her to be with him.

"What about you, Megyn?"

Nothing.

He babbled on. "I'll get flights to San Francisco and get you home." He didn't know if she had a condo, a house, an apartment... "I could stay a couple of days. We could go to Mountain View, get some sushi..."

His voice trailed off. He waited. He felt the longing for her, to be together, connected, man and woman. Bonded. Fused.

She said, "I need to call you back."

He nodded. She was visiting family, he remembered. A couple of hours—two?—outside of Wuhan, she'd said. Probably safe there. Everything—the murder, the bomb—had been on school property.

Why there? he wondered.

Regardless, Blake was in the thick of it here. Across the street. Literally. And the killer had seen his face: looking down from the classroom, and maybe on the mountain earlier?

"I need to book flights, Megyn. The sooner, the better."

"I know," she strained. "It's... complicated. I need some time, Blake."

He felt angry.

"Look," he explained, "I'm sorry about all this, especially the class. I know you helped put that together, but none of what's happened is your fault. The students will just have to read the last of the materials on their own. You can apologize for me to the University. Maybe they'll pro-rate my fee or something. But with all that's happened, I really don't care."

Megyn's tone was insistent. "I need to think. The school is... I'll talk with Xiaosheng. He's the head of the department that's paying for this. Dr. Gu Xiaosheng. It's his budget, so it's really up to him."

"Dammit, Megyn, it's *not* up to him. It's *my* life. *I* decide what I'll do. You can call Fu... Tu... whatever his name is, but tell him I'm leaving."

"Blake, please," she moaned. "Give me time to think this through. You're not getting on any airplane in the next five minutes. See what flights are available. That's fine. But don't book anything. Not yet. Let me do some things and call you back first."

It was Blake's turn to stay quiet.

"Please?" she said. "I really care about you, Blake. It's just... It's complicated. I can't explain. Please? Do this for me?"

Blake hated being manipulated. Julie'd done it a lot, and it really pissed him off. When is being wimpy and pussy-whipped, versus bending with the wind that might diminish in time?

But Megyn was... Could be...

All of Blake's insides, all his being wanted to be with her, somewhere private, door locked, "Do Not Disturb," cocooned under blankets in their own universe, bodies and souls joined...

"All right," he gasped. "Just hurry. We need to get out of here."

The taxi bumped up the hotel's ramp.

Blake was sitting on the bed with suitcase and computer bag when Megyn called.

"Good news," she announced in a cheery voice. "Class is on for tomorrow. They're moving you to another building."

Blake's jaw dropped.

"Megyn, I'm leaving. Tonight. Half of my class got hit by glass and debris. Some of them are dead..."

He stopped, dumbfounded.

"It seems crazy to me, too," she said, her voice a lot more animated than he remembered. "Dr. Gu said the University Provost talked with the Police and got the go-ahead."

Blake worked his jaw but the words wouldn't come.

"Are you watching TV?" Megyn asked. "The Department for the Comprehensive Management of Public Security was just on TV from Beijing. Their emergency team said it was definitely an underground gas explosion. Some local company repaired the pipes in the tunnels last month and did something wrong, they said. The man who supervised the work has been arrested and charged. Xiaosheng says it's important for your class to go on, to avoid unnecessary alarm.

Blake wanted to yell but kept it in check.

"Unnecessary alarm?" he repeated. "Megyn, that's not right. I was there. I saw it. Something exploded on top of the concrete, not underneath. It left a big round black mark on top of the concrete."

Blake looked out the window. The dirty-yellow sun would set in an hour. The longer he waited, the fewer the flights going out.

"Megyn," he said, louder than necessary, "I'm leaving. I don't know where to but I'm not staying here. I'm a citizen of the United States. Doctor... Ku... Bu... Doctor Fuck-You can't stop me!"

Megyn corrected him in a calm voice. "It's Gu. Doctor Gu Xiaosheng. He's a friend, and a nice man."

"I'm sorry," Blake said, exasperated. "You're right; I don't know the man. I'm sorry for calling him... those names."

"Gu. Doctor Gu Xiaosheng."

"Thank you. Gu. Doctor Gu."

"I've known him since college," Megyn explained. "We had classes together. He understands how you feel, Blake. Really. Xiaosheng and the Provost talked about your best course of action. They're trying to see this from your perspective. They don't want you to do anything rash, something you might regret. I told them I would forward their concerns, and if you agree to a meeting, I can pick you up. Are you at the hotel now? I'll go with you to meet Dr. Gu."

Blake fumed. Did Megyn feel the same way about him that he did her? Her loyalty, if that's what it was, seemed to be to the school, to this other person. It made him a lot less sure than when they'd made love or had breakfast in bathrobes the next morning. Was he wrong? Was that just a one-nighter to her? Blake shook his head. He wasn't like that. He couldn't do that. Sex wasn't just the physical act. He'd felt... But there was no word for what he'd felt in his heart, in his soul that night. *Oblivion* wasn't it, but there was some of that. *The Universe* wasn't right either. And it wasn't *one* or *two*. It was something... so much more, so... complete.

Megyn's voice became gentle. "Blake, this affects both of us. I handle the US side of these seminars. Dr. Gu said future sessions could be affected. I know what's happened is a big deal, but they might cancel the program entirely. Blake, this job pays for my trips home. It gets me into China."

And pays for it? Probably both ways? And maybe a stipend as well?

Blake's anger ratcheted up. Was it just dollars to her?

But she managed a group of software engineers in Silicon Valley. They weren't cheap, and her salary would be as much or more. For what? Twenty years? Living alone? With any decent savings, probably a matching 401(k) plan, and the rise of real estate there, she ought to be relatively well off.

Certainly, better than me, he thought.

And what about the school's actions? If they had a problem with what he was doing, they should damn well talk to him. Trying to manipulate him through Megyn was... disgusting.

He couldn't decide if he was angrier at the school for twisting her arm, or at Megyn for letting them do it to her?

"They're using you, Megyn. I don't like that. They're bullying you to get to me. That's just chicken-shit."

"I know," Megyn sighed. "I don't like it either. But won't you at least talk to them, listen to what they say? I'll be there in ten minutes."

Blake straightened in surprise. Her family's home was on the other side of Wuhan, one, maybe two hours away, she'd said.

"Where are you?" He asked.

"I'm at the University. Watch for my car. Ten minutes, tops."

The closed roll-up door of Sartaq's shop thundered.

"Closed," he shouted. "Go away!"

He stuck his hand inside the forge and felt the surface. Stone-cold. He'd have to rake out the black, stony residue before restarting. But that wouldn't be today. The next trip, the big one to Singapore, was only a couple of days away. He had plenty of goods to sell in the meantime, and after the trip, if that was successful... The possibilities were enormous.

The banging on the metal roll-up came again.

"What?" He barked.

"Open up. It's me."

It was Lili's voice.

Sartaq scowled. He wished he'd never involved her, but her people enabled the money.

Tehran had liked his idea but complained that Feng Min's electronics were too expensive. They wouldn't pay for them. He figured that was the end.

But a month later, on Lili's annual trip when he'd confided his frustration, she volunteered to finance the electronics.

"My friends in America," she'd said, "have money. And attack will work for them, for what they want, as well as for your Xinjiang friends."

Sartaq didn't care one yuan for Lili's movement, for the democrats as she called them. They were just a bunch of academics who'd failed thirty years ago and had done nothing since.

But they had money.

And what that enabled had been his dream since Xinjiang.

Forty years? he wondered. If he really needed the number, he could figure it out with a piece of paper and a pencil.

But now, in hindsight, he should've known what Lili would be like.

"No," she'd said when he told her they could just go to Singapore like tourists, "It needs to be in secret. You'll have to smuggle yourselves in. Afterwards, leave same way so no one ever knows you've been there."

And then, about the money for the border crossing into Vietnam, there was "That's too much. Make it smaller." And he really didn't know. So maybe she was right.

Then she'd change it. "When you get there," she said, "offer less. Say that's all you have.'"

But after telling him to save money every step of the way, she'd say it was okay to throw it away. "Let your recruits, your soldiers, as you call them, enjoy their last few nights on Earth. That's nice hotel. Get many rooms. Enjoy pool. Have fun in Casino."

But they were going to die, he wanted to remind her. Why waste money on dead people?

There was no outguessing her. Anything he planned, she redid.

And everything she did made things harder. More steps, more risk, more to remember...

But she had the money.

And Islamic State in Tehran was essential. They had the only way to get the needed explosives into Singapore. It was far more than he could steal and transport all that way. And they had to have a demonstration. And that required Feng Min's electronics, which only she would finance.

More and more complicated.

So, he went along with her ever-changing plan.

And then Islamic State sent the explosives too early. They said it was the only time they could line up everything.

And they didn't send what he wanted.

Fan Zixin said to get "C-4." They'd seen it in lots of movies. "Powerful," they said. Fan looked on the web and came up with the amount. "Six pounds, one per column."

But IS said they needed to use dynamite. Twenty pounds of it.

"Dynamite pushes," they said in the message to Lili for her to explain. "C-4 only fractures. Need to push columns out. Make one side of the building no support."

Sartaq didn't understand, but too late, the stuff was on its way. The arrival date was fixed by some ship's schedule and would be arriving two weeks earlier than they needed. So, as usual, Sartaq had to fix the problem.

Lili fumed about the added expense, but finally agreed to pay for the two fake passports and stolen credit cards, and round-trip air tickets with different names. So, he flew to Singapore, got the box of explosives, hid it, and then flew back home.

The metal door of his shop's roll-up thundered.

"All right, all right," he shouted. "I'm coming."

He pulled the roll-up halfway and then stopped. He could see scarlet toenails in open-toed white shoes waiting in the light outside.

"Duck under," he ordered.

"Not in skirt."

"Damn!" He cursed for her benefit but yanked the roll-up shoulder height.

Clad in shades of white, Lili crouched and scuttled under.

He shoved down hard on the handle and then put his foot on it to keep the roll-up from bouncing open again.

She stopped next to his shoulder, arms and hands folded to her chest as if afraid to touch anything.

He turned and raised an ash-colored hand to speak, but she jumped back and bumped into the table. The repaired kitchen gadgets on it skittered and clanged. Immediately, she twisted around, looked at the seat of her skirt, and yelped.

"Damn! Look what you made me do."

She turned. A dark gray streak ran across the back of her white skirt.

Sartaq couldn't help but grin. He took a step to brush it off, but she stopped him.

"No! You'll just make it worse. Club soda will work if it's not ground in. Just leave it alone."

Still amused, he backed up and shrugged.

She tilted her head and blinked at him in the light from the shop's bare lightbulb. The lines in her face smoothed.

"You did good today, big brother."

Praise from his little sister was rare.

"Seventy dead," Lili reported. "Some regular students, of course. That's unfortunate. But there were several ranking Party-parents at meeting. Not enough to make big difference, but couple of seats for next Congress is good." She smiled at him. "And that was huge blast! Tehran have no doubt now."

Sartaq beamed. The victory was sweet, but this was just the first act. There were problems to be handled.

He tried to sound casual. "I saw your American again. He was looking out of top window of computer building."

"And he saw you, too," she said. "Dancing."

Sartaq narrowed his eyes and shook a charcoaled finger at her. "You told Mother you would kill him."

Muscles rippled in Lili's jaw, and her nostrils flared.

Not waiting, he gestured toward the closed roll-up. "I'll kill him for you, Lili. He's at hotel across street. I can watch from here. When he comes out—"

"No," Lili stamped a white shoe. A chuff of dark gray ash puffed up and coiled over to land on top. "He's mine. You leave him alone. Sending him to library was mistake. Mother's idea. But I need him to get into Singapore. Alone, they would be suspicious. But with him, they'll hardly give me glance. Rich American with Chinese woman. They see plenty of that from Hong Kong. And besides, my dear brother, you need me there to handle unexpected contingencies. That's why I will be there. Now it's even more certain that you need my help."

She opened her purse and took out her iPhone. Clicking the button, the screen lit up. She looked at the display for a moment, then clicked the button again and put it back in her purse.

"It's time," she said. "Let me out."

Sartaq pulled the roll-up all the way. She stepped out, stomped dust from her shoes, crossed at the light and disappeared into the neighborhood where they'd lived as kids. He guessed she'd left her rental car somewhere there.

Sartaq nodded to the hotel. If little Lili wouldn't kill the American, he'd do it. One good chop with a machete, maybe the same one he'd used for Wang, would do it.

Dr. Gu Xiaosheng was all smiles as Blake and Megyn entered his mahogany office.

Wearing a baggy gray suit, white shirt, and plain blue tie, the short man had a thin, triangular face that was smooth and even. He looked twenty years younger than Blake, not what he'd expected of one of Megyn's college classmates. His squat, rectangular glasses accented the unusually wide, fleshy space between nose and upper lip.

After introductions and handshakes, Dr. Gu directed Blake to the chair in front of his desk. Megyn, an odd gray smudge on the back of her skirt, walked automatically to one at the side.

When Dr. Gu scooted into the chair behind his desk, his head remained at the same height as standing. He grabbed the edge of his desk with both hands and pulled himself close. A green-shaded lamp, a blank pad of paper, and a yellow pencil with a perfect point sat in geometric alignment on the polished top.

"Dr. Gu," Blake said, eager to get going, "after what has happened, I'm sure you will understand why I am leaving. Tonight."

"Now?" Gu squeaked and pouted. "But you still have another day of class."

Blake decided to try a calm, reasonable approach first.

He leaned forward and spread his hands.

"If the terrorists that blew up the library are after publicity, then I'm likely to be a target. Dead Americans in foreign countries make news around the world."

Megyn wore a perfunctory smile.

Blake added, "I saw the man who did it and he saw me."

Gu's eyes flicked to Megyn and back. "Did you tell this to the Police? They interviewed you after the explosion, yes?"

He looked down. "Actually, they rushed me off to the hospital, so no, I haven't. Not yet."

Megyn chimed in, "He's afraid they might think he's involved."

Gu looked at his fingers holding the pencil. "That would be... inconvenient." He started turning it end-over-end. "And you feel threatened?"

Why was Gu being obtuse? A terrorist attack on his campus had killed several dozen people. How could he ignore the danger?

Megyn's shoulders moved in what might've been a tiny shrug. Eyes down, she said, "It's hard to know someone's background, why they do things. And there are undeclared wars—revolutions —going on all the time."

Blake's face pinched like he'd tasted something bitter. What was she getting at?

"For God's sake," he said, "that man murdered college students, kids who haven't made their mark on the world."

Megyn refolded her hands. Gu tapped the eraser end of the pencil on his desk three times, paused, turned it until the eraser was down again, and then tapped three more times.

He reminded Blake of managers in big companies that tracked projects and reviewed expenses. To them, underlings were resources. They were to be monitored, minimized, and ultimately removed from the ledger's debit column.

Blake straightened and began the statement he'd been rehearsing.

"Dr. Gu, the University invited me under false pretenses. The situation here is not what was represented. There's been nothing in the American news about any danger from terrorism in China, but that is the reality. According to contract law, a dramatic difference or sudden change in circumstances is more than sufficient grounds to rescind an agreement."

Gu balanced the pencil on his fingertips and tapped it. The pencil twirled like a helicopter. When the twirling slowed, he gave it another flick.

"Terrorism?" Gu asked with the third stroke. "This is the first I've heard anyone use that word." *Flick.* "My understanding is there was a gas leak in one of the service tunnels under the building." He caught the pencil between thumb and finger. "Something—a student's cigarette, perhaps?—ignited it." He put the pencil down and sighed. "A terrible accident, yes. The maintenance engineer may have failed in his duties. I believe he's been detained pending the outcome of the investigation."

Blake swallowed his exasperation. "Dr. Gu, circumstances—the destroyed classroom, in particular—have made class impossible."

He waited for Gu.

The pencil-helicopter twirled again.

Blake took a deep breath. "Sir, performance of the terms of our contract has become impossible. Our agreement is hereby terminated."

He stood up. Alone.

Gu smiled, but his tone was ominous. "Well, if you *really* want to do that, there is a way."

Blake waited for the shoe to drop.

Gu set the pencil down and pulled open the center drawer of his desk. He took out a single sheet of paper and laid it on the desk.

"I believe you've incurred some expenses. Your air travel, for instance. If, as you say, our contract is void, then…"

Blake had never seen the bill for the round-trip airfare. The University had made all the arrangements. He'd just shown his passport at the airline desk and boarded.

He didn't need to look at the sheet. It'd have the Shanghai hotel, the Feng Yi hotel, nearly two weeks of three meals a day, his binge after the beheading that gutted the minibar, probably William's rental van, Sunday museum excursion, dinner for five at Tsing-Tsing, ...

The total would almost exceed what they'd agreed to pay, and now wouldn't. He'd be deep in debt for a long time despite his top-level expert fees, assuming they let him out of the country so he could resume making a living.

But a thought came. Once he was out of the country, they couldn't collect so long as the US didn't extradite him. He wasn't sure of the US/China arrangements in that regard, but with his defense industry connections, maybe he could just throw away the bill? Or get it cut way down? It wasn't like he'd stiffed them and delivered nothing. He'd taught class. And they had copies of his lectures.

He smiled and sat down.

"I'll make you a deal," he said. "I delivered the training for the first week, and then four days of the second. How about a nine-ten split? You pay nine-tenths of the expenses and that much of my fee, and I'll pick up the rest of the expenses."

Gu rolled the pencil on his desk under a finger. "We have some additional concerns."

Now what? Blake wondered.

"Discussing guns with your class, for one. While not illegal, there are those among our patrons who might consider that... seditious?"

Blake kept his jaw clamped shut.

"And I don't believe you've spoken with the Police about today's unfortunate event. Some of the students—the ones who went with you to the site of the explosion without authorization—said you made quite a fuss about one particular spot. I believe you told them it looked like a bomb had exploded there?"

Blake tilted his head. "And you're claiming it was a gas leak?"

Gu gave a chin wag. "Are you an expert in forensics?"

"But the students, they saw it, too. You just said..."

"Ah. I think you have misunderstood me. The students reported what *you* said. They testified to the burning gas jet. From a broken main. The one that failed, perhaps?" Gu smiled. "To report otherwise—especially with no evidence or expertise—would be tantamount to calling the Chinese government a liar." His smile dropped. "The penalties for giving false testimony are quite severe."

Gu's chair squeaked as he shifted his weight.

"But if you still feel you must leave, I understand. That is your responsibility, and I would not attempt to tell you how to live your life. If the contract is, as you say, cancelled, your responsibility would be for the expenses—*all* the expenses— incurred to this point."

Using the eraser end of the pencil, Gu pushed a button embedded in the desk.

"The other matters will be for the Police... or Beijing... assuming they arise."

The door behind Blake opened.

A beefy Asian man in a drab gray suit stepped in and closed the door behind him. He was about Blake's height, but thicker and heavier. His arms and legs stretched the fabric of his suit taut as he stood, arms crossed, blocking the door.

Gu's eyes flared and the corners of his mouth pulled up ever so slightly. "This gentleman will hold your passport while you decide."

Blake's throat clamped shut. Without the passport, he wouldn't be able to board an international flight. They always checked. Same for trains that crossed borders. He couldn't even rent a car and drive his way out.

Gu's eyes narrowed behind his glasses. "Mr. Blake, your papers, if you please?"

Blake turned to Megyn.

She met his eyes. "I'm sorry, Blake. This is beyond me."

The large man stepped next to Blake. His hand, open like a waffle, waited.

Blake took his passport out of his shirt pocket and held it up. The big man plucked it away, turned, and left.

After the door clicked, Gu said, "Of course, should you decide to teach tomorrow, that would complete your contractual obligations. Assuming these other unfortunate matters don't come up, it would please us to fulfill our part of the contract."

He motioned to the sheet on his desk. "We will then pay all your expenses. Your students have been very complimentary. Your fee will be paid in full, and it will please Mister Kim to return your passport. Where you go after that, well, that is up to you. I understand you wanted to do some sight-seeing. You should capitalize on your good fortune of already being here."

"But the classroom?"

Megyn spoke. "They've set up another one. Students have been told where to go."

Sitting at the desk in his hotel room, Blake frowned at his notebook's LCD.

His original flight home, booked by the school, was prepaid. It couldn't be changed, cancelled, or refunded. And it wasn't for another ten days.

"Screw that," he said to the room, and started trying to make new reservations. But with the short notice, a Friday night departure from a busy airport, required a lot of gyrations.

An hour later, he'd spliced a high-speed train to Guangzhou with an overnight stay, then a train to Hong Kong and a red-eye to Beijing with another night in a hotel, and finally a flight back to San Francisco to kiss Megyn goodbye, and then home to Phoenix.

Everything except the high-speed train required a reservation. He booked fully refundable, and the hotels with cancel by 6:00 PM. He hoped Megyn would go with him, but he could adjust things either way.

But there was still no word from her.

If he left by himself, would he ever see her again? Would she feel like he'd abandoned her?

"What do you want?" he asked aloud in frustration.

He wanted Megyn. Close. He wanted to reach over, touch her arm, feel her warmth, feel her move while keeping his touch. Part of him. Be in his life from now on.

He typed up the itinerary, attached it to an email, and sent it. Then he sent a text message to be sure she'd see the email.

Leave tmw after class. Complicated and pricey but do-able. Don't worry abt money. Advise ASAP. Miss you. A lot.

He almost added "Love", but after much consternation, didn't want to complicate things anymore.

Out his window, the sulfurous glow of the sky reminded him of a hotel he'd used in Orange County. It overlooked a metal scrap yard that clanked and crashed, its incinerator flaring, all night. It had been like looking into hell.

Depressed, confused, and exhausted, he curled on the bed with his back to China.

Chapter 15

Friday, November 3
Wuchang, and then in-transit to Guangzhou

Blake awoke before his alarm clock. The white LED blinked on his cell from the bedside table.

The text message from Megyn was a single Emoji, a heart.

It could only mean *Yes*, and *I love you*, and *I want to be with you*, and *Take me with you*, and...

Blake's grin held through the shower, packing, and checking out.

But standing outside, his eyes tracked across the mostly brown trees of Mount Luojia behind the shops across the street. His unease returned. He stayed close to the front of the hotel and panned his head left and right watching for anyone's approach.

A chilly gust up the hill from the lake smelled of rotting vegetation. He frowned and zipped his jacket. The weather map on the lobby TV showed a blue-edged, white blob oozing down from Siberia. It covered all of Mongolia and reached well into central China covering Wuhan. The single digit "9" for the city told today's story.

High of forty-eight, his mind converted. Compared to yesterday's upper eighties, the change was stunning. But right now, it was close to freezing. Blake pulled his windbreaker tight.

A two-tone gray Hyundai tooted in front of him as steam puttered from its exhaust. The trunk popped open and the side window whirred down two inches.

"Put your luggage in," Megyn said. "Heater's on." The window shut.

Inside, he clicked his seat belt. "You're much prettier than William." He started to turn and lean toward her, but a glance stopped him.

She punched the gas. He put a hand on the dash as she jockeyed into a center lane gap on the far side and then shunted right twice to get to the curb lane. Fifty feet later, she turned into the university's open gate through the high stone wall.

When they passed his previous building, there was a yellow-plastic accordion barrier across the entrance. Megyn continued up the road. From the remembered map, they'd reach the lake soon where it curved around the north side of the campus.

Water in sight through the trees, Megyn went left, then left again, then braked moments later on loose gravel in front of a single story, red brick building.

It was older than the four-story computer software building, but not ancient. Blake guessed it was from the 50s. It's aluminum-framed windows were like his high school shop building where he'd learned Ohm's Law.

I equals E divided by R, echoed in his mind. "Don't waste your time with digital computers," Mr. Schneider, his high school electronics teacher, had told the class of teenagers in his drop-jawed Brooklyn accent. "Unreliable because of those hundreds of transistors. Analog computers are the future." Moving to the greenish chalkboard, he scratched K-I-S-S in yellow chalk and then underlined each letter. "Keep It Simple, Stupid." The man became Blake's idol, his mentor, and the patient, caring father figure he needed but didn't have at home.

But about computers, Mr. Schneider couldn't have been more wrong. Analog computing disappeared in the next decade, and microelectronics took over with computer chips as transistor counts rocketed to the millions and then billions. Blake's cell phone was a common example of the enormous leaps in sophistication wrought by the semiconductor industry.

Megyn shouted through an open slit of window. "Here for lunch." Her tires churned the gravel as she left.

Inside the building by the door, the six toggle switches were up but the room was dark. He flipped them down, three at a time, with the side of his hand. The fluorescent lights snapped on, right then left.

There were the same long, gray tables, but no Sony monitors or computers this time. Everything else was the same except the projector bolted to the ceiling. It was huge, the size of a 1950s television and stereo-turntable combo. On its side, three graceful Chinese characters appeared to have been hand-painted.

Blake hooked up, and not finding a wand, walked to the projector and pressed its red button by hand. Moments later, the image from his notebook appeared on the screen behind him, in green and black. He wiggled and pushed the cable tight against his notebook and the projector flicked to full color, but when he took his hand away, it went back to just green.

He shook his head. He just wanted to be done.

The clock on the back wall twitched to 8:25.

Half an hour to kill, Blake walked outside. The chill air pushing through from the lake felt good. Looking up, the tops of the taller trees had been raked bare. He guessed this building had been shadowed from the shock wave by some hill, but not the highest tree branches.

A few minutes before the hour, students began arriving on foot, alone or with a classmate. Nobody made eye contact even when he nodded and said, "Good morning."

At nine, he stepped inside and counted heads. Twenty-seven. There'd been over two hundred every day before.

"We'll wait a few more minutes," he announced from the back. A couple of faces turned to look, their expressions neutral.

Ten minutes passed, but no one else arrived.

He marched to the front. "Let's get started."

He began as he always did, talking around the slide's points and giving examples. At the bottom of the first page, he looked up for questions. All the faces were down, at cell phones, notebook computers, anything other than him.

They were present, he was sure, for the same reason he was: the powers-that-be decreed it.

With no one listening, he said less. Eventually, he started doing what he despised in others: He read the lines on the slide aloud.

"Any questions?"

Nothing.

Next slide.

No faces, no questions, no objections.

No one paid any attention.

Not even him.

At Noon when they broke for lunch, Blake counted pages to the end.

Thirty.

The day would be short.

Megyn was waiting in the back. "How's it look?"

He closed the lid of his computer and turned off the projector. "I'm gonna be a couple of hours short."

"Let's get something to eat," she said, rising. "Have you tried the student cafeteria? It's... edible." She grinned.

He went American. Big mistake. They burned the outside of the beef patty but left the center bloody and raw. Brown-streaked, limp lettuce and a tiny slice of green and yellow tomato completed the burger. He nibbled a few fries, then pushed the tray to the side.

Megyn's plate of Moo Goo Gai Pan came from the steam-line.

"Chicken?" He asked, wondering if he should go back.

"Edible." She slid her plate toward him. "Might be turkey."

There wasn't enough for two. He shook his head and decided he wasn't hungry.

"We're going to finish early," he said, "maybe three o'clock if I stretch. Do you think that'll be enough?"

She swallowed and started bulldozing another bite with her chopsticks. "You followed through and finished the job. A compromise or two along the way is Okay."

"Do you think Dr. What's-his-name will give the Okay?"

Megyn gave him a mildly impatient look. "Gu Xiaosheng," she supplied. "Do the last slides and answer questions. You're done."

Blake guessed that was a "Yes."

She pushed a thin piece of meat on top of a slice of water chestnut and scooped them up. "What about Singapore?" She popped the bite into her mouth.

Blake felt shaky, no doubt from yesterday's explosion and the aftermath. He'd slept some, on and off, but probably only a couple of hours. Megyn seemed unaffected.

"What?" He asked, more to see if she was really that disconnected from what'd happened than to repeat the question.

She chewed and swallowed. "Singapore. We talked about it on the flight to Wuhan, remember? We could go there and unwind? You and me?"

He chin-wagged a yes. "All the reservations I made can be rebooked, so all we need are seats on a flight and a place to stay. Once we get there, I know a guy. He knows the good places."

She pushed up a stack of vegetables and delivered them intact into her mouth without leaving red lipstick on the chopsticks. She set them on her plate and slid her hand over and down the inside of his thigh again. He definitely liked her overtures. "Singapore is nice this time of year. Very warm."

"I've been there. Did I mention that?"

He put his hand on top of the one on his thigh. She squeezed his leg in reply.

He cleared his throat to keep his voice from wobbling. "Have you heard of Boat Quay? I had some huge prawns there, big as lobsters. And the waiter went and got me a pint of Harp from the bar next door."

Megyn beamed. "Singapore for a few days." Another squeeze. "Just the two of us."

Singapore was ninety degrees with ninety percent humidity year-round. Nobody wore long sleeves. Clean shorts with a short-sleeve shirt were the norm in most places. Wonderful food, smiling people, a clean beach...

He wondered what kind of bathing suit Megyn would have? Had she packed one from California? He imagined a string bikini, jet black. Or maybe one with tiger stripes? But maybe she'd be coy; a modest two-piece to reinforce her public instead of private personae?

He'd need to buy a swimsuit, something loud and garish to match his giddiness. Or maybe he should go for reserved and mature: a James Bond look with plain navy trunks and a flowers-and-palm shirt? Blake's bicycle-hardened and tanned legs would show well in shorts, the shorter the better. And brown leather loafers—sock-less, of course—on his feet, with Ray-Bans for his eyes, mirrored with black frames, of course.

The Orchard Road stop on the MRT would have everything needed.

Then, they'd take the subway out to Beach Station on Sentosa and change there. He'd guide her to Siloso Beach Walk and let her choose a sandy spot across from one of its three tiny islands. Two were swimmable from Sentosa, while the third could be accessed by a small footbridge. He'd frown at that one. On the far side of one of the first two, they could wade out chest deep with no one watching. He'd turn her to face him, draw her tight, and dissolve into a deep kiss. He'd feel her legs snake around and then climb up his thighs. She'd envelope him, and under the water...

Dishes clattered on the next table.

"I know someone there," he repeated. "Mickey will know the interesting places to eat." He grinned. "Have you ever tried Durian?"

Megyn beamed like she'd won the lottery. "We'll re-book when we get to Hong Kong," she said, obviously excited about the junket. "Air, hotels, everything."

Back in the classroom, Blake finished the last slide at quarter past two.

The classroom was empty in two minutes except for the big man from Dr. Gu's office who'd come in to wait in the back. When Blake approached, he took an envelope from inside his jacket, put it in Blake's hand, and left without speaking.

Inside were Blake's passport and the check—a cashier's check—for $7,000.00 in US currency, his payment for the two weeks. He was ready.

Tires crunched on gravel outside, and Megyn waved from the driver's seat. With his suitcase and computer bag stashed in the trunk next to hers, they followed the road back to the lake. She pointed through the window. Across the lake, a brown and white building the shape of an ice cream cake stood taller than anything nearby.

"That's the new high-speed train station," she said. "Three minutes."

Four chocolate and French Vanilla columns with massive inverted-pyramid caps soared up to the train station's overhang forty feet above the turnout. Hertz curbside was at the far end.

Inside, the station was marble, glass, and steel. Flashing electronic signage, animated LCDs for cosmetics, jewelry, and notebook computers filled every shop and kiosk. Around the edges of the high-ceiling main hall, stainless-steel frames bore sign tiles in blue, green, and orange. Graphics pointed to exits, restrooms, stairs, elevators with handicap wheelchair symbols, and slanted escalators.

Compared to the Feng Yi and the rest of Wuchang, Blake felt like he'd re-entered the modern world.

He poked the American flag on the ticket machine's display and punched up two tickets, First Class for Guangzhou North, that departed in twelve minutes.

They followed the signs and escalators to Line 4.

A smiling attendant corralled their four cases at the front of their carriage. At their third from the front row, plush tan-leather seats rivaled First Class on any airline.

And no seat belt.

There would be no turbulence, no bumps. Just a smooth glide atop burnished steel rails welded into continuous strips hundreds of kilometers long.

Blake chuckled as he wriggled into his seat. "This is the nicest train I've ever seen."

"Competition has been motivational," Megyn explained like a guidebook. "Japan's Shinkansen started the trend. Korea and Singapore copied and improved on it, then Malaysia and Thailand upped the ante. China's high-speed train is the latest, the fastest, and as you can see, the best."

Megyn's face was glowing. She might be a rebel to the Communist government, but the pride she showed in what her people had accomplished was undeniable. Zoey in the classroom had that same pride, albeit attributed to "the Party" instead of "the people." She hadn't shown up for the last day of class. Blake wondered if she was still alive.

Blake turned his head against the memory and focused on the scenery outside. Multi-story apartments and wide avenues morphed to compact single-family dwellings and narrow, angular streets. Farther on, the paved roadways straightened, the houses shrank, and widening fields with varying shades of produce between them.

Inside, at the far end of the car, a digital display on the wall incremented past 100.

"Sixty," he converted. "Miles per hour. What's the top speed, do you know?"

Megyn took out her cell. After a couple of pokes, she turned it toward him.

"Three-fifty," he read aloud, then told her the number his brain had just told him. "Two-ten miles per hour." After a moment, he added another data point. "Two hundred and twenty would be a mile every seventeen seconds."

Outside, houses strobed between the blink of fields.

Blake mused, "Wuchang reminded me of the south where—and when—I grew up. Family oriented, but also class and race conscious."

Megyn nodded. "There's much here that's a human characteristic, something deep that makes us label some people as *Other*. The Uyghurs, for example, up in the Northwest, are victims to that. And the Tibetans. The Han—my people—have their unofficial enclaves, just as the other ethnic groups have theirs."

She leaned closer.

"The Party is the problem," she said, her voice just loud enough to hear. "Elected officials amass wealth and power rather than working for the people. They're neither Socialists nor

Communists anymore. Instead, the Party is filled with Capitalists. They control the elections to keep themselves in power. We used to have Premier, President, General Secretary. According to the original Constitution, they had to be different people. But the Party has promulgated new Constitutions several times—that's easy to do here—and because it's a single Party system, changes always pass. Now, one person holds all of those offices. It's become a dictatorship. One man with all the power. Much worse than when I was in school."

In the far distance, a two-story home with white pillars across the front panned by. Down the hill from it were a few brick shacks of different shapes and colors.

Blake pointed. "Those are kind'a like the big estates in Mississippi, but the sharecropper shacks would be wood. It's cheaper than brick."

Megyn shook her head as the scene disappeared to the left. "Those could be a century old. Generations of occupants have cobbled them together from what they find. Wood is for cooking."

Megyn cupped a hand to Blake's ear. "The Party is self-perpetuating now. They no longer enable the people."

He waited.

"When I was a student," she said, "we would sit under the trees and talk about how things were going to be when we got the democratic reforms."

She gazed in his eyes. "Blake, I trust you, more so than anyone I've ever known."

His heart swelled. It was almost as good as saying she loved him.

That will come, he thought.

"Megyn, anything you tell me is safe."

She began.

"We were young. Ignorant. Did what we were told. The Party, the school, people on the street, all filled our heads with ideas. Every day, every moment, over and over. You didn't hear anything else. Only what they wanted you to think. No discussion, no comparison. Just the same—slogans and ideas—over and over.

"But when I went home, it was different. Mom and Dad—they

didn't say much outside the family. They were... Afraid isn't the word. They just didn't say what they thought. It was more for us so we wouldn't repeat something we weren't supposed to think. But not think, as in right and wrong, but more in degree, a shift in direction, an inflection on what to do or how to get there. The Party can be very subtle.

Megyn shook her head. "Mao's gang of four and their experiments—they were terribly destructive. If you didn't do what they said, you disappeared. Sometimes people were killed right on the street. It happened. And you couldn't talk about it because the same could happen to you. Secrets on top of secrets."

Her lips crinkled like she was spreading lipstick, evening it out.

"But that was the world," she said with a sigh. "My childhood, my comrades, those I thought of as my sisters and brothers... We just didn't know any better."

She straightened her back, flattened her shirt with both hands, and then focused on her knees.

"They murdered my father."

She said it so softly, Blake wasn't 100% sure she'd said that.

"Murdered him?"

"I was still a baby, so I don't remember it. Momma told me years later. Sometime after that, a neighbor we trusted confirmed what'd happened. She said it changed her—Mother, I mean—hardened her heart. The neighbor said she was never the same again.

"The night he didn't come home, she asked the school if they knew anything. At first, they said, 'No.' Then one of them said he'd run off with another woman.

"That was a lie," she protested. "Such an honorable man..."

She blinked hard.

"I could see Momma's rage when she told me that part. That anger, that all-consuming hatred... That was all new to me. I was afraid of it, of her, for a while.

"Anyways, she kept the bookstore open, but then the fire ended that."

"Your family owned a bookstore?"

"The Feng Yi Hotel you stayed at? It was right there, along with some other shops, like the ones across the street. We lived two blocks behind that.

"After the fire, the school said we couldn't stay because the house belonged to the school. 'Reserved for faculty.' Mom moved us—me and my older brother—out to Shenjiawan. That's where her family, the Shen's, had been for a very long time. She still lives there."

She grinned.

"Our mother runs everything."

She took a breath and resumed before Blake could ask what she meant.

"Remember how the Party took everything and redistributed it to the people? Well, Momma ended up managing... In America, in the south, what do you call them, people who work the land owned by others and get part of the crop and a place to live?"

"Sharecroppers," he said, thinking of the big Mississippi and Arkansas plantations he'd seen as a child. "They also had to pay rent, and like those working in coal mining towns in the Smokies where everything was owned by the company, it was hard, maybe impossible, to save enough to get out."

She nodded.

"The same here but imposed by the Party as much as the system," she said. "Momma supervised them, all the land around Shenjiawan according to Party rules. My brother and I attended school out there. It was very parochial—backward—not like around the University."

"And your father?"

She shook her head. "When I got to the University, I tried to find out, but there was nothing left by then. According to the records, no one with that name had ever taught there. There was no birth record, and nothing at the schools he should have attended growing up. He'd been erased. Others, too, we found out."

She grimaced, and her eyes flared.

"Mao was evil. Hitler, Stalin, Pol Pot... They said they were doing good for humanity, but they were murderers, thieves, madmen..."

She took a loud breath and put her head back to gaze at the ceiling.

Outside the window, things rocketed past. The digital speedometer alternated between 358 and 359.

Megyn looked lost in memories. He picked up her hand and laced his fingers with hers. She leaned on his shoulder. The scent of her hair reminded him of a good Pinot Grigio: light, spring flowers, nothing heavy or mysterious.

Minutes passed.

"Megyn," he finally murmured, "could we talk about something, something that's been on my mind?"

She murmured something affirmative.

"Megyn," he whispered, "I think…"

Say it!

"I love you."

She didn't move.

Maybe she hadn't heard?

He took a breath.

A little less softly, he let it all out. "Megyn, I want you with me, beside me, to share my—to share *our* lives, whatever those might be. I'll take care of you when you need it, help you, and I'll let you help me when I need it, everything. From now on."

Silence.

Was she deciding? Trying to figure out how to say no?

"Megyn, I want to spend the rest of my life with you."

Nothing.

Ask her.

He turned to get his face as close as he could.

"Megyn, will you marry me?"

Finally, she turned to look into his eyes. She smiled. "You're sweet," and then put her head back on his shoulder.

Part of his mind went blank.

Another part didn't.

Sweet?

He felt like he'd been patted on the head.

Wait, his inner voice warned. *Don't jump to conclusions.*

Sometimes he hated how his mind worked. All those thoughts

coursing around different neuron loops competing to see which could get into his conscious mind.

His lower back ached.

Stress?

Words came: *Ease up.*

He nodded.

It'd been an insane two weeks. Murder and a terrorist attack. Megyn was going through something with her family. And no doubt, his cutting their trip short didn't help her any. Maybe he just needed to be patient. Romance was... Oh hell, he was terrible at romance.

In his mind, a gossamer angel pirouetted in a rainbow of color.

But, Megyn...

He smiled at the remembered moment.

A voice near his ear spoke. He turned to look. The refreshment cart was at his elbow. The glass bottles clinked gently as the train's wheels shifted a centimeter or two between the glass-smooth tracks.

He needed to pee.

"I'll be back in a minute."

Chapter 16

Afternoon and Evening
On-board Train

Sartaq closed his eyes against the flashes of countryside. She must've walked up then.

"My brother," Lili wore an impish grin, hands on her hips as she stood in the aisle, "I saw you follow us onto the train. This is not where you belong."

Her hair and makeup were immaculate, as always, and her clothing was smooth, spotless, and perfectly coordinated. A scent —fruit blossoms?—came to him.

She accused, "You are supposed to be with students on way to Singapore."

"I am," he barked. "Just not way you said."

She glanced forward to where the American had disappeared into the train's bathroom, then pushed in past his knees and sat down.

"You need to be there in two weeks," she reminded him.

Sartaq gritted his teeth. Why did she always think him incapable of planning? Hadn't he carried out Wang's execution without leaving a single trace? No blood, no body, nothing?

Of course, there was the witness... But that was her fault. She'd brought him—American—to China. He needed to be dead.

This morning, he'd left his apartment early to follow them into the campus. The curving paths through the campus made it easy to keep up on foot. And after Lili left the American, Sartaq was ready to strike, but he stayed in plain view of passing students. No chance. And after class, Lili'd been the one to take him out of reach.

He fell behind when they left the campus, but luckily, he could see her car as it went around the lake, and that road ended at the train station. He'd read their plans on the glowing screen of their ticket machine and bought a seat in the same car.

He felt Lili's eyes on him, waiting.

"Oh," he exclaimed, "My students are in van like you planned. They're driving now to Guanzhou. Lin Yusheng knows neighborhood at train station."

"Lin? The boy that uses lemon juice on his hair to make it white?"

Sartaq nodded. "They meet me there."

Lili's eyes narrowed. "I don't know. The ship won't wait if you're late. Do you have envelopes?"

Sartaq tapped his shirt. "Yes."

"And you know when to use?"

"Yes, yes." He took a breath and stood up. "So, I'll kill American now, and—"

She grabbed his arm and pulled.

"I need him to get into Singapore."

Sartaq sat but shook his head. "Lili, you not needed there. Go home. I do everything. American mess things up. He in bathroom now. Perfect place. I know what to do."

Lili's jaw dropped. "What? Here? In train? You can't attack here." She paused. "And what would you do with body, throw it out window?"

He almost answered.

Her eyes stretched wide. "My dear, dear brother, I was being facetious."

Lili threw in big words to prove she was smarter. Whatever that meant, it wasn't good.

She tapped the window beside her. "Look."

A smear of orange—roof tiles, he guessed—shot past the window.

"Glass," she tapped it again. "It doesn't open except for emergency. And lavatory has no window."

A muscle in his cheek quivered. He wanted to shout he'd smash a hole in the wall and squish the body through. He could bend aluminum like what this car had on the outside with his bare hands. Pulling and pushing it to make a hole, he'd shove and force the body through.

Lili was shaking her head. "Haven't I kept him from doing anything? Leave him to me. I know how to handle him."

Sartaq fumed. "Well, it doesn't have to be here. When we get to Guangzhou, I will—"

"No!" Lili stamped her foot.

The man across the aisle glanced over. Lili stopped and leaned back in the seat. She hissed, "There are too many dangers, Taq. Leave him to me."

Lili's beautiful face and gold-sparkling green eyes, her dark brown hair, and the gentle sweep of her shoulder left no doubt in Sartaq's mind of his little sister's persuasive abilities.

But there was more to it this time, and it was Lili, not the American, that bothered him the most. She'd described the man as an old friend. But when Sartaq found out he was the same man that witnessed the execution and specially when she started protecting him, he knew there was more.

And this afternoon when they'd waved with her in the car and him inside in the classroom, there'd been a look in both their faces. It was the same as lovers leaving the Feng Yi in the morning.

She loves him, he cursed to himself.

"All right," he lied, "I won't kill your American."

She squeezed his muscled forearm, leaned in and kissed his cheek in front of the scar.

"I love you, big brother," she said.

"I love you, too, little sister."

She peeked between the seats, squeezed out to the aisle, gave him a last smile, and then walked back to her seat.

Lili makes the plans, he repeated to himself. *I make them work.*

Megyn's seat was empty when Blake returned. He looked to the rear, but the aisle was empty. Maybe she'd gone to the next car for a lavatory.

Blake climbed into the window seat.

He turned to look out just as another train, going full speed in the opposite direction, blasted past. The *thud* of its shock wave reminded him of the bomb blast passing through the classroom. He remembered everything moving in slow motion, his chair pitching back, white dust falling from the ceiling, shards of glass punching through the green window shades...

Megyn was back. She must've slid back in while his mind wandered.

But she looked odd. Her cheeks were a bluish gray instead of pinkish yellow. Spindly branches of wrinkles fingered out from each eye, and three dark crevices ran across her forehead.

She looked ten, twenty years older.

He joked, "I thought you'd left me for another man."

She didn't move or speak.

"Megyn?"

He touched her arm. Her body twitched once with a passing shiver, and she frowned.

"Is it the train?" He asked. "Are you motion sick?"

"Blake, I..." She turned to him and laid a hand on his forearm. She started patting it like a mother burping a baby.

It brought back a memory.

When Blake was eight, he'd shoplifted a bone-handled folding knife from the display case in a sporting goods store. When his mother saw it on his dresser and asked where it was from, he tried, "I won it in a bet with Bebop." His mother shook her head. "This is way too nice for Arthur Bishop." She tapped it with her finger. "Where did you get this?" Accompanied by a torrent of tears, he blurted out the truth. She made him wash his face and then said that tomorrow they would drive to the store, and he would explain what he'd done. Horrified at the thought and terrified of what the store's owner would do to him, he'd shouted,

"No! You do it." His mother tried putting her arm around his shoulders and cooing, "He won't hurt you. Don't worry." But he was frantic. She tried soothing him by patting his forearm, but her face said she didn't know what to do. The patting went double-time march and made it that much worse. He bore as much of the drumming as he could, then pushed her away and screamed, "Get out!"

Blake grabbed Megyn's hand to stop it.

"I'm sorry," she said, looking down. "I've got a... family complication. It's something I thought settled, but now, well, now I'm not so sure."

Perhaps she'd received a phone call or text while he was in the bathroom? Something wrong with her mother, maybe, or a conflict over taking care of her? Blake had never dealt with aging parents, his mom and dad passing within a month of each other, a fast cancer and then a stroke.

The muscles in Megyn's cheek and neck stood out.

Before he could ask, she hissed, "You're right. You can never tell anyone. Never!"

He blinked. "What?"

She pulled her hand loose and resumed patting his arm, her face tense.

A terrifying thought came to him. He'd read that a stroke could cause sudden emotional and behavioral changes. The furious patting, her out-of-the-blue statement, her changed appearance, the odd reply—"you're sweet"—to his marriage proposal...

He remembered two tests.

He scooted forward and turned to face her.

"Look at me, Megyn," he commanded. "Show me a big grin."

She gave him a quizzical look. On the side closest, the curve of her mouth ascended. But on the other side, her lips drew a straight line.

Uh-oh.

He took both her hands. "Squeeze my hands, Megyn," he ordered. "Squeeze them. Hard!"

The sudden crush, both hands, and the flare of anger—on both sides of her face, equal and even—caught him unprepared.

"Ow!" He pulled away.

She flashed him a huge, false grin—equal and even—that showed Hollywood teeth and pink gums. It fell as fast as it had gone up.

"I'm not having a stroke."

"Oh, okay," he mumbled, not sure he should trust her self-diagnosis.

He flexed his fingers and scooted back in the seat, but kept his head turned so he could watch her.

She put her head back and gazed, eyes unfocused and face limp, toward the front of the coach. After a moment, her eyelids seemed to narrow, and the wrinkles and crow's feet crept back into her face.

She put her hand on his forearm.

The patting resumed.

"It's all right," she said mechanically, her face a pale mask. "We're on our way now. You'll be safe with me. We'll just mind our own business and be out of this soon."

He wanted to jump out of his seat and yell, *What the Hell is going on with you?*

But he ground his teeth and said nothing.

It was dark when the train glided to a noiseless stop at Guangzhou North.

Blake and Megyn gathered their bags and followed the exit arrows. Just outside, they stopped by a bicycle rack and Blake looked down through a park from the station.

Sparsely lit, the concrete and planter-filled space was bordered by single lanes on each side paved in cobblestones like some old European street. Overhead lamps would light their way if they followed a zigzag path.

"I checked on Google-Earth," he said, pointing. "We turn right where that traffic signal is. The hotel is second on the right after that."

He started down the steps, but Megyn didn't follow.

"Is something wrong?"

She was facing into the station. "No," she chirped, angling her head as if looking for something.

Turning, she followed.

They joined a fresh surge from the station and merged in behind someone towing a green roller bag. To their left, a woman pulled a wire shopping basket with one hand while tugging the arm of a tired, four-year-old girl with the other.

They stayed with the pack and reached the bottom of the park in a couple of minutes. Most of the pedestrians stopped to wait for the light. A few went left, and a few right, but one of them, a man in dark-green work clothes with a duffel bag draped over one shoulder, bolted out against the light. A taxi swerved and just barely missed him.

Blake shook his head, but then pointed to the right toward a brilliantly lit, orange building. "That must be our hotel, the one with all the lights."

They were there a minute later.

The garish, twenty story building had a curved front that arced around a circular driveway. It looked like something from the Las Vegas strip. Half a dozen Romanesque columns supported a covered walkway. Across the top of the walkway, three gigantic Chinese characters glared in bright red. Next to them in glowing white, smaller English letters spelled out "Mayor's Plaza." Above that, the orange marble façade glared in the blue-white mercury-vapor floodlights.

After processing their passports and credit cards, the check-in clerk handed Blake the keys to both rooms and motioned toward the elevator.

Megyn asked, "What floor?"

Blake looked down at the keys in his hand. "Seventeen."

When the elevator doors opened at their floor, a young woman rose from behind a desk in the hallway and smiled. She held her hand out, palm up. Blake handed her the keys. She looked at each one, the clock next to the elevator, and then wrote something in an open notebook on her table. She stepped backwards down the hall and motioned for them to follow. It reminded Blake of a White House tour he'd attended years ago between gigs in northern Virginia.

Megyn translated the girl's introduction.

"Welcome to the Mayor's Plaza Concierge floor. There will be tea and coffee in the lobby in the morning. Please dial one-seven-zero-zero during the night if you need anything. Breakfast is self-serve from seven to eight. We hope you have a pleasant stay."

Megyn added, "She apologizes for her ignorance of English."

Well down the hall, the woman stopped and waved her hand toward two doors opposite each other. She hesitated, then handed both keys to Blake. She bobbed her head, added a small bow, and marched back up the hall.

Blake didn't want to get his hopes up, but they were hundreds of miles from the horrors and dangers of Wuhan.

He held out one key and asked, "Are you okay? Do you want me to come in?"

"No."

Blake winced at her abruptness. He'd allowed his hopes to rise with the mileage from Wuhan, but it seemed to have done the opposite to Megyn.

She frowned at his reaction. "It's Okay. Everything is all right. I just have a lot to think about. Family stuff."

She kissed him on the cheek, took the offered key, but then had to push with her shoulder to enter her room. The door slammed behind her like someone shouting, "Keep Out!"

Julie used to cut him off like that. End of discussion. Not even a "talk to the hand." Closed door, closed subject, closed marriage.

Blake sighed and shoved open the door to his room.

Apparently decorated for kids in an American cowboy theme, the twin-beds had polyester covers with brown ponies grazing on yellow grass. They sided to opposite walls, presumably for siblings accustomed to sharing a room. At the foot of each sat a varnished, lift-top chest with cattle horns branded with a hot iron into the wood. Nightstands of the same blond wood, one for each bed, held lamps with clear bulbs. They projected the western street scenes printed on the shades to re-appear on the dirt-colored wallpaper with Monument Valley outlines, a rusty-red monolith rising from the top of the saloon.

Showered and in fresh boxers, Blake turned off the lights and sat on one of the beds. The glow from the mercury-vapor streetlights below painted two blue-white stripes on the ceiling.

He closed his eyes, drew air through his nose, then exhaled through his lips as if blowing a flute on a Coke bottle. One at a time, he called up his worries, and then visualized each one drifting away—two breaths in-and-out to pull it into focus, then in-and-out once more to let it dissipate into nothingness.

Two quick raps on the door interrupted his meditation. Three more sounded before he could reach the door.

Through the peephole, an enormous eye—green and blue with gold flecks—waggled and blinked.

"Blake," Megyn's voice hissed, "Little Miss Monitor has her pencil out but doesn't know what to write. Let me in to inspire her journaling."

Blake felt confused. The way she'd rejected him in the hallway —what was that, an hour ago? But his hand, following a silent order from his libido, had already turned the handle.

Bare feet. Crimson toenails. A sheer white robe swirling as it entered. The steel-safe *kerchunk* of the door sealing them in was followed by cascading scents of soap, lavender, and clean skin. Her arms snaked around his waist and pulled him tight. One leg up encircled the back of his thighs and snaked up. Her head tilted up, mouth open, red lips waiting.

He merged into her deep, moist kiss.

"Some music?" She suggested, pulling away and surveying his room. "Something slow, I think. Beethoven, maybe? Moonlight Sonata? The Adagio Sostenuto?"

Blake smiled. It was another pleasing but undiscovered facet to this complex woman. She knew classical music.

He tapped the face of his phone and stated the title aloud. In a moment, YouTube began a melancholy piano.

She listened for a moment, then shook her head. "Try the Friedrich Gulda performance. It's much more..." She sighed. "I want to be in anguish, not just melancholy."

Their lovemaking started with the artist's hesitant, tentative, lingering touch. Memories of the week faded. Guangzhou disappeared. The hotel was gone. Even the enveloping room vanished.

Only their bubble of reality remained, a universe of touching, caressing, little sounds…

"I want your baby," she whispered.

A breeze swirled odd bits of paper around the alley as Sartaq snugged the cardboard around him. Folded under on three sides, it would keep out the wind and chill. The Guangzhou alley smelled of damp concrete and plaster dust. His chosen spot for the night was down an alley next to a gray-marble office building glowing blue and orange from the hotel's reflected floodlights.

He'd have no trouble spotting them when they came out in the morning. His warriors in the van would be here by then, and once the American was dead, they'd make a quick getaway. Lili's plan would then get them to Singapore.

He imagined the American's neck in his powerful hands, the man's tongue turning black, his eyes rolling back, the body convulsing before the final collapse… Sure, the man looked fit and capable, but Sartaq had dealt with others. The key was instant savagery.

Wang had been easy. The boy was weak, frightened, and totally submissive. He'd walked beside Sartaq without resistance to his own execution. Only when the blade began its work did he react.

But this American would not be easy like Wang. Lili said he was very smart. "An engineer," she'd told him. He made things with computers. When she'd first described him months ago, he'd replied, "I use computers, too." He reminded her that the money she sent from the United States went to an HSBC branch in Wuchang, and he used A-T-M—"That is computer."– to get cash. But she shook her head. "Taq, he teaches computers to fly airplanes. Can you do that?"

At least, she kissed his cheek to apologize.

The American got away, but that was because Lili's plan and Tehran's schedule forced the trip—get and hide the dynamite—to Singapore.

"Not again," Sartaq mumbled, his nose and mouth beneath the edge of the cardboard as another breeze, cooler than before, drummed his make-shift shelter.

"I need weapon," he mumbled to the dark alley.

He climbed out of his warm cocoon and edged up the alley. Behind a new office building was a jumble of broken red bricks. Hit in the head with one of those, the American would go down. Another blow would crack the skull. A couple more and his problem would be solved.

Sartaq picked up the biggest chunk of brick. He brushed away the dust and hefted it for balance.

A deep voice commented from nearby, "That'll do."

Sartaq froze.

Somebody unseen, possibly with an unknown weapon, was bad. If Sartaq needed to strike, it would have to be sudden and savage, but where? He slid his gaze into the black shadow where the voice came from and waited as adrenalin primed his body.

"Of course," the voice offered like they were sharing a meal, "you must be close."

Sartaq barked his only warning. "Get away!"

The voice chuckled, "My dear, brightly illuminated friend, it's my alley, not yours."

In the shadowed triangle, Sartaq saw an orange glint slide down a shiny metal edge.

Knife! On right. In shadow's left hand.

But how to get it? A plunge into the black abyss was out. Too many unknowns. He needed to stop that hand first, but how was the man sitting? Knees up? Facing me? Turned halfway? Exposed? Cardboard shield?

Sartaq turned and tilted his head so his ears could pick out more location details from the voice.

He probed. "You have knife?"

"Maybe," the voice paused. "Interested?"

At the back of shadow, probably against the wall. That'll limit his moves.

Sartaq grinned, "Maybe," and shifted his head again.

The voice inhaled and said, "You don't look like you can afford it." Dirt and small stones scraped on top of concrete.

Slightly left of center. Voice higher than if sitting. In poop squat?

Roles reversed, Sartaq would keep his knees together and square on for defense.

He turned the brick in his hand for a good grip. He'd throw for the mouth as he went in, press back the shoulder and grab the arm with the knife and quickly slide his hand down to find the wrist. Twist hard to break it, and then use the knife. In, twist, up —

A metallic click froze his thoughts.

Sartaq knew metals. He knew their looks, their voices, everything about them. That sound was high-quality steel on steel under the pressure of a strong spring.

Gun cocked.

"Relax your arm," the voice commanded.

Knife and gun, Sartaq thought. *Wait and watch. Better chance later.*

Sartaq shrugged and rotated his body to show his right hand. He let the arm sag and slowly passed the brick to his left hand in full view, and then dropped it into the big pocket on his thigh. He smiled and turned out both hands to show they were empty.

"What about that?" Sartaq nodded toward where the gun must be. "For sale?"

"Could be," the shadow said. "But not free like brick. And more than blade. Much more. You have money?"

Sartaq had it: the bribes in Lili's envelopes. And he was used to haggling street vendors. But this would be for a lot more than he'd ever spent.

But a gun worked from many paces, long before the American could try to take it away.

After a quick trip to his duffel bag and the exchange of thirty-three crisp 100 Yuan bills, Sartaq held the revolver in his hands. He ran his fingers over the beautiful carbon steel and then raised it to his nose.

Machine oil. Clean. Fresh. Not used oil from car or truck.

Regular Police didn't carry guns in China, so most likely, the owner was in the People's Armed Police. They did riot control, terrorist attacks, and other internal security issues. The former owner of this gun was probably rotting now in his pine green uniform.

Back at his duffel bag, Sartaq snugged under the cardboard with his two weapons. He was ready for the American in the morning when they came out of the hotel. He could be up close and silent with the brick. That would be best. Or use the gun if he was far away, but he'd want the van near for his getaway because the noise would draw attention.

A breeze made his cardboard blanket gently drum on the hard dirt of the alley. It reminded him of the sound of Lili's bare feet racing across the path that followed winding ridge of Luojia. Three years younger, her short legs moved twice as fast as his, but after showing him she was faster, she would then slow. When he caught and threw her into a bowl of soft leaves, she'd squeal with delight.

So pretty. So pure. So long ago.

His chest ached. He felt like crying, but he hadn't done that in a very long time.

"Children cry," Mother Shen would say. "Grownups fix problems."

He'd fix this one tomorrow.

Chapter 17

Saturday, November 4
Guangzhou, China

A sound tugged Blake from his warm cocoon.

His face under the sheet, he licked the air. It was salty, spicy, and... musk like that of a wild animal?

He rolled his face on the sheet where she'd been, flooding his mind with the night, with her, with their scents merged, union, one...

The sound jangled at him again.

Phone.

He sent out a hand and groped the night table.

"Mmmmm," he said, the cold glass of the cell phone's display on his good ear.

Megyn's statement from the tiny speaker was pragmatic.

"Coffee."

Blake flipped the sheet down and glanced around the room.

"Where are you?"

"In the lobby. You were all curled up in the brown pony bedcover." Her voice was smiling. "Did you have a cowboy room like that when you were little?"

He closed his eyes to remember.

"Two silver cap guns in a double holster and a black Hopalong

Cassidy hat. But no boots, chaps, or other cowboy stuff. A model train that took smoke pellets running on tracks screwed down to a plywood table stored under my bed. A science fiction novel—Heinlein, Asimov, Clarke—on my night table, flashlight in the drawer so I could read under the blanket. My Army men camped in a box also under the bed, and plastic model airplanes flew from the ceiling on string—"

She interrupted with a laugh. "I'm ready to go. And I've got a list of flights from Hong Kong. We can be in Singapore for a late dinner. Coffee now or down here?"

Blake rubbed grit from one eye and looked at his finger. "We don't have to check out for hours. Why don't you come back up here?" He smiled. "We can shower. Together."

"I already did," she said, and then whispered, "You have delicious skin."

Her sudden switch left him speechless.

"But not now," she continued, "I want to get through security and into Hong Kong as soon as we can. I'll bring up your coffee. You get ready."

"Lots of cream," he added before she hung up.

He stood up, naked. For a middle-aged man, he thought he looked pretty good. His stomach was only a little rounded, and while his legs were bulgy with muscles in comparison to his upper body, he had a nice face with everything in the right place and in correct proportion. On the downside, the abrupt end of the tan on his arms and legs showed the limits of the shorty socks, riding shorts, and the dense t-shirts he wore on his morning rides.

He peered out the window. The sky was bright and the sun a blindingly clean white for a change. Still low on the horizon, Guangzhou's tall buildings cast long shadows and left the streets in deep shadow. But the arch over the entrance of the train station gleamed as if in a spotlight.

From a teaching gig two years ago, Blake knew the slow train from Guangzhou to Hong Kong took an hour and a half to reach the checkpoint where, even though Hong Kong was now part of China, Beijing still treated it like a foreign country.

Blake was just out of the shower with a towel—she'd left him one, exactly one—around his waist when the room's door slammed.

"Damn!"

Blake leaned back to look.

Megyn stood frozen, hands out with two paper cups, as coffee dripped from both.

She wore yet another outfit he hadn't seen. A tan linen jacket hung loose over a satin white top with an immaculately creased, pleated skirt. The white canvas walking shoes with brown laces and soles matched the belt around her waist except where a brown dot had spread on the toe of her left shoe. But her lips, fingernails, and toes were the same bright red as yesterday.

The bright sun, softened by the room's translucent drapes, made her face unusually radiant. Was it her makeup? Or was she glowing?

On the plane to Wuhan after their lovemaking in Shanghai, he'd worried that he hadn't been prepared. But where and how would he get condoms? Ask the front desk at the hotel? What if it'd been a woman? What was the social norm for such questions in China? And if they didn't speak English, what was Chinese for *prophylactic*?

But last night, her "I want your baby" settled the issue. Blake was sure that would be the most wonderful thing in the world.

"What?" Megyn said, still holding the cups at arm's length.

He tried to imagine her, tummy bulged out, in an appropriately tailored suit. He chuckled and waved his yellow Bic razor. "How many wardrobes do you pack, or are you shipping ahead?"

"Just my usual." The corners of her mouth twitched up. "Nothing special."

He tossed her a face cloth from the back of the toilet and turned to the mirror to shave. In the reflection, he watched as she wiped the bottom of one cup and set it on the desk. He shifted to keep her in the mirror as he lathered his face.

"You should shave before showering," she said. "More efficient."

"Shower softens the bristles," he explained, chin high as he scraped one side of his Adam's Apple then the other. "Closer shave this way."

In the mirror, she took a sip from her cup, her eyes down toward his ankles. Was she checking the tan line where his shorty socks would end?

"I'd like to get into Hong Kong," she said, sounding a little impatient.

He wanted to linger here, but she'd already rejected that. Now, she was pushing to get going again.

Was she worried about the killer, the terrorist?

"Wuhan is hundreds of miles away," he said, pulling the skin taut to get some fuzzy bristles. "He could've gotten me at class yesterday. And on the train, or if he followed us, walking through that park last night. But none of that happened. He must have other things on his mind. I think we're safe."

She didn't look convinced.

Coming into the room, he smiled. "Okay. Let's head to Hong Kong, out to the airport, and see what we can get to Singapore."

Computer bags identically propped on top of roller suitcases, Blake and Megyn turned left out of the hotel's entrance. Three blocks later at the cobblestone roadway, the sun beamed through gaps between buildings and zebra-striped the park leaving dark hiding spaces.

"We'll stick to the roadway on this side," Blake said, pointing to the cobblestoned lane. "It'll get the light sooner."

Walking uphill, steam chuffed from the exhaust of a white van halfway up the slope. Inside, two silhouetted figures shifted in the front seat.

The words of Blake's self-defense instructor echoed in his mind: *When you feel something's not right, pay attention.*

Hemmed in by the block wall on the left that was punctuated by deeply shadowed alleys and the alternating glare and shadow in the park made escape routes difficult to plan.

A scattering of people walked uphill toward the station, including a man in lime green and black Lycra astride a bicycle who stood on one, then the other, pedal. Blake wondered why he hadn't downshifted. That seemed suspicious.

The deeply shadowed alley coming in just ahead would be next to Megyn. Another concern.

Blake stopped and motioned for her to cross. "Trade sides."

Megyn stopped, but only straightened her computer bag on top. She said, "You don't need—"

From the left, a man with black hair wearing dark green clothes flashed out of the nearest alley. His arm was up. It held something red.

Blake gasped to shout a warning, but it was too late.

The man leaped to go over Megyn's double-stacked cases, but one of his yellow-booted feet snagged on the computer bag. Mid-air, his body rotated sideways as it pitched forward. His outstretched arm looped Megyn's neck and yanked her backward. But Megyn's grip on the computer case was solid, so as she went down, she yanked the case with all its contents from her regular suitcase. The smaller bag arced up and over by its handle like a heavy, black iron skillet. The two of them hit the cobblestones side-by-side. An instant later, the computer case smacked into the man's chest.

He exhaled with a loud *whoof.*

The red object flew up from his hand, bounced, and then twanged into the front spokes of the bicycle. The rider, already stopped, jumped back at the sound, and a fractured piece of brick rolled to a stop.

Blake had let go of his own bags and started toward Megyn, but when he saw the attacker's face with the wide-set eyes, round head, and the long white scar in his hair and cheek, he stopped in shock.

"Oh!"

Megyn scrambled to get up, but her shoes kept slipping on the cobblestones.

"Stop!" the killer yelled in English. He boosted himself up using Megyn, who went back down. He reached into a pocket and pulled out a black revolver.

Blake's mind cataloged the specifics:

Service pistol.

Six shot.

Four-inch barrel.

Probably double- and single-action trigger.

Blake knew only two who could shoot double-action with precision, and they were High Masters.

For a double-action shot, the trigger finger had to do three things, in sequence, and all of them different. First, it had to push hard to raise the hammer. In a revolver, that also rotated the cylinder. Then second, it needed to slow or even pause for a last check of sight alignment on the target. And finally, the finger then had to add pressure again to release the hammer. And that pressure needed to be perfectly straight to keep from disturbing the sight alignment.

Double-action shooting was immensely challenging.

Single action was much, much easier. For that, you cocked the hammer without touching the trigger. Then, you could wait all day to aim and then gently push it to release the shot.

Single-action was easy-peasy by comparison.

This man in green coveralls and clumsy work boots did not look like a well-practiced Bullseye marksman.

But then again, he was only a few feet away from Blake. A complete miss was possible, but not guaranteed.

Should Blake try to disarm him?

He blitzed through the memorized instructions.

Option one. Charge to the backside of the gun hand while grasping the gun and then rotate it up and away to peel it out of the assailant's grip.

Option two: If the hammer is still down, grab hard over the top of the revolver to lock the cylinder in place. Twist the assailant's hand in the opposite direction to force open his palm and trap his trigger finger inside the guard. Keep going. It'll break. Release the pressure and take the gun as he reacts to the pain.

Blake had done each of them, in practice, more than a year ago, once.

Undecided, his attention came back when Megyn shoved out both hands like dual stop signs.

"No!" she bellowed.

Then, she turned her head away from Blake and yelled three

syllables. The first was "Taq!"

Blake peered around Megyn for the gun. It shifted toward his face.

Megyn shouted at the other man, "No, Taq. No!"

The man coursed his eyebrows and shifted his gaze from Blake in to Megyn. He tilted his head and smiled at her, then moved it side to side in a slow but definite "No." He stepped to the side and re-aimed at Blake's face.

Blake was looking square at the end of the barrel. He could see the silvery-looking copper tips of the bullets in the cylinder, and the gun's front and rear sights, silhouetted on the killer's face. As he watched, the cylinder rotated a little, stopped, and then rotated a little more before again stopping. Each time, the end of the muzzle aimed at Blake's face moved down and to the side.

Blake's eyes flared in recognition.

The man was going to jerk the shot!

Whenever he tried squeezing the trigger, he also tightened his grip. That moved the gun down and to the side.

Blake remembered GTSOOI, Grip The Shit Out Of It.

If you gripped the gun hard as hell, when you pressed the trigger, your grip would already be at maximum. It wouldn't move the gun.

The man's eyebrows furrowed in exasperation. He opened his fingers, re-gripped the gun, and tried again. The same thing happened.

Blake grinned as the man's frustration grew and grew.

But he also knew that, eventually, the man would shoot no matter what. If Blake was going to wrest the gun away, he'd better do it now.

Blake shifted forward onto the balls of his feet and tensed his body, but Megyn was watching.

"No, Blake!" she shouted. "This is my brother. Let me deal with this."

Blake stopped, one foot a few inches forward.

"What?"

"My brother," she repeated. "This is my brother, Sartaq. I'll handle this."

Blake shrieked, "Your brother?"

He looked from Megyn to Sartaq, back and forth.

Sartaq was a big man, ugly as sin, with brown-red skin and a horrible scar, but Megyn was petite, beautiful, and with a flawless porcelain complexion.

"This is your brother?"

Sartaq barked a dozen syllables in roller-coaster Cantonese. He flicked the end of the gun to motion her aside.

She shook her head. "No, Taq."

She told Blake over her shoulder, "He wants to kill you."

No shit!

Blake cocked his head to peek around Megyn. The man's eyebrows—Sartaq's eyebrows—pinched inward over his nose. Blake did that when concentrating.

After a long moment, a sly smile pulled up the corners of Sartaq's mouth. He winked at Blake, then shifted his eyes to his sister.

The end of the revolver's muzzle shifted from Blake to Megyn.

What? Is he going to shoot Megyn, shoot his own sister?

Megyn's fingers balled into tight fists, and she stretched up on her toes. The heels of her shoes rose a full inch from the cobblestones.

And then she roared like a lioness in Cantonese. The avalanche of pitch-wobbling syllables went on and on.

Sartaq twitched back from her tirade. His face went from sly conniver to a teenager being read the riot act by an irate parent, his gun hand drooping each time her verbal pommeling continued after a quick breath.

It was like a Chihuahua making a Great Dane shrink back.

But then, Sartaq's expression changed. Something she'd said must've struck a different nerve because his face twisted into a snarl, and a moment after that, his eyes opened wider as if a light bulb had come one, and his mouth morphed into an evil grin.

An instant later, Sartaq bolted to Megyn, captured her about the waist, lifted her up, and then shook her like a rag doll. He turned so Blake could see both their faces, raised his revolver, then aimed it, muzzle down, into the center of her skull.

She grimaced as he pressed it into her scalp.

Fired in contact with a body, a shot could kill three different ways. In this case, the bullet would first drill a hole through the middle of Megyn's brain. Second, it would shatter bone and send them rattling around inside her skull slicing and dicing the flesh. And third, the incandescent gasses that pushed out the bullet would then enter her head.

The balloon would pop and spatter everything for a dozen feet.

Pressed in hard, the muzzle would be jammed in place. A contact shot never missed.

He'd seen Julie's dead body, draped with a white sheet when he'd identified her corpse. She'd OD'd on narcotics and alcohol, so her body was intact, but her expression was anything but peaceful. Blake knew he'd neglected her, ignored her, somehow caused that terrible frown. And because of all that, because of what he'd done, she killed herself.

And now, the woman he'd found to love again was about to be murdered, obliterated beyond recognition. And all because he'd gone for a mountain hike on a Saturday morning and stumbled into something. If he'd stayed in the hotel that morning, none of this would be happening. Again, it was his fault.

"No!" He raised his hands and stepped forward. "Kill me," he shouted. "Anything you want."

But Sartaq wasn't interested. He turned and barked something over his shoulder.

The white van idling a few yards back jerked into motion, then slewed to a stop two steps away. It rocked back on its springs and the sliding door banged open. Carrying Megyn, Sartaq stepped back, twisted and threw her like a bag of onions into the van. Hands and fingers grabbed and pulled her deeper into the shaded interior.

Holding the gun on Blake, Sartaq scuttled around to pick up a duffel bag, then returned to the van. He sat in the open doorway and swung in his legs.

Megyn's tan outfit shone in the light reflecting from the block wall. Held by two men on van's middle bench seat, one with his arms around her shoulders, and the other splayed across her lap.

A third person, his hair, a stark, unnatural white, slapped and pushed at the first from the van's third row.

Megyn was shouting, too. From the tone of it and the anger in her face, she continued to berate her brother. He wagged his head and argued back, but Megyn's ferocity was clearly beating him into the ground.

"Okay," he bellowed. "Stop!" And then half a dozen syllables in Cantonese.

Everyone stopped.

Still sitting in the doorway, Sartaq pushed the barrel of the revolver up into the pale skin beneath Megyn's chin. He glared at Blake, and without looking, cocked the revolver.

Single action, Blake's mind said.

His eyes on Blake, Sartaq spoke in Cantonese. As he did, Megyn nodded from her imprisonment.

"If you want to see me alive," she translated, then stopped, barked something at Sartaq, and growled, "I don't believe this!"

Sartaq drew back the hand with the revolver, rapped her forehead with the muzzle, and then poked the gun under her chin again. A rivulet of bright red started down Megyn's temple.

Sartaq resumed calmly in Cantonese; Megyn translated, "If you want to see me alive, tell no one. No Police. Not your embassy. No one."

The blood dribbled into her eye. She flinched and flipped her head sideways, but that just made it worse. She scrunched the eye closed. But the sharp motion had speckled her tan jacket with dark, crimson spots. The drops soaked into the fabric and blossomed out.

Megyn continued translating her brother's words.

"Be in the lobby at the Marina Bay Sands Hotel in Singapore in two weeks. Sunday at Noon. He says he'll release me then."

She nodded to her brother. He shifted his feet in and moved to sit on the middle bench seat next to her.

Leaning forward, she said, "Blake, I—"

The van's sliding door cut her off.

The van lurched forward and accelerated down the hill toward the traffic signal, the street full of morning traffic.

* * *

Blake's paralysis broke.

"No!"

Ten feet ahead, the man in lime green and black straddling a stripped-down bicycle turned to look. His Lycra outfit and tiny backpack unmistakably identified him as a bike courier in the Guangzhou's business district. For quick communications in congested areas, bicycles easily beat taxis.

Blake bolted to him, grabbed the handlebars, and wrenched the bicycle forward pulling it out from between the rider's legs.

"Hey!"

Blake ran two steps and bounded on. His feet, long practiced at the mount, meshed with the already rotating pedals. He powered one, then the other, and in four strokes, the wind whistled in his ears.

It felt great to be moving, guiding his own path, in control of what would happen next.

At the bottom of the park, the van had already disappeared into a clot of traffic. Blake arrowed right and into the gap next to the parked cars. He veered to miss side mirrors on one side and the jockeying traffic on the other. He stretched up to scan ahead while still pumping the pedals.

Half a dozen vehicles away, the hind quarter of the white van popped into view. Its brake lights flashed, held solid for a moment as the rear end bobbed up, and then the lights winked off, and the tail of the van dipped. Ten seconds later, it repeated the dance.

Brake, then speed up. Over and over.

The van's driver jockeyed to escape, but the traffic boxed him in.

And Blake was used to vectoring around rocks in the Agua Fria river bottom. This bike seemed even lighter and more agile than his Cannondale.

The van tilted right, then swept out of sight to the left.

If they turned left, he would lose sight of the van.

Blake veered. Something steely blue with chrome honked as tires made a single *skritch*. Blake yanked to center his front tire on the white line one lane over, then stood and pumped the pedals to shoot forward, stretching to look again but his feet were almost going as fast as he could pump. He needed a higher gear.

He looked down but the shifter wasn't on the handlebar. He tilted his head to check along the top tube, then the diagonal tube going down to the sprocket.

No control, no shifter, no brake.

Fixie! His mind shouted.

A *fixie* had no gears. Instead, the pedal sprocket was chained directly to the back wheel. When the bike moved, the pedals turned. Back pressure could slow the rotation; that was how you slowed. Or jamming hard on both pedals at the same time would skid the back wheel for an emergency stop or make it easier to kick it out and then jet off in a different direction. Instant starts, stops, and turns. The combination made the bike more nimble than any other. It thrived on spurts and jumps in heavy traffic.

Blake grinned. In the morning crush, he had the advantage.

Two cars ahead in the center lane, the white van jagged and dipped like a prizefighter. The traffic light at the next intersection turned red, but the van sped up and swerved to get through.

Blake veered right and yanked the front wheel up to mount the curb to the sidewalk.

"Move!"

Pedestrians scattered like chickens.

But one of them, a man twenty then ten feet dead ahead, was completely blocking the way.

Deer in the headlights!

The man froze, his eyeballs and mouth opened wide, and his legs split shoulder width apart.

It was too late; the bicycle took him straight on.

The handlebar's head tube pressed into the soft flesh before finding the hard bone of the man's pelvis. Blake and the bike continued forward, and the man's torso began folding over the handlebars, his head skating down Blake's shirt, *thwaping* over his belt buckle, and striking the crossbar with his forehead. But before it could rebound, the solid crank drove Blake's knee up into the man's chin—*clack!*—and shoved his upper torso back up, completely off the bike and tumbling backwards into the pavement ahead of the bicycle. The man landed askew on his back. His eyes dropped to Blake's front wheel as it rolled for his privates.

Through the handlebars, Blake felt soft flesh and rubber tire compress to their respective limits. The front wheel bounded up. That was followed by the impact, compression, and similar bounding of the rear wheel.

"Sorry," Blake called over his shoulder as he thumped back down onto the sidewalk.

He scanned ahead. The van crept forward only half a block away. He'd be there in a few moments.

Then what?

Force it to stop?

Make everyone get out?

Grab Megyn and run?

He shook his head and focused on the cargo door. Get it open, then... something?

After three hard strokes on the pedals, he grabbed van door's handle and yanked. The rubber seal around the door made a sticky sound, and the door started back. But before it'd gone six inches, it reversed and slammed shut. Blake heard a solid *kerchunk* inside the door.

Up in the passenger side mirror, a face with round-lens glasses and long shaggy hair looked back at him as the van surged ahead.

Blake commanded his legs faster and faster with the maniacal pedals.

Plan? What's my plan?

They would expect him at the side door this time and maybe greet him with a bullet fired from inside. He needed a different spot.

Doors locked, the side windows, passenger and driver's side, were the only possibilities. He'd hit the passenger side sliding door already. Better switch sides.

Smash driver's window. Yank steering wheel. Crash van. Get Megyn!

But he knew that car windows were special; they are not plain glass. You needed a sharp point and a lot of pressure to break through auto glass. Blake remembered a YouTube of a man hammering the broken porcelain top of a spark plug into a car window. The voice-over explained that the hard-baked ceramic, when broken, had edges only a single molecule wide. Thrust or thrown hard into a car window, all the energy would transfer through a one molecule point. The window would shatter.

But Blake had no spark plug.

What else could he use?

In his shirt was a ball-point pen. No. Too blunt, the metal too soft.

Coins in his pockets? No. Copper, nickel, silver, and aluminum. Too soft. And rounded edges.

His ring of keys from home?

The key to his gun safe!

It had four coded ridges spaced around a central shaft for security. And made of high-carbon steel for strength, it had a sharpened point. Blake had used it to chip ice from frozen car locks, and to break up ice in a hotel's plastic bucket.

He joggled his hips to keep the bike on track as he fished out his keys. He positioned the safe key in his right fist, point down, ready to stab.

He chuffed as he pushed the pedals and shifted over to the van's left side. In the side mirror, the driver was hunched forward over the steering wheel. He glanced out as Blake powered up to the window. Over in the passenger seat with a map in his hand, another man with big, round glasses gestured at something ahead. The driver glanced ahead and nodded.

Blake cocked his right arm and drove the tip of the key into the side window.

It banged but skated off the glass.

Blake and the driver both looked at the point of impact.

No mark.

Force equals mass times velocity.

Blake slewed the bike left and then back right and hard into the van. Blake's arm, already primed, stabbed at the glass.

White fractures popped out in rays two inches long.

The driver's eyes stretched as his muddy complexion turned

noticeably darker.

Blake shimmied to regain his balance, raised his arm, tightened his grip, and bobbled the bike out and back, then jabbed at the starburst.

The glass exploded in a shower of tiny pieces!

The van jerked right half a lane.

Blake followed, thrust his arm through the now empty window, and grabbed the top of the steering wheel. He leaned and shoved the wheel right.

The van lurched away, but with Blake's hard grip on the steering wheel, he held on.

The driver used one hand to swat, slap, and try to peel Blake's fingers from the steering wheel as he fought with the other to correct the swerve. The van swayed and reeled, threatening to suck Blake and the bicycle under or throw them off.

The man in the passenger seat gestured ahead and shouted something for the driver. The boy and Blake both looked. A paved ramp, empty of traffic, led up to an overhead roadway that crossed at a right angle over the main street.

The van's front tire bounded through a pothole and shimmied.

The wheel in the cupped housing... it reminded Blake of a baseball pitching machine. It used a tire with a stationary shell kind'a like the van's front wheel. A ball tossed into the gap between tire and shell would rocket around and then shoot out the other side.

What would happen with something too big? Something manufactured with welded metal tubing? With needle-thin spokes? A steel chain? Metal sprockets like Ninja throwing stars?

Blake let go of the van's steering wheel and veered out five feet. Focusing on the gap behind the front wheel and its housing, he forced two grunting pumps on the pedals, veered in, and jumped straight up on contact.

There was a sound like thick cardboard grinding against hard rubber, but then it ratcheted up to screeching and grinding as the van's front wheel ingested the bicycle. The wheel ratcheted left making the van lurched into Blake on his way down. He had one set of his fingernails had the roof's rain gutter but most of his weight was on the other hand where he held himself up by the driver's outside mirror.

Something—the driver?—hit the brakes as it continued left. Blake flipped around to the front windshield. He pawed the smooth roof of the van and scrambled with the toes of his shoes for purchase.

The front wheel spewed mangled parts out the front, cleared the last of them, and then shot back to straight. The van seesawed as the driver fought for control. Perched on the toes of his shoes atop the front bumper with nothing to hang on to except windshield wipers, Blake tilted and wagged with the van's gyrations.

He looked in through the windshield and saw the one in the passenger seat thrust an arm to the right. The driver yanked the steering wheel with both hands that way. The van swept right and yanked the wipers away from Blake's fingers.

His feet hit the pavement first, but the backward momentum threw him down on his butt. He bounced, completed a three-quarter backflip, hit on his feet again, butt again, and skidded to a stop with his legs spread-eagled.

He turned to see the van bound up a steep ramp, crest at its top, and then vanish.

Megyn was gone.

Chapter 18

Minutes Later
Guangzhou and Points West

Lili slapped at Sartaq's gun.

"Put that away," she barked as the van loped across the next expansion joint in the elevated roadway.

"Careful," Sartaq yelped. "It might shoot!"

She flared at him. "How dare you kidnap me."

The morning sun beamed through the van's two back windows as it headed west from downtown Guangzhou.

"You've ruined this," she accused, pulling at her linen jacket to show him the blotches of blood. "And you left all my things. What were you thinking?"

Sartaq shrugged.

She was right; he didn't think. Kidnapping her was pure impulse. It came to him in a flash, so he just did it.

But now, after the American's ridiculous rescue attempt, he knew it was right.

"This is working," he grinned.

From the third-row seat behind Sartaq, Lin tapped Lili's shoulder.

"Let me see," he said.

She turned for him to examine the jacket. He shook his head.

"Hydrogen peroxide will take it out, but it'll bleach color." He glanced at Sartaq. "You ruined it."

Sartaq growled at the boy but said nothing.

Lin looked down to paw in his purse and came up with his make-up mirror. Lili nodded and reached over the seatback for it. Checking her forehead, she gave a huge, angry sigh.

"My make-up kit is back there, you know?" She shook her head. "And my passport. How do you expect me to get anywhere now?"

Sartaq hadn't thought of that. "I..." he started, paused, and then said, "We'll have to—" He clamped his mouth shut and shook his head. Stumped, he dared not admit it with his soldiers right there.

"Leaders lead," his mother lectured. He needed to lead, and leaders don't make mistakes.

Lin slid forward and handed his purse to Lili. She pawed through and discussed his makeup, what would work with her complexion and what wouldn't. They agreed his base would be too dark, but the blush, liquid eyeliner, pencil, and the brightest of his three lipsticks would work.

Turning to Lin when she finished, the boy did a meticulous inspection, then tossed back his shock of white hair and grinned.

"Royal princess!"

Lili grinned, but when she turned back to the front, it fell.

"Blake is loose now," she said, shaking her head. "What makes you think he won't call Police?"

Sartaq nodded slowly. "I saw how he looked at you. You did good job, Lili. He's hooked on you."

Lili took a breath to speak, but Sartaq held up a hand.

"American believes I would kill you. I made sure of that. As long as he thinks you are prisoner and I have gun to kill, he won't tell."

"Dammit, Taq, I had him under control. You didn't need to do that. Everything was set to get me into Singapore with him as my escort. I need him for that. I had it all planned out."

"*You* planned it all out," Sartaq said. It was a statement, not a question.

She fumed. "Yes, I planned it, with help from others, from very smart people. Taq, we've been working out options for years.

Singapore is your idea, yes, but details, exact steps of who, what, and where, had to be worked out. Dozens of people are involved, all working together to make this happen."

She took a breath. "Taq, you are tip of spear. Everything was proceeding as planned, but then you made up your own plan. You broke everything."

The five students were looking outside in different directions. None of them spoke.

Sartaq hissed back at her, "Because you leave things out. You always do. It's me that solves problems, makes your plan work."

They all leaned and put out hands for support as the van arced too fast around a long ramp.

"Sorry," Guo called back from the driver's seat.

Next to him, Zhou leaned forward to look up through the tops of his glasses at a huge green sign with white lettering. "Yes, this is it," he said, a finger on the map in his lap. "We stay on S15 to G15 South, then G80 West to Nanning. Five, maybe six hours. We get gas somewhere."

The van slapped across the joints between concrete slabs. When Guo merged them behind a gray Mercedes, he looked in the mirror at Sartaq. "Radio okay now?" He asked. "Good station here. Plays American—"

Lili's simmering boiled over again.

"What about that gun? Where did you get it? Did you pay money for it? With what I gave you? We need all of that. It's budgeted." She shook her head. "Taq, you've ruined everything."

"Look," he growled, "I did you favor. American boyfriend *should* be dead. He knows too much."

"Besides," he continued with a nod, "I'm working plan. Brick and gun make sure plan goes forward. Lili, I see how he looks at you. He'll stay quiet as long as you hostage."

"I don't know," she wagged her head, but seemed to calm down. "He's engineer, Taq. Very creative. And troubleshooter. He solves problems."

Sartaq guffawed. "With bicycle?"

"That was desperation," she conceded, her voice softening. "But he tried. That just proves what I'm saying."

Sartaq snorted. "No. American is—" He turned to the front and called louder. "What is English word? Means clumsy-stupid?"

"Klutz?" Guo called back from the driver's seat.

"Dickhead!" Lin offered shaking his white mane.

Zhou offered, "Boob?"

"Asshole?"

"Fuck brain?"

Yang won the prize: "Pussy-face, tit-face, dickface?"

They all laughed.

Lili was unable to dismiss her grin, "But what about money you spent for gun, Taq? We will be short."

He asked triumphantly, "Who can get money at A-T-M?"

All five recruits raised their hands.

"See?" Sartaq laughed. "We don't need silly envelopes. Never have. Need money? We get money."

Out the back window, Guangzhou's taller buildings had disappeared behind the nearby shorter ones.

Sartaq took two envelopes from his pocket and handed them forward. "But here's Lili's envelope for tolls, and one for gas and food. How much more do we need?"

Yang summarized their upcoming expenses. "For bribes and budgeted supplies, ten thousand RMB here and in Vietnam. Another thousand in Singapore dollars when we get there. But an extra 25% in each currency might be good idea."

Guo kept to the right lane at the posted speed limit. The divided highway was smooth and nearly empty.

After a while, Sartaq asked in a loud voice, "When do we get to shipyard?"

Zhou studied the map. "We leave toll road at Nanning, but next highway winds in mountains." He looked back over his shoulder at Sartaq and shrugged. "Dirt road across border is not on map, but after that—"

Lili interrupted. "Beishan Mountain should be on map. Islamic State arranged our crossing there. When we exit from toll road, zero trip odometer. Envelope for border has written distance to turnoff."

Guo looked back in the rearview mirror again at Sartaq.

"Dinner?"

"Snack when stop for gas. Lili's plan says we make crossing tonight before Eight."

She clarified. "Islamic State set it up."

"Eight o'clock should be easy," Zhou said, holding up the map.

Sartaq announced. "Supplies and late dinner in Vietnam."

"They recommended Lạng Sơn," Lili supplied.

Sartaq warned everyone. "That'll be last regular meal for long time."

After a moment, he leaned forward and squeezed Lili's shoulder. "I know you didn't plan being with us. We get you extra supplies for ship. Anything you want."

Lili flipped a lapel of her linen jacket with her fingers. "My ensemble is not exactly designed for two weeks roughing it."

"We get new clothes when stop for supplies."

"In Lạng Sơn?" Lili shook her head. "Jungle-camo fatigues maybe, but not likely my size."

Lin Yusheng frowned but chuckled. "Greens and grays with your complexion? I don't think so."

"No, thank you," Lili said to Sartaq. "I'll have to get by in these until Singapore."

Guo glanced back. "Now can I turn on radio?"

Sartaq nodded.

Short snatches of words and music tracked the radio's tuning. Finally, a fuzz-box guitar riff with a pounding drum filled the van.

Zhou trumpeted, "Steppenwolf!"

All five students started moving with the heavy acid beat. Yang, sitting next to Lili, drummed on the back of Guo's seat. Zhou slapped a quarter-note beat on the paper map in his lap. In the far back, Lin flung his head left and right playing air guitar. On Lili's other side, Fan, his eyes closed, thrust his chin forward with the beat.

At the chorus, they all sang together.

Lili translated for Sartaq: "Born to be Wild."

But as the kids sang and danced in their seats, it seemed odd to Sartaq that they could be so exuberant while knowing they were going to die in a week. He wondered if they weren't so committed as they claimed to be? The trio at the library that he'd had to prepare in a rush, setting off their explosives two minutes ahead of schedule guaranteed success. And he had the parts if he needed to do that again.

Seemed like a good idea. He'd still need them to put their explosives in the right place, but as he'd done for the Old Library, he'd blow them all up two minutes early.

And if they thought they were fooling him for a trip to Singapore, they'd be pulverized before realizing they'd made a mistake.

Sartaq frowned. They wouldn't know he'd beat them.

But dead is dead.

He smiled at the music and started nodding with the beat.

An hour after bribing their way into Vietnam, Lạng Sơn lay before them on the side of a meandering river delta. Traffic on the main roads looked dense, and shops were busy.

They pulled into Big C's graveled parking lot after crossing 1A and bouncing over a berm with railroad tracks.

Sartaq handed out the shopping lists.

"Get everything," he said, then nodded toward Lili. "And extra blanket and food."

"And more cash," Zhou reminded them. "Each one get twenty-four hundred RMB from ATM." He pointed toward the Currency Exchange booth. "I'll exchange mine for Singapore dollars."

After stepping out, Lin stopped and faced back to Lili. "Anything special? Makeup, ladies' needs, pink army fatigues with mint-green combat boots?"

She grinned and shook her head. "No but thank you. I'll be fine."

After Sartaq's five soldiers headed off to shop, he slid the door shut.

"Sorry I was rough today," he said, Lili's face looking paler in the bluish light coming in through the windows. "The American had to believe it was real."

Lili's hand went up to the black scab on her forehead. "This is probably going to scar, you know? You could've given me warning."

"It just came to me," Sartaq shrugged.

"You were improvising?"

He nodded.

"Well," she took a breath, "That's not how I would've handled it. All we can do now is hope you're right."

Sartaq almost laughed. "I am. He's hooked on you. Anyone can see that."

"Maybe."

Sartaq shook his head. "That bike he tried in Guangzhou against our van? That was stupid."

Lili looked thoughtful. "I'll bet he went back and bought new one for owner."

Sartaq's jaw dropped, but he said nothing.

Lili's voice was gentle, her eyes downcast. "He's good man, Taq."

Sartaq huffed, "Waste."

Lili turned. Her gaze flicked between his eyes like she was looking inside.

"He's what you and I used to be long time ago."

"I was never like that."

"Yes, you were. Once. He makes me feel comfortable and safe. Like you did."

"We don't need him."

"I do, Taq. You don't travel so you don't know. He's my excuse... *was* my excuse to get into Singapore." She glanced out the window. "Guess I won't need that now."

Sartaq took a quick breath. "See? I told you we don't need him. He mess things up."

She didn't move.

"You will get over him, Lili."

She took one of his muscled hands in both of her small, pale ones.

"I've never lost my feelings for you, Taq. You're my brother. We grew up together. I know you're angry about Blake, and I understand what you must be feeling. But please trust me, he's not taking your place. He's just... different... In my life, I mean. I can't explain. I've never felt like this before. But no matter what, Taq, you will always be my brother, my big brother who takes care of me."

Her soft eyes always worked. He didn't feel like a big brother. Instead, he wanted to lay his head on her shoulder, feel her hand stroking his hair, hear her voice making those little animal sounds like when they were little. She was the one that would comfort him when their mother raged. She was the one who calmed him when the neighbors called him names.

"And," she said softer, "what we're doing is so important. Remember why we're doing this, for your people and for mine. We've worked all our lives for this. We're going to bring good things to China, you and me."

He thought she understood. "Lili, I don't care about China. Singapore is for Xinjiang independence, for East Turkestan."

Lili said nothing.

"East Turkestan is my country, Lili, not China."

She laid her hand on his cheek and turned his face out of the light.

"Taq, you are as Chinese as I am."

Sartaq laughed and pulled away. "I am not! You've been in America too long. Lili, I am Uyghur, not Han. Mirror shows me; neighbors in Wuchang tell me; face tells me. I am not like you, Lili."

He leaned into the light again.

"And I am *piroytki*. Half-breed. Some like you, some not. My father was Uyghur. I look like him, like his father, aunts, uncles, and cousins. Their ancestors are Uyghur. They live, father to son to his son, many times over. All Uyghur. Their country is East Turkestan not Xinjiang, Lili, and not China. It is East Turkestan. Beijing is locking up Uyghurs, millions of my brothers and sisters, in their *re-education camps*."

She tried to turn away, but he took her jaw and turned her head. "Lili, look. This is Uyghur!"

She pulled her face loose from his fingers. "I wish you wouldn't say that, Taq. You're my brother. We have same mother. You are Han, family Shen like me. Our fathers are dead, but they don't matter."

"No!" Sartaq's shout made the van vibrate.

"Father matters! I am Khan. My father was Khan Batu. I am Khan Sartaq. My family, my grandfather—all of them—live in Kashgar. I was born in East Turkestan. My life began there, and that is where I found out what my life is for. I have Khan blood, the blood of Genghis and Kublai. Warrior blood!"

His chin and lips felt wet. He wiped them with a hand and shook his head.

"You do what you want, Lili, but I fight for East Turkestan. Later, what you do with China—make it democracy or make it hell —I don't care!"

Close to midnight with the van swaying from the supplies and the seven of them, Guo slowed the van and crunched to a halt before a closed gate. Its sign read, "Doan Xa Terminal and Bonded Warehouse, Haiphong."

The guard, addressed as Michael and bribed with an envelope of money, walked the gate open.

Guo drove the van slowly behind him and deep into the storage yard where the guard unlocked and opened a second gate. After another fifty paces, he stopped at the small end of a dark red, twelve-meter-long shipping container.

Using a key from his pocket instead of those on the ring at his waist, he opened a circular padlock on the door, cut a stiff wire with pliers, and undogged four locking bars. The double doors shuddered when he yanked them open.

In the van's headlights, the inside looked like a steel dungeon. Corrugated red panels made up the walls and ceiling. In the center of the plywood floor, a four-level pyramid of white cardboard boxes were stacked on two pallets. Z-shaped, bright yellow clamps had been screwed into the plywood on each side, and thick hemp ropes tied the stack to steel-loop tie-points in each corner. The rest of the container was empty.

This would be their home, their campground, for nine days.

Sartaq directed the transfer: toilets in the back, living and sleeping in front, and general storage to next to the pyramid.

Van empty, Sartaq instructed Guo to drive five minutes, park somewhere legal, and throw the keys into a wooded area as he walked back.

"Everyone inside," Sartaq ordered. "Close doors."

Everything went pitch black when the rubber seals on the doors mated with the container.

Light flickered through the blades of four fans at the far end. Lin spoke like he was reading from a book. "Adults need cubic meter of air every four or five minutes. For seven of us, that's two cubic meters per minute."

Fan picked up the calculations. "Small computer fans move three cubic meters per minute, but those are bigger. We get plenty of air."

An hour passed before footsteps, two pairs, crunched through the gravel outside and stopped near the double doors. Jerked open, Guo nodded to the guard before stepping in.

The guard waited.

"Bathroom break," Sartaq ordered. "One bucket. Last person put on lid, but not close hard."

Lin unwrapped the six-pack of Febreeze and set them near the buckets.

Five minutes later, Sartaq bobbed his head to the waiting guard. From the outside, he worked each door deep into the rubber seals, and from the sound, he dogged each of the four floor-to-ceiling latches on their steel prison. The padlock's *scrape and snap* preceded a noisy scratch of steel wire being threaded through steel. There was a final, squeaky *scrunch*.

"Lead inspection seal," Zhou's voice confirmed in the dark.

The guard's footsteps crunched, faded, and were finally gone.

"Toaster oven camping," Yang announced.

Lili sounded confident. "Sharmarke loading will be early. It's scheduled to depart at 7:40 on its regular circuit."

"All right," Sartaq ordered. "Get blankets and sleep. No talking."

Sartaq spread his in the dark and covered himself. Rolling onto his side, he used an arm for a pillow. Lili settled down next to him. Her breath, warm and sweet like a summer night, drifted across his face. He loved her as the little sister she'd always been, and he would protect her. But all grown up, he couldn't hug her; his body always responded to her beauty, to her scent.

He listened. Her breathing became slow and deep, like an exhausted kitten. Her throat made a puttering sound. Sartaq had never heard a woman snore, had never slept with one. Laid down, yes. Fucked and been fucked. But there was money. His money.

Her purring made him feel... He wanted to cry but didn't know why.

A reverberating clang jolted Sartaq awake.

Overhead, something bounced, metal against metal, then skidded and screeched.

Brilliant sunlight strobed through the blades of the ventilation fans. Lili sat wedged into a corner, her eyes bright within blackened hollows.

Smudged eye makeup?

She stared at him, wide-eyed with her fingers gripping the edge of the plywood decking.

A bang like a hammer sounded in the corner above her head. She ducked. Then, another bang sounded in the corner above Sartaq's head, and finally two more at the far end.

Outside, a voice shouted, "Yo!"

Their world—the container and everything in it—launched straight up. It paused and bounced for a moment, then racked upwards and then sideways. The howl of distant electric motors added to the zing of steel cables.

Lili stage whispered. "Sharmarke. We're being loaded."

After a long, sideways trundle, their shipping container plummeted, bounced once at the end of a springy cable, then slammed hard and flat onto steel.

"Ow!" Sartaq grimaced, rubbing the bone at the bottom of his spine.

Four metal-on-metal shots came up from below, followed by squeaky ones overhead. Electric motors chorused again, but this time, their world stayed put.

Clangs, shots, and the howl of big electric motors continued for a while but grew distant. The slits of flickering light through the fans crept down the wall. Only pencil-thin slivers of light remained when all the noise stopped.

Sartaq felt a low rumble beneath them.

"Ship's engine?" Guo guessed.

They were underway. A little over a week to Singapore with one stop.

"Depending..." Lili had said.

Chapter 19

Sunday, November 5
Singapore (Equator)

"Blake, over here!"

A compact Malaysian man in a bulky gray suit, white shirt, and blue-striped tie waved from the crowd. His upraised arm, bare to the elbow, was dark and muscular. Most others in the Arrivals area wore t-shirts, shorts, and open sandals.

Two degrees north of the equator, Singapore was hot, humid, and lush year-round.

Blake carefully balanced two sets of luggage, his and Megyn's, on their wheels before taking the offered hand.

"Hi, Mickey. Great to see you again."

Mickey squeezed like he was gripping a Bullseye pistol. Blake grinned and responded in kind.

When they shook, something heavy bounced under Mickey's jacket on the left.

Nine-millimeter automatic?

They'd met two years ago at Ohio's Camp Perry. The National Guard training facility occupied a wide stretch of shore near the Toledo-end of Lake Erie. The NRA ran the National Championships, rifle then pistol. The contest, always around July 4th, had repeated annually for a hundred years except during war time. It attracted the best rifle and pistol shooters from around the world.

Assigned to adjacent firing points two years ago, Mickey and Blake became good friends.

Blake glanced at the shiny top of Mickey's head.

"What happened to your hair, Inspector Chee?"

Micky blushed through his sienna complexion. "Completely gone on top now. And the fringe on the sides is thinning fast." He straightened his jacket in a mock huff. "As compensation, however, you may address me as *Senior* Station Inspector."

Blake put up his hands. "No chewing gum, Officer. Honest."

Mickey pouted. "But I like Juicy Fruit." He pointed to Blake's two stacks of luggage. "Can I take one of those?"

Outside the airport, Blake stopped to inhale the heady aromas from the profuse greenery. Nearly daily rainfall and lots of sun made Singapore's untended areas dense jungles. But the meticulously manicured landscaping along the roads and in public areas showed the city's constant attention. Excellent roads, a light rail transit system second to none in the world, and constant attention to cleanliness made Singapore a pleasure to visit.

The snack on the four-hour Cathay Pacific flight from Hong Kong had done nothing for Blake's taste buds. He was ready for something *interesting*, and he knew Mickey and Singapore would not disappoint.

Mickey nodded toward a four-story parking structure. "Car's this way."

The two nearly identical stacks of luggage, each with a black computer case atop a black wheeled bag, clacked on the expansion gaps as they walked.

Blake felt wet under his arms within seconds. Teaching at the Paya Lebar Air Base, Blake had needed two clean shirts per day, and then another for dining out after. He bundled laundry for the hotel's exorbitantly priced overnight service twice a week. It was a helpful deduction on his Schedule C tax form to offset some of the income.

This week, however, he would be spending his own money.

"Camp Perry was, what? Two years ago?" Blake asked. "You out-shot me by ten points and four Xs."

"Sounds close," Mickey said and punched the button for the elevator. "I earned my Master Class certificate that week. It's on the wall of my cubicle."

"Congratulations," Blake said sincerely. A Master-class shooter would score 95 out of 100 on almost all his targets. Blake hadn't made it there yet. "I'm still Expert," he confessed.

They stepped in when the doors opened, and Mickey pushed the button for the third floor.

"I was Expert for eight years," he said. "You just have to keep at it. But you know that." He glanced up as the floor indicator flicked to three. "Do you ever see that redhead, the one you cross-fired in the finals?"

It was Blake's turn to blush.

"Colleen. We'd just finished 45 Slow Fire. In my 'scope, I could only find eight holes. I thought I must have two doubles, but then I heard her complain. 'I've got twelve holes. Anybody need two?'"

Mickey laughed, pointed down a long row of expensive-looking cars, and started walking.

Blake confessed. "There were two 8s in her target. Probably my shots. All hers with 9s, 10s, and Xs. She was understandably pissed and chose to re-shoot the whole target. I was so embarrassed. I butchered my next target."

Mickey nodded as they walked.

Blake realized this was the first time he'd thought about anything other than Megyn's kidnapping. He'd been re-running what'd happened, what he did, what he didn't do, and especially what he should've done ever since.

Singapore might, for a little while at least, be a distraction.

And when he got Megyn back in two weeks...

The trunk on a white Volvo S90 popped open a few steps ahead. Mickey let Blake put his stack in first.

"Nice car!"

"*Senior* Station Inspector," Mickey answered. "Rank hath its privileges."

Blake hesitated. "I don't mean to pry, but I thought cars were expensive here. You dealing narcotics on the side or something?"

Mickey grinned. "The permit costs more than the car, and no, it's not mine. Belongs to the department."

Police Department, Blake reminded himself.

Sartaq's threat had been clear. He'd kill Megyn if Blake talked.

Mickey was a cop. A *Senior* cop with decades of practice listening to people and knowing when they lied, when they were hiding something.

Stupid.

He agreed with the thought. This was really stupid. Last person on Earth he needed to be around was a cop.

Blake closed his eyes. *Stop*, he answered the argument in his head. *Mickey's a good friend. I need that right now. I just have to be careful.*

He walked to the right side of the Volvo, opened the door, and stopped. In front of that seat was a steering wheel.

Mickey was standing behind him. "Sorry, but I can't let you drive. Department rules."

Blake laughed at himself. He'd forgotten Singapore had been a British colony. They stayed left on the road, so the driver sat on the right.

"My bad," he said and went around to the other side and climbed in. It felt vacuous and empty with no steering wheel in front of him or pedals on the floor. He wanted to hold on to something but knew from experience that the feeling would soon pass.

Mickey leaned forward to turn the ignition switch. As he did, the slit at the bottom of his jacket opened to reveal the handle of what must be another small automatic in the small of his back. Mickey carried two guns, one in a shoulder holster and the second in an IWB, In-Waist Band. Blake guessed he might have a third carry, a snubby most likely, in an ankle holster. Blake resisted the urge to look down at the cuffs of Mickey's pants to see which leg it was on.

Mickey flashed his Police ID badge at the tollbooth, and the attendant waved them through.

They entered the divided highway at a sign marked ECP South,

"East Coast Parkway" Blake knew from his previous visits. English was the official state language in Singapore, but Mandarin, Cantonese, Malay, and Tamil would also be heard on the streets. But outside of the ethnic districts, most signage would be in English. It was an easy country for Americans.

Out the car's window to the left, a dozen large ships dotted the smooth surface a mile or so out, their decks universally stacked with containers. Singapore was an ideal drop-off and pickup location, much like airline's hub-and-spoke systems. Shipping going west from China, Japan, and eastern Russia had to go right past the tiny island state. And container vessels from Africa, India, and dozens of small nations around the Indian Ocean rounded the Malay horn headed the other way.

For millennia, Singapore had been the home of sea-faring pirates, thieves, and murderers.

The British Navy civilized matters in the nineteenth century. Illegal piracy stopped. But its legal form, government taxation, replaced it. And that proved to be even more lucrative.

Container freight revolutionized shipping. Companies could lease a container, fill it with their goods, and then contract an expediter to move it from point A to B. They would then rent space on ships with regular routes, and shift the container across multiple legs, dropping off and picking up at intermediate ports for the next ship. Singapore's dock yards passed thousands of containers and taxed each one.

But it was the burgeoning aircraft maintenance industry that brought Blake to the little island twice before. As airplanes aged and newer, more efficient models took off from the factories in Everett Washington, Toulouse France, and Hamberg Germany, the older planes were sold, and most often to customers in Asia.

Singapore hosted a dozen refitting companies, many of them at the Paya Lebar Air Base five miles west of the international airport. Walking in the mornings from the security entrance to one of his teaching assignments, Blake took the long way so he could peer into the giant hangers and marvel as the huge aircraft were bathed, painted, and relabeled.

Blake fingered the Volvo's dash vent to aim the air at his face.

He closed his eyes and leaned back. When the car rolled over a bump, it brought back the image of Megyn being tossed into the open maw of the white van. He clamped his jaw tight, shook his head to dispel the vision, and opened his eyes.

Mickey was looking at him.

"Sorry," Blake confessed. "I'm a little pre-occupied."

"If I can help..."

"Thanks," Blake started, then stopped himself.

He's a cop. He'll know you're hiding something.

"Problem at work," he lied.

Mickey nodded.

Blake turned to watch the streets outside. After several minutes, they turned from Ang Mo Kio Avenue 3 into Ang Mo Kio Avenue 10. And, shortly thereafter, onto Ang Mo Kio Street 44.

"Is this area Ang Mo Kio?"

"Yes. It comes from a *rambutan* orchard that used to be here. Literally, it means red-hair, like the fruit. But it's all HDB now— Housing Development Board."

Mickey turned his face to watch the back-up LCD and maneuvered them into a numbered parking space.

He hooked a thumb over his shoulder. "My building is behind us: four sixty-seven."

When Blake got out, he looked up at the fourteen-story tan and red high-rise with "467" painted near the top. Around the parking area were four more tan and red structures. Only the numbers differed.

Mickey pointed between the buildings as they rolled the two sets of bags onto the concrete walkway. "The hawker center is about three hundred meters up that way. There's a McDonalds a little farther on if you'd prefer."

Blake shook his head. "The hawker center will be great, and I'm starved. Is it a big one or just three or four lunch counters? What about a grocery? And a fruit stand, maybe? I could do with some Durian for dessert."

He'd eaten the spike-skinned fruit twice and enjoyed its overripe taste and pudding-like texture. One of his students at the air base told him the flavor depended on the eater's genes; either you enjoyed it, or you had the gene that made you puke.

Mickey grimaced. "Not me. But you're in luck. There are eight booths in our hawker center. Everything from Malay to Indian, sushi, and American hamburgers with fries and shakes. And in the market area, you'll find a vendor with several kinds of Durian. I'm told his prices are high, but everything is supposedly fresh. Eat that by yourself, though. And don't bring it inside my place."

They rode up the steamy elevator in the center of the building. Blake's face was dripping again by the time they reached the open-sided balcony. Mickey's apartment, 916, was small with haphazard looking furniture. Nothing matched. Blake guessed they were leftovers from Mickey's divorce. That was another bond between them, being single. Again.

There was a good size central room with kitchen appliances on the left wall. Three doors to what he presumed would be two bedrooms and a bath were on the right. On the far wall, a dark brown striped couch sat behind a glass-top coffee table with two black faux-leather chairs. Next to Blake's right hand was a long and low, blond-wood table with a huge LCD television, DVD player, and an iPod stereo flanked by two small speakers. A white plastic saucer with a brass key sat nearest his fingertips.

"That's for you," Mickey pointed to the dish. "Singapore looks safe, but don't you believe it. Take the key and keep the door locked all the time, in or out."

Blake chuckled. "Just like home."

He followed Mickey to the right and into the second bedroom.

A trio of musical notes came from Mickey's jacket.

"Excuse me," he said, retrieving his cell phone. He tapped it once.

"This is Chee."

His voice sounded deeper, more officious than in the car.

"Yes," he said into the phone. "I read the report."

He gave a half-wave to Blake and stepped back into the main room.

Blake looked around his bedroom. He'd have a queen size bed with what looked to be a polyester blanket. Behind it was a dark headboard leaning against the wall. It looked like standard fare for a Holiday Inn Express. On the right side of the bed was a small square table with a lamp. On the left, nothing. Against that wall near the foot of the bed was an ornate Asian, black lacquer armoire with brass hardware. Against the wall on the right, magazines sat on the carpet in four stacks.

Mickey came back in. "Consider this your home." He swept his hand around. "I did the sheets yesterday. I'll be working during the week and whenever they call, which is often as you can see. Get yourself settled, and as soon as you're ready, we'll go down to the hawker center for dinner. I'll show you the ATM there if you need cash. None of the vendors in this block take credit cards. You'll need Singapore dollars or Chinese Yuan. Afterwards, we'll walk down to the MRT and I'll show you how to get around on the train."

"I've ridden it," Blake huffed and was surprised at his impatience.

"Mickey," he apologized, "you're being very generous. I'm here for two weeks. If that's too long, I can shift to a hotel."

That was a lie. There was no way he could afford a Singapore hotel for that long. The money he'd budgeted before leaving was for China, not Singapore. Expenses here would be five, maybe ten times as much.

"No, no," Mickey shook his head, "two weeks is fine. It'll be good to have some company. Gives me a reason to get out. I spend too much time cooped up here. Singapore has a lot. I'll enjoy showing you around. You knew the good places around Camp Perry, so now it's my turn." Mickey's face brightened. "Come to think of it, let me check something."

He walked out of the guest bedroom to the kitchen. Blake followed.

Mickey put his finger on a one-month, computer printed calendar hanging by plastic-flower magnets on the front of the refrigerator.

"Yep. There's a 2700 Friday after next. Would you be up for that?"

Blake's mind flashed up the image of Sartaq pointing a gun at him with Megyn standing between them, her arms out. If Blake had had a gun then, he would've used it without hesitation and according to all his drilled combat sequences. Sartaq would be dead, and Megyn would be here. But he didn't have a gun then, and he didn't have one now.

"I'll loan you guns," Mickey offered.

"Is that legal?" Blake asked. "Aren't firearms forbidden here? You're a cop, but..."

"Yes and no," Mickey shrugged. "The permits exist, but they're difficult to get. Basically, you have to know someone. But since I'm a cop—a *Senior Station Investigator* cop—I'm in. There's a dozen of us who shoot both Bullseye and International, so I've got all the hardware you'll need.

"But," Mickey added, "this'll be strictly at the range. Anywhere else and you'd get locked up for several years. Our laws are quite severe in that respect."

Blake nodded. A match would be a distraction from his worries. The concentration needed over a full-blown match would blot out everything else. It was every bit as effective, more so perhaps, than a Buddhist meditation or a bottle of wine.

Mickey continued in a mock-whisper. "There's one thing. Don't ask about the ammo. My boss has the S&W 38 and the 45 ACP custom-loaded in Indonesia. He puts it down as practice ammo in his department expense reports. And it's good stuff. It'll hold an inch at fifty yards if the gun is up to it."

Blake had shot Bullseye in Chicago with a gun borrowed from the uniformed officer at the next firing point. If a cop said it was okay, that was good enough for him.

"Sounds great. Count me in."

Mickey grinned, "The Chief of Police calls the line. We rarely get guests, especially one that can actually shoot a respectable score. Everyone will enjoy it."

Twenty minutes later, Mickey had changed to a blue and white squiggly-print shirt with khaki long pants and running shoes. But compared to everyone else in the outdoor picnic area next to the hawker stalls, he looked very dressy. Blake's plain shirt, blue jeans, and similar shoes left no doubt he was American.

Blake looked at Mickey's tail-out shirt and asked, "You carrying?"

Mickey nodded. "People hold grudges."

Back in Phoenix, some of Blake's Bullseye pals were LEOs, Law Enforcement Officers. They carried everywhere, too.

Mickey pushed rice around a chunk of curried lamb on his paper plate, smoothly picked it up with his chopsticks, and asked, "Were you teaching last week in Hong Kong?" He popped it into his mouth and started chewing.

Blake shook his head as he tried the same with stir-fried chicken in a dark brown Malaysian glaze, but the rice wouldn't stay put.

Mickey asked, "You want a spoon? The soup place has them."

Blake pushed chicken and rice into a corner, worked his chopsticks under, and then bent over to shorten the lift to his mouth.

"Just passing through from Wuhan after a night in Guangzhou," he said around the food.

He suddenly felt uneasy, like he'd said something he shouldn't.

But the words just kept coming.

"We were on our way here," his mouth continued, "after two weeks at the University."

Mickey stopped, his chopsticks mid-air. "Last week? At the University? Wuhan University?"

Blake kept chewing but wondered if his unconscious had taken over to unburden itself, share troubles with a friend?

But he also knew this would be a bad idea since his friend was a cop.

"Uh, yeah," Blake said. "The kids were great, but, well, some things happened. Overall, I'd have to say it was a mixed experience."

Mickey put his chopsticks down and put one hand atop the other across the slight bulge of his stomach. He waited.

Blake looked around, then finally down to his plate. "Awful, really." He chased a piece of chicken but couldn't get a good grip on it. "Actually, other than my wife's suicide, this was...." He paused. "No, this was worse."

Blake silently cursed himself. Part of him knew he needed to get this out, to talk it through with someone. But this wasn't the place, and it sure as hell wasn't the right person.

Mickey's intense stare made Blake squirm.

"I've seen little TV," Blake said. "And everything was in Mandarin. Nothing in English, so I don't know what's been on the news here."

Mickey reached across the table and stopped Blake's chopstick hand.

"How much did you see, of the bombing, I mean?"

Blake shrugged with a nod. "A lot."

Mickey waited.

Blake took a deep breath.

"The blast came through at an angle, behind from the right." He pointed with his chopsticks. "Shattered all the windows. I was right next to a concrete pillar, and I guess it shielded me from the glass. But it hit a lot of the kids. No warning, and they were looking almost in that direction; three-quarter, I'd say. One boy, his name was Alex—they take American names for their English classes, was right in front of me. A big piece of glass—"

Blake's throat cramped. He grimaced, closed his eyes, and turned his head.

Mickey asked in an even voice, "Did you see the blast site itself?"

Blade nodded. "Fifteen, twenty minutes later I'd guess, after the emergency crew got to our classroom. Some students walked over with me. There wasn't anything left. Just big piles of wrecked things. Off to the side, this huge blue flame was roaring up from the ground. Natural gas, I think. They said it was the main feed to the building. In the middle of what my students said was the building's main floor, it looked like someone had swept it clean with a broom. Nothing at all except a few leaves that'd blown in. And right in the middle, a big black scorch mark. I could scuff it with my shoe."

Mickey's eyes narrowed.

Blake added, "They said it was a gas leak in an underground

service tunnel, but I don't think that's right. That would've pushed up the concrete up from below, but I didn't see anything like that."

Mickey's eyes gazed in the distance for a moment.

"Blake," he said, "I'm going to tell you something. It's confidential. You cannot repeat it."

"Okay. Confidential," Blake said with a shrug.

Mickey's forehead furrowed. "I'm not kidding. You could be locked up if you repeat this."

"Okay," Blake said, much slower.

"We received an advisory from ICB; that's our International Cooperation Bureau. Chinese State Security has confirmed it was a bomb. The did a residue analysis of that blackened area you mentioned. Nitroglycerin and a stabilizer. You'd call it Dynamite. Their comparing the composition to known manufacturers."

Blake nodded slowly. "I'm not surprised. But why didn't they just come out and say that?"

Mickey tossed imaginary fluff with one hand. "The CCP doesn't advertise its internal problems."

"Chinese Communist Party?" Blake asked to be sure.

Mickey nodded. "When their senior members come here, they keep us informed."

He continued. "The communique said there were two explosions not quite twenty meters apart, one several times bigger than the other."

Mickey squinted his eyes in thought for a moment.

"Two bombs that close together, they would've needed det-cord to make sure the detonations were synchronized."

Blake's mind latched onto that last word.

"But in an open, public place like a college library," Mickey said, apparently thinking out loud, "that would not be possible."

"How close?" Blake asked. "How close in time would the two have to be triggered?"

Mickey shrugged. "How fast is a shock wave across twenty meters? A few hundredths of a second? Maybe thousandths?"

The math was easy but involved several guesses. It started out at several times the speed of sound—Blake decided to use 5X—but slowed quickly. For the distance, he'd use the number Mickey'd just mentioned and assume the velocity a constant. So, 20 meters divided by about 1750 meters per second—make it easy, he thought, make it 20 divided by 2000. Ten milliseconds.

Alex's boxes were two orders of magnitude, more than 100 times, better than that.

They used WiFi. Blake remembered Sartaq's dancing in the walkway just after the blast. With only a ten second delay, he would've had a transmitter with him.

Blake nodded slowly. Alex's receiver in the classroom would've synchronized with it. They'd seen the actual countdown.

Blake grimaced. If they'd only known!

Mickey was still going. "Witnesses reported three students at a table under the building's central dome. It's pretty sure they were the bombers at the biggest explosion. The smaller one—I'm guessing now—maybe it was a latecomer or someone chickening out? It's an intriguing oddity."

"Poor kids," Blake said.

"And another thing," Mickey said, his face scrunched. "The report listed the casualties in an adjacent auditorium before those in the main building. Why'd they make two lists? The first one also mentioned the auditorium was below grade—two meters, they said. I suppose that explains the difference, but why tell us?"

Blake picked up his chopsticks, put a piece of chicken in his mouth, and started chewing.

"Anyone claim responsibility?"

"Always," Mickey chuffed as if Blake had made a joke. "The usual suspects."

Mickey put a hand behind his neck and rolled his head. "Maybe some religious zealots like that Buddhist monk that burned himself up? Or a group of militant students? China has its internal issues, but you probably haven't heard of most of them. They keep things zipped up pretty tight."

Blake wanted to say that he'd seen the perp after the explosion, but if he did, that would lead to the next detail. He'd better stop now, or he'd tell Mickey everything, and Sartaq would kill Megyn. He couldn't risk it.

What happened in China was China's problem, and Megyn was his. What would happen in Singapore would be Mickey's problem.

Blake would play along.

He smiled at Mickey. "That all sounds very credible. Afraid I can't add anything."

Mickey scratched under his nose and folded his hands. He looked at Blake and smiled. There was an intensity in his eyes.

"A moment ago, you said, *We*. '*We* were on our way home.' Who is *we*, Blake?"

Blake tried to shrug casually. "A friend, that's all. We met years ago. Work stuff. Her family's in China, somewhere outside of Wuhan, she said. She's visiting them. I didn't see her very much on the trip."

In his mind, he saw again her twirling figure wrapped in colorful silk with Shanghai glittering through...

Mickey was watching him.

Blake's voice wobbled as words came out. "Mickey, she's... I think... We're... I hope..."

Mickey waited, his eyes not moving.

It rushed out. "She's coming here in two weeks.".

A tiny corner of Mickey's lip twitched up.

"And," he pried, "you already have her luggage. How convenient."

Blake's mind reeled. Another mistake. What else had he leaked?

He made up a story. "She's home with her family. We thought it would be easier, less embarrassing, if I brought a few of her things now. She said her mother is very traditional, and since I'm not Chinese..." He let it drop.

To his relief, Mickey backed off.

"I see. Well, let's get you some rest, my friend. You can show her around when she gets here—with another suitcase or two. In the meantime, you'll have my apartment all day while I'm at work. No one will disturb you. Sleep, hit the food court, ride the MTA, whatever you want."

Mickey paused, then leaned forward with a friendly smile on his face. "But don't think the memories of what you witnessed in Wuhan will go away. That explosion, those kids in your classroom, the destruction you saw... Those things won't go away on their own, my friend. They'll change you, and not in a good way."

Blake bit his lip and nodded. After Julie's suicide, he'd spent nearly a thousand on grief counseling. And the help that man provided, the listening, the ways he helped Blake move through the grief, of putting Julie's actions—Julie's actions, not his—in perspective, was worth every damn penny.

"I deal with trauma a lot," Mickey continued. "Try me when you want to talk. Blake, we've shot side by side. You know that takes trust. I'll do what's best for you, no matter what."

Blake nodded, but until this was over, he knew that wouldn't be possible. "Maybe later."

He craned around to look into the lighted tent behind him. "I'm gonna get some Durian," he said, getting up. "Sure you won't have some?"

Mickey winced. "Eat it over there. And use the soap and water next to the stand to wash your hands. I'll be here having ice cream."

Inside the Durian tent, they'd stacked the spiky, green fruit into pyramids. Blake chose the one at the top. The owner split it open and handed it to Blake on a tray with a plastic spoon.

He sat at an empty table and scooped out a bite of the pudding-like, yellowish goo. The texture reminded him of overripe bananas, and the scent was worse, but Blake knew to hold his breath when taking a bite. He did the same with Stiltons and Surströmming. And the taste made it all worthwhile.

As with the other two exotics, it was revolting and wonderful at the same time.

When Blake returned, Mickey was still at their original table, his cell phone face down in front of him.

Chapter 20

Six Days Later, Saturday, November 11
Sarawak River, Port of Borneo

Sartaq took a deep breath, pressed his lips against the anger he felt, and blew it out with a loud hiss.

The ship had stopped in Sarawak longer than Lili'd said, and they had no way of knowing why, or when they'd continue to Singapore. But it sure wouldn't be on schedule.

The meeting in Singapore wouldn't wait for them. The hundreds of senior Party members, the agenda set for China's next five-year National Congress, would head home. Midday next Saturday was the last guaranteed time they'd all be in one place.

He looked at Lili and flared his eyes.

"We'll make it," she said, smiling and confident. "Sharmarke sails regular schedule. Same places. Customers rely on it. We'll be there Thursday. Plenty of time."

Lin Yusheng, his white hair seeming to glow in the lantern's dim light, flipped it back from his face. "I don't see why we didn't just fly. We could be sitting around swimming pool instead of..." He waved a hand at the interior of their shipping container.

Yang, a law enforcement major and Sartaq's *de facto* Sergeant at Arms, looked up from where he sat near the locked doors. "Lili said you grew up in Wuchang? How did you get involved with

East Turkestan? That's thousands of kilometers away."

After a week at sea with the seven of them—five students, Sartaq, and Lili in that tiny, smelly space, any talk drew everyone's attention.

"Born there," Sartaq said with a sigh. "My father, Khan Batu, was Uyghur, descended from Mongolians. He fought Communists, but they murder him."

"So, you followed in his footsteps?" Yang asked.

Sartaq did half a chin wag. "When I was older, yes, but I was only one year when he killed." He nodded toward Lili. "Mother moved us to Wuhan. There, we lived with Shen grandparents until Mother married Zhang man. He is Han. Lili's father."

"A Professor," Lili supplied. "Chinese history. We lived—"

"Across from campus," Sartaq interrupted. Lili's eyes flared, but she stopped.

Continuing his story, Sartaq said, "Growing up there, Lili and me played on Luojia, swam in Donghu, ran on same streets—"

"You swam in that water?!" Yang exclaimed, a smirk on his lips as his eyes flicked around the edges of Sartaq's big head, his wide-set eyes, and then tracing the white scar in his cheek and hair.

Lili inserted, "It was clean then. People use it for cooking, catch fish for dinner... It was very nice before Communists."

Sartaq coughed to get their attention. "Big change for me came when I was twelve. The school gave me something to learn in the Red Book, but it made no sense." He shrugged. "I refused, and they kicked me out."

Lili glanced at him.

He flared his eyes back at her.

"Twelve?" Yang asked, looking confused. "You were grade six? Learning Mandarin for six years?"

Sartaq's eyes cast about on the floor. How to explain?

Lili saved him. "Schools were broken," she explained. "Cultural Revolution. Mao closed all schools. Teachers hung as traitors. Our father—my father—didn't come home one night."

"He was good man," Sartaq allowed.

She continued, "When they reopened schools in 1972, my brother and I started in same class."

"First and Sixth grade together?" Lin asked.

Lili shook her head. "Schools closed before he started. When re-opened, we were in First Grade together."

Lin nodded.

She continued. "Nobody want to be teacher. They remember what happened before. The Party had to assign people to teach. No experience. No training. And most books destroyed."

Sartaq gave a loud sigh. "So, we only had Mao's Red Book. Everybody got one. Then, there was meeting with parents and teachers in front of whole school—"

"Annual recital," Lili explained.

"—I was supposed to say mine from memory, but it was stupid, what it said. It didn't make any sense." He shrugged. "So, I just said, 'this is stupid' and sat down. That's when Party leader..."

He remembered the moment, the insult, the rage he felt. He sighed hard, an animal sound escaping his mouth.

Lili finished for him. "Party Leader was horrible. Berated my brother in front of everyone. Called him names, said my father abandoned us—that was lie—and then started to say something about our mother, and—"

"I hit him."

It was Lili's turn to blush. "Yes. My brother hit him in front of whole school. One punch." She grinned. "Smack on his nose. The man flopped down like dead pig."

Sartaq gave the next detail. "They sent me to next province. Work on farm."

"In Anhui," Lili specified. "They made it sound all nice, that he would *share* what he'd learned in school about how to run farm, but we'd never studied anything like that. It was just way for Party—"

"Party Leader Chen," Sartaq inserted.

"—to get even, to punish my brother."

He grinned, "So, I didn't go."

Lili bragged. "All by himself, he went to Xinjiang Province. Thousands of kilometers, all on his own."

Sartaq leaned forward. "I found my father's Khan family. Some of them were Muslim, but not very much. I learned to work farm."

Lili supplied the next step in the story. "That's where he met Major Qassim."

"There was accident," Sartaq explained with a glance to be sure Lili wouldn't say differently. "Major Qassim saved my life. He became like father. He worked against Communists like my father. And I learned about our country, East Turkestan, even though Communists call it Xinjiang. And he told me about my Khan ancestors."

Zhou asked, "Your Major... He was *Mu'min*, a Believer?"

Sartaq opened his hands, palms up to the ceiling. "Allah blessed me," he said, playing his role. "Learned scriptures like Guo." He nodded toward the boy who returned the gesture. "Major Qassim was Imam, my teacher. He inspired me, helped me find warrior spirit."

"His Mongolian heritage," Lili explained.

"The Khans Genghis and Kublai," Sartaq completed. "And it was in Major Qassim's yurt that I received Allah's calling. We were making *polu*; that's mutton with carrots and onions in rice. Very good for cold night. Major Qassim was standing beside me stirring rice and water when I felt deep shiver. He later said that must've been Allah sliding inside to take me. At that moment, I knew Allah would guide me, and that I would do whatever He willed."

Guo bobbed his head. "Allah be praised."

"Allah be praised," Sartaq echoed.

Zhou asked, "What about Singapore?"

Sartaq scanned the waiting faces of his five suicide bombers. "We were in dorm and Lin was showing us new TV—"

"I remember," Lin interrupted. "We were watching YouTube. Twin towers victory. When first airplane splashed through, we cheered, but you stopped us. You raised your hand for silence. 'Allah is in me now,' you said. We didn't understand. You closed your eyes for long time, then suddenly you shouted, 'Allahu Akbar!' I remember it startled me so much, I couldn't breathe."

Sartaq nodded. "Allah was hugging you. And he is in you now, in each one of you."

Lin nodded and sat down. "You went into some kind of trance

until second tower started down. You awakened and told us what Allah was saying to you: 'This is way!'"

Sartaq raised his hands and face. "Allahu Akbar."

"Allahu Akbar," they all repeated.

Sartaq peeked at Lili. Her eyes were open but squinted. They flicked across the others before stopping on his watchful gaze. Her eyelids gave the tiniest flicker of acknowledgement.

It was as if she'd said, *Good job.*

Lin interrupted the moment. "Imam, you have guided many to Allah?"

"Yes, many, but I am not Imam. They are appointed by men, and they can refuse. But what Allah gave me, I could not deny. Allah gave me holy duty."

Lin nodded. "You are *Nabi.*"

Sartaq closed his eyes, and they all waited in silence. When he opened them, he smiled and looked at each of them, one at a time.

"Many years passed," he said. "I don't know why. Perhaps it was Allah's way—sometimes it comes in subtle ways—Lili mentioned Party's Five Year pre-planning meeting in Singapore. Lin showed me picture of big hotel they would use—"

"It's huge," the boy interrupted. "Three broad, tall towers, all glass on sides with each one's skinny end almost touching skinny end of next one, like mahjong tiles waiting to be played."

Sartaq nodded. "I sent message addressed to Major Qassim, but Islamic State had taken over then. He was out; they were in. IS leaders read my message. They said to go ahead, and that I will lead attack."

He smiled and nodded toward Lili. "So, my dear little sister make plan and bring money from her Chinese Democracy-friends in America. That's what is in envelopes, Chinese Democrat money. Islamic State then lined up shipping explosives to Singapore and the route we travel. All we do is give money at each step."

Lili shifted forward, and one at a time, looked each of the five in the eye until she had all of their attention. "You are sharp point of Allah's sword. It is you who will start new China history."

Sartaq echoed Guo's lead as they all—all except Lili—repeated, "Allahu Akbar!"

* * *

"I've been in the United States for several decades," Lili said. "What you don't know is our network. We have members in United States, and in Spain, Turkey, Somalia, Zimbabwe... many places."

Sartaq could see Lili turning her head as she spoke and making eye contact with each person. She was good at this.

"For many decades," she said, "our network has been grooming people, preparing them to be instruments in bringing about change. Our goal is for our people to take over Party Congress. Once in, they can change Constitution. China will be democracy.

"The trick," she smiled, "is getting our people into Party Congress.

"As you know, next Five Year Planning Committee meets about year from now. At that meeting, they will elect two thousand members of Politburo. Two hundred of those are then chosen for Central Committee that elects Politburo's twenty-five. Politburo then picks seven members from Standing Committee to run country on daily basis. They also choose General Secretary, President, and Vice President. Each level designates allowed candidates for next."

She smiled. "It has become self-serving."

Zhou nodded. "Incestuous."

"Exactly!" Lili smiled. "But there is loophole."

Everyone except Sartaq perked up.

"It's in first part of Constitution, about election of members for Five Year Planning Committee. Party recommends who you should vote for, but Constitution says you can write in others. Nobody does, or it they do, it's not coordinated. So, vote is always close to unanimous."

Several nodded.

"But if many people write in same extra candidate, that person come in second."

Zhou shrugged. "So?"

Lili's smile turned into a grin. "Constitution says if first place winner dies, second place moves up."

"Oh!" Zhou trumpeted, upsetting his glasses. "You wrote in your people in many places? Yes?"

Lili nodded.

"So," he went on, "when we kill those just elected, your people move up!"

"Exactly!" she said. "In more than five hundred districts, we received enough write-ins for our people to come in second. Some are former college students I knew twenty years ago at Wuhan University, or at Shanghai University, or indirectly at schools in Beijing, Guangzhou, Xian—" she looked at Sartaq, "—even Kashgar University in Xinjiang."

Zhou shook his head. "But only five hundred... The Party Congress has more than two thousand delegates. You won't have majority."

"True. But we believe support for democratic principles is present in many other. They've just been afraid to speak out, to propose or vote for those kinds of changes. Once we have five hundred pushing for democratic changes, they will happen. And remember they elect Central Committee who then elects Politburo, then they decide the Standing Committee and all our top leaders."

She leaned forward. "Remember student demonstrations at Tiananmen Square? I know it's not in your Party-sanctioned history books, but I'm betting many of you read about it on Internet. Even though Party tries to block websites with story, there are just too many websites, too many blogs that show the *Tank Man* picture. And there are new ones cropping up constantly. The Party can't keep up with whole world!"

Lin and Yang both nodded with Zhou. He said, "Didn't they arrest students back then?"

Lili nodded but said, "Worse. But with good proportion of Politburo speaking out, we believe we can start the changes, and once started, others will join in."

Sartaq leaned in to be seen. "And once they have majority, they will set East Turkestan free!"

The back of Lili's head wobbled.

"There will be many things to do, Taq, but yes, your province's future is extremely important. We need their votes to help keep tide of change going, but if they eventually vote for independence... Well, we'll cross that bridge when we get to it."

Yang rocked side to side rubbing his back against the steel wall as he gestured toward Lili. "You've been active for long time, then?"

"I was your age when we started," Lili answered, "an undergraduate at Wuhan. I kept our group's secret membership records. And to make certain they stayed secret, my name never mentioned. And I didn't attend open meetings. No one outside of core knew I was part of movement. Even after I received Master's degree in Management and moved to Shanghai for job, I continued to work secretly for movement."

Sartaq suppressed a scowl. It was okay to sway these kids with her ideals, but the Party's old, hard-core Communists would stop them. Guns, tanks, and secret executions overruled any thoughts or words that didn't line up like a good little soldier. They'd done it to before, and they'd do it again.

Lili was still talking. He let her go on, hoping they'd eventually see the weaknesses of her plan.

"After a year, my employer, Comac, moved me to Silicon Valley in California. That's near San Francisco. In California. I worked in the daytime for Comac, but in evenings and weekends, I helped organize our people in America. We expanded to other countries as members moved. I also became Treasurer. Supporters sent donations to me in United States, and I invested it. Some went to plain savings accounts, but also some went to US stock market. My job at Comac and people I met in Silicon Valley taught me about high-tech industry. I had contacts all around south bay. I knew what companies were doing, I watched market, and I managed our investments. Our portfolio grew by as much as twenty-five, thirty percent in good years."

Fan's eyes widened. "You must be wealthy woman!"

Lili shook her head. "No. Everything extra went into movement. That's what my life is about, bringing democracy to China."

She stretched her back.

"I sometimes bring cash for our secret workers in China. That's how we started promoting our people to get to where they are today. It's been very long road and lot of work."

"Party never suspected your visits?" Yang asked.

She smiled. "I use simple technique. I chose American engineer to teach seminar at University, and then I escort him into China. At border I show contract for him signed by me. They let us in every time."

Sartaq scanned across the faces of his five suicide bombers. Something about how they were looking at Lili made him uneasy. It was like the tricksters in the street that got you saying *yes* over and over then slipped in a question you should refuse but you say *yes* instead. Lili was good trickster. It was time to get their thinking back on track about East Turkestan.

"The Uyghurs," he said, "are our brothers and sisters, but they locked in re-education camps by Beijing. Millions of them..." He glared at Lili making sure they all saw him do it.

"Her way take too long. Besides, Party lines-up vote before first one is cast. Other ballots get lost? Dead people vote? Sick people who can't hold pencil sign names? All lies." He slammed a fist into an open palm. "The only way is hit them. Hit them, again and again." He pounded his palm.

He stood so the gas lantern projected his giant shadow on the inside of their shipping container.

"What Lili says sounds okay, but long before they get around to us, we will already have our independence. That's because we will seize it!"

He gestured at Lili sitting on the floor. "You and your college friends can do whatever you want in your little meetings. Wave hands, make speeches, we don't care because we'll be gone."

"Taq," she said, her voice turning soft and pleading. "Xinjiang will be able to vote; every man and woman as they wish. The Province can do whatever it wants."

Before Sartaq could answer, Guo said, "No, whatever *majority* wants. And must come to vote first. Takes time. Much time."

Sartaq grinned as Lili's eyes flashed in anger.

Yang hadn't spoken for a long time. He sounded cautious. "If our suicide takes five hundred delegates, how long would your democracy take if we only killed two hundred?"

"Longer," Lili acknowledged.

"Or fifty?"

"Longer still."

"Or none?"

Lili paused before she shrugged. "Most of us think it is inevitable."

"Well then," Zhou said with a huff, "I don't know about you, but I like being alive."

Yang and Lin nodded, Guo looked sick, and Fan was frowning.

Sartaq exploded, "No!"

Everyone jumped.

"You're missing point. Democracy is not way. Takes too long. Maybe never. Look at Xinjiang now, today. What is happening there, and what has already happened? Millions of Uyghur brothers and sisters arrested, taken away, locked in prison camps, brain-washed. Beijing is killing their minds. It's like, like, like ..." He turned to Lin. "What's it called when a farmer—" he made a violent slash with one hand "—cuts off the boy parts?"

"Castration?"

Sartaq nodded vigorously. "Yes. That's what we must do to them, cut off their..."

Fan perked up. "Nuts?"

"Balls?" Yang said.

"Jewels?"

"Man eggs?"

Sartaq fought back his smile. He slammed his muscle, bone, and sinewed fist into his palm. "We hit them!" He smacked his palm again. "Hurt them!"

He looked to Fan. "What is it Americans say when they beaten, when they want you stop, when they give up?"

The boy offered, "Uncle?"

"Yes," Sartaq bellowed, "make Beijing cry *Uncle!* Hit them, hard, over and over, and they will do what we want. Why? Because it hurts! They will fear us. We will make them fear us; we will hurt them," he continued pounding his palm. "We will castrate Party in

Singapore. They will then be..."

"Eunuchs," Fan supplied.

"And they will do as we demand. Keep hitting them—Kunming, Urumki, Aksu, Hotan, and next week, we hit them in Singapore!"

Through the soles of his feet, a deep vibration shook the floor. Everyone looked back toward the fans, their only view to the outside world. A loud clanking, the same they'd heard before leaving Haiphong, rang through the vent openings and in their feet and seats.

"Anchor going up," Lin rejoiced. "We leaving."

All five looked relieved.

But not Lili. She was glaring at Sartaq, her eyes filled with red rage.

He glared back at her and then smiled his victory.

PART THREE

PUSH COMES TO SHOVE

*"Being deeply loved by someone gives you strength,
while loving someone deeply gives you courage."*
Lao Tzu

Chapter 21

Friday, November 17
Police and Military Range, Singapore

Blake grunted to hoist the gun box onto the firing-line table.

His mental and physical state had plummeted over the nearly two week wait. Terrible dreams, constant second guessing, and ever worsening self-recriminations plagued him night and day.

Alcohol blurred the middle five days until Mickey locked it away and threatened to do the same to Blake.

Today's Bullseye match at the Singapore range could be the dose of reality Blake needed. And if he could muster it, the mindless concentration of "front sight, rear sight, target, pressure" would, at least for a few hours, quiet his mind.

Blake scooted the gun box Mickey had loaned him to the left side of the table but didn't open it. Centered in the tabletop, a stenciled "8" matched the number on his target fifty yards downrange.

To Blake's left, Mickey set his zippered-shut gym bag atop the "7" on his table.

And to Blake's right, a dark-complected man with the sharp features of a movie star boosted a gun box to the "9" position. He glanced at Blake, nodded without smiling, and stepped back to sit on the long bench.

Mickey had said everyone today would be an experienced Bullseye shooter. Re-titled by the NRA to Precision Pistol a few years earlier, most still called it Bullseye as it'd been called for a hundred years.

Blake rolled a "foamy" into a thin stick and quickly worked the end into his busted eardrum's outer canal. Hearing on that side had returned to normal but he didn't want to take a chance. He waited for the foam ear plug to expand and fill the canal. After doing the same on the other side, he added Mickey's electronic hearing protector headset, and then turned up the volume until his surroundings sounded normal. The electronics would instantly mute gunshots, but conversations would come through at a comfortable level.

The PA system crackled from speakers behind him.

"Shooters, your three-minute preparation period starts now."

Blake wondered if they always shot Bullseye in English, or if it was a concession for him?

Mickey's boss, Singapore's Police Chief, was calling the line. Blake snuck a look. An older man with white hair held a microphone at a table just back from the middle of the line. In front of him was a slope-fronted control box and a large darkroom-style timer. The second-hand rotated counter-clockwise and the minute-hand crept down from the three-minute mark.

Blake unlatched the side-opening gun box and swung the lid up until it latched vertically on top. Attached to a swing arm inside, he loosened the set screws and rotated the spotting scope into position. He peered through and shifted box and scope to center his #8 target.

He loaded two magazines, five rounds each according to Bullseye tradition, and set them on his table next to Mickey's Smith & Wesson model 41, the first of three handguns, ninety to a hundred rounds each, that he'd shoot today.

Blake raised the empty 22 pistol and sighted it—front sight, rear sight, target center—on the black circle in the middle of his target. He wriggled his wrist to get it settled in his practiced orientation and re-checked the alignment. A little low on the target, Blake moved his rear foot back about an inch to raise the gun.

Mickey shot center aim and set his sights accordingly. Blake preferred a six o'clock hold, but didn't want to disturb the sights on Mickey's loaners. He'd just have to remember to hold center for each shot.

"Gentlemen," the line caller's voice declared over the PA, "Your preparation period has ended."

Blake lowered his arm until the model 41's muzzle touched the tabletop. His off-hand thumb was tucked behind the belt buckle of his pants, his feet placed slightly wider than his shoulders, and his body standing so that gun recoil would travel straight up his arm and shove his body straight back without twisting it. That would leave his gun on target when it came back down from recoil.

He was ready.

Don't think, he thought. *Empty mind. My body does the shot plan. Don't think. Just watch.*

"Shooters, this is the first target of the Slow Fire portion of the twenty-two match. Ten shots Slow Fire, ten shots in ten minutes." The Chief of Police paused for about a second, then added a single word: "Load."

Up and down the line, twelve shooters inserted their magazines of five rounds, pulled back and released the slides of their guns to charge their weapons. Twelve guns and twelve shooters were ready to fire.

Unlike the more recently invented "run and gun" competitions, Bullseye came from a time of honor and trust. It was implicit in the sport. Eyes and mind focused on your own sights and target, you simply trusted every shooter standing next to you up and down the line. You trusted they would shoot safely, and they trusted you to do the same. Nobody watched anything except their own target.

"Is the line ready?"

The Police Chief started the familiar cadence.

Don't think, Blake told himself.

In the three-second pause mandated by the rules, Blake followed his shot plan and took a deep breath in through his mouth and then puckered slightly to blow it out. The breath would charge his blood with oxygen and keep his shooting eye and brain in communication for one shot.

"The line is ready."

Another three second pause.

Blake took a second deep breath, this time in through his nose, then out through his lips. The regimented process he'd followed hundreds of times stilled any thought in his brain.

"Ready on the right."

Shot plan, he allowed his brain to remind him. *Let your body do it. No thinking.*

Blake automatically raised his gun arm, shimmied his hips to perfect the balance in his body, and verified the gun's aim remained close to the center of the black bullseye. His sights meandered on the target's black center. Blake ignored the motion.

Everyone wobbled. Holding the arm completely still was impossible. The goals took that into consideration. First, aim so that the wobble remains centered on your aiming point, and then second, watch for the wobble to momentarily slow or cease. That's when you wanted the shot to break.

"Ready on the left."

Don't think.

He closed his lips and breathed through his nose, deep, slow breaths.

"Ready on the firing line."

Another slow breath in and out through the nose.

The front sight of the Smith & Wesson model 41 meandered slowly in the fuzzy black circle fifty yards away. Up an inch on the face of the target, down and left, up, a little right... On its slow excursions, it often passed through dead center.

"Commence fire."

Nothing happened.

This was Slow Fire: ten minutes for ten shots. With a minute for each shot, he could wait for the pause in the wobble each time.

Blake inhaled, let half out, and locked his throat to trap the air in his lungs. The inflation pushed his arm up slightly. He expelled a tiny puff, closed his throat, and his aim came down. The path of the wobble still seemed a little high.

Let out a little more.

He did and the sights continued meandering, but now they passed, slowly, through the center "X" on the target.

On the pad of his forefinger, he felt the curved face of the trigger. His body was holding a slight pressure on it; that helped lessen the wobble. Blake kept his attention on the sights so his eye/brain/wrist would keep everything perfectly lined up. He felt the pad of his finger beginning to squish on the trig—

"Bang!"

Seven o'clock, eight ring, some part of his brain reported.

Blake lowered the end of the pistol and peered through the spotting 'scope. A small white hole, smaller than a pencil, shown through the target about three inches down and left of center in the "8" ring.

He frowned.

For a right-handed shooter, down and left meant he'd probably jerked the shot.

A beginner mistake.

He blanked out the critique, shimmied his hips, and raised the gun to make his second shot.

Up and down the line, the sharp cracks of carefully aimed shots to targets fifty yards away punctuated the progress of the Slow Fire match.

Blake finished his ten shots with a minute or so to spare. He set Mickey's empty Model 41 on the table with the muzzle pointed downrange and threaded a foot-long piece of orange weed-whacker cord through the barrel. The ECI or Empty Chamber Indicator gave visible proof that the gun was not loaded.

Peering through the spotting scope, Blake tallied his score. 89-0. Eighty-nine points with zero holes in the X-ring.

I can do better, he thought to himself.

A loud buzzer sounded from the Chief's table.

"Cease firing," he commanded on the PA as per the rules even though everyone had already finished like Blake. He added, again as per the rules, "Unload."

Blake picked up his blank score card, clipboard, pencil, and staple gun from his table and stepped back behind a red line on the floor. Up and down the line, the other eleven shooters did the same.

"Is the line safe?" The Chief asked.

Anyone with a problem was expected to sing out.

Silence.

"Is the line safe right?"

Silence.

"Line safe left?"

Silence again.

"The line is safe." The announcer added.

Then not from the NRA rulebook, he said, "Gentlemen, you may go downrange, score and repair your targets. The repair centers are in the box behind the berm at the short line."

There were eight targets to go with the 22, then nine with Mickey's revolver, and another nine with a 45 caliber 1911 that was Mickey's pride and joy, a Masuda 1911, named for the skinny gunsmith in Hawaii who'd built it. Blake had no doubt that gun would strike the center X with every shot.

He just hoped he'd be reasonably good and shoot his mid-ranked *Expert* classification.

At the mid-morning break between matches, Blake sat on the bench amidst the other shooters. Next to him, Ray's dramatic features, black mustache, and shy blue eyes invited attention.

"You could be a movie star," Blake said.

Ray ignored the compliment. "You're with Chee?" he asked with the British accent common in Singapore.

"Mickey and I met two years ago at the Nationals in Ohio... In the US."

"Why are you in Singapore?" Ray's tone sounded like Blake shouldn't be here.

"Just getting some R&R. Resting up after a two-week job in China."

Ray's eyes examined Blake's face. "What did you do in China?"

Blake thought about changing seats.

"I was teaching some college kids. Beginner stuff. But my usual customers write the software that pilots military and civilian aircraft." There, Blake thought, that should impress him.

"My brother-in-law is a chemical engineer in KL. He makes more than anyone here. You?"

On Blake's other side, Mickey leaned in. "KL is Kuala Lumpur, an hour northwest of here flying." Louder, he added, "Ray's in our STAR team, Special Tactics And Rescue."

"Hunter," Ray said.

"Designated Marksman," Mickey clarified. "Sharpshooter."

Ray shrugged. "Sniper." He nodded toward the range where they'd moved the targets out to fifty yards. "We have to show pistol proficiency at short range."

Fifty yards with a pistol was not short range, but Blake decided not to nit-pick.

"That's like SWAT in the US?"

Ray blinked. "Your people get more action,"

The pupils in the man's blue eyes were perfectly clear. Blake imagined him scoping a target at a thousand yards, gently squeezing the trigger, and then watching the silvery tail of the bullet for two seconds until impact.

Blake offered, "Singapore seems like a Garden of Eden compared to LA or Detroit. I wouldn't have guessed you'd need such a group."

"We get terrorists here, too," Mickey answered. "We just handle them a little different."

"More directly," Ray amplified, glanced at Blake, and added, "D-R-T shot."

Blake furrowed his eyebrows. He didn't know that abbreviation.

"Dead-Right-There," Ray clarified. "Severs the spinal cord."

Nearby conversations had stopped.

Ray went on. "With no signals getting through from the brain, the body relaxes. They either bleed out, artery or vein cut, or suffocate. Trachea."

Mickey leaned out and said, "Maybe we should change the subject."

"It's Okay," Blake said. "It's interesting information. I sometimes deal with crashes. The bodies are gone by the time I get there, but it happens."

Ray turned to Blake. "People should know. Bad people, in particular. Maybe they'd think twice."

"When I first started carrying," Blake said, "I mentioned to my wife that arms and legs were relatively small, so we aimed for the center of mass. More likely to score a hit. She looked at me like I was a monster."

Ray gave an equivocal chin bob. "Sometimes, if someone's standing in the way of our actual target, we can aim for a leg. They don't move as much as arms. Then, with the way cleared, we can get to the business."

Blake wasn't sure what he'd just heard. "Someone's in the way?"

Mickey leaned in. "Ray, this is not—"

But the sharpshooter was undaunted.

"Look," he said, his voice emphatic, "you make choices in life. Sometimes it's between bad, really bad, and... horrible. You have to do what you can, when you can."

Blake was sure this man had killed. Probably several times.

Ray wasn't done. "With all due respect to Officer Chee, arrests, reports, and trials don't always work. Sometimes a direct and permanent solution is best."

Mickey forced a smile. "Ray is, perhaps, over-simplifying? By the time his team is called in, it's already extreme. They're trained to do what's necessary."

Ray put a finger on Blake's chest.

"Your country is turning crooks—convicted and sentenced criminals—loose on the public. They're running the streets, selling drugs to kids, shooting innocent people in their homes..." He shook his head. "What kind of government is that?"

In the corner of his eye, Blake could see Mickey trying to wave Ray down. But it wasn't working.

"That tells criminals they can do whatever they want—rob, rape, kill, whatever. No goddamn consequences in your country, so why the hell not?"

Mickey sighed and leaned back.

Ray took his finger back and crossed his arms. "Well, that isn't gonna happen here, I can promise you. You do something bad, there's gonna be a consequence, a *permanent* consequence. I get one of those bad guys in my sights? D-R-T, mother-fucker. D-R-T."

Chapter 22

That Evening
Mickey's Apartment

Back in the apartment, Mickey spread a pair of old, stained towels on the glass-top coffee table next to the gun cleaning supplies.

"You start with large calibers," he said, "I'll do small."

Mickey picked up the Ruger 22, made sure the chamber was empty, and clicked the trigger. With a fingernail, he snagged the end of the housing latch and had the major parts loose on the towel in a few seconds.

Blake picked up the 45, Mickey's Masuda.

It was, without question, the finest gun he'd ever fired. Mickey said he'd waited two years for it. And that was after paying in advance. Ed Masuda, a skinny, little Japanese man, performed his magic in Hawaii. When he finished, the gun's original brand no longer mattered. It was now a Masuda.

Blake took it apart Bullseye-style: press back the slide slightly, press the slide stop on one side then pull it out from the other, and then ease the slide off the receiver. With the tension removed from the recoil spring, the barrel bushing turned with finger pressure.

"That was fun today," Blake said, sliding out the barrel, "a perfect distraction."

Mickey looked through the one from his Ruger. He dipped a white cotton patch in the fragrant dish of Hoppes #9 cleaner on the table. Holding it over the end of the jag, he pushed it through. The sides of the patch came out streaked with black.

"Everyone knew you were shooting unfamiliar guns," he said, dipping and running another patch through. "You did good."

"Thanks," Blake said and began on the Masuda's barrel. After half a dozen patches through the nearly half-inch diameter barrel, he held it up and looked through. Near the chamber end, a reddish streak hugged one of the polished helical grooves.

Blake pawed the box of supplies. "Copper cleaner?"

Mickey shook his head. "Just Hoppes #9. I don't want to risk scratching that barrel. Just keep running patches, a new one each time. I have plenty."

Blake ran a dozen more, checking each time to see if the red streak was gone. It wasn't.

Meanwhile, Mickey had reassembled his cleaned and lubricated Ruger and pulled the trigger to release tension on the mainspring. He moved on to the S&W 625 revolver he'd shot in Center Fire and started working a brass brush dipped in the cleaner on the soot of the revolver's cylinder face.

"I don't mean to pry," Mickey said casually, his eyes checking the underside of the top strap, "but if you need someone to listen... What you experienced in Wuhan, for example?"

Blake clenched his teeth. Other than the first target or just after it while sitting with Ray, he'd gone through most of the day without thinking about any of that. Mickey's question resurrected it.

Blake said, "No," but it came out angry.

Mickey shrugged and switched to the Colt 1911 he'd used at the end of the match. It was a fine gun, collectable by aficionados of the brand. It was eminently shootable, but not the pinnacle example like the Masuda Blake was still patching and checking.

Finally, a long, hair-thin helix of copper pushed out with a patch. Blake looked through, and the red streak was gone.

Blake ran two more patches before saying, "Have a look," and handing it to Mickey.

"Perfect," he nodded while looking through. "Thank you." He handed it back, then picked up his bottle of Orion beer. He tipped the open end briefly toward Blake, and took a long, gurgling draw. "I never could get my ex to the range either," he said, leaning back on the couch. "Like yours, guns terrified her."

Blake said, "My wife killed herself."

He snapped his lips tight. The confession had come out for no reason.

Mickey asked in an even voice, "Did you know she was suicidal?"

Blake felt askew like he'd awoken to some emergency from a dreamless sleep.

"Not really," he said. "Julie and me were married—if you can call it that—for not quite seven years. Toward the end, I knew she was sleeping around, but neither of us were into confrontations. I ignored it hoping she would stop, and she ignored me ignoring it. Pretty stupid, huh?"

Mickey shrugged. "People do things for lots of reasons. Sometimes it's for stupid ones, but more often than not, for something they don't yet realize."

Blake went to the refrigerator for another Orion.

Mickey added in a louder voice, "We're more creature than intellect sometimes."

"Megyn is different," Blake said after sitting and taking a swallow.

Mickey's head bobbed as he dotted the end of the oil bottle along his Colt's slide, spread it with his fingertip, and then started reassembling the gun.

He asked, "Megyn?"

Blake explained. "I only saw her in the Bay area at first. And then we were in Chicago at the same time. I don't remember who texted who. We were both there for business, me up in Schaumberg, her in Naperville. I took her to dinner at Clara's in Downers Grove." He turned to Mickey. "There was nothing going on between us. Just friends..."

Mickey racked the Colt's slide and pulled the trigger. Its hammer clicked on the back of the firing pin and drove it forward, but with no cartridge in the chamber, nothing happened.

In front of Blake, the parts of the Masuda still lay on the towel. Mickey had cleaned three guns while Blake was still on his first. But it was the Masuda and well worth the extra care.

Blake carefully guided its barrel into the upside-down slide.

"So out of the blue last August," he said, continuing the Masuda's re-assembly, "she contacts me for these classes in Wuhan. It was good money, real good money. And they covered all the travel, lodging, and food. So, I agreed, and a couple of months later, I'm in the San Francisco airport for the outbound flight and—Bingo!—there she is at the gate."

He smiled.

"She's beautiful, Mickey. A real China Doll. She tells me she's going to visit family in China and is on the same flight to Shanghai. She's at the same stopover hotel there—a one-nighter—and then the same flight to Wuhan. She even got the seat next to me on both flights."

Mickey's face gave no clue to his thoughts. "I see," he said, upended his beer, and set the empty on the table.

Blake went on. "Megyn and me, we like the same things, food in particular. Sometimes she surprises me."

Blake felt Mickey's eyes on him again.

"In Shanghai, before we get off the plane, she hands me this envelope and asks me to carry it through Customs."

Blake paused. Just how much should he tell Mickey? Everything had seemed normal enough up to that point. And even then, Megyn explained herself, justified—in a normal, rational way—everything she'd asked him to do.

"It was money for her mother, for her workers. Chinese money, some from Singapore, and another one... some skinny Asian with a beard."

"Ho Chi Minh?" Mickey offered. "That'd be Vietnamese. Plastic money. And you agreed? You must've suspected something was fishy, otherwise why would she ask?"

Blake remembered the warm squeeze of her hand on the inside of his thigh. And then there'd been the caress of her gown as it flowed across his abdomen in her hotel room that night. Even now, the memory gave him a flush of warmth.

Chemistry.

Mickey was watching Blake. "Yeah, that happens," he said, his face amused. "Obviously, you made it through Chinese Customs. Being American probably helped."

"What do you mean?"

"In some countries," Mickey explained, "a foreigner accompanied by a citizen would get a little extra, but polite, scrutiny. But in much of Asia, a Chinese woman with an American man, especially a beautiful one with someone who looks as American as you... Asia can be very sexist. Did Megyn—I assume that's her American name?—did she tell you about her family?"

Blake nodded. "They live nearby, a few miles from Wuhan. She had a rental car. Megyn's Chinese name is Li, Li Zhang. I mean, Zhang Li."

Mickey shifted in his chair as if he'd reached a decision.

"Blake, we talked about the explosion at the University. I wouldn't ask again, but it's important."

Blake racked the Masuda's slide, pointed it down and away, and pulled the trigger to check the action.

Mickey reached over and put his hand on the gun.

"The library, Blake? Someone blew it up?"

Blake gave a one-shoulder shrug. "I was teaching the seminar, day four of five, in the second week. The building—the Old Library—was two, maybe three hundred yards west."

Mickey's silence and penetrating eyes made him uneasy.

"The blast wave—we were up on the fourth floor, so it came through unimpeded—shattered all the glass in the windows and blew it through the room. It killed several."

The shudder began in Blake's gut like he was going to puke, then it spread to his chest and shoulders, his vision narrowed, and everything went black.

When Blake opened his eyes, he was flat on the couch looking at the ceiling.

"How do you feel?" Mickey asked, sitting beside him.

"What happened?"

"You fainted. Any aches or odd feelings?"

"No."

Mickey nodded. "Stress. You popped a circuit breaker. Has that happened before?"

"No, but I've been having nightmares. With all that's happened, though, I wasn't surprised."

Mickey nodded. "Good that you understand them, but that doesn't make them go away. It's a reaction to severe stress. It won't go away by ignoring it. People act out without understanding why. You need to take care of that."

Blake remembered the worst of the two weeks, the Saturday on the mountain when the boy's eyes in the detached head had gazed around.

"All right," Blake said. He'd let that out. Maybe that'd be enough.

Blake told Mickey about the beheading, all the gory details, how he'd bolted, drank himself to oblivion, and then what Megyn had said.

Mickey's first comment started, "A lot of people would've freaked out—"

"I did!"

"—and stayed that way, but you got it back together. Mostly. And she was right. China's police would've locked you up. Depending on the political climate, things could've gone terrible for you. Unofficially, you probably did the right thing by getting out of China."

"Then on Thursday right after the bombing," Blake said and glad to have another person on his side, "I looked down from the classroom. A man was spinning, his arms straight out and his head tilted to the side. I could see the scar on the side of his face. Even before he stopped to look at me and then point, I knew it was the same man. His name is Sartaq."

"Sartaq?" Mickey raised an eyebrow. "You *know* that?"

"Yes," Blake nodded vigorously. "On the mountain, they said it twice. Clearly. And the way they used it, I'm sure it's his name."

"And you're sure it's the same man?"

"Yep. Same white stripe in his black hair turning into white skin down his cheek."

"Stay here," Mickey commanded. He walked to his bedroom and came back with a notebook computer. He pushed back the towel in front of Blake and set it on the table. When he opened the lid, the screen lit with a graphic: a white crescent moon on a red background with a pentagon of five stars. In the center, a gray box waited for a login. A dozen taps and clicks later, Mickey angled the screen toward Blake.

"This guy?"

The camera was looking down from a few feet away, but the wide eyes in the bulbous head turned up toward the camera with that long, white scar were unmistakable.

"That's him." Blake exclaimed. "Sartaq!"

Mickey chewed the inside of his lip.

"Is this from China? Did they catch him?"

"No. This is here, not quite two weeks ago. Sunday morning at a hotel check-in. He used a passport at Immigration that was legitimate in our database. But since then, it's been tagged. Issued to an Afghani, his body was later identified. The killer mutilated his face to slow things down. We have a shot of your man at the entry check booth, and then a little later walking through Nothing to Declare, but this one at the hotel is the best we have. Someone did a good job replacing the photograph in the passport. That's not supposed to be possible, so our people missed it."

Blake's eyebrows scrunched. "Which Sunday?"

Mickey right-clicked the image and read the box that appeared. "Twelve days ago, 6:37 in the morning. Probably flew in on a red-eye. His reservation was for two nights, but he never checked out. Credit card belongs to the same dead man, but again, that wasn't flagged yet. Their security got involved because the infrared sensor for his room's air conditioner never triggered the second night. They checked the card again, and by that time Visa had flagged it. Unfortunately, he'd disappeared by then. We're guessing he left on a different passport. We're checking images, but getting out is a lot easier than getting in."

Blake's grin was filling his face.

"That's it," he mumbled.

"What?"

"He was here on Sunday, not there. We went to some museum that day and then to dinner. I kept looking over my shoulder, but after a while I figured, with the crowd and all, he didn't recognize me. You know how sometimes everyone looks alike if it's a kind of face you're not used to seeing? People say, 'they all look alike.' So, I guessed that was it. But if he was here instead, that explains it. Turns out, I was perfectly safe, just like Megyn said."

"And you didn't see him again?"

Blake was nodding and grinning. "Not until the Saturday after that, in Guang—"

Stop! His mind shouted. He clamped his eyes and mouth shut, and turned like he'd been slapped.

But Mickey latched on.

"Guang...What? Guang-dong? Guang-xi?"

Blake confessed. "Guangzhou."

"Okay," Mickey's voice shifted into interrogator mode again. "Now tell me what happened in Guangzhou."

But Sartaq had said he would kill Megyn—his own sister—if Blake talked, and this was the last.

Blake saw him murder that boy on the mountain. And he blew up a bunch of people at the library.

And whatever they had planned, Blake was not likely to stop them. Getting Megyn away from six captors also seemed unlikely.

His mind said, *I can't beat all that.*

Mickey and his people knew about terrorists. They had the personnel, the weapons, and the training. That's what they were for. If they could take care of Sartaq and his personal gang of five, Megyn would be safe.

There was no way Blake could do that by himself. He'd been a fool to hold back. Mickey and his troops were professionals. Let them do their jobs.

Blake took a big breath.

"We were leaving Guangzhou," he began. "Megyn and I were coming here for a romantic getaway. But then Sartaq kidnapped her, his own sister."

Mickey's eyebrows shot up, and his chin dropped. "What? Megyn is his sister?"

"Sorry," Blake said. "So many details. She told me he's her brother; Sartaq is Megyn's brother."

Mickey guffawed.

"Jesus, Blake, when you fuck things up, you sure don't mess around!"

Blake opened his mouth to say that none of this was his fault, but Mickey put up a hand. "It's Okay. She set you up, pal. Big time. But—Wow! And you didn't see any of this coming?"

"See it coming?" Blake exclaimed. "See what coming? I took a simple job in China to teach some college kids. And it was good, but not ridiculous, money. Everything was on the up and up. I still debug and fix computers sometimes, but seminars are my bread and butter now, and this one was a no-brainer. I could almost do it in my sleep."

Mickey gave him a sympathetic smile. "Well, they duped you, my friend. Big time. These people are terrorists and murderers. They'll say and do anything to advance their plan."

Blake shook his head. "Megyn's not part of it."

Mickey leaned toward him, an accusing look in his eye. "That money she gave you to smuggle into China? How much was it? And in three currencies? Did you actually see her give it to her mother or her family?"

"She didn't want me to go out there..."

Blake felt his feelings come together.

"I want to marry her, Mickey."

Mickey's jaw drop was instantaneous.

"Blake, come on. She's playing you."

"Nope," Blake wove his head back and forth, his lips tight. "She's a manager for a high-tech company in Sunnyvale. Responsible for a group of engineers for twenty-odd years. She's not the type to get sucked in as a courier for some terrorist group."

"Blake," Mickey warned, "if for any reason she carried money into the country to finance some part of what happened, China will execute her. They don't screw around. Court, sentencing, and execution will finish in a few days, a week at most."

He argued, "But what if Sartaq is tricking her? Or blackmail?

Extortion? Do this or I'll murder our mother? The man's a monster, Mickey. Remember, he kidnapped his sister at gunpoint. The man is nuts."

Blake spread his hands.

"He's a master manipulator. He convinced several college students to carry bombs into that library and blow themselves up. That's no small feat. If he can do that, I'd say there's a good chance he's controlling his sister, too."

Blake rocked his head from side to side, the kidnap incident replaying in his mind. "In the van, there were several college-age men. Five of them. When Sartaq threw her in, they grabbed her —"

This is another set of suicide bombers, Blake realized. Another target.

And why would Sartaq specify that hotel and that exact time? The answer was obvious.

Singapore is next.

Blake's empty stomach convulsed. He gasped hard several times and just barely kept the beer inside.

Five suicide bombers, this time. Bigger target. More dead.

And Sartaq with a gun. Pointed into Megyn's head.

Singapore, Noon Saturday, she'd translated.

Ray's abbreviation flashed in Blake's head: *D-R-T, Dead-Right-There.*

Ray and his team would kill the terrorists with a shot through the neck to sever their spinal cord.

That's what Blake needed, Sartaq and his killers dead, and Megyn in his arms.

"Marina Bay Sands Hotel," he told Mickey. "Twelve o'clock. Tomorrow. That's when they're attacking."

"How do you know that?"

Blake nodded fast as he spoke. "Sartaq said he'd release Megyn then, but now that I think about it, they must be planning another attack. He was very precise about where and when. That must be it. He's going to kill Megyn and me, along with everyone else."

"Shit."

Mickey picked up his notebook, walked into his bedroom, and

shut the door.

Blake was on the couch when he Mickey returned.

Clicking his pen, Mickey sat down.

"A couple of points," he said, his notepad ready. "First, do you think you'd recognize them, the others, I mean?"

Blake nodded slowly. "The one on the passenger side with a map in his lap? Yes, for sure. He had big cheekbones and round glasses, and long, shaggy hair instead of the usual close crop. Not so much the driver. He was a little older than the rest, but he looked like any other Chinese. But there was a guy all the way in the very back next to Sartaq. He had stark, white hair that flopped around, and pretty, not handsome, but *pretty* facial features."

Mickey flipped through his notes, chose a busy page, and wrote.

When finished, he said, "You know you should've told all this two weeks ago. Withholding information like this is a criminal offense, and not just here."

Blake was shaking his head before he spoke. "He said he'd kill her. I couldn't take the chance."

The air conditioner thrummed to life.

"Blake, you need to understand something." Mickey took a breath. "He can't release the woman. She's bait. He thinks it'll keep you quiet—it's a good thing he was wrong about that—but it's also intended to get you there, and then to make sure you're killed. Unless he's planning on killing himself—which he did *not* do at the Wuhan University library—he can't leave you around. You're a loose end."

Blake nodded and dropped his gaze. It stopped on the Masuda 1911 in the gun box.

Mickey leaned forward. "There are some incongruous details in the report from China," he explained, flipping back several pages in his notes. "In the library debris, they found pieces of electronics that don't belong to anything that should've been there. One fragment is part of a circuit board for a tiny computer known as a Raspberry Pi. It's a low-cost—"

"Alex!" Blake shouted. He remembered how the boy's control box had come to life and ticked down to the explosion. It all made sense now.

"It's one of the control boxes that Alex made," Blake said in a rush. He put his head back and grinned at the ceiling. "I can't believe... That kid. So smart. Sartaq must've sucked him in, blackmail, whatever..."

He rolled his head to look at Mickey. "Alex built them a set of remote-controls."

He remembered Mickey talking about the students that were at the center of the Old Library just before the explosion.

"My God," he said, "he murdered his own people. What did he tell them? What did they think they were carrying?"

Mickey flipped pages in his notebook and started writing.

Blake galloped on. "The transmitter could command many receivers; Alex said that was one of its shortcomings because you couldn't confirm how many receivers there were, too few or too many. Sartaq wouldn't have known the one in my classroom had connected."

Mickey was scribbling like mad. Blake waited for his pen to stop.

"They use the lower, 2.4 gigahertz, Wi-Fi band. There's a hundred-milliwatt amplifier in each box for added range. Probably a few hundred yards in the open."

Mickey's eyes were half-closed in concentration, "Are you sure about that, the Wi-Fi, lower band?"

"Yes, yes," Blake gushed. "And I'd bet Alex didn't know what his boxes were for. He's a nice kid. Very smart. This Sartaq is superb at manipulation."

Mickey bobbed his head like a rowboat on a rough lake. "We have a jammer with a setting for WiFi, either or both bands. And it doesn't affect our radios."

Blake nodded. "To be certain, your transmitter will need to be close. Inside the lobby. That's where he's expecting me."

"It's a hundred watts," Mickey added. "The instructions say to stay at least two meters from the antenna. Makes me nervous." He nodded toward the apartment's kitchen. "Like standing in front of my microwave with the door open."

Blake shook his head. "There's an interlock. And the screen in the glass, because of the higher frequencies, stops almost all of it. Even so, at WiFi frequencies, it'll be line of sight and not through any substantial amount of metal."

Mickey nodded. "If Sartaq has the transmitter, he's the key. If we stop him, we stop the bombs."

Blake didn't hesitate. "Mickey, I can certainly recognize him, and probably some others. That boy with the white hair, for example."

Mickey cautioned, "That'd be great, but understand Blake, this will be dangerous. We'll try to keep you out of the action, but if things go bad, you could be killed. We can't guarantee anything."

"I have to be there, Mickey. For Megyn."

"And I should tell you." Mickey continued as if reading an official announcement, "Our duty is Singapore and its citizens."

"Of course."

"If we have to use force," Mickey continued, "people may get hurt—other people, not just Sartaq and his little cadre of would-be terrorists."

"Okay," Blake said, "I got it. A stray bullet could hit me, blown up by a bomb, I understand that. And I know everyone will do their best, but—"

Mickey waved a hand and shook his head.

"That's not it. What I mean is, if we only have seconds to stop them and like Ray told you, if someone is in the way, we will make them be no longer in the way."

Blake emphatically bobbed his head. "Yes, yes, I got that. You might have to wound someone, and that includes me and Megyn. I understand."

Mickey hissed, "And that's only the first part. Ray meant more than that. Those guys are pretty worked up about stopping bad guys—"

"And that's just what Sartaq deserves."

"You didn't let me finish," Mickey complained. "I was about to say, 'bad guys and girls.' If your Megyn financed this, if she brought the money for this operation, then she's as guilty as her brother."

Blake's eyes opened wide.

"But she's not," Blake automatically objected. But then he remembered all the oddities: the money, how she'd said to go to the library at 4:30 and then stay for an hour, and then that bomb went off at only 5:00 pm. If they'd done as she said...

Mickey was standing, notepad in hand. He gestured toward the kitchen clock.

"It's Eight now. That gives us sixteen hours. We've practiced setting up in the Marina Bay. It takes one hour. I'll start them now and they can monitor for Sartaq using the still picture from his earlier visit. They'll alert me if he shows up. Before that, we should get some rest."

Mickey tapped his cell phone and put it to his ear. He said, "I hope you're right about all this," and walked into his bedroom and shut the door.

Megyn, Blake thought.

He knew he wouldn't sleep.

Chapter 23

Same Time
A Couple of Miles Away

They listened to the *bang* and *scree* somewhere near their shipping container, but everyone jumped when the hoist's frame slammed onto their roof.

When the frame's locking bolts fired, Lin said, "Hope they don't drop us."

Everyone braced an instant before their steel box bounded into the air and began racking sideways.

After twelve days of imprisonment, freedom was almost at hand.

But the crane operator dragged their container sideways in the gravel making it tilt and then skid before slamming down. Inside, there was a pop and the sound of water. The smell reached them a moment later.

"Damn!"

"Oh, God."

"Fuck!"

Sartaq covered his nose and mouth against the stench from the spilled toilet bucket. He scooted up to a squat in case the liquid headed in his direction.

Hours passed, but no one asked about dinner.

Yang pressed the button on his wristwatch for the umpteenth time.

"Three minutes after midnight," he whispered. "Shouldn't they —"

Footsteps crunched in the gravel outside and stopped at the container's steel doors.

Steel screeched against steel through them as something turned. It repeated three times.

Suddenly, both metal doors popped open, rattling on their hinges.

Standing on the gravel, a uniformed guard clamped a hand to his face, gagged, and staggered back.

Sartaq, his five followers, and Lili bolted out of the steel container and fell onto the shipyard's gravel. Gulping air like fish from Donghu Lake, they coughed, grinned, and shook their heads at one another.

They'd survived.

The guard tucked the envelope inside his jacket pocket, closed the gate behind them, and walked back into the yard.

"Avoid each other," Sartaq said with his back to the paved road. "Find big street and make your way to hotel. Big, off by self, next to water. Reservation for Lin. He will check-in for both rooms. Ask for room number when you get there."

Lili shook her head. "They won't tell you that. Use house phone and ask for him by name. He can answer from room and tell you number."

Outside the shipping yard gate, the road split. Lin and Zhou went left, Yang, Guo, and Fan right, and Sartaq and Lili kept going straight.

Sartaq's duffel bag with the remote-control boxes clanked as he walked. Now and then, Lili would look toward him as if she wanted to ask something.

"What?"

"Ten seconds?" She said in the dark, one of her shoes scuffing on the pavement. "Is that long enough?"

"There is exit near our column. We go out there, over short

concrete wall, and then squat. I'll push button then. Very important: open mouth and yawn for explosion. Also look up. Silver bubble quick but pretty. Then stand and watch as buildings fall."

Lili looked confused. "Maybe we should tell them."

"Tell them?" He asked.

"Fan, Zhou, Yang,...Your *madrasa* graduates?"

"My what?"

"*Madrasa.* Your little Islamic college for terrorists."

"Ah. My soldiers. Tell them what?"

"About ten second delay. If they put their bombs next to columns, they can leave. You can trigger bombs after they are gone. No need to die."

Sartaq smirked.

"Lili, you know what Mother says. 'Soldiers die, but leaders lead.' We are leaders. We live to lead others. And they are soldiers. They supposed to die."

"Do they know?" She asked.

"That they die? Of course. But sooner than they expect."

Lili looked at him, their faces dimly visible by a distant streetlight. "I meant, do they know you are running away?"

He stopped.

"Lili, they must not know these." He patted the duffel bag. "They can't. They believe they control bombs. It's only way to be sure they do what we need."

She didn't look convinced.

"Lili, each of them believes he controls own life. I gave them push buttons and said they make bombs explode. They will take the bombs and put them in place. After that, they will wait. And they will think about running away. But they will wait until time almost gone. And two minutes before time up... Boom!"

Lili looked skeptical but nodded. Sartaq knew part of her was still that little girl that ran barefoot on the mountain. They'd both seen evil and cruelty as children, but back then evil was black, and good was white.

Lili'd never grown up. Not all of her.

He loved the innocent part but knew better. He knew thieves, whores, and murderers. And now he was a murderer. He could do the hard things. And he'd do them for her if she couldn't.

They resumed walking.

After a while, she said, "Sacrificing yourself for good cause is noble. That's what your father did. Mine, too."

"Lili, when the hotel falls, more will die than on America's 9/11. That was three thousand. We will kill ten, maybe more. Beijing will be terrified at our power."

"And Blake?" She asked, glancing up at him as they walked. "You told him to meet us there. At Noon."

Sartaq wagged his chin. "Oversight. I should've said two minutes before. That's when everything happens. My five, and hopefully, your American. No more problems."

"So," her voice lifted, "what if he's not there?"

Sartaq harrumphed. "He will be. Engineer, you said. Some of my students are engineers. Very precise. American will arrive early, watch clock, then pop up at exact time."

A car was coming toward them. It had a sign with four English letters on the roof.

"Taxi!" Lili shouted, her arm waving.

As they climbed in, Lili said something to the driver in English. Her American accent was so strong it took him several seconds to realize it was "Marina Bay Sands Hotel."

When they entered the lobby, Lin and Zhou were at the check-in desk. The others were there, too, spread out as Sartaq had instructed.

"How can they check-in?" Lili whispered. "Won't they check for Singapore entry stamp in their passports?"

"They have them," Sartaq said, grinning. "I sent Lin and Zhou here month ago and they entered legally. Then, when they got back, Guo erased exit stamps. Easy to remove. If anyone look, passports say they've been here whole time. Long holiday!"

She made a silent "O" with her mouth.

Lin and Zhou turned from the check-in desk and walked toward the elevators. Zhou flashed two white-plastic keys and mouthed, "five, zero," and gestured up.

* * *

When the elevator opened on the fiftieth floor, Sartaq nudged Lili out. His five soldiers were already waiting. They followed Fan down the hall until he pointed to doors across the hall from each other.

"Lili and I will take this one." Fan tried the key and the lock on 5054 churned. Sartaq pushed it open, took the key from Fan, and then shrank back as Lili swept past like a little animal zooming into the safety of its burrow.

Inside, he let the door close on its strong spring. Lili marched into the bathroom. "Don't come in," she said and shut the door. He heard the lock click, and then water started running.

Sartaq set his duffel bag on the bed nearer the door and sat to wait. Through the closed door, he could hear an occasional splash and the squeaks of bare feet on tile. But there was something else. It took him a few moments to recognize the sound. Lili was singing to herself, the same as when they were children.

It brought up memories from so long ago. They made him feel
—

No!

This wouldn't help with what he needed to do. Tomorrow was the most important day of his life. He couldn't let anything get in the way, not even Lili.

He stepped across the hall and knocked on the door of the other room. Yang opened it.

"Come with me," Sartaq ordered.

Lili's little girl singing continued from the bathroom. He rolled the desk chair near the door and told Yang, "Sit here. Be nice, but don't leave. When she comes out, show her you have this." Sartaq handed him the revolver. "You know to how use?"

Yang nodded.

"She may not leave," Sartaq finished. "I come back soon."

Many minutes later, he was back with the "XMAS" box. He set it next to his duffel bag, Lili's shower still running.

He crossed to the bathroom and rapped on the door. "Hurry up."

There was no answer.

He banged. "Hurry up!"

Lili shouted something back that he didn't understand. It sounded like English. He looked at Yang, who was grinning, but then quickly frowned and shook his head.

Sartaq sat on the bed between his duffel bag and the box of explosives. Yang sat in his chair by the door. They waited.

On the digital clock between the beds, the minutes digit progressed from 1, then 2, 3, and every number to 8. The sound of running water stopped.

Six more clicks of falling tiles sounded from the clock before the bathroom door finally swooshed open.

Steam ballooned out and Lili, wearing a huge, fluffy white robe, stepped out. Only her head, two graceful hands, and two tiny feet were visible. Draped back across the collar, her dark hair glistened in a long ocean wave ending halfway down her back. Fragrances of flowers, green grass, and fresh loam accompanied her into the room.

At the desk, she smiled at Yang. "May I have chair, please?"

Yang scooted it under her as she sat before the mirror.

"Thank you."

Sartaq offered, "I will have Lin get you some new clothes when shops open."

She wasn't listening.

"Dry, very dry," she said to the mirror, turning her face left and right.

They both heard Yang's sigh. Lili smiled at him in the mirror, a coy, girlish smile. His face had a dreamy, curl-up-and-snuggle look, and his hand with the revolver drooped.

Sartaq coughed and glared at the boy.

Yang jumped, righted the revolver, and straightened his back.

"Nobody leaves," Sartaq said.

In the bathroom, Sartaq washed his clothes in the sink using half of the only soap left, a tiny, plastic bottle marked "Body Wash." And then finished the bottle with his shower. One face cloth on the back of the toilet was the only thing left to dry himself. He then dabbed as much as he could from his squeezed-out coveralls and put them back on, wet skin through wet fabric. It did not go easy.

Back in the room, he took the gun from Yang and sent him across the hall to wait.

Lili glanced at him. "You're dripping."

She resumed threading her fingers through her hair and letting the strands fall in long streaming cascades, over and over. It glistened and shimmered like liquid mahogany.

Dirt and makeup both gone from her face, she glowed.

She pouted at him in the mirror. "Why you give gun to Longwei? Don't you trust me?"

Chapter 24

After Midnight
Mickey's Apartment

It was after midnight when Mickey opened his door again.

Blake turned off the TV.

"It's set," Mickey said in a weary voice. "The team is deployed. We have a few hours before we're due, but when we get there, your job will be to spot them. That's all. I don't want you moving around if things happen."

Blake gave him a nod.

"We roll at Four," Mickey said, pointing to the kitchen clock. "Get some rest."

He went back into his room and shut the door.

Blake stayed on the couch until the light under Mickey's door turned off, then headed for his room, undressed in the dark, and lay in bed listening. It didn't take long for Mickey's snoring to start. Blake counted the inhalations. When they became as regular as a pendulum, he counted. After a hundred in a row, he figured Mickey was in Stage Three, the deepest sleep.

Blake slid out from the covers and used his hand to follow the cord of his alarm clock down behind the end table. He wriggled the plug loose. The red digits—1:17—dimmed but continued to glow. Holding it out as a flashlight, he padded to the bedroom door, silently opened, and watched as several tiny red glints sparkled back from the coffee table. He padded across to the shiny, clean guns.

He needed to stop Sartaq long enough to grab Megyn and run. Mickey and his crew could then deal with the rest.

The chromed 38 revolver was out. Although it was extremely accurate like all the Bullseye guns, its special bullets were wad cutters. They were slow and not good for much more than punching pretty holes in paper. And worse, Blake jerked it more than once. A seven or an eight might score points at the range, but on Sartaq it might be a miss, or not slow the big man down enough.

Blake had shot best with the 22, but the little bullets had very little mass. They were used by assassins, but only when several shots could be accurately placed, preferably to the head.

The .45 caliber Masuda 1911 would be best. Firing standard "ball" ammo, that gun and that ammunition had been the US Army's choice for decades. They switched to 9mm later, a decision that was still frowned upon by many. The official explanation was that fewer sizes of ammo in the field would guarantee more ammo for the troops, but many objected because of the decreased stopping power.

Blake sat on the couch with the alarm clock's red glow facing toward the gun box. He took an empty magazine from the magnetic strip and quietly inserted seven of its standard round-nose, copper-plated bullets. Blake guided the full magazine into the 1911's grip and pressed, then released, the slide latch as it seated to avoid the click. He carefully racked the Masuda's glass-smooth slide back to load the top round from the magazine into the chamber. Then, he removed the magazine, added back a round for the one now in the chamber, and re-inserted it. The gun was loaded 7+1: eight shots ready to go.

All for you, Sartaq.

He put his thumb under the safety and was about to push it up, when he remembered that Bullseye shooters rarely used it. They preferred the ECIs as they'd done at today's competition to prove the gun was "safe." Because it was rarely used, the Masuda's safety latch would be stiff, and hence make a loud click.

But carrying a loaded gun with the safety off was extremely dangerous. It was an easy way to shoot yourself.

Blake knew what to do. Holding the gun in his right hand in the normal way, he put his left over the top of the slide and positioned his thumb in the space between hammer and firing pin. He squeezed the trigger, and the hammer gave a whispered *thump* when it hit his thumbnail. He grasped the sides of the hammer, withdrew his thumb, and gently let the hammer go the rest of the way down.

Pulling the trigger now would do nothing. The hammer had already fallen.

With a round in the chamber but de-cocked, it was safe to press the trigger.

He'd have to cock the hammer with his thumb if he wanted to shoot.

Blake crept back into the guest bedroom. Temporarily, he concealed the 1911 in the right front pocket of his cargo pants on the chair by the bed. He spread his garish Hawaiian shirt with green and yellow palms on top. In the morning, he'd move the gun to the small of his back under the shirt's tail to conceal it.

The alarm clock brightened to 1:32 when he plugged it in again.

Blake lay in bed, eyes wide open, and started engineering solutions to every problem he could imagine.

Chapter 25

Same Time
Marina Bay Sands Hotel, Singapore

"Of course, I trust you," Sartaq lied. "Fan only here to protect you." He jerked his head toward the door. "Those easy to break."

"Actually," she said as she started another sheaf of wet hair cascading through her fingers, "they're steel in a steel frame. Quite strong."

Sartaq changed the subject. He pointed to the box of explosives from the housekeeping closet. "I'll make these ready."

Opening the flaps, inside the cardboard was another, smaller box completely wrapped in clear tape. A red label warned in several languages, "Fragile: Do Not Drop."

Sartaq used a fingernail to slit the tape along the edges. Inside, red tubes sat like sausages on the University cafeteria grill.

Lili obliged his "Look" by glancing over to one he held up, then went back to her mirror and finger-combing.

Sartaq unzipped a pocket of his duffel bag and removed the folded page of Feng Min's instructions. Before the library attack, he'd glanced at it, nodded, and gave it to Tan Ling. He watched over her shoulder, but when she commented that the connectors only went together one way, he realized anyone could do it.

"I showed Tan Ling for library," he lied. "It's easy."

Looking in the mirror, Lili divided her attention between her hair and what he was doing.

He counted out the dynamite sticks into six piles, followed by the contents of his duffel bag, the six boxes, one for each pile.

He held up the seventh box. It was different. "This is order giver." He said to her reflection. "It tells others what to do." He straightened his back and stretched himself up. "I told Feng Min to make these. He good but very young. Doesn't know world. I am like father to him."

Lili turned and nodded at the bed. "Lots of parts."

He shook his head. "It's simple. Only hook up one way."

Lili looked skeptical, but it didn't matter. She didn't need to know about dynamite or bombs or Feng's remote detonators. That was his job. His job was the doing.

Sartaq picked up a wiring harness and one of the bricks containing five 9v batteries. He positioned the lined-up connectors in the harness to the top of the brick and then pressed all five connectors into place with what sounded like a cricket's single chirp.

He held it up for her to see, but she was looking at the instruction sheet he'd tossed.

"You're doing it wrong," she warned. "Batteries are later."

He blinked.

She read aloud. "Very Important. After assembling harness to equipment, verify Arm/Disarm switch. It must be in Disarm position before connecting batteries."

She held up the page for him to see.

"Feng made these," he objected. "It doesn't matter when you put in batteries."

Lili's eyes flared. "Your boy, Feng, says it does. He wrote, 'Very Important.'"

"Lili," he fumed, "this is my job. I know what I'm doing."

She stood and stamped a bare foot on the carpet. "Dammit, Taq, you could blow us up right here."

He stood and glared back, the batteries swinging at the end of the harness in his hand.

After several long, silent seconds, her eyes narrowed ever so slightly. Her face relaxed, the smile came back, and she shuffled the same foot on the carpet.

"Taq," she cooed, "I love you. You're my big brother. You're stronger and more powerful than me. Always have been." She nodded toward the door. "And I'm very proud of how you've trained those boys."

"Soldiers," he corrected. "Yes, I trained them and they're ready to die when I tell them."

Lili walked, her tiny feet taking baby steps, until her little round toes touched his big, yellow boots. She reached up and cupped her small hand on his scarred cheek. It felt cool against his fiery face.

His head automatically turned to nuzzle into her caress.

"You are helping me, aren't you, Taq?" Searching his eyes, she asked, "You always help me, don't you? Helping little Lili?"

She gave him the little girl pouty look.

He felt his head nod in her hand.

"So, let me help you, too, my big, powerful brother. You are doing so much already. Let me do this one thing? For you, yes?"

She tilted her head the other way, waited, and then blinked once.

"How about I read?" She asked. "Remember how I helped you in school? I would read, and you would say it back? You were good student. If they hadn't kicked you out, you could have gone to college just like me. I know you are smart. Can you let me help you again, Taq? I read and you do it?"

Sartaq felt his head nod.

An hour later, six fully assembled bombs, all set to Disarm, lay in a straight line on the bed. Each one was about the size of the ball used by students when they played American football in the university stadium's infield.

"Now," Sartaq grinned, "see my special addition."

He reached into his duffel bag and brought out a tangle of yellow and green wires with several blue-sparkle, bicycle handlebar grips.

Extracting one, he held it up with his thumb poised over a red switch in the end of the bicycle grip, and a twist of yellow and green wires trailing out the other end. "These are mine. Not even Feng Min knows about them."

Sartaq picked up one bomb, stuffed the butt end of the wires into the middle of the bundle, and then added two rounds of black tape to secure it.

"This," he said, holding the bicycle grip again with his thumb poised, "gives soldiers courage!"

He mashed the red button.

Nothing happened.

"See?" He pumped it. "It does nothing!"

Lili frowned but nodded. "I'm impressed with your understanding of human psychology. Mother will be, too."

Someone rapped on the door.

Sartaq glanced at the clock between the beds. It was after two in the morning.

"What could they want?" Sartaq said, guessing it was one of his warriors from across the hall. He peered through the peephole.

Something white—a cart?—waited just out the door. Behind and looking like he was far away, a man in a hotel uniform with a very dark complexion waited.

"What?" Sartaq shouted, his eye to the door.

"Room service."

"We didn't—"

"Taq," Lili interrupted, "That'll be hotel porter with dinner. I ordered some things."

Sartaq turned and growled, "Fan let you use phone?"

"Yes, but don't worry. Your faithful follower had your gun on me."

Strong aromas drifted under the door. They made Sartaq's mouth water. They'd lived on ramen, dried fish, and candy bars for nearly two weeks.

He swallowed and shouted, "Wait."

He crossed to the bed and pulled the top of the bedcover down towards the foot. The six bombs clanked as they rolled together before the cover hid them.

"Jesus," Lili warned, "Be careful!"

Sartaq scanned the room before opening the door.

"Good evening," the porter said, pushing the cart into the room.

Lili pointed to the small table with two chairs in front of the floor-to-ceiling and wall-to-wall window.

He wheeled the cart next to the table, lifted one end of the cloth and used the toe of one shoe to set a wheel lock. In two minutes, steam was rising from seven dishes of food arranged on the white tablecloth along with two place settings facing each other. A glass vase with three yellow petaled flowers at the ends of lime-green stems sat nearest the window.

Sartaq leaned over to sniff. They were real.

The porter stepped back. "Anything else?"

Lili surveyed the table. "Pepper oil?"

He motioned with an open palm. "In metal pitcher with dipping spoon. Would you like more?"

"We'll call if we do. This looks fine. Thank you."

The porter handed a flat leather pad to Sartaq. Embossed with the outline of the hotel's three buildings and the curved swimming pool across the top, a tongue of paper and the end of a pen stuck out.

Sartaq pulled out the paper and glanced down at the list. He could read only the numbers. The last one said, S$256.23.

He handed it to Lili. "What's this?"

"It's our dinner. Let's see, there should be Hainanese Chicken Rice—" the porter leaned in to raise the lid on a dish with pale slices of chicken laid atop a mound of white rice garnished with tiny rings of sliced green onion"—and Guangzhou-style Hor Fun—" another lid revealed wide, almost translucent rice noodles with sliced Bok Choy and Enoki mushrooms in a reddish-clear broth— she glanced at him, "—and Moo Shoo, with shredded pork and vegetables and pale, thin pancakes with caramelized sugar and soy sauce."

Sartaq swallowed the flood of moisture in his mouth. He drew Lin Yusheng's name at the bottom of the receipt, and the porter left.

Lili stepped to the clock radio and turned it on. American rock music played into the room as Sartaq lifted two of the Moo Shoo pancakes onto his plate, added a spoonful of pork and vegetables to each, then one of sweet brown sauce. He rolled them into tubes with his fingers and lifted it to his mouth after folding the bottom end so nothing could fall out.

"Fan mentioned this radio station," she said, waving a hand toward the radio. "Okay with you?"

He nodded while swallowing his first bite. "Sure," he said, "We listen, same kind music, when I visit students in dorm."

He stuffed the rest of his first Moo Shoo roll into his mouth. "This," he said around the ingredients, "is wonderful."

Thirty minutes later, Sartaq and Lili both leaned back in their chairs. The plate of pancakes and most others were empty, but with enough left for breakfast.

Another knock sounded at the door.

"Oh," Lili exclaimed, standing up. She batted her eyes at Sartaq. "That'll be my personal shopper that concierge suggested. I asked to bring me some things."

"Personal shopper?" Sartaq glanced at the alarm clock. "At three in morning?"

Her hand on the door handle, Lili pouted at him. "I only ordered what I had to have. Nothing more."

She held the door as a long clothes rack rolled in like a train. A pert woman with immaculate makeup, pearls around her neck, and wearing a crisp, black dress followed the porter, who guided the rack just short of the dinner table. He left with a nod.

A new song began on the radio. "Oh!" Lili exclaimed. "That's one of my favorites. Do you mind if I turn it up?"

The music had an old-time sound like something that would be in what his students said was *film noir*. He imagined the singer would be an American woman in a slinky, shiny dress standing at a big microphone on a silver stand.

"It's Madonna," Lili said. "*Sooner or Later.*"

Without waiting for an answer, she turned to the woman in black, snugged the belt of her robe and turned all the way round with her arms out. The woman watched, nodded, and then began pawing through the rack.

Sartaq watched in fascination while the sultry singer's voice tickled his ears like a seductress in a Wuhan alley. The stern woman in black would select a dress or blouse and hold it next to Lili's neck and face as she stepped and turned with the music. "No," and "Definitely not" went to the end of the rack. "Maybe" and "Very nice" garnered mutual smiles and sometimes a twirl from Lili and a happy glance. Laid with a graceful swoop on the empty bed next to the previous candidate, only "Yes" would remain.

"If you would, sir?" The lady said, inclining her head to two boxes on the bottom of the cart.

Sartaq knew he should look away or find something else to do, but the finery of the undergarments stunned him. Meticulous needle work swept around each cup of the silk bras. And the sheer panties, not the black ones but the light cream with a hint of tan, matched Lili's complexion. If not for the lace—he felt himself blush—they'd be invisible on her. Lili plucked and fluffed through the box until one perfectly matched set lay across the top of the bed, as if waiting for a spirit to materialize and inflate them.

Sartaq realized that both Lili and the woman were looking at him and waiting.

"What?" he said.

Lili put two hands on the rope holding the robe closed and raised an eyebrow at him.

"Oh!" He turned away and looked toward the window. There was nothing to see in the dark except Lili's figure perfectly reflected. Madonna's voice beckoned from the radio.

Lili pulled open the robe's belt. Sartaq closed his eyes and turned his face to the right.

But now she was in the desk mirror. The robe dropped from her shoulders, swept down her lithe arms, past her rounded hips...

On the radio, Madonna gasped. She held her breath between two words.

Sartaq put a hand over his eyes, but the vision lingered.

His little Lili was an astonishingly beautiful woman, and in the full flower of life.

Sartaq felt confused, aroused, guilty, proud, and ashamed.

As he waited, eyes covered, fabrics rustled, zippers zipped, and unzipped. There was more rustling, more zippers, on and on. The only words were, "Yes," "No," and "Try it with that."

Finally, they were done.

"You can look now."

Gathered around her neck and reaching only to the top of her thighs, Lili wore a pale yellow, and mercifully opaque, robe. Matching yellow, poof-ball slippers adorned her tiny feet. He thought of a fluffy poodle, trimmed and primped for show.

He was sweating and felt deeply uncomfortable. Maybe it was the rich dinner?

He walked to the radio and turned it off.

On the bed lay tomorrow's selection. There was a pink and light tan, sheer silk top with spring flowers to be worn over what Lili had said was a *camisole*. The plain linen skirt matched the pink of the flowers in the blouse. There was an off-white sweater—"A cardigan for this chilly room." She'd insisted he feel how soft it was.

Sartaq picked up a shoe from the bed. It was tan—Lili said, "nude"—had a hole in the front—"peep toe"—and straps—"sling back"—that would loop around and behind her delicate ankle. The heels looked taller than the length of her foot. In the instep were gold English letters. "Jimmy Choo," she told him.

Makeup came from another box. Aligned on the desk— "Dressing table"—were half a dozen tiny bottles, flat plastic packs, little tubs with screw tops, and two fold-open pads like artist's kits with pencils, short-handled brushes, tweezers, tiny scissors, and flat-paddled tools with intricate ivory handles.

At Sartaq's scowl, Lili stated she would need everything there before she could possibly leave the room. The woman in black sternly agreed.

She handed an electronic tablet to Sartaq. As with dinner, everything was in English except the amounts. She held out a short plastic stick and said something in English.

Lili translated. "She wants you to sign."

On the line below S$2,473.43, he drew Lin Yusheng in Hanzi.

Twenty minutes later, with the new wardrobe hanging in the bathroom—"To steam," she said—and the bombs lined up on the desk, Sartaq and Lili lay in separate beds. Lights off, and backs toward each other, there was no sound unless one of them moved under their sheet.

Nearest the window and looking out, Sartaq's gaze settled on a yellowish light that seemed far out, probably on board some ship sitting in the ocean. But his mind kept going back to Lili, her beauty, the clothing, her secret garments, the scents from their dinner dishes, the soap and shampoo Lili had used when bathing...

My little sister...

Chapter 26

Before Dawn
Saturday

A few minutes before four, Mickey's stirrings sounded through the wall.

Blake got up, dressed, and tucked the Masuda into the small of his back. Hidden under the tail of his Hawaiian shirt, he'd have to remember not to expose it by bending over. He entered the living room and waited by the apartment's door. When Mickey opened his bedroom door, Blake called, "Over here. Ready to go."

Mickey never glanced toward the coffee table.

In the Volvo, a sign with 90 in a red circle shot past Blake's window. He glanced over at the Volvo's speedometer: 150.

"Surveillance is up." Mickey said, shunting onto the shoulder and around a car.

"Black helmets and clothes?" Blake asked, the steel muzzle of the gun digging into the unprotected center of his plumber's crack.

Mickey shook his head, his eyes far ahead on the dark road. "Not the ones in public. You won't know who's who. But you'll be in the van watching the monitors, so it won't matter."

Being stuck in a police van was not in Blake's imagined scenarios.

"I'd do better in the lobby," he suggested. "Direct observation."

"No. And for lots of reasons: He knows you; you can only be in one place; you'd be exposed if we have to engage... The monitors in the van will give you better views than you could get on your own."

Blake said nothing. *Adapt or perish*, he remembered somebody's words. Blake had no problem with that approach. Circumstances change; plans must follow.

Blake was an engineer. He shoved back against the sense of impending failure.

I can do this.

The car veered left under an overpass for an exit. Mickey braked hard but then held their speed as the tires sang around the 270 degree arc up and over the highway they'd just left. Coming out of the curve, he glanced right, then left through the trees, and powered through a red light.

"You job," he said, "is to spot the terrorists. That's all. Leave the rest to us."

Far ahead, the broad faces of the hotel's three buildings glittered across an inlet from Singapore's downtown.

Mickey glanced at Blake. "Fifty-seven stories," he volunteered. "There's a restaurant and swimming pool on the roof. They say it has an invisible edge. Looks like you would swim right out into space."

"Not quite six seconds," Blake said without thinking.

"What?" Mickey asked.

"The fall from the top would take just under six seconds."

Mickey glanced at him.

Blake explained, "Fifty-seven stories at ten to twelve feet per floor plus a tall lobby, so that's six hundred feet up. Then thirty-two feet per second, per second acceleration starting from zero. Total is about six seconds, but you'd reach terminal velocity, so a little less than that."

Mickey gave him another look.

"You do that in your head?"

Blake shrugged.

"It just happens. The numbers come to me."

Mickey leaned forward.

"Out on this end," he pointed up, "there's a deck sticking way out. They say it's strong enough to hold a thousand people."

Blake nodded as he peered up. "Looks like a surfboard."

Mickey slowed to guide the car past the narrow end of the first tower. A uniformed doorman looked up momentarily as they passed.

Ahead on the wrong side, a brown van sat next to the curb. Bright yellow letters on its side advertised, "Mr. Sparky Electrical Services."

Mickey cut across the centerline and stopped behind it.

"Come on," he said, getting out.

He rapped twice on the back of the van. When the door cracked open, Mickey held his badge in the light that streamed out.

"In here." Mickey climbed up the step and into the van.

It looked like a television studio. Video monitors covered the wall on the right above a waist-high slim tabletop that ran front to back. Three police officers in dark blue wore headsets and boom microphones as they sat in rolling chairs.

Mickey squeezed past Blake and into the doorway to leave. He said, "Remember, you spot the terrorists and let us know. Nothing else."

An officer standing next to Blake held out a black belt with a small box connected to a wire and earpiece.

"Take off your shirt."

Blake shied away. "What's this?" He couldn't let them see his gun.

"The little part goes in your ear," the officer explained. "You can talk and hear through it. The box goes on your belt with the wire under your shirt."

"Thanks," Blake said, taking the radio. "I can do this. Don't let me keep you from the monitors."

Thirty seconds later, with his back turned away, Blake finished belting and plugging himself into the Police network. He put a finger on the earpiece in his ear. "Testing, one, two, three?"

"Nope." The officer at the console shook his head. "You're not transmitting. Did you turn on the microphone? It's a slide switch on the top of the box."

Blake reached around, felt for it on his belt by the Masuda, and clicked the switch to his right.

"How's this?"

The officer gave him a thumbs-up and gestured toward the front of the van. He went back to his computer screen. Blake sidled up and squeezed into the only empty chair.

The officer next to him—female, round face, button nose— turned and said, "I'm Dian." She offered a hand. "D-I-A-N but pronounced the usual way. Glad to meet you, Mr. Spencer."

"Blake is fine," he said and shook her hand.

She pointed to the four TV monitors, one atop the other, in front of her. A small paper note beneath each screen, neatly printed in English, described each one's view.

This bank of four covered the lobby. The stack of monitors to its right showed Check-In, Cashier, Concierge, and Bellman. Next to that were views of elevator doors numbered 1 through 4. And a fourth rank showed North and South entrances, inside and outside views. The final bank, next to the door he'd come through, was unlabeled.

"We connect those on an as-needed basis," Officer Dian explained. "Three restaurants, several rooftop cameras, kitchens, laundry, you name it."

Blake nodded in approval. "All the floors and hallways, too?"

She shook her head. "Way too many. With fifty-four guest floors across three buildings, it's just too many. We concentrate on the prime areas."

Blake examined the people in the lobby monitors. Most were sitting or standing, alone or with someone. Everything looked normal. He leaned back to survey all five ranks, the monitors in the last occasionally flicking to a different camera.

Knowing what the cameras could and could not see would be important when he left. The random ones... Well, he'd just have to watch for the cameras and avoid them.

"This is amazing," he said. "I assume the cameras are pretty small?"

She nodded. "Most are two-centimeter cubes. If you aren't

looking, they're almost invisible. The ones with gimbals are bigger because of the mount, but there aren't many of those."

"And those people?" He pointed to the lobby monitor in front of them. "Which ones are yours?"

Dian looked for a moment. "Mostly our's," she said, then leaned forward and tapped the glass on the second monitor on a man in a blue business suit. "This guy's not one of us. That's not him, is it?"

Blake leaned forward to look. The man was stocky and bald.

"No."

Dian motioned back over her shoulder, "If you're hungry, there are sandwiches and drinks in the mini fridge. Coffee and tea are on top. Starbucks. Might be a donut left. Milk's inside if you want it."

The digital clock at the top of the wall said 4:27.

Noon was a long time off.

A ham and cheese on white would have to suffice for his breakfast. There was only one yellow-mustard packet left. Blake squeezed it out onto one triangular slice, smeared it on the other half, then reassembled his sandwich. He poured a coffee, added the last of the milk, and sat down to eat in the Police surveillance van.

"They're opening the pool."

Officer Dian's voice echoed in Blake's ear a fraction of a second after she spoke aloud right next to him.

From the delay, Blake knew they were using a computerized digital radio. The engineers he'd taught in Ft Worth a couple of years ago were designing one. He knew the basics.

Blake leaned over to Dian and tapped his earpiece. "How many channels do you run?"

"We're using two today," she answered. "*All* and *CC*, Commander's Conference. Everybody's transmit goes to the computer simultaneously but on different frequencies in tenth-of-a-second chunks. It re-transmits each chunk a tenth of a second later on the two channels we're using today. You won't notice the delay unless you can hear both the radio and the person directly.

Inspector Chee and three others are on the Commander's Conference channel. When they select that one, they hear only each other."

"I assume," Blake asked, "that I won't hear that one?"

Dian nodded and pointed toward the back of the van where the officer who'd given Blake the radio and earpiece sat. "Prakash manages the routing. He can change it when ordered. It just takes a moment."

Blake thanked her and checked the van's digital clock.

5:59.

Two hours down, six to go.

He pushed his chair back, stood and stretched, and then sidled behind the chairs to the back of the van.

On the last bank of monitors, a digital title, *Pool Cabana*, floated in front of the image on the top screen. It showed long shadows running straight out across lounge chairs and disappearing into the water beyond. Near the bottom left corner of the screen, two men, one in black swimming trunks, the other in red, spread towels on lounge chairs. One of them walked over, tested the water with his foot, then slid in to his waist.

The officer assigned to that monitor zoomed in and turned to Blake.

The swimmer had a round, somewhat reddish face, distinct frown lines between his eyebrows, and neatly trimmed hair. There was no scar when he turned.

"Nope," Blake said, stifling a yawn. "Not even close."

He shifted back to the front and refilled his coffee.

Before he could open a creamer, the pool officer beckoned. "More swimmers. Want to look?"

He carried his cup and the creamer with him. On the screen, three people stood with their backs to the camera. Two of them, their bodies lanky and youthful, wore loose-fitting, knee length trunks in solid, primary colors with sharp creases on the outside of each leg. They dove in together and stroked away to the right. The third member of the new group wore a badly wrinkled green shirt and pants. His broad-shouldered back to the camera, he walked to one of the lounge chairs, gripped the top with one hand

and spun it around effortlessly. Shading his face from the morning sun, he sat with the back of his head toward the camera.

Blake felt his chest tighten. He leaned forward and touched the man's image on the screen. "Can you zoom in?"

The picture bloomed until the back of the man's head filled the screen.

"I need to see his face. Left side."

Three chairs away, Dian said, "Roof Cabana, make the guy in the lounge chair turn left. We need to see that side of his face."

A moment later, an unknown voice boomed in Blake's earpiece, "Sir, may I get you something?"

The head on the monitor bolted up and out of the camera's view. The officer in front of Blake began dashing his hands over the controls.

A gruff voice that sounded like it was several feet from a microphone barked a couple of sharp syllables.

Cantonese? Blake wondered.

The camera found the man again. He was shaking his head and gesturing at a man in a hotel uniform.

But the scar was unmistakable.

"That's him!" Blake shouted. "That's Sartaq!"

"The leader?" Officer Dian shouted, her hand jerking to her waist. "Are you sure?"

"Yes, yes. Get him!"

Dian's voice in the van said, "We've got him, sir." Her words echoed in his earpiece. "Attention. Attention all stations! The leader is on the roof. Positive ID. Repeat, positive ID." She reached to her waist. "Yes, sir." She twisted that arm. "Roof Cabana, break away and get us a complete description."

Mickey's voice sounded in Blake's ear. "Elevator Control: Where did the last delivery to the roof come from? Man in green work clothes, plus two college age in new swimsuits."

Blake leaned forward and shook the officer's shoulder. "That's the guy. Grab him!"

Another voice crackled, "Lift three, middle tower. Pickup on fifty, direct to the roof. Three passengers, as described. Nothing else to the roof for nine minutes before that."

"Shoot him!" Blake shouted. "Get him now! And the rest of them," he bellowed, "they'll be with Megyn on the fiftieth floor."

He wondered if Mickey could hear him.

Officer Dian was waving her hands at him. "Sir, please stop yelling. Be quiet and let us do our jobs." She returned to her monitors.

The man next to her pressed a button and leaned into his console microphone. "Elevator: I've got the videos. What are the timestamps?"

"Six-fifty-nine pickup at fifty, then seven-oh-two at the roof."

Blake clamped his lips shut and crossed his arms, but it was impossible to stand still. He fidgeted in place, craned down to look at the bottom monitor, and then back to the pool camera.

Nothing was happening.

The rooftop police officer's voice droned in his ear. "Hundred-seventy centimeters, seventy-five kilos, messy black hair three centimeters long with a centimeter wide white scar in left hairline continuing in the skin down his cheek to the jawline. Round face, large, wide-spaced brown eyes, mixed-Mongolian complexion, plain green work shirt and slacks, brown belt, yellow construction boots."

The officer in front of Blake typed on his keyboard and hit the Enter key. The inside of an elevator appeared on the top monitor in front of him. He put his finger into a small depression on the top of a knob and twirled it clockwise. The time code at the bottom of the screen counted up. When it reached "6:57:50," he slowed but continued forward. On the monitor, the doors snapped open, and three men leaped in like Keystone Cops. The operator stopped and spun back a couple of turns. Men jumped out backwards and the doors closed. The operator pressed a green button on the console. At normal speed, the three men looked down and stepped over the gap into the elevator. They turned as the doors shut. Only the tops and backs of their heads were visible. The one on the left wore a green shirt, the other two were bare-chested. The one on the right pressed a button high on the wall next to the elevator door. In the playback, the digital floor indicator counted up. After "56" the indicator changed to "RF" and a chime sounded from the van's main speaker. The man in green pointed to his wristwatch and said something Blake didn't understand. A moment later, the doors opened, and they all stepped out.

"No faces," the video operator reported to the radio.

Blake shook the man's shoulder. "What did he say? What did Sartaq say?"

The man glared until Blake removed his hand.

Officer Dian translated. "'One hour, no more.' I didn't get everything after that, but he mentioned the gift shop and ten o'clock. Now, please, stop interfering and let us do our work."

Blake couldn't believe what was happening. The Police were doing nothing about stopping the terrorists. Sartaq was the head guy. If they stopped him, the attack would stop, and Megyn would be safe.

It would be easy, he was sure, to check the registration for the fiftieth floor where they'd boarded the elevator. A group like that —five men plus Sartaq plus Megyn—would be obvious. Ray and his team could storm the room, shoot any bombers they found, and rescue Megyn. Sartaq and these two on the roof would be easy shots. D-R-T. Game over.

And Megyn would be safe!

But nothing happened.

Instead, the van settled back the same as it'd been for hours. Dian watched her monitors and sipped tea. Officer Prakash pushed his mouse around and occasionally pecked at his keyboard. Someone in the van mumbled something in another language, and they all chuckled and nodded.

Why doesn't Mickey give the order?

In his loud, start-of-class teaching voice, Blake commanded, "Mickey! Take Sartaq now. He obviously doesn't have the explosives. Shoot him, or grab him, but do it now!"

Mickey calmly replied. "Stay off the radio, Blake. We've got this."

Blake shook his head. Were they going to let the terrorists carry the bombs into the lobby? Show up with the gun held to Megyn's head again?

At the back of the van, Officer Prakash touched a hand to his ear and said, "Yes, sir." He began mousing and typing. A few seconds later, he flicked a glance at Blake but then turned away.

Mickey's voice came out of the van's speaker. "Roof Cabana, when those two in the pool get out, get them to look up at the towel stand so we can get their faces."

"Roger."

Blake realized he'd heard none of that in his earpiece.

Mickey's voice came out of just the speaker again. "Elevator Control: when the terrorists arrive in the lobby, I'm going to need everyone there. That includes you. You'll shift to," there was a pause, "position four, Lobby South. I'll say when but be ready."

"Yes, sir."

"I'm not hearing this on my radio," Blake complained, tapping the earpiece.

Dian gave him a patronizing smile. "We have to consider the entire group, not just the leader. If they're all together at some point, then... But we don't know where the explosives are. If one of them gets to the lobby and sets off a bomb... Right now, we need to watch and see what they're going to do."

"I need to hear what's happening," Blake demanded. "Turn me back on. They've got Megyn somewhere. We need to find her."

Dian smiled at him. "Is that her name? Megyn?"

Blake coursed his eyebrows, but she went on without waiting. "We practice for situations like this all the time. We know how to handle this. We'll get her out. Don't worry."

Blake's jaw dropped. She'd actually said, *Don't worry*? How could she say such a thing? If he'd learned anything in life, when someone said that, you damn well should!

He flexed his back in frustration. The grip of the 1911 rubbed his back.

Sartaq was a murderer. He should be killed like a rat, but that wasn't Blake's job. That was for Mickey and his people. Same for the college boys. Deluded and confused maybe, but again, not his job.

Only Megyn. And just Megyn. That's why Blake had come to Singapore. That's why he was here in the Police van. For Megyn.

Not for Mickey, and not for Singapore.

The Police had their job, and he had his.

And he needed to know what they knew, and what they were planning in order to work out what he could then do.

He closed his eyes, took a deep breath, and forced his shoulders lower as he exhaled.

He smiled. "I'm sorry, Officer Dian, about my outburst. I shouldn't have yelled. I know you're all just trying to help."

She gave him another fake smile. "It's hard for everyone. But that's why we train, so we do the right thing."

"I know, I'm sorry."

She reached over and patted his hand.

He tilted his head. "Would you ask them to let me monitor things again?"

She frowned.

"It helps me to know where to look," he said. "There are three more terrorists, plus Megyn, to find. If I see something, I'll just tell you. I promise. It's your job to decide what to do about it. I understand that now."

She didn't look convinced but said, "Let me see what I can do."

Her hand went to her waist as she conferred with someone, probably Mickey, on the radio.

Eventually, she looked up and winked. "All right. You'll hear everyone, but when you speak, only Inspector Chee will receive."

Moments later, the methodical chatter of voices resumed in his ear.

Blake said, "Thanks. I'll go check the pool camera again."

He side-stepped to the back of the van.

In the last set of monitors, Sartaq and his two students were still relaxing on lounge chairs.

With all the officers focused on their work, Blake reached around to the radio on his waist. He slid the microphone switch to off.

He leaned over and tapped Officer Prakash's shoulder.

"I need to poop," he whispered. "Where's the toilet?"

\Blake closed the door of the stall and sat, pants on, to avoid the tiny camera cube he'd spotted in the top corner of the bathroom. In his earpiece, "No activity" was becoming monotonous.

Sartaq and his swimming buddies had come from the fiftieth floor, but which room? Or rooms?

Blake flushed the toilet, waited a moment as if fastening his pants, and then kept his camera-side hand up as if to brush his hair as he left the bathroom. In the lobby, he kept close to the wall as he edged around to a dark area opposite the elevators.

He waited.

There were more people milling about than he expected this early, but as Dian had said, many would be undercover.

A man in a blue suit by the Concierge desk holding a travel brochure seemed extra stocky. *Bullet-proof vest under his jacket?*

A woman in tan, bell-bottom pants and a loose jacket carried a huge purse.

Semi-automatic in the purse? Snubby on her ankle?

A couple with two kids in bathing suits near the main door, some innocent bystanders waiting for a taxi who'd be shredded in the blast? Getting them out and gone should be a priority. But people scooting them out and into buses and taxis would be a giveaway.

God help the innocent.

A bell chimed and the up arrow above a closed elevator door turned on.

With a hand across his brow like the bill of a baseball cap, Blake kept his face down and strode toward it. Glancing between his fingers as the door opened, he spotted the tiny camera at the top of the elevator's back wall. He entered, turned, and pressed the button marked "50." The doors closed.

When they opened, he stepped out to the fiftieth floor. Predictably, the long hall had numbered doors on both sides, odds on the left, evens on the right.

With seven people, Sartaq and his crew probably used at least two rooms.

But which ones?

He huffed in frustration. He'd just have to wait.

Blake stepped into the alcove to his left. It had a soft drink machine, an ice maker, and a tall, glass-fronted vending machine with chips and other snacks. In the twelve-inch gap between ice maker and soft drink machine, two white PVC pipes dripped into a floor grate.

Blake checked his watch: 8:07.

Almost four hours.

He was about to fish in his pocket for change to buy a bottle of water when an excited voice in his earpiece reported the two terrorist swimmers were getting up. It said the man in green was still dozing in his lounge chair.

A minute later, the elevator monitor said, "Two coming down, middle tower, headed to fifty."

Blake pushed into the gap between the machines. The horn of the 1911 made a loud scrape on the side of the ice machine. He shifted to shallow chest breaths to keep it from moving.

The *ding* for the elevator was followed by the *fwap-fwap, fwap-fwap* of two sets of flip-flops. They passed the alcove and dwindled down the hallway.

Blake blew out to empty his lungs, pulled in his stomach, put his hand around back to cushion the Masuda, and slid out. He tip-toed to the edge of the hallway and peered around the corner.

Two shirtless men, their backs to him with towels around their waists, one with green flip-flops, the other in pink, stopped halfway down. As one raised his hand toward the door handle, the other casually turned his head back up the hall. Blake yanked himself back, his heart pounding.

A few seconds later, the solid *thunk* of a door closing reverberated in the hall.

Blake peered around the corner. The hall was now empty.

He had a rough idea where they'd gone—halfway down on the left. But that didn't tell him exactly, nor Megyn's location, nor that of the other three terrorists.

Patience, he told himself.

Minutes passed before the same excited voice in his ear shouted, "He's getting up!"

Mickey's tone was calm and efficient. "Don't get excited. Just tell me, who is getting up, and where is he now?"

The first voice continued just as fast. "Yes, sir! The head guy—Up at the pool?—he's up now. And he's walking toward the elevator..."

Mickey answered, calm and unperturbed, "Elevator Control: When that car gets to the roof and he boards, if he's alone, take him to the floor he wants. Exclusive and express service. No stops to pick up anyone else."

"Yes, Sir."

Mickey's voice continued, "Blake, get a good look at him. Make sure it's Sartaq."

Standing in the alcove, Blake wondered if he should say, "Okay," but before he could, his earpiece announced, "He's in the elevator by himself. Headed down to fifty. Express service."

The radio was silent for several seconds.

"Blake?" Mickey's voice sounded urgent. "Is that Sartaq? Can you see his face?"

Blake clenched his jaw. Ice clunked in the ice maker behind him.

Mickey commanded, "Anyone in the van, turn on Blake's microphone. I can't hear him."

"Um," Officer Dian's voice warbled. "He's not in the van, sir."

"Arriving at fifty."

Blake heard the chime out in the hallway. He pressed into the gap between the machines again.

"Blake," Mickey's voice barked in his ear, "where are you? We need you in the van."

Heavy boots stomped by the alcove and kept going. Blake slipped out from between the machines and hugged the wall next to the opening.

Dian's voice squeaked in his ear. "He went to the bathroom, sir, but that was quite a while ago."

Mickey's "Shit!" came through loud and clear.

Blake grinned.

The boots stopped. Blake snuck a look. About the same distance down the hall as the students, but at the door on the other side, Sartaq was inserting a card in the lock.

Two rooms across from each other, kids versus grown-ups. That made sense.

"Blake, where are you?" Mickey demanded in his ear. "Report your location."

Sartaq stepped through the open door.

Blake sprinted down the hall. The door slammed ten feet ahead of him.

He slowed to a walk, but kept going, his eyes on the door numbers: 5053 and 5054 across from each other.

He coursed his eyebrows but kept walking.

But where's Megyn? One of those? Or somewhere else?

In his gut, he was sure Sartaq would keep her close.

Unless he'd already killed her. Blake ground his teeth. Either way, that made Sartaq his goal, his target.

He pushed through the emergency exit at the end of the hall and into the stairwell but caught the door before it shut. Trying the handle to be sure it wouldn't lock him out, he eased it shut.

Mickey's voice quivered with anger on the radio. "Take Blake's receive off the main ch—"

Blake's earpiece went dead.

After several seconds, Mickey's voice came on again. "Blake, you're off the net. I can hear you and you'll hear me, but only when I want."

Whatever trust they'd built at Camp Perry, here on the range, trading divorce stories, and telling Mickey everything he knew, that was all gone now. Blake hoped Mickey would cut him some slack because of the situation, but that would be later, if ever. Megyn was the only one that mattered now.

Blake clamped his jaw tight and hardened himself to the task at hand.

Megyn. Get Megyn.

"Pal," Mickey gloated in his ear, "I can hear you breathing."

Blake jumped as if someone were behind him.

"Where are you?" Mickey taunted. "And what are you up to?"

Blake put his arm around back to feel the microphone switch. It was still off.

He shook his head. They'd enabled his microphone despite the manual switch. Like the camera and microphone on his computer, he wasn't actually in charge of them. The computer was, and Mickey gave the orders.

But Mickey was asking where he was. He didn't know. Either their radios didn't have GPS, or the metal in the building blocked the satellite signals.

"Damnit, Blake," Mickey boomed in the earpiece, "This is dangerous enough. Don't make it worse!"

Two beats passed.

"Blake?"

The radio had become a liability.

Blake plucked out the soft rubber earpiece, yanked loose the wire, and ripped open the Velcro fastener. He dropped everything down the center of the stairwell. Eight seconds later, they *cracked* and *clattered* from fifty stories below.

He'd expected six.

Lower terminal velocity.

Chapter 27

Fiftieth Floor
Marina Bay Sands Hotel

A door slammed in the hallway.

Blake edged up to the small window in the Emergency Exit door. He expected to see someone walking toward the elevator, but the only person was a young man scratching his back and knocking on a door on the left side of the hall.

From Blake's angle, he couldn't see the room number on the door, but it was in about the right place if Sartaq was in the one he'd guessed.

The door opened, and the man went in, but didn't stay long. Coming out, he took the elevator down.

Blake waited, the hall empty.

Minutes later, the elevator chimed again. The same man stepped out carrying a tan bag with a wooden-loop handle. The bag bulged slightly but bounced as the man walked. Whatever it held didn't weigh much.

At the same door, he went in for a moment then came out empty-handed. He crossed the hall, knocked, and disappeared.

Blake checked his watch: 11:13.

He crouched down with his back to the concrete block wall. He needed Megyn alone or with only Sartaq. The other five had to be gone before he would have any prayer for success. Would Sartaq send them out one at a time, or would they all go at once?

He could only wait and hope.

The clock between the beds flicked to 11:15.

Sartaq stood up. "Time to get ready."

The souvenir bags Zhou brought, five folded inside the one he carried, sat on the nearest bed.

Sartaq turned one bomb upside down and flipped the power switch where it stuck out of the black electrical tape. The green LED on the control box glowed through another small gap.

Each bomb went in its own Eco bag with the control box hidden on the underside. On top where it'd be obvious, he bunched the yellow and green wires and placed the blue-sparkle bicycle grip with its red pushbutton.

He phoned across the hall. "All of you: Here."

Zhou, Fan, Yang, Guo, and Lin filed into the room, their faces drawn and somber.

Sartaq pointed to the Eco bags on the bed. "You will each carry one. They are armed and ready, so be careful about red button on top."

Yang and Guo nodded. Zhou and Lin looked sick. Fan didn't seem to be paying attention. Instead, he looked at Lili and scanned her from head to toe. She noticed his appraisal and curtsied while turning for his appreciation. He smiled and tucked his chin in approval.

"When I tell you," Sartaq said, glaring at the boy, "all of you will take your bags to lobby. When you get there, read travel brochure, look at people, whatever you want, but also watch hotel clock over check-in desk."

He scanned their faces. They were all looking at him, even Fan.

"At three minutes before hour, arrive at pillar. Stand with back to column and set bag on floor behind you. Do silent prayers in secret. No movements."

They'd all be dead with the hotel collapsed a minute later. What he next told them would never happen.

He smiled.

"Wait for ten seconds before Noon on clock. Quickly take out grip, think but do not say, "Allahu Akbar," and when second hand straight up, push red button. You will feel nothing as you join us all together again in *Firdaus*."

He forced back a chuckle and continued the fantasy.

"Listen for singing. You will hear Allah's voice, and we will be together in his arms."

Zhou whimpered, his face near panic.

As long as they placed their bags, they could stand there in stupidity, cry, run, or hide, but they'd all die ten seconds after Sartaq pushed his transmitter's button.

He swept his hand toward the bed. "Pick up your Godly presents."

Sartaq took the last one. He put his arm through the handle and folded his arms across his stomach.

He walked to Yang, bowed slightly and then spoke, his voice full and resonant like the Imam at the mosque.

"Yang Longwei, you are enforcer. Use this weapon to bring about Allah's will."

Yang gave what might have been a tiny nod.

Sartaq side-stepped to the next.

"Guo Manchu, of all of us, you know best that Allah is with you."

Guo, his chin high to look up at Sartaq, raised it even higher. "We are *Mujahid*," he said, loud and strong. "It is written, 'And he who fights in cause of Allah and is killed or achieves victory - We will bestow upon him great reward!'"

Sartaq shifted.

"Fan Zixin, this will be championship, ultimate game, and you will win. Allah is with you. Enjoy your victory." The muscles in the boy's jaw rippled, but he said nothing.

To Lin Yusheng, he said in a softer voice, "Allah forgives sins of youth. You will enter *Firdaus* like rest of us."

Zhou, last in line, waited with his chin quivering. He put out his hand like an American. Sartaq shook it. The boy nodded, but another whimper escaped his lips.

"Allah is with you," Sartaq said sternly.

"Can I go with Yusheng?"

They'd bolt, Sartaq was sure, out the door and pitch the bombs who knows where. Yusheng would have to be the last sent to the lobby.

He shook his head.

"No. Allah decreed this test for you. You will succeed by your own efforts." He leaned close and whispered, "Remember, in Heaven, you will be with Yusheng. Together forever."

The boy sniffed, stretched taller, and nodded.

Sartaq clamped his jaw to keep from smiling.

The room's alarm clock flicked to 11:45.

"Zhou Guang," he said, "You go first to lobby. Do as Allah expects."

Zhou opened the door, glanced back at Lin who nodded, and then left. The door slammed.

Sixty seconds later, the clock flicked to 11:46.

Sartaq directed Fan to leave.

Over the next three minutes, he sent them out, Yusheng last.

Sartaq reached into his pocket, brought out the revolver, and pointed it at Lili.

"Get up. We're next."

She scowled at him. "You won't need that."

Dressed in the finery from last night and wearing a full hour of meticulously applied makeup, Sartaq could only think of one word for her: *Elegant*. But then *treacherous* came to mind. And *scheming*. And *manipulating*.

She glided to the door in spite of the tall heels on her shoes and reached for the handle.

"Wait!" Sartaq stopped her. "I'll tell you when."

He then lied. "When we get to lobby and I say so, you may go to him... If he shows up."

Her eyes looked both hurt and angry, but she said nothing.

The Eco bag hanging on his gun arm, he put that hand in his pocket with the muzzle obvious where it pressed the fabric.

The clock switched to 11:51.

"Now."

Lili mashed down on the door handle. It squeaked.

* * *

When the fifth student disappeared down the elevator with the same kind of bag, Blake was sure only Sartaq and Megyn remained. He crept down the hall, squatted down across from their door, braced his feet against the wall like a sprinter, and prepared to launch himself.

The latch squeaked.

Blake's bicycle-hardened legs launched him across the hall and into the door, turning so the back of his shoulder plowed his body's mass into it. Energy would then transfer into the door and frame assembly. They would pop out as a unit. He'd then scramble up and shoot Sartaq.

But with the latch turned, there was practically no resistance.

Blake glanced off the door hastening its opening. He stumbled in as something pink and tan flew back from the other side. He fanned the air with the 1911 to regain his balance for several steps, but then his legs struck the edge of a bed and stopped. His upper torso, however, continued forward, twisted sideways and down. One foot snagged the bottom of the bedcover, and he fell, his rotation continuing, as the polyester cover wrapped him like an Egyptian mummy. His gun hand with the Masuda tightly bound between the bedcover and the outside of his right knee, he fell on his back between the beds.

Beyond his feet, Sartaq stood eyes agog and yanking at something in his pocket. One of the wood-handled bags the boy had brought from the lobby bounced heavily on his forearm.

Blake could feel the Masuda's trigger on the pad of his forefinger, but hidden by the bedcover, he couldn't be sure where it aimed.

Fabric ripped and Sartaq's hand came out of his pocket with the revolver. He whipped his arm down like a cowboy ready to fling wild shots at galloping Indians.

Blake's mind screamed, *Shoot!*

He mashed the trigger thinking it might blow off his kneecap but at least there was a chance he might get Sartaq.

Two guns fired over Megyn's scream.

Blake felt his body yanked back by his left arm. Particles and heat from the revolver's blast hit his face. He snapped his eyes shut remembering a bright spot of silver flashing on the bathroom's door frame behind Sartaq.

An animal scream made him force one eye open. Sartaq was in mid-air, the revolver high and coming down toward Blake's face like a brick. Blake tried to scrunch into a fetal position to avoid the blow, but a loud *klunk* was the last thing he remembered.

Blinking furiously and rubbing his eyes with the back of his fists, Sartaq growled, "Damn, that stings!"

In front of him, Lili squeaked from where she knelt between the beds, "Is he... dead?"

Sartaq continued to grind his eyes, the revolver waving in that hand as he did. "Hope so."

"I don't see blood," she said. "Where did you shoot him?"

Sartaq struggled to keep his eyes open. The American, all wrapped in the inside-out bedcover, reminded him of something.

His eyes squinted, he pointed and laughed. "Moo Shu man!"

A splotch of red appeared on the side of the bedcover.

Sartaq frowned. "Shot in arm."

He cocked the revolver. "This time, I'll be sure." He aimed.

Lili crashed into his shooting arm. The gun fired, and the glass bulb in the bedside lamp flared and went out.

Sartaq automatically lashed out at her, but she dodged back. The horn of the revolver's hammer scraped her cheek.

She fell on the second bed, a hand to her face. Several seconds passed before blood appeared between her fingers.

"You cut me!"

A memory flashed in his mind. Lili, nine years old, dirty knees, sitting in yellow and brown leaves, hand to her cheek, and blood.

Her accusing look now was the same as then.

"All right," he shouted. "I won't shoot him."

The relief on her face confirmed everything he'd suspected, everything he dreaded.

She loves him, not me.

The tiles in the bedside alarm clock clicked to 11:53.

He needed to trigger the bombs in five minutes.

"Lili, we must go."

She crossed to the desk and plucked out three tissues to dab at the cut on her cheek.

"Lili, please."

He held the door as they left.

Chapter 28

When the elevator opened to the lobby, Sartaq propelled Lili out. His bomb, hanging in the Eco bag on his gun arm, bounced against his thigh as he walked her to his pillar.

"This is ours," he said, then pointed across to the outside wall. "See door below green sign? That is way out. When I tell you, we go very fast."

Lili swung a leg out in front and wriggled it. "I can't run in these, Taq."

"Take them off. Run better barefoot."

"That was forty years ago, Taq. Besides, this skirt..."

He shook his head. "Figure it out. We must go fast so others don't see. And after push button, only ten seconds."

A large Asian man in a shiny gray suit with a slim young woman in a long jacket both looked in their direction. The woman then pointed to a rack with travel brochures and said something. They picked out two, unfolded them, and looked at the pictures. The woman glanced up and met Sartaq's eyes, then immediately went back to her brochure.

Sartaq leaned down to Lili. "Are they watching?"

"It's probably okay, Taq, They're not used to Uyghurs in

Singapore."

A dozen paces to their left, Zhou was standing near his assigned column. He was kneeling and tying one of his shoes, the round handle of the bag with his bomb looped on an arm. Farther down, Yusheng leaned against his column, eyes closed, lips moving, and his bag next to his foot.

The minute hand on the Check-In clock said it was three minutes before Noon. Time for all his soldiers to be in place, but he could only see Zhou and Yusheng. But the lobby was quiet, and people milled about. Everything seemed like it was going to plan.

Thirty seconds later with the second hand pointing straight down, Sartaq squeezed Lili's arm.

"Get ready."

He leaned back against the wallboard covering his column and bent his knees to place his Eco bag on the floor. He pushed it tight against the column with the heel of his boot.

He took the transmitter from his left pocket. All three LEDs were dark. He thumbed the power switch to "On."

The green LED came on.

He felt giddy this time knowing what was to come. At the library, he'd been nervous that something would go wrong. But this time, he knew it would work.

Waiting for the yellow LED, he shifted his weight from foot to foot.

Once the yellow came on, he'd pull Lili across to the Emergency Exit, push open the unlocked door, and then trigger the ten second countdown. There'd be just enough time to the two of them behind the concrete barrier.

Seconds passed.

Many seconds.

The LED had come on almost immediately at the library. He shook the transmitter.

Green, yes, still no yellow.

He huffed through his nostrils and watched the box.

Nothing changed.

He turned the power off, then on again. Green LED.

He waited.

No yellow.

He glanced down the lobby. Guo was watching the clock. His bag sat at his feet against the pillar, and through the weave, the brightly glowing green LED was easily visible. But no yellow.

The clock over the Check-In Desk twitched to 11:59. In seconds, Sartaq's soldiers would retrieve their fake detonators, and moments after that discover that they did nothing.

Sartaq had to do it now.

He raised his arm and mashed the GO button.

Pandemonium erupted.

Men and women in business clothes, Hawaiian shirts, shorts, and sandals were suddenly waving shotguns, rifles, and handguns.

"Freeze!"

"Hands over your head!"

"Lie down!"

At the next column, Zhou was furiously mashing the button on his blue-sparkle bicycle grip. He looked up to Sartaq, his eyes and mouth widening, and was bowled over by a man in a dark, brown suit followed by another man, this one in bathing suit and running shoes who scrabbled into the bag at that column and pulled out the bomb. He turned to place it inside a thick, woven basket carried by what looked like a man-size, green-fuzzy bear. The creature flopped the lid closed and began walking, basket at arm's length, toward the near end of the lobby.

The large businessman and athletic lady with the travel brochures now stalked toward Sartaq, short barrel rifles up and aimed at his face.

"Drop box," the man shouted in Cantonese.

"Step away," the woman ordered, also in Cantonese.

"Face down on floor."

"Arms behind head."

Lili raised her hands, but Sartaq stuffed the transmitter into his pocket and grabbed the handle of his Eco bag from the floor. He swept his arm around Lili's waist and let the bag slide up that same arm. In almost the same movement, he pulled the revolver from his pocket and pressed it to Lili's head.

"Stay back," he shouted.

He hauled Lili up and off her feet, and then started across the lobby toward the gray emergency door.

"Stop," Lili protested, wriggling to break loose.

"Don't worry," Sartaq said in her ear. "I'll take care of you."

"No, Taq, no," she pleaded, twisting her body and pushing against his arm. He hoisted her even higher, the Eco bag on his forearm bounced on her stomach as she struggled.

The man and woman with rifles followed but did not shoot.

At the door, Sartaq shifted Lili sideways so he could push the panic bar with his hip. It went in but the door wouldn't budge. Instead, a red light over the door began raking the lobby, and an alarm horn started to blare.

Lili was saying something, but the horn and shouting drowned her out.

Sartaq shoved his hip again and again against the push-bar.

What good's an emergency door if it won't open in an emergency?

Lili yelled, her body jerking with the effort, "Fifteen second delay."

The man and woman with rifles started fanning out, one to each side. The woman's rifle pointed at Sartaq's neck, and the man's was aimed at Lili.

Trapped, Sartaq opened and closed his mouth as they closed in.

A white light blinked across the lobby. Sartaq looked at it.

"Elevator," Lili jabbed an arm as the doors opened. "Keep gun on me, Taq, but go! Go quick. And look crazy, same as Guanzhou!"

Clutching Lili, he scuttled backward across the lobby, the rifles tracking their progress but not firing. When they reached the elevator, its doors were still open. Inside, Lili squirmed in Sartaq's grasp to hit the button for the top floor. Both the man and woman with their rifles continued shouting, but then the doors closed.

Silence.

They were safe.

But not alone.

A man with grayish-brown hair, a mustache, and a small graying beard stood in the far, back corner. His left arm hung limp and a rivulet of blood traced down his forefinger to drip in a puddle on the elevator's polished marble floor. In his right hand was a shiny gun, half again bigger than Sartaq's black revolver. It was pointed at them.

The American!

Blake stared.

"Is this for real or what?"

Sartaq pulled Megyn tighter and wagged the elbow of his arm with the revolver to emphasize the muzzle against Megyn's scalp. He growled something Blake couldn't understand.

"I see it," Blake said. He flexed his fingers on the 1911. It was pointed and ready, but there was no way he could shoot. As small as Megyn was, she covered enough of her brother to keep Blake from shooting.

She looked into Blake's eyes for a long time as the numbers over the elevator door incremented up.

Then, she began saying things as if thinking aloud, but in Cantonese.

After a few more floors, Sartaq nodded. She kept talking. When the indicator reached "26," the big man frowned and shook his head. Their ascent continued, and now and then, he'd mumble something. She'd give an eye roll then sound like she was backing up to repeat something with added emphasis.

Sartaq's reddish-brown face grew darker, and his head shakes became more and more emphatic.

When the floor indicator flicked to "41" he barked—in English—"Bitch."

Red flooded up through the translucent skin of Megyn's neck. She wrenched loose from her brother's arm, landed on her feet, and spun to face him.

A fist on each hip and stretched up on her tiptoes, her tirade dressed Sartaq up and down. The big man winced and blinked as she pummeled him with words, the harangue driving the language's dips, sweeps, and drones to new highs and lows of pitch and intensity.

And she pushed forward as she raged, pressing him back, chest against belly with the bomb mashed between them, toward a corner of the elevator.

As Sartaq drew back from her verbal assault, his gun-hand also withdrew, turning upward as if also trying to escape.

Blake glimpsed an opportunity. Hoping to startle the big man into yanking the trigger and shooting himself, Blake stamped his foot on the marble floor and shouted.

"Hey!"

Sartaq jumped, but instead of clenching his fist and firing, his gun-hand sprang open. The revolver flipped out and landed on the shelf of Megyn's breasts where she pressed against him.

They both looked down at it.

Using two fingers as if touching something filthy and vile, Megyn picked the revolver up by its handle and handed it back to Sartaq.

Blake exploded. "What?"

Megyn snapped around to him.

"Butt out!"

Blake's jaw and arm dropped.

She was the reason he was here. She'd invited him, signed the contract, flown the same planes, slept in the same hotels—in the same bed... They'd made love... Shanghai... Guangzhou...

"I..." he sputtered.

"Honest to God," she swore, fists on hips and looking back and forth between the two of them, "if it wasn't for me, you two would accomplish nothing!"

Sartaq looked as shocked as Blake.

A chime sounded and the indicator over the door changed to "RF."

Sartaq and Blake both closed their mouths.

Megyn put a finger to her lips, took her brother's arm, and pirouetted back into his grasp again. She grasped her brother's gun hand, maneuvered it up, and then angled it down so the muzzle pointed into the top of her head.

Same as before.

The elevator door opened.

* * *

Singapore's Noon-day sun poured its blazing glory on the huge, curved-surfboard of roof deck atop the Marina Bay Sands hotel.

It was hot and gorgeous, as usual.

Megyn pressed Sartaq to back out of the elevator and into the light.

Blinking against the glare with the Masuda hanging loose in his right hand, Blake followed. Sartaq was a murderer and deserved to die, but now it was Megyn in charge.

When was she acting? When had she been sincere? Had she orchestrated everything all along? Was this attack her doing? What about the school library? All those kids? And her brother's execution of that boy on the mountain? Was that her plan, too?

To Blake's left, a cabana-covered sitting area split the deck with the pool filled with slowly bobbing heads, all of them either bald, or covered with black, shiny hair.

To the right was the side of the platform. A hip-high, metal railing marked the boundary into nothingness.

Megyn continued pressing Sartaq back. They passed the cabana area toward a sea of orange umbrellas and plastic chairs. A breeze flapped the fabric over seated families; Dads in garish short sleeve shirts with wide collars; Moms in long, colorful sun dresses or florid shorty robes over one-piece bathing suits; and kids with bare-chested boys in bright swimsuits and little girls in flat-chested bikinis, all of them bare foot, feet kicking and swaying above plastic flip-flops that'd been shed to the deck.

Somewhere ahead, a woman's voice screeched, "Shee-ung!" Another voice crowed, "Chee-ung!" The two words, differing only in their initial consonants, repeated through the crowd like rapid fire on the Bullseye firing line.

Plastic chairs scudded back, many flopping onto their backs. Men's voices bellowed and mothers grabbed small wrists. Kids shrieked in pain, surprise, and anger. Forks, spoons, and chopsticks clattered on ceramic plates. Fingers pointed, heads bobbed to stare, and everyone pressed back as Sartaq and Megyn approached, the revolver pointing down and into her head. Mickey's 1911 at the end of his arm must've seemed far less dramatic.

Hemmed in by the pool on one side and fifty-seven stories of emptiness on the other, the crowd surged backwards into the long expanse of the cantilevered deck, a dead end.

Mickey'd said it projected out a hundred and fifty feet over nothing but space.

Six hundred feet down, grass and dirt would be as unforgiving as hardened concrete.

Sartaq shifted glaring looks at Blake, over his shoulder to the deck behind as they backed, and then down at Megyn. He said something into her ear, the swish of syllables unknown to Blake. She answered in kind and continued pressing back.

"Megyn," Blake pleaded, "there's nowhere to go."

As the far side of the crowd reached the tip end of the surfboard shaped deck, they began squeezing out sideways. When the leading escapees came even on the side with Sartaq, Megyn, and Blake, they broke into panicked runs still hugging the rails.

Seconds later, the tenor of shouting behind Blake changed from high-pitched panic to bellowed orders and angry protests.

Blake glanced around.

The elevator from which they'd emerged squirmed with people, the doors unable to close. Inside, arms held children up from the crush of bodies fighting to get in. Small, high-pitched voices cried and screamed in panic over the shouting and barking.

Farther away, another mass of bodies pressed against the side of a white building, an open doorway in its middle. Bodies were moving into that doorway, but much too fast. More screaming and cries of panic echoed out from the doorway.

Blake remembered the clatter of the police headset and control box at the bottom of the steel and concrete stairwell. Six seconds, he remembered. These would take only that unless they hit and bounded from rail to rail on the way down.

There were no black-clothed snipers, no plain-clothes cops with rifles in the crowd.

Mickey's order to the elevator monitor moved him to the lobby. Mickey'd concentrating his forces for the bomb attack. Blake guessed he'd done the same for the ones at the pool cabana.

The rail at the end of the platform, devoid of people, lay just ahead.

Blake shouted, "Megyn, it's a dead end. There's no place to go!"

Sartaq reached it and stopped. Looking left, right, and then over his shoulder into the space beyond, he bellowed something at Megyn. The muscles in his arm bunched and slid beneath his skin as if he was working his grip.

Blake started again, "Megyn—"

"Shut up," she shrieked at both of them. "Years! I've worked years for this. Today, this day," she waved just her forearms like a miniature T-Rex, her upper arms pinned in Sartaq's grasp, "China would've changed..."

Sartaq was yelling, too, at her.

Megyn gritted her teeth and tried to bat his gun away. She struggled to turn in his grasp but shouted at him anyway.

Blake watched as brother and sister escalated, rocketing up the anger and vitriol.

Spittle flew from Sartaq's mouth. Megyn, one hand grasping her brother's gun hand atop her head, the other wiping the side of her face nearest his mouth, grimaced as she barked at him.

Blake suddenly realized the revolver's hammer had risen to fully cock; Sartaq was going to fire, to blow his little sister's head apart, to obliterate this person known as Megyn, as Lili.

Far in the distance behind Sartaq and Megyn, Blake heard the familiar churn of passenger jet engines. A tiny glint of silver rose up behind Sartaq's head. An airliner—*Boeing 757, Rolls-Royce engines*—climbed out from Singapore's passenger airport a few miles away.

If he could startle Megyn, Blake realized, if he could make her bend around to look, she would no longer cover Sartaq.

And Blake could fire.

It was his only chance.

Blake morphed his face into panic and horror.

"Oh God!" He jabbed his wounded arm, gritting his teeth against the pain. He pointed beyond them toward the rising dot and its roar. "Look!"

Megyn's eyes sprang wide. She twisted sideways in her brother's grasp to peer around and beyond him.

Blake's right arm with the Masuda in his gun hand swept up like he was shooting the four-second round of five shots for International Rapid Fire. The Masuda's front and rear sights arrived in perfect alignment on Sartaq's face.

The first shot bucked hard in Blake's hand.

A single, dark spot appeared on the target slightly above Sartaq's two enormous eyes.

Twelve o'clock, ten ring.

Blake's "GTSOOI" grip brought the sights down and into perfect alignment. His finger moved forward to let the trigger reset. He pressed to fire again.

Another dark spot appeared in Sartaq's face.

Eight o'clock, nine ring.

A puff of red spray haloed behind Sartaq's head but then blanched to pink against the blue sky before disappearing. The big man's head cocked back, and his knees began to buckle. Sartaq's body collapsed to its knees on the deck behind Megyn less than a foot from the rail.

D-R-T, Blake thought.

Megyn screamed, "No!"

She turned and pulled Sartaq's bloody head to her breasts.

"Taq! Taq!" She rocked, blood streaming out through the flowers of her blouse, the translucent fabric sticking to her skin and outlining the edges of her bra.

She opened her bloodied hands to look at them. They glistened in the noon-day sun, the color dark and thick.

"Why?" she cried. "Why?"

Blake opened his mouth but had no words.

She wailed at him. "He wasn't going to hurt you!"

Blake choked to stop the words that wouldn't come.

She pleaded, "I wouldn't let him. I love you. You were safe."

"Megyn, I..." Blake started.

She sobbed, cradling her brother's head as the blood pooled on her skirt, then overflowed down her pale leg.

"Megyn!" He gestured toward the panicked crowd behind him. "It's women and children, not just Party members. Families, teenagers, nine-year-old kids, some only four and five, and babies in carriers, infants in blankets nursing at mother's breast..."

But it was over.

Because he'd killed her brother.

Blake dropped his eyes from her tormented face, from the anguish he'd brought upon her.

His eyes stopped on two bright points gleaming through the side of the Eco bag still looped on Sartaq's dead arm, one green, one yellow.

His eyes slowly widened in recognition.

The bomb was armed.

Megyn tilted her head at him, and then followed his gaze down. Cradling her brother's head in one arm, she reached inside the Eco bag and brought out the football-sized bomb. The LEDs on its detonator box, one green and one yellow, beamed despite the midday sun.

She coursed her eyebrows. "How?"

Blake shrugged automatically. "Must be a transmitter."

The police jammer was fifty-seven stories below, through a maze of metal beams, walls, floors, and miles of copper wiring.

Megyn leaned forward, reached into her dead brother's pocket, and drew out a gray box. It was one of Alex's transmitters. Its LEDs matched those on the bomb resting in her lap: green and yellow on, red off.

Mickey's WiFi scrambler was fifty-seven stories below through a maze of metal that blocked its effect. And Sartaq's transmitter was no more than a few dozen inches from his bomb. The devices had synchronized. The bomb was ready.

Megyn's eyes narrowed. She leaned slightly to one side, her eyes focusing on something far behind Blake. He watched as her eyes flicked about also. She was watching things move about.

The screaming and shouting behind Blake reminded him of the panic taking place. More than a thousand trying to escape down one elevator and one emergency staircase would take time. A lot of time. People, lots of people, would be stuck on the roof with nowhere to go for a long time.

Megyn's expression hardened.

"Run," she commanded.

"I'll give you as much time as I can," she said. Shifting her eyes beyond Blake, she calmly gave him instructions. "Go around behind the elevator housing. It's closest. Then lie flat and face away. It will shield you enough, I hope."

"Just turn off the switches," Blake pleaded. "The bomb squad can take that one apart when they get here."

She still gazed beyond him as she shook her head. "It won't be thousands, but there's, I don't know, several hundred? Maybe a thousand? My people, the replacements for those, will move up for the next Congress. It won't be a majority, but," her Mona Lisa smiled appeared, "it's progress."

He started, "Megyn, you can't—"

The smile disappeared. "Go now. Before the police get here."

"But it'll kill you!"

She wagged her chin. "This is what my life's been for."

He heard himself bark, "No!"

"I have to," she said, raising her arm with the transmitter control box higher. "All my life..."

He heard the button's click.

The red LED on the transmitter and the one on the bomb's receiver burst on simultaneously. They began their dance of microsecond-precision, synchronized destruction.

Ten.

"Megyn!"

She casually tossed the transmitter, its purpose fulfilled, over the rail behind her back. It disappeared.

"It's done," she said.

Nine.

Detonated here, the shock wave would rocket across the deck at many times the speed of sound. It would fracture anything hard or rigid, like bones and internal organs. The force would push people across the deck, some falling fifty-seven stories to their deaths, while others would succumb to ruptured spleens and livers, and brains shattered into disconnected chunks inside their fractured skulls.

Blake lurched for the bomb.

Eight.

But she saw him coming. She bent to curl over it, extending one leg as she tucked and hugged the bomb.

Seven.

There was no time for a wrestling match. He needed the bomb, and he needed it now!

Ray had said, *Clear the field.*

Blake shifted the Masuda's aim to the calf of her long white leg and fired.

Six.

She screamed in agony and her body unfolded automatically, her arms and hands reaching toward the wounded leg.

Blake grabbed the bomb and flipped the power switch off.

Five.

Green and yellow stayed on. Red continued to blink.

Damn!

Alex said it was like a burning fuse: once triggered, the receiver's control box couldn't be turned off.

Four.

He thrust the bomb away from him, up, forward, and over the rail.

Three.

Fifty-seven stories. Six seconds. Not enough time. How far?

Two.

His mind supplied the answer. *A hundred and fifty feet, as far down as out.*

One.

Blake dropped his gun and pulled Megyn to his chest. "I love you."

Zero.

Straight down from the tip of the platform, a logic output from the Raspberry Pi board inside Alex's receiver went to active-low. Sinking current through the coil of the relay, its contacts snapped closed. Five times nine volts—forty-five of them—pushed trillions of electrons into the match head-size initiator inside the silver detonator. It flared with intense heat and ignited the detonator's tiny explosive charge. The shock and heat from that burst into the first stick of dynamite. The shock cascaded the moderated nitroglycerin into the primary explosion. That set off the remaining five sticks.

Everything was over, as far as the bomb was concerned, in a few thousandths of a second.

To anyone looking in the right direction at the right moment, a fleeting white bubble appeared in the air well below the deck a little way out from the side of the building. Singapore's thick, humid air made its surface opaque, like a white birthday balloon. But it expanded faster than the speed of sound and reflected perfectly from the side of the building. Metal wall studs on the outside walls dented in as if hit by a huge medicine ball, and planks of tile began sheeting off the building.

When the rising top of the supersonic shockwave reached the underside of the cantilevered platform, it shoved upward with a single, massive pulse. The end of the deck rose almost a meter then fell back. Tossed in the air, Blake and Megyn crashed back down onto the still shuddering deck.

Seconds later, the sound of the massive explosion echoed back across the inlet from Singapore's downtown skyscrapers.

The rolling ball of orange fire and smoke from the dynamite churned slowly upward. Reaching the projected end of the platform, it pushed out in the center, with little wisps curling inward along the edges.

Looking up, it reminded Blake of an orange and black hooded viper contemplating its prey.

Chapter 29

Two Weeks Later
Surprise, Arizona

Blake sat on his couch, bare feet on the coffee table, computer in his lap.

Since returning, he couldn't bear to be around anyone. They might talk to him, ask a question, expect an answer.

Drapes closed, and shades down, he didn't go out except for frozen dinners, beer, and toilet paper. He'd stopped mail delivery before the trip. Bills would be past due.

"Fuck 'em," he said to the room.

He was both a hero and a criminal in Singapore. Officially expelled, they'd paid his First-Class ticket home the next day.

But Megyn was unreachable.

Her phone got a recording: *The number you have reached has been disconnected.*

Texts were rejected: *Message cannot be delivered.*

Emails came back: *User not found.*

He'd ruined her life, killed her brother, and then shot her, too.
Hopeless.

He sent email to Mickey, but his friend's reply said it was going to take a while. Everyone wanted—demanded—jurisdiction. Diplomatic dealings between Singapore and China were complicated, Mickey explained. And with the United States chiming in because of Megyn's dual citizenship, her fate became a three-way wrestling match.

Megyn had used him, but it'd been for something much greater than herself. She'd fought the Communists all her life, and this was going to be its culmination, a victory for democracy.

If she could sacrifice herself for something heroic, shouldn't Blake honor that?

And she'd told him how to save himself: Wasn't that love?

He pulled the closed curtain aside for a moment to look out the front window. "One day at a time," he said to the sunny residential street and the sunbaked houses with their rock lawns, closed shades, and battened down garages.

His computer dinged from the coffee table.

The email was from Mickey.

Dear Blake,

How are you, my friend?

Good news!

Your State Department has prevailed. (Apparently, you give us better fighter jets and missiles than China.)

Megyn has been deported. She should be back in the USA by now, but with a new identity. China will kill her if they can so don't expect to hear from her. They'll be watching you for that reason.

Sorry, pal.

Hope to shoot with you again someday but don't come here. My government would not like that. Camp Perry maybe next summer.

Ray and the others ask about you from time to time. They admire what you did. It was heroic even though you really, really pissed me off. You'll have to buy me all the beer I want as penance.

10s and Xs, my good friend.

Without thinking, Blake launched the browser and typed, "YouTube, Don't Explain, Billie Holiday."

Her voice reached into his chest, wrapped its fingers of unconditional forgiveness around his heart, and slowly ripped it out of his body.

www.ingramcontent.com/pod-product-compliance
Lightning Source LLC
Chambersburg PA
CBHW020332180626
46812CB00001B/162